# The ShadowHunter

*Witch Bound*

*Book Two*

Opal Reyne

Internal Illustrations: Etheric Designs

# <u>Author's note on language</u>

I'm from AUSTRALIA.

My English is not the same as American English.

I love my American English spoken readers to bits. You're cute, you all make me giggle, and I just wanna give you a big 'ol hug. However, there are many of you who don't seem to realise that your English was born from British English, which is what I use (although a bastardised version since Australians like to take all language and strangle it until it's a ruined carcass of slang, missing letters, and randomly added o's).

We don't seem to like the letter z.

We write colour instead of color. Recognise instead of recognize. Travelling instead of traveling. Skilful instead of skillfull. Mum instead of mom. Smelt is a past participle of smelled. We omit the full-stop in Mr. Name, so it's Mr Name. Aussies cradle the word cunt like it's a sweet little puppy, rather than an insult to be launched at your face.

Anyway, happy reading!

To all the princessy DragonFuckers out there,

This book is for you.

Sometimes we just want to wear a fancy dress, play cat and mouse inside of a palace, and get chased by a Dragon that wants to tear our clothes off.
*So run, rabbit. Run*

*They took my sister...*

Valerie Faerydae stood on the only path for carriages travelling through the Everlye Forest. Dirt crunched beneath her dainty slippers as she threw applebye berries, turnip slices, honey oats, and mugwort leaves across the well-used path.

*I will find her.*

Lifting her hands towards the oncoming carriages, she allowed the magic that rippled beneath her skin to cascade down her fingertips and into the air.

Two horse-pulled carriages were steadily coming closer. One held nobles, the other most likely servants. Beside them, eight armoured riders served as guards.

*I will take her back.*

"Move, you silly woman!" the coachman yelled.

Ignoring him, Valerie continued to quietly chant, barely moving her lips as she spoke the precious words she needed.

Perhaps she should be frightened of the horses and carriages that could barrel over her. Perhaps the coachman was worried about not stopping in time and hurting her. She wasn't.

Once she finished chanting, she lowered her arms, softly clasped her hands in front of her hips, and waited. *I will bring my sister home... no matter the cost.*

Four of the soldiers on horseback galloped towards her to move her out of the way. Travellers were often wary of strangers on the roads. With dark Witches afoot, she didn't blame them.

"Whoaaa," all four commanded to their horses as they reared back onto their hind legs.

When the first coachman noticed the commotion, he pulled back on the reins to slow his speed.

The riders tried to get their horses to do as they were commanded, but they neighed and turned away to show they didn't want to approach any closer.

It was a harmless spell, nothing of any danger except for the caster. It was designed to ward off animals, to halt them from approaching unless they were truly fearless – these horses weren't.

The two carriages stopped behind the four riders while two of the other soldiers came forward to inspect the commotion.

"Who do you think she is?" one of them asked, pulling on the reins to calm his horse.

"The horses will not approach," one stated, eyeing her carefully. "She might be a Witch."

Three of the soldiers' faces paled at his words.

They pulled their swords from their scabbards before jumping down from their horses and approaching with caution. The carriages remained a safe distance behind, with two riders to guard them.

Valerie gave them a bow of her head. "You are correct. I'm a Witch."

She truly meant no harm if they did what she wanted. All six surrounded her, the tips of their swords pointed at her torso. Two vials rolled from the sleeves of her dress into her palms without them noticing.

"*Ad mentem imperium,*" she chanted.

She pulled on the corks of both the vials in her hands. Just as swiftly, she blew a concoction of stolen pixie dust and her own dried blood into their faces.

All six soldiers stood frozen; they would remain frozen until she gave them a task. It was dark magic, a spell of mind control that only the powerful and the few knew.

Valerie had never done such a spell before this day, and she was pleased to see it worked.

Before her sister was taken, she had been a white Witch, just like all her family. *As the eldest, I must make the sacrifice to save Kaeylyn.*

For the last two weeks, Valerie had done unspeakable things to get to the truth, to find out who had stolen the youngest family member from their small coven. She'd stolen pixie dust and fairy blood, had used blood magic to discover who took her.

Not once did she kill the small creatures who were no larger than the palm of her hand, but she'd extracted those parts without permission. She needed the mischievous properties of pixie dust to overtake these men, and she'd needed the fairy blood for two reasons.

One was to look back in time for a vision.

The second was to create a powerful illusion of all senses. It required one last ingredient, and she planned to obtain it now, among other things...

With this particular spell, the soldiers would have no memory of what was occurring until she released them, which she didn't plan to do any time soon. She walked around them to approach the carriages, and the two remaining soldiers unsheathed their swords and pointed them in warning.

"Lady Cecily Dyèrie, I come with a gift," Valerie called

once she stood in front of the two soldiers. "I come with the answer you seek."

She knowingly eyed one of the knights in front of her.

"No, dear child!" a man fretted when the front carriage door burst open. It slammed against the side with a loud bang. "You must not leave the wagon."

"Quiet, Uncle. She has not attacked us, and I wish to know what she wants," a woman snapped.

Her brown hair waved around her pale, yet tall, features as she stepped out of the carriage. She was clad in the finest fabric money could buy, frumpy and flaunting her father's wealth. Cecily proceeded to stomp in front of Valerie until they were a metre apart and shoved her hands on her hips.

"Who are you? What do you want?" Cecily rudely questioned.

Valerie's eyebrow twitched at her courage.

This was the only daughter of Duke Grayson. She thought she was above others, that the grand title of her father would be enough to protect her. Although Cecily was a vain, eccentric woman, she was also brave in a brutish sense. She had wit, though sometimes dull, and she always walked with an air of superiority only money could buy.

"I'm Valerie Faerydae, and not too long ago, I was a white Witch of these lands ruled by your father."

The young woman scoffed and rolled her eyes. "My father does not allow Witches on his lands. We have burned many of you on our pyres."

A large man, much older than his niece, stepped out of the wagon to stand beside her. His full tuft of hair blew in the soft wind while his right hand rested on the hilt of his sword, ready to unleash it at a moment's notice.

"Ah." Valerie held up a finger before slowly waving her hand to the side. "You cannot burn what you don't know is there."

Cecily pursed her lips in annoyance. Then she brushed her hair over her shoulder before folding her arms under her small chest, making her breasts look plumper – something Valerie had seen her do to catch the men around her off-guard.

"You said you come with a gift, the answer to which I seek. You would have to know what I want to give me that."

Valerie pouted her lips into a knowing smile. "You don't wish to go to the selection gala." Cecily's eyes widened a fraction. "You don't wish to marry the king of the north because you are already in love."

One of the knights in front of her turned his head to Cecily.

"So? I'm a woman. What I want does not matter." Her eyes briefly met the knight's, and Valerie could see the pain-filled look she gave him. "My father has demanded I win the king's heart and become queen to strengthen our alliance and wealth."

"Your father once blessed your marriage to this knight, until he learned of the king's search for a bride." She gestured to the young soldier in front of her, then motioned to the frozen soldiers behind her. "What if I could give you an alternative? Already, I have taken control of the men behind me, and by doing so, I can add their confusion to our façade."

"You wish to take my place," Cecily whispered, taking a step back. *Ah, there is that quick wit.* "Why do you want to become queen?"

"I don't," she answered. "This charade would only last until the gala is finished. Your chance to become queen would end, and I would get what I wanted."

"And what is that?"

"Something was stolen from me, and I *sincerely* want it back."

Cecily paused to think, her eyes falling over the noble knight she obviously longed for.

Valerie had come up with this plan as she walked through

the town closest to her home.

Over the course of the last two weeks, the king of the north had issued scrolls to the five dukes of his lands, asking for a presentation of their daughters. He didn't trust the kings of the other kingdoms and therefore didn't wish to take a princess.

It was the talk of many human towns. Valerie thought it might be her opportunity, since out of the five dukes, two of their daughters looked like her. The other one had been much too far away for her to travel to in time, so she'd chosen Cecily.

With that knowledge, Valerie cloaked herself in invisibility to sneak inside the Dyèrie manor to investigate.

She'd watched Cecily sob to this knight in her room about their broken marriage proposal. The duke didn't care who his daughter married, so long as he was a noble, and this knight was of high-born blood. Unfortunately, the temptation to unite his family with the throne was too much for her greedy father. He was selling her off for more wealth and fortune.

"You cannot seriously be considering this, Cecily," her uncle argued, shaking his head. "This is treason. We would be hanged."

"Quiet, Uncle. I'm thinking."

"A Witch has taken over your caravan, brain washed your soldiers, and is forcing you to submit. That does not sound treasonous if you play it correctly." Valerie raised her chin. "The alternatives are I kill you and take your place." Their eyes widened as Valerie rested her hand on her sword hilt. "Or, I take over your minds and leave you to wander the forest without thought. Mayhap you will live until I break the spell, or you will be robbed or killed."

"What do you plan to do to the king?" the uncle asked, his face turning a dark shade of red in anger or frustration – she wasn't sure which.

"Nothing. I just want information, but what I seek will not

come easily. If I ask for what I want directly, they will know what I'm. I will have to find what I want without them knowing."

"As an invited guest, that gives you the freedom to search," Cecily commented, nodding her head as though she understood.

"I don't intend to kill the king or anyone in his castle. All I want is what I seek and then to leave. When I find it, I will release the spell on your soldiers. They will be confused and have no memory of what has happened. If you say you were also released from a spell, no one would question you. As long as you remain hidden, of course."

Cecily cocked a perfect brow. "How will we know when the spell has been broken?"

"You will not. Your role is to arrive after the final day of the gala to tell the king you have regained your minds, that your last memory is of a Witch taking over your caravan. I will have left by then. If I have not, then I will release the control I have over your soldiers and flee."

"Why are you giving me the option? Why would you not just do what you have done to my guards to me?" Cecily asked, unfolding her arms to raise her hands in question.

"Because, my ladyship, I require your permission to share blood."

"Excuse me?"

"During my stay with the king, I will have to suppress my witchcraft, which I can only do if I share the blood of a human. It will make my magic untraceable while making me appear human to those who can sense it."

*Whether they be another Witch or... a Dragon.*

This was the danger of Valerie's plan. She didn't know who the king had under his employment. Another Witch would be able to sense her if they tried. They could alert the king if they were loyal to him or using him for their own gain.

Dragons... Well, they were creatures who could transform into humans with an ancient spell. They liked to place themselves in locations that often led to hunting her kind.

A stray Witch seeking to kill or steal from the king could actually be entering the hunting ground of a Dragon.

*I will not be able to spot them without my witchcraft.* Even with it, telling the difference between a Dragon and a human was near impossible for those who had never come across one before – which Valerie hadn't.

"Will I be able to use magic?" The noblewoman's eyes lit up with excitement.

"No. You will not be able to share in the power of the spell. It only works for the Witch, but both parties must be willing."

There was a long pause as Cecily thought, her dull green eyes scanning the forest next to the dirt road surrounding it.

"Okay, I will do it. If it means I can be with my Godfrey, then I will do it." Her eyes fell back on her knight, who gave her a soft, caring look.

Valerie crinkled her nose at the two of them. *I have little aspiration for what they share.*

"Cecily, my dear, you cannot do this!" her uncle yelled, pulling on his sword to unsheathe it. He tried to push her behind him protectively.

"Quiet, or I will have the Witch cast her magic on you as well. You can follow me around like a mindless dog."

She gritted her teeth as she stormed around him to face Valerie. Once more, she placed her hands on her hips, but this time, she stomped her foot like an immature child.

His face paled at what she was suggesting. He was also coming to the realisation that he wouldn't be able to fight her on this and Valerie could very easily take his say out of the matter with witchcraft.

"So, it's settled." Valerie clapped her hands together. "We will share blood and I will take your place. Tell no one of this conversation, or, as your uncle put it, you will be hung for treason. Betray me and I will make sure your entire family line is wiped from existence, because, dear lady, my entire coven knows I'm here and what has occurred on this day."

A complete lie; nobody knew what she was up to.

With a nod, Cecily came forward so Valerie could do the spell. Finally, the last ingredient was in her grasp.

*I don't like having my witchcraft locked away,* Valerie thought
as she was rocked around the carriage.

Staring at her hand, she assessed the inability to feel her
magic whatsoever. It felt like there was a piece missing from
her, a vital piece that instantly made her feel broken. She was
at least relieved that if she needed it, all she had to do was
release it.

Sighing, she turned to look out the window while ignoring
the man travelling inside this uncomfortable transport with
her.

For five out of the six men she'd used the mind trapping
spell on, she commanded them to think of her as the duke's
daughter. Immediately, they begun to act as though she was
the girl, confused as to why they were pointing their swords
at each other. She'd done the same to the two servants with
them.

She'd picked one of the six men who looked like Cecily's
uncle, Vermont, and commanded he act as though he was
Cecily's uncle. He was there to escort her to the king. *He's my*

*glaring vulnerability in this plan.*

Valerie had been teaching him all that she knew about being a duke in the day they'd been travelling. Hopefully, with her magic enchanting him, he would be able to act the way she needed. He certainly looked the part.

Before she'd done the spell with Cecily that would suppress her magic, she put a glamour on him, one that filled in the blanks for those who might know the real Sir Vermont.

*Using dark magic feels wrong.* The way her power flowed from her crawled across her skin rather than cascaded gently.

*But there is nothing I can do about it. This will not be successful without it.* Even the spell with Cecily was blood magic, which was against her teachings.

Once the binding contract was made, Valerie went through the noblewoman's travel chests to select dresses and jewellery she could wear to signify her false status. Cecily had received a drawstring bag of gold coins in payment for the items, something Valerie had stolen from a different caravan of carriages. Then, she handed the girl her sword, knowing she couldn't take it with her.

*It's lucky that we look similar, even in age.* Although the life spans of Witches were different to humans, they were able to live almost two hundred years thanks to their ancestors.

Valerie didn't look older than twenty-eight years old.

Cecily was twenty-six, but Valerie was sure if Duke Grayson had a younger daughter, he would have sent her instead. Alas, he didn't, and could only send Cecily.

The ageing state of his daughter was why he originally allowed her to wed the knight, knowing she was crawling away from the age where he could pass her off as youthful. *She's still quite a beautiful girl.*

Valerie pulled at the waving hair that flowed past her shoulders, down to just below her waist. Cecily had added two braids that came from the corners of her forehead just above her ears to the back of her hair, intertwining there. The braids were small and left most of her hair free, which she was thankful for.

Cecily's hair was a lighter brown than Valerie's dark locks, and although they both had green eyes, Cecily's had been brighter. Even Valerie was able to tell that her own pale skin covered daintier bones.

*It's lucky that she rarely left her manor.* She informed Valerie she hadn't seen the other dukes' daughters since she was an early teenager. Instead, she'd been surrounded by other dukes and their sons, those who didn't have daughters, since Cecily didn't get along with other girls.

They found her brutish and snobbish because she refused to play her role with women of the same status. *The girl is a flirt. No wonder a knight of her own guard fell for her.*

It worked in Valerie's favour, though. Most wouldn't know that she and Cecily were not the same person.

Resting her arm on the windowsill to look outside, Valerie thought on the vision she'd conjured.

Without her coven – consisting of her mother and two other sisters – knowing, she'd taken some of Kaeylyn's hair from her brush. Then, in the darkness of night, she'd called upon the fairies who lived near their home.

They came to her joyfully, since they had grown to trust her family over the generations they lived in the same house and forest lands.

Valerie still felt terrible about betraying them. She'd trapped them and stole their blood, knowing they wouldn't give it to her willingly.

She hadn't needed much, only a few droplets, but, to something the size of her palm, it was devastating. It was added to a potion of herbs with a small chant.

When she drank it, it allowed her to see back in time by a day. She saw through her sister's own eyes.

She'd been playing, chasing fairies around the forest in the dark of night when she should have been in bed. Unfortunately, she travelled too close to the road and was spotted. Her sister had been frightened, crying and screaming for their mother.

Valerie's hand clenched into a tight fist. *She cried for me as well...* She hadn't called out for anyone else.

Valerie never saw the faces of the men, but she'd seen the house emblem on their shields and armour. All she saw before the vision faded was her sister, bound with rope, seeing the palace through a wagon window.

They were planning on gifting her to the king.

*Why, Kaeylyn? You silly girl!* Valerie's hand clenched tighter. *Why did you have to sneak out of bed to play that night?*

Valerie had tried scrying for her first, but all she could see of her sister was that she was in an empty room, chained. She was a little girl, innocent of any crimes whatsoever, terrified, all because she was a Witch.

Valerie was doing this alone, because she didn't wish to endanger the rest of her family. If she'd told them she was leaving, they would have tried to come along. She couldn't risk more of her sisters being captured and their mother couldn't go. Their mother was their coven leader, and her sisters still needed the guidance she provided.

No, the only person who had the knowledge, power, and freedom to do this was her.

*Now here I'm, approaching King Bradwick's palace to find you.*

She could see it in the distance, the road curving just enough to see it out the window.

The palace was grand. Even in the distance, she could tell it was one of the largest buildings she'd ever seen. It was so tall, it seemed like the architects wanted to touch the heavenly sky.

There were four square towers on each corner, just slightly taller than the rest of the square-shaped palace, except for the main building.

The grounds took a while to ride through, and they passed lush grassy fields on either side. Crow's nest trees lined the driveway, thin but bushy trees that looked perfect for climbing. More had been planted along the metal fence line of the grounds.

Eventually, they reached the actual fortified palace entry.

The coachman, who was also under her spell, was approached.

"Halt. Who goes there?" one of the royal guards asked.

"Duke Grayson of house Dyèrie received an invitation for his daughter to participate in the king's royal gala. I bring Lady Cecily of house Dyèrie and her uncle, Duke Vermont of house Dyèrie."

"May I see the invitation?"

Valerie handed her version of Duke Vermont the invitation she'd taken from the real Cecily.

Like he understood what he needed to do, the man exited the wagon. Her heart remained steady, confident in the magic she'd cast. This was just the first step, and she had faith it would be successful.

A small conversation followed before Duke Vermont returned. He gave a singular nod.

The coachman was instructed to go through the gate and drive the inside square loop of road until they reached the other side of the grounds. The carriage began to move.

Valerie sat poised in her seat like a noble, instead of peering out the window with curiosity. *I must play my part.* Eyes would be watching, and she couldn't afford to slip up.

She could just barely see the large grassy field in the centre, surrounded by the square palace walls. The carriage curtains were open enough to allow her to see in the evening light.

The sun was setting, and servants were walking around to light lantern poles with flames.

When their carriage came in front of the main building of the palace, they were once again stopped. A similar conversation played out, guards asking who they were and to see their invitations.

Valerie took in a long, calming breath when Vermont reached inside to take her hand and help her out of the carriage.

The man wasn't as fat as the original, but he had a similar brown tuft of hair. His eyes were such a dark shade, it was hard to tell whether they were green or blue. He had a well-cared-for beard, which the original did not, but she was certain it would be better to hide his real face.

With assistance, Valerie walked down the three steps that had been pulled out from underneath the carriage.

"The gala has already begun," Vermont stated. "We are late. A ball has been thrown and we must attend it instead of resting."

He walked in front of her as they made their way towards the palace entrance. Their five soldiers surrounded them to make sure they were guarded from all sides.

This wasn't optimal; she'd been hoping to slowly integrate herself into the people here.

Squaring her shoulders and raising her chin to show brash confidence, she lifted the skirts of the dress she'd taken from the noblewoman. It was a dark maroon and, although simple, elegant.

The shoulders were crinkled from a V in the back between her shoulder blades to a low-cut V in the front. A silver broach with a dangling blue jewel sat in between her cleavage. Her breasts were small, but they gave her just enough femininity to show she had them.

The gown was sleeved and long, hiding the flat, black shoes she wore. Her feet were larger than Cecily's, and she hadn't been able to acquire more.

Valerie had turned her nose up at any of Cecily's glamorous dresses, anything that had too much lace or frills. Instead, she'd chosen something sophisticated, anything that showed the woman wearing it was more interested in showing the qualities she already had than hiding behind a dress.

The real Cecily hadn't understood such a mindset.

Valerie had taken make-up, although she didn't normally wear it. She had to conform to the class she was playing. Rather than hiding her pale, alabaster skin behind colouring powder, she used a white cream to mask any impurities.

Her cheeks naturally had a slight pinkness to them, like she was always warm. She didn't feel the need to add anything there.

She'd donned a maroon eye shadow, darkened her lashes, and put liquid coal along the rim of her eyes. Her lips were already a pale brownish red, and she felt if she'd donned anything on her lips, it would make her appear like a jester – or that she was trying too hard.

A soft horn sounded, informing all those inside that guests were arriving.

"Now entering, Duke Vermont and Lady Cecily of house Dyèrie," introduced a servant before stepping out of the way.

She found it difficult to see over Vermont's shoulders and the guards surrounding her.

People moved out of the way to allow them to greet the king, women and men on either side trying to peer around the guards to see her. She could only see them between the guards' shoulders.

Her eyes quickly ducked up to the glass dome ceiling and the crystal chandelier hanging above. It was lit with candles and reflected rainbow fractal patterns across the glass before it became a stone ceiling of painted images.

The ceiling was alive with images of the heavens, of mountains surrounded by clouds and sky. Painted creatures like birds flew around the glass dome, like they wanted to escape and fly through it.

To someone like her, who had never seen such wealth and elegance in a simple ceiling, she had to refrain from being entranced by it.

Once they were firmly inside the room, the guards fell away to reveal her, like she was something precious.

Vermont continued to approach the throne. It was only now that she could see him, King Bradwick, sitting on his affluent chair.

His long blond hair was tied back at the base of his skull before the length of his ponytail came over one of his shoulders to rest against his chest. A golden crown encrusted with red jewels sat on his head and not a single hair was out of place.

His face was clean shaven, his eyes such a rich colour of brown they appeared molten copper.

Under his royal suit of white and blue, he looked lean yet strong. A bright grin crossed his features, making his cheek bones appear more prominent, his jaw wider.

He was handsome, dazzlingly so.

He sat on his throne with an air of arrogance. His legs were outstretched while his hands laid on the armrests made of the highest quality timber. The light blue cushions looked plumper than any chair Valerie had ever seen.

"Duke Vermont! I have not seen you since I was a little boy. Look at how fat you have gotten." King Bradwick chuckled, making his guests chortle along with him.

*Perfect, the glamour is working.* She felt the twitch of a grin at the corner of her lips but snuffed it out fast.

"Good evening, your Royal Highness," Vermont greeted, placing his hand over his heart before bowing his entire body until he showed the man the back of his head. "We, at the house of Dyèrie, would like to formally thank you for this opportunity to visit you here at the palace, and for the invitation to your gala."

King Bradwick peered at his hand for a moment, as though he was more interested in his own fingernails.

"Well, I *am* looking for a wife, and I knew that Duke Grayson had a daughter, since you only bore sons." He returned his gaze to Vermont, who was still bowing. He waved his hand dismissively to the side so Vermont would stand normally. "I'm offended that he did not come to introduce his daughter himself. Does he hold no respect for the throne?"

Valerie's gaze fell to the crowd, who began to chatter around the room, many pairs of eyes looking her over. Immediately, she could see the judgement in them.

"We were unsure if you were aware that Duke Grayson's wife is gravely ill, your Highness. He did not wish to leave his beloved in case she passed while he was away."

Valerie already knew this. She didn't react, not even when more whispers circulated.

The spell was working with the knowledge he had, and she realised that he must have been a high-ranking guard with how well he was speaking with the king.

*This is perfect. He will know enough to pass as the real Vermont.*

"Oh." The king's brow creased. "I did not know; news often takes time to travel to me. My condolences to your family. I shall pardon his impudence, considering the circumstances, and I appreciate your effort in taking his place."

"Thank you, your Highness. You are too gracious." He

gave a light bow in thanks. "May I please introduce my lovely niece?"

"Please do," he answered, his eyes finally falling upon her.

Valerie took a deep, steady breath through her nose before she stepped forward.

*I stand here for my family.* Her family wasn't here to support her, and if anyone discovered she wasn't meant to be here, she would likely be killed.

She had yet to truly take in the room, the guards, the people watching her. As soon as the king had been in eyesight, she refused to take her eyes off him.

*For my sister...* She continued to step forward until she was a step ahead of Vermont. *I bow down to the king upon the throne.*

At the last moment, her eyes flicked to the man standing off to the side of King Bradwick. There was a fierce glint to his eyes that caught her attention, and she noticed he kept his hand rested on the hilt of his sword.

She quickly averted her gaze from him and back to the king.

Valerie crossed one leg behind the other and curtsied, bowing her head by tilting it gently. She kept her head down as Vermont spoke. "This is Cecily Dyèrie, the eldest child of Duke Grayson Dyèrie and Duchess Edrea Hardringe."

The moment he was finished, she lifted her head high and rolled her shoulders back to present herself. She forcefully held his stare, meeting him eye to eye without fear. The look she gave him was one of unwavering determination.

He raised a brow, rolling the pad of his thumb over the tips of his fingers while examining her.

*While I'm here, my life is his. If I falter, I will not escape. If they discover what I am, I will not have the power to flee this palace.* She knew it. Only an incredibly powerful Witch could stand against an army.

"My, my. I did not know Grayson could produce such a woman from his loins," King Bradwick stated with a shake of his head. "You are quite stunning to behold."

Valerie didn't smile at his compliment, but she did dip her head. "Thank you, your Highness. Not many believe I'm his daughter. I took after my mother, thankfully."

He chuckled, causing lines of laughter to crinkle at the corner of his eyes. They made him appear younger, like he may have a tenderness to him.

"And comical too. Then again, I would hope for the same thing if I were his child. He is rather, how to put it eloquently... grim?"

He laughed again, but this time with a bellow. She got the impression he thought he could say whatever he pleased.

Her eyes flew to the guard beside the king as he folded his arms across his muscular chest.

She quickly brought them back to Bradwick. The men were staring at her with an inspecting and intense gaze, but she refused to show a shred of bashfulness in front of them, or anyone here, for that matter.

He waved his hand forward for her to step back next to Vermont, done speaking with her.

"You arrived just in time for the first night's events. I imagine your travels were long and tiresome. Drink, converse. Tomorrow, I will begin getting to know the daughters of the dukes of my kingdom."

Vermont bowed while she did a small curtsey, her head turning away to fall on the eyes already upon her. Vermont stepped outside so he could help a palace servant escort their guards, and Valerie was left alone in the middle of the room.

Without hesitation, she approached a waiter with a serving tray, calmly taking a chalice of wine with a strawberry inside of it.

She made her way to one of the eight white pillars in the

room so she could stand in front of it. This still put her near the centre of the hall, but it meant her back would be shielded from behind. No one could startle her there, and she wouldn't appear like a feeble woman with her back against the wall.

Like she knew they would, three women approached, even when Vermont stood next to her.

She knew who they were. They were the other dukes' daughters, ones who would be attempting to gain favour with the king and receive his hand in marriage.

The first to speak was the woman Valerie had considered taking the place of over Cecily. Now that she was looking at her, she was glad she hadn't.

Her hair was such a similar colour of brown to her eyes, they were easy to lose if her large curls fell in front of them. She was also darker in skin tone than Cecily was, and more voluptuous than Valerie could try to pass off.

"Hello, I'm Charlotte, youngest daughter of house Sazerac," she greeted with a smile, revealing mostly straight teeth. "How are you finding your evening in the palace so far?"

*She's not very bright,* Valerie thought, as the black-haired woman in front of her said, "She just got here. Her night has barely started yet."

"Well..." She seemed to think for a long moment.

"I'm Wyetta, the youngest daughter of house Haywarde," the black-haired woman said, cutting off Charlotte.

She got the impression the woman was sick of the younger girl already. Charlotte barely looked of age, whereas Wyetta was in her early twenties.

Wyetta had stunning green eyes that were darker than her own, but they held far more warmth. She had high cheek bones with pouting lips. Her skin was a deep brown, making her curly black hair stand out against her face, highlighting her beauty.

Unfortunately, she held most of her femininity in her face. She had a similar body to Valerie – petite in the ways that men seemed to care about.

"And I'm Savannah, the only daughter of Duke Colbolt Fairbairns," greeted the last woman, her frizzy hair a dazzling shade of red, her eyes a beautiful honey brown.

Her hair was tied back into two tight braids, like the servants that dressed her found it unwieldy. There were a handful of freckles dotting her face, making the bored expression she wore in her brown eyes seem softer. Like Charlotte, she was well developed, but held a brutish beauty in her face that made it seem like she would be playful if someone of interest spoke to her.

"I feel as though introducing myself would be rather pointless at this stage, but, as you all know, I'm Cecily Dyèrie." Valerie took a sip of her drink, eyeing it carefully as she absorbed the fruity taste. Then she let her eyes scan the room. "Please, tell me about your homes and your travels."

She was hoping to get them to talk so she could spend the rest of the conversation in silence. Valerie wanted to examine her environment.

Charlotte began to happily chatter away about her life in her manor, some place off to the west of the northern kingdom.

*Multiple guards on every wall.* They each had their arms straight beside them, unmoving like they were nothing more than statues. She could see their eyes moving, though, watching them all carefully.

The great hall was filled with women and men of noble blood, all obviously comfortable and relaxed. Valerie understood enough about royalty to know they surrounded themselves with a court, people to entertain them. She imagined the majority of people in this room lived permanently within the palace.

There were more than she had anticipated. *It will be hard to search the palace with so many people here.*

Savannah began talking with Charlotte about her home, asking her questions about her life. It figured that the two younger women would take a liking to each other.

The eight pillars in the room were grand, holding the ceiling by spiralling up. Painted lace designs circled them, a contrast against the cold brown marble floor.

Long glass windows reached from her hip height all the way to the top of the ceiling, allowing them to freely look outside into the dark of night. Blue curtains with silver embossed stitching had been tied back beside them, and they draped against the ground, causing an unsuspecting man to trip and fall.

People laughed at him.

Three steps ran circular at the back of the room where the throne was, thrusting it higher than the rest of the room like a podium. Bradwick was still seated there, watching them all converse while talking to a handful of men who had joined him, lazing on the steps in front of him.

*They must be his most trusted companions.* Valerie would avoid them as much as possible.

*Who was that man standing next to the king, though?* Valerie knew it might be her apprehension making her wary. She needed to be cautious of all those who could pose a risk.

*He is gone.* The guard she'd barely had the chance to look over was no longer posted next to the king. She let her eyes wander the large crowd of guests in the hall, trying to find him.

"You have yet to tell us about yourself, Cecily," Charlotte said, bringing her focus back to the conversation.

While she spoke with these women, she remained poised like a proper lady, refusing to slouch her back or shoulders whatsoever. She couldn't say the same for all of them.

"As you would have heard, my mother is ill and has been for a while. I have been taking care of my two brothers and running the house in her stead, so I rarely get to leave the manor."

"No wonder you are so late to marry then," she giggled, showing a hint of rudeness. "You are still rather pretty, so hopefully the king can see past it."

And there it was, the true game. They wanted to bring each other's confidence down.

"We have no idea what he seeks in us. Perhaps he's searching for a beautiful woman with ample breasts and perfect child-bearing hips like you." The girl batted her lids with a blush, happy with Valerie's compliment. "Or, perhaps he's searching for a woman who is not dull of wit and has learned much in her time already running a house, someone who can help run a kingdom, since she will be a queen."

Valerie tilted her head when the girl's mouth fell open. The insult had been there, but since she never mentioned who she was speaking to, none of the women could truly be offended.

Wyetta's lips perked into a small smile while Savannah's torso lightly twitched, as if she was snuffing a laugh.

"Beauty fades," Wyetta agreed, even though her face was just as stunning.

Valerie let her eyes fall to them all when she spoke.

"If one cares more about her fleeting beauty than becoming knowledgeable, what does she have left to give when the sons are born, other than a wrinkled face and lack of conversation?"

"Are you so forwardly insinuating that we are stupid?" Savannah frowned, taking the trailing of her eyes over them as an attack.

"I don't believe I said such a thing. We were merely discussing the fickle views of men that we must endure as women." That placated the girl, although Charlotte was still, deservingly, offended.

"We each have something to offer, and it's solely up to men if they find that desirable or not," Wyetta added, as if she understood what Valerie was talking about.

"Yes, and it's not our choice. We may foolishly love a man, but he could seek something as vain as beauty on his arm."

"And yet, they don't understand we often seek the same thing," Wyetta laughed before she leaned forward to whisper. "The size of their purse is often helpful in deciding."

All of them laughed except for Valerie, who merely gave a false smile.

"Perhaps, but there is more to a man than his purse and his face."

"You are talking about treatment," Savannah said, taking a sip of her wine. "It's true that some men can be brutish. Most lack the ability to be romantic, or to not think with their dicks."

"I would not take a man if he could not be faithful," Charlotte blurted out.

"Only a woman who can handle men and satisfy them can stop their husband from taking a mistress," Wyetta told her.

That was something Valerie already knew about human nobles. The men often liked to take up other women. Doing it openly meant they lacked respect for their wives, but there were many reasons why they hid their disloyalty.

"I agree with Charlotte," Savannah said, allowing a frown to cross her features. "It should not matter. To take up a wife is to be loyal to her, especially since we rarely get the opportunity to choose our husband. If they sought us, they should remain ours."

"What do you think, Cecily?" Wyetta asked with a raised brow, obviously disagreeing.

"I believe karma is a wonderful medicine," Valerie answered, causing all the women to lower their lips in silent gasps.

Valerie was talking about fighting adultery with adultery. They wouldn't know she also wouldn't allow a man to beat her, or treat her horribly either, without retaliation.

She appeared dainty and feminine, but she was strong. Her mother had taught all her daughters how to fight with a weapon, since white magic was rarely used to harm.

These words were also a message to not cross her. She wouldn't hesitate to retaliate freely.

Turning to Vermont, she tugged on the sleeve of his dress suit to grab his attention. She wasn't bothered by her own statement, how it wasn't seen as proper, but she no longer wished to be a part of this conversation.

"Uncle, I believe you promised we would dance when we arrived." No promise had been made.

"Of course, niece." He offered his arm so she could take it.

She pulled away from the women, looking each in the eye before turning.

Placing her empty glass on a tray offered by a servant, she put her hand on his shoulder while the other she allowed him to grasp.

The king was still seated on his throne, and from the corner of her eye, she noted he was watching her now that she was out in the open. There were already other dancers, and they joined in an easy waltz, mirroring them.

She knew how to dance, knew how to be proper. Most importantly, Valerie knew how to act *human*.

"Perhaps you will be too much for those girls," Vermont whispered, leaning forward. "I think they underestimate you."

The power of the spell was working perfectly. *He truly thinks he's Duke Vermont and I'm his niece.*

"They will come to learn that I have fangs," she answered, keeping her face relaxed.

Other guests turned their heads in their direction due to the bellowing laugh he released. He shook his head with a grin.

"Perhaps you should be more cautious. If you wish to gain the king's hand in marriage, you would do well not to upset the court, my dear."

Valerie became quiet with thought. Even though she had no desire to earn the king's marriage proposal, she needed to get close to him to find the answers she sought.

*It does not matter. I intend to avoid the court as much as possible.* She didn't need to change.

Valerie also didn't want to pretend her personality wasn't what it was. She already had to pretend to be another person; changing who she truly was to play a soft woman would add confusion.

They were moving in a slow circle. Eventually, she was able to peek over her pretend uncle's shoulder to see the king upon his throne once more. Her focus drifted to the guard, who had returned to his position next to him.

Their eyes met, and she held his gaze, since he refused to look away. Folding his arms across his chest, his head reared back very slowly, lifting, while his brow raised.

He appeared tall and muscular under his black dress suit. Ten red felt buttons ran in pairs up his coat while that same red was stitched into the seams, including the thick collar.

The hilt of his sword was silver, held by a mahogany brown scabbard. The hilt wasn't fancy, but she could tell by the size of the thing that it was a claymore.

*He has the eyes of a killer.* Predatory, cunning, with a shining blue that almost appeared silver if he moved.

His inch-long hair was unruly, as though he didn't care about it, yet it was such a dark shade of black, it almost appeared blue in the light.

Along with a sharp clip of jaw was a curved nose that almost looked as though it was buttoned with a triangle rather than a circle, making him look fiercer. His cheeks were not as high as the king's, but there was a rugged edge to him.

She expected him to be stone cold with the way he looked, but the king leaned his head back and to the side to speak with him, and the guard's eyes lit up. She could tell he gave a warm chuckle, turning his gaze away to speak to the king.

Now that the eye contact was broken, she allowed Vermont to continue their circle so her side was facing them.

The reason Valerie had met his eyes for so long was so he would know she wasn't afraid of him, and to leave her alone. Men didn't appreciate women like her, women who might cause trouble if they were approached wrong.

It was a silent warning that she would cause trouble for him at court, would cause strife with the king if he bothered her.

She gave similar looks to other men in the room who gazed at her while she danced. They shied away much quicker.

There were only a handful of women who could grab the attention of someone like Geryon within the first moment.

Watching this beauty – who appeared as delicate as a butterfly and walked with the elegance of a deer, all while wearing the stare of a snake – approach the king to bow to him was truly intriguing.

There was something about the cold, calculating look in her pale green eyes that made it hard to look away. She was focused, even when her eyes darted to look at him standing just off from the king, before she gracefully curtsied and bowed her head.

There was no smile when she was complimented by King Bradwick, nor did she grow rosy in the cheeks under the scrutiny of the court.

*She's different from the other ladies.* Then again, they were all different.

The black-haired one had been easy to make smile with a simple compliment – the king had spoken such tender words to each of them. She also held a certain grace, but she lacked a fierce gaze that would have grabbed his interest.

The redhead had been dazzling when she was introduced. The subtle lick at the seam of her lips and the inviting eye she gave would have made lesser men crawl over each other to bed her.

The female with light brown hair had not only curtsied, but she had almost gotten to her knees to do so. The complete dip in her bow allowed them to see straight down her dress – which was already low to accentuate her femininity. The roaring blush with a flutter of her lids at being complimented was an attempt to show she was flustered.

He could tell she was used to such words.

The only one who didn't seem to care about the king's affectionate words had been this woman. Then, her chin had lifted ever so slightly at Bradwick's rude words about her father, like anything he said was insignificant.

As soon as the word came to mind, that's when he realised the look she gave all of them was just that. It was as though they were all insignificant. Beneath her. Inferior.

Other than that cold look in her eyes, the other aspect of her that caught his attention was her long, slender neck. *Like a swan...*

Unlike the other females, who he'd already decided what kind of prey they reminded him of, she was the only one who resembled multiple. He couldn't decide on which one to call her.

Why did Geryon like to think this way about women? He didn't. He thought this way about all people, especially men.

If he thought of a man as a bear, he knew to be just as brutal back. If the man was catty, he knew to be cunning and quick-witted around him. If he reminded him of a pig, all he needed was to direct a woman into his lap, give him meat, and he would be a good little piggy.

Women were the same. A mouse would mean he needed

to be careful of her skittish nature. If she was a viper, he knew how to keep her in line. A gazelle would indicate to him that she must be treated properly to be compliant.

He had to know these things about the people of the court, since he was a rather... special guard for the king. His task was to keep him alive, as well as to council him.

Geryon had offered his services many years ago. After gaining Bradwick's respect, he had allowed him to stand by the king at court.

Bradwick wouldn't dare tell him what to do, and understood that although he protected him, the king didn't rule him. Geryon wasn't like his servants or other guards. He wasn't on the same level as the people here.

He also didn't truly care about Bradwick, since he had his own reasons for being here.

Once again, Geryon's eyes trailed over the woman being presented to them.

She was petite in bone and body, but not in stature. Even though they weren't on the same ground level, he thought she may be a little taller than him – a feat all on its own.

*She does not appear weak.* He could see the press of feminine muscle through the sleeves of her long dress, despite her slim figure.

The features of her face were soft around her pointed chin and jaw, but her cheek bones were high, her brow bone prominent. Her eyebrows were dark like her hair, arched with a defined point at the end. Although she obviously wore make-up around those cold, pale green eyes, it wasn't overdone on the rest of her face.

Something dangled from her ears, but he couldn't see them with her hair in the way.

*The other women are prettier,* but they didn't hold his attention as well. *Perhaps she will be boring like the others.*

When she was dismissed, Geryon took himself from the

rise he was on to follow.

He'd done this with each of the newcomers, wanting to understand them, since they were strangers.

She turned her back to a pillar, and he brought himself to the side of it, leaning the bottom of his boot and back against it. He kept himself out of view, listening to the conversations of her and the man who travelled with her.

Her uncle was as he expected: calm and intelligent, easy to stir to laughter by other men. The conversation hadn't once brought up the king, but his brother was readily tossed into the conversation. They made fun of Duke Grayson until the conversation turned darker, speaking of the strange illness that had overcome the duke's wife.

*He reminds me of a tiger, cunning yet sharp fanged.* He'd seen muscles under his suit, even though he had a small, fat gut. He obviously trained and had fought many battles in his life.

As a man, Geryon should have been offended by the conversation of the women, as well as with the things Lady Cecily had freely said. He wasn't, although it did cause his brow to raise.

*She has wit and is well-mannered, yet insolent.* He brought his hand to his chin to rub his jaw thoughtfully. *If she speaks so forwardly with Bradwick, I'm unsure if he will like her.*

The king was arrogant. He liked to surround himself with men of high intellect, but Geryon was unsure what kind of women he preferred, since he rarely took the time to speak to them. He didn't care if people laughed at his jokes, so long as he found them hilarious, but he did like people to be entertaining.

He wasn't sure if she hated men or if she just understood the unfair justice of her place as a woman. *If she does understand and adhere to the hierarchy, then she would be a valuable person at court.*

He'd thought the same thing of Wyetta.

"I do believe karma is a wonderful medicine," she answered to Wyetta's question.

She had said it so calmly, no undertone of humour or snarkiness, but he understood the warning behind it. *She will not tolerate being ill-treated by anyone.* Knowing that made Geryon grin.

*If she does not entertain the king, she will surely entertain me while she is here.* He hoped to overhear further conversations. *I hope someone crosses her; I'm interested to know how she reacts.*

That spark of enjoyment from his eavesdropping was stolen when she was taken away to dance with her uncle.

With a scowl, he returned to stand next to the king.

"How were they?" Bradwick asked as he rested his cheek against his enclosed fist.

"You will enjoy conversing with Duke Vermont. He laughs easily but speaks with intelligence."

"His niece?" This wasn't the first time Bradwick had asked him questions about those he snooped on.

"Sharp of mind as well as tongue," he answered truthfully.

"Is she funny? She appeared to be when I spoke with her, and I do so love that in a person."

"The conversation did not allow me to know." Geryon never called him by his title or spoke formally, like everyone else was forced to. He couldn't remember if the words 'your Highness' had ever fallen from his mouth.

There was a silence between them. The men at his feet began to pull apart her looks. They were studying both the negative and positive aspects of her face and body.

Geryon crinkled his nose at the turn of the conversation and ignored them. Instead, he brought his gaze forward to sweep over the court.

That's when he connected eyes with Cecily, and she

blatantly held his. Surprised that she would, he raised his brow and folded his arms, expecting her to avert her gaze.

She didn't. *She has the nerve to stare me down?* He couldn't believe the audacity, even more so when she further deepened it by narrowing her eyes.

*This woman is dangerous.* Not to the king, but to a man like him. He ran his tongue behind his lips before tonguing the point of a human canine tooth.

Her look had been a warning, but he saw it as an invitation to cause mischief. He didn't like being told what to do, and it was unfortunate he couldn't cross any boundaries with her.

She could potentially become the queen consort.

"I'm not surprised she hates you already." Bradwick snorted. "How do you manage to make everyone dislike you without ever needing to speak to them?"

Geryon chuckled, turning his head down to him since he was being spoken to. "They sense I'm hazardous without understanding why they feel that way."

His eyes fell back to the woman, expecting to find her joyfully dancing with her uncle.

He almost growled when he realised the same gaze she had just given him, she also gave to other men around the room. He didn't like that what he saw as an invitation was given so freely to others.

She refused to look at him for the remainder of the evening.

Valerie separated from Vermont so he could lead them back to her pillar once the other ladies disappeared. He left to grab her a drink at her request and eventually returned with two women in tow.

"Cecily, I would like to introduce you to Countess Nicole of house Celoncrea, and Baroness Victoria of house Ashwold." They all bowed lightly in greeting to each other. "Nicole and I have discussed it quickly, and Cecily, my dear, Victoria will be your lady-in-waiting while you are within the palace walls."

*What is a lady-in-waiting?* Valerie tried not to show her lack of understanding.

"Each of the invited nobles was assigned a court assistant," Nicole said. "We were not sure if all of you would turn up, but King Bradwick made sure we were prepared."

"Of course. I expected the head of the house for the king would be so organised," Valerie answered smoothly.

"Thank you, I do try." She leaned forward to cover her mouth as she whispered, "The fact that he has finally decided to marry means I won't have to do so much. I can finally relax." Her smile was warm and genuine behind her hazelnut hair and blue eyes. "Now, if you will excuse me, the evening grows late, and I must take my drunken husband from the room before he embarrasses me."

Nicole departed, leaving Victoria behind, who stood clasping her hands together like she was awaiting something.

Valerie was interested in the countess, considering her current path. She was making a steady beeline straight to the king and the men at his feet.

She curtsied for Bradwick before she crooked her finger at one of the men, who gave a roll of his eyes. The man who had been sitting closest to him on the floor got to his feet with a huff.

"You wish to dance, dove?" he said with obvious cheer, boisterous enough that even Valerie could hear him.

Nicole gave a shake of her head, but he grabbed her hand and forcefully spun her around. His hold on her was tight as they began to waltz. He drunkenly stumbled over his own feet, but she indeed laughed, letting her head fall back.

*Court is not as serious as I thought it would be.* She'd always been told functions such as these were boring and proper. *Perhaps only for those who are not a permanent part of the court.*

"Uncle, the hour is late, and I wish to retire to my room."

"Yes, my lady," Baroness Victoria answered instead. "We have already arranged for your chests to be brought up to the room, and I'm happy to escort you if you are ready."

"Are you ready to retire yourself, my Lord?" a male said as he stepped into Valerie's view.

He'd also been anointed a lord-in-waiting.

"Yes, our travels were long, since we are one of the furthest provinces from the palace. I wish to remain with my niece until she is more comfortable within the palace walls."

"Please, follow me then," he answered, turning away to lead them from the main hall.

The baroness walked behind them and made sure she was always a step behind Valerie.

*This place is far larger than I expected it to be.* It would make searching harder. She doubted she'd be able to cover the entire square building in the time she was here with how far it went.

They were taken to a section of the palace on the second floor, where they had their own private seating areas separated by a long hall. It was not part of the main second floor, though; it was sectioned off by itself, only accessible by a staircase from the first floor.

Her own seating area, her parlour, had been arranged to be feminine. It looked clean and well dusted. *My living arrangements are awfully private.* There had only been two guards posted, and they were those she had travelled with.

Valerie hadn't asked Victoria to follow her inside her room, and she was confused when a moment later, women carrying steaming buckets entered as well.

She jumped when Victoria began to undo the tie at the back of her dress, unused to people touching her so informally. She'd also been expecting the servant woman she'd brought here – someone she trusted.

Valerie swiftly turned around. "What are you doing?"

"Oh, my apologies." She bowed her head with a crinkle of her brow. It was hard to tell if she was sincere. "I assumed you would prefer to bathe to remove the night and your travels before you slept. I was instructed to make sure you were well relaxed."

*She's acting like the personal servant girl I saw following Lady Cecily around her manor.* Valerie's eyes widened as she realised the woman had been commanded to follow her around like a dog.

Once her bath had been filled, Victoria once more began to undo her dress. Understanding the woman's position better, she allowed her to do what was necessary.

She stepped from her dress when it fell to her feet and hopped inside the bath.

"At first, I thought you had been shy, but it seems you were merely confused." Victoria said this because she had stepped from her clothing without a blush or a shred of bashfulness. "Did you not know what a lady-in-waiting was?"

Even though she had three sisters, which meant being naked around women didn't bother her, she wasn't shy about nudity in front of men either.

"I did not know someone of noble blood would be attending to me."

The woman came to kneel behind the tub to start unravelling the braids in her hair.

"I often forget court is startling to those who are unused to it. That's why I have been assigned the task of assisting you while you are here."

"It's fine. I eventually realised it myself."

"So, you don't need me to explain any of it to you?"

Valerie shook her head. "No, since I will be changing your duties."

"How do you mean?" She could hear the frown in the woman's voice.

Valerie turned in the water to face her and placed her back against the other tub wall. Resting her elbows and hands on the edge of the tub, she tapped it while she thought, deciding on what she wanted from the girl.

"I don't wish for you to follow me around the palace. However, I will expect you to be here in the mornings in case I wish to go somewhere in particular. At that time, you will also inform me of news and the events for the day. Once I'm done with you, you will only come to my side if I join the court. No matter where they are in the palace, you are to remain with them."

Victoria's brows crinkled. She was a sweet-looking woman with freckles dotting her skin heavily. Her hair was an ashy blonde, while her eyes were such a dark colour of brown, they almost appeared black from far away.

"People will ask me why I'm not with you, since I'm supposed to be attending to you."

"I don't care what you tell them." She held the woman's eyes with a crinkle of her nose. "Unless it's something unpleasant." She let her warning features fall to soften her look. "I have always been a person who prefers her freedom and privacy. I wish to explore the palace on my own and without distraction, unless I have been called for."

"But how will they know where to find you?" The girl's frown deepened.

"That's why I want you to know the events of the day by the morning, so you may inform me where and when I'm required to be present. The rest of the time, I wish to be alone. If there is another party like there was tonight, you are to be there with me. If not, I will expect you to wait for me in my parlour area to help me prepare for sleep."

"What do you wish for me to do while I wait for you?"

Valerie paused, letting her eyes sweep over the baroness, who was obviously deeply confused by her demands.

"Do you know how to read?"

"Somewhat. I have been taking private lessons."

"Then read, paint, bring your husband if you have one. I don't care what you do to entertain yourself. I don't care if I find you asleep, as long as it will allow me to explore this beautiful place on my own." She gestured to the walls around her.

Victoria gave a cheerful smile.

"The palace is remarkable, is it not? I understand your

desire to wander it. I often do when there is no court business to attend." Her smile grew brighter. "Perhaps it's fortunate I'm the one who will be attending to you."

"How so?"

She gave a giggle. Then she raised her hand to the side of her face like she was intending to whisper something private, yet she spoke with the same loud volume as before. "I have often been ridiculed for being missing or late to functions because I have gotten lost in the palace." She then did lower her voice. "Or I fell asleep somewhere on the grounds."

*This is wonderful. The baroness will cover for me while I look around.* She snuffed the desire to smirk.

Everything was happening easier than she imagined.

"But I will suggest to you, my lady," Victoria said while she obtained a towel, since Valerie had finished bathing, "that you do attend the separate functions that some of the court women hold. It will reflect better on you in the eyes of the king if he sees you are able to blend in with them. It will be one of the factors that will help him decide on his wife. If you ladies are unable to assimilate into his company, it may not bode well for you."

"Should they not accept us, since we will be the potential queen?"

"No." She shook her head before she knelt to go through one of her chests for a nightgown. "They may go out of their way to make sure you stick out, so they can assure a queen they can manipulate."

"If that's true, why would you tell me when you are one of them?"

"Because, my lady, while you are here, my task is to inform you of such things. I can also already tell you will not treat me horribly, like some high-handed noblewomen have. I will try to assist you as much as I can for that reason alone."

*She is trying to gain my trust.* Valerie didn't know if it was merely a ruse, but she didn't particularly care.

"Thank you." Valerie inclined her head in gratitude. "I shall consider you an ally during my stay, then."

"You are welcome." She walked over to the bed to untuck it, pulling the corner out carefully and folding it back, then turned with her hands clasped in front of her waist. "Do you need me for anything else? I can brush your hair or—"

"No, this is fine. Please, enjoy your evening."

Once the woman was gone, Valerie let out a sigh and walked over to the window to stare at the night sky.

Finally, she could have a moment to relax, to breathe. The charade she was playing was tiring.

The waning moon bathed the long, wide, grassy field in the centre of the square palace walls with light. She touched her sternum, like that was where her magic was hidden away inside of her.

*I don't remember a night where I have not done a moon ritual.* It was something her entire coven performed every night to give tribute to their ancestors, to thank them for their power.

There was also a ritual for the sun she would miss in the morning, a tribute to the power of fire and those who wielded it.

Witches were the product of humans and Dragons mating; their witchcraft came from their mystical ancestor. Dragons had the ability to take a human form through a spell, and over a thousand years ago, one had decided to take a human female to slake their lust.

Witches were created by accident, since it hadn't been known Dragons could breed with humans. Once they discovered they could, they became interested in the creatures they could create.

The result was a thing with a human body, but with magical properties like them. They were curious. Breeding with humans became a regular thing until there were hundreds of Witches.

Dragons taught them how to use their magic, how to access the world and nature around them to grow it, how to create potions, and cast spells. From there, they began to teach themselves, and their Dragon parents were entertained by their powerful little human-like children.

Apparently, life had been peaceful.

The Faerydae family, her family, to this day prayed to their ancestor in thanks for life.

*It's also our way of apologising.* Her eyes fell upon the moon once more, before looking over the stars. *Their hatred is well deserved.*

Just over five hundred years ago, one of their kind, Strolguil the Vast, turned on his Dragon parent. After learning he could grow his magic by pulling apart fairies and pixies who wouldn't have been apprehensive of her kind at the time, he ate them.

Once he realised this increased his power, the villain turned on his own Dragon parent, killing him to consume his parts. He became the first dark Witch and extended his life through evil magic.

He taught others how to do this, how to steal essence from magical creatures through violence. It permanently tainted their souls, corrupted them.

Now, Valerie knew there were more dark Witches than white.

She also knew Dragons hunted Witches to rid themselves of the evil they had mistakenly created, while evil Witches hunted them so they could extract them for parts.

It was a constant cycle of hate, a war between the species, and one she didn't want to join. Unfortunately, that choice may be taken away from her.

*How long will it be before I desire nothing more than*

*power?* She was waiting for the tingle to begin, or at least something to indicate she was turning, the poison of corruption taking over. *I have committed disgusting acts to be here. How long until I turn?*

Valerie feared it. She dreaded it like a cold sweat dripping down her back, even though she knew she would no longer care when the darkness started growing inside her. *But I don't wish to turn corrupt.*

This was one of the reasons she hadn't let her sisters join her in finding Kaeylyn. She couldn't allow any of her pure, magic-wielding sisters to fall to darkness, just to save the youngest. She was the eldest, and it was her duty to protect her younger siblings.

*I will be the first Faerydae to become a dark Witch.* An overwhelming amount of shame washed over her. *I will taint our family bloodline.*

She pulled away from the window with slumped shoulders.

Taking in the large room littered with wealthy furniture and a grand bed, she felt out of depth with her task.

*I'm not used to this.* In all her life, she'd never been waited on by a servant or slept in a bed this soft. The expensive, wealthy quality of everything made her feel as though she'd break anything she touched.

She turned her mind away from the daunting room, knowing she needed her rest for whatever torture this place was going to force her to endure tomorrow.

5

Valerie sat upon the backless cushioned stool in front of the vanity in her living quarters. Victoria was styling her hair while she spoke of the events that happened after Valerie's early retirement.

It was only this morning that she fully took in the extravagant room.

The bottom half of the walls were painted a pastel purple with golden embossed designs, and the top half were plain and cream coloured. Paintings of nature covered each wall, like they were there to make it seem this vast room was larger than it already was.

A giant brown carpet with red floral designs was laid down over oak slats, and it almost spanned the entire size of the room to hide the wooden flooring.

There was a writing desk in front of one window, overlooking the field in the middle of the palace. The window she had stared out of the previous night was empty of any furniture. The vanity table she sat at was on the other side of the room, on the wall with the door.

The bed had a canopy frame, with purple curtains tied to each spiral pole holding the frame up.

There was a single lounging bed up against the wall, behind a table with two chairs in the centre of the room. It was like she was supposed to entertain guests in her room, which she thought was preposterous.

*I doubt I will want anyone in here.*

There was a serving tray with warm tea that Victoria had brought up with her. She'd been woken when an eating tray was placed in her lap with a large breakfast.

"...And Lady Gracie tripped over due to the wine. She knocked into a servant holding a full serving tray, and it all came tumbling down on top of them, red all over her dress and the floor." She was giggling, like the embarrassment of others was something to be ridiculed and laughed at. "I'm sure she will be quite red-faced today."

*This is what this woman considers news? I don't want trivial gossip.* "And what of the other dukes' daughters?"

"Well, Lady Wyetta left not long after you." Placing the brush down, she twirled her hair and pinned the long length of it. "Savannah and Charlotte left at the same time."

Valerie frowned. "Why?"

"They left the party once King Bradwick retired to his room."

"They wish to be under his constant gaze, so the rest of us don't have a chance to be alone with him if possible."

"It would appear so, yes."

Victoria didn't plait or braid her hair, but she made a small, tight bun on the back of her head off to the side. It was behind her right ear, clipped so that the waves of her hair were controlled to rest over one shoulder and down her chest. It tucked underneath her jaw when she applied more pins to make it appear thicker. Pulling her hair like this to one side highlighted the pale flesh of her neck on the other side.

"They are rather devious, those two," Valerie said, raising a brow through the mirror's reflection.

Now that her hair was done, she was instructed to turn around so she could do her make-up.

"You saw how I prefer it last night; I wish for it to be similar around the face. You may apply it as glamorous as you please around the eyes. There, I don't care."

With a nod, she began her task. Valerie closed her eyes so that they could be painted, the dusty make-up cold against her eyelids.

"Are you worried about the other women participating in the gala, my lady?"

"Not at all. We can call it a gala, but it's really a competition. We will all play the game how we see fit, and it's up to King Bradwick as to what he decides is titillating."

It was a game Valerie would be pretending to play, and she had been strategizing since she arrived. It was also one she wasn't invested in at all.

*If I play mysterious, it will give me the freedom to search while also garnering the king's interest so I can get closer.* It could backfire, though; he might see her as disinterested.

She opened her eyes when Victoria was finished, nodding in approval. A soft brown had been painted on her lids. Her eyes were shinier, while the rest of her face appeared natural.

"You have yet to tell me what today's events are," Valerie said, watching Victoria pull dresses from her clothing chests.

"King Bradwick seems to prefer blue. If I were you, I would dress accordingly."

"I don't care what his favourite colour is," she answered dully, moving one of her legs so it rested atop the other. This made the girl pause in surprise. "I wish to wear the grey dress."

It was pale in colour, but it would stop her skin from washing out if she were to walk into the sun. It had a multilayer skirt, which would fluff out so it would be comfortable to walk in. There was brown stitching over the chest that came to a V near her navel, while the rest of the torso was plain. That same stitching danced along the sleeves.

"Yes, ma'am. Sorry to be so untoward." She grabbed it, airing it out of any dust, while Valerie stood to remove her nightgown. "You are to attend court while Bradwick makes up his mind on what he wishes to do."

"There is no plan for the day?" She thought he would have some clue as to what he was doing.

"He does for the rest of the week, but I believe he's unsure for today, since it's technically the first day of the gala. He does not know you ladies, so please be patient with him."

*Ah, so he's unsure how he wishes to approach us. I would be overwhelmed if I had four men fawning over me.*

Valerie felt pity for the king.

"Do you not have any other shoes?" Victoria asked as she gestured to the plain black slippers in her hands.

"No. It seems my servant forgot to pack them." *Cecily's feet had been too small.*

"Oh no, this cannot be tolerated." She walked over to one of the sofas and matched the bottom of the slipper against her own foot. "I believe I'm a size too small."

"It's fine, Victoria. I can make do with one pair. I, at least, chose to wear something comfortable in my travels."

"You are trying to impress the court, my lady. They will ridicule you if they discover you only have one pair." She helped put the slippers on Valerie's feet before she stood up to place her hands on her hips. "Clothing and footwear often go missing. I will try to find something that will fit you." Then, her eyes darted up to Valerie, who towered above due to their height difference. "Perhaps something that lacks a heel, though."

"Much appreciated," Valerie answered, with a bow of her

head to show her thanks. "Am I ready now? Or is there something missing from my ensemble that you wish to criticize?"

The baroness had been creating a fuss for most of the morning, wanting to make sure she looked beautiful. She felt like a porcelain doll.

The woman blushed. She'd made many comments about Valerie's lack of fancy dresses, jewellery, and footwear. Valerie was thankful she'd gone through Cecily's travel chests and thrown out everything over the top.

"No, I believe you look fashionable."

"Splendid. Please lead the way."

Rather than being led to the main ballroom, she was taken down a long, wide hallway, filled with people of the king's court already chatting away. They were acting merrily, but she noticed their gazes peek at her when she walked past.

She didn't feel the need to lift her chin. She didn't want to seem like she was snubbing them, but she did carry a firmness in her shoulders.

There were large windows to the left, while the doors to a few rooms were open to her right, allowing her the opportunity to peek in as they passed. More people were littered inside of them.

Valerie was taken to a large room with an assortment of seating. Women sat with their husbands at a large round table, conversing with each other and laughing. Lounges allowed those seated to speak with those on the floor, or to those standing close by.

From the corner of her eye, she could see Vermont speaking with a small group of men on the balcony. *As much as I want to keep an eye on him, it does not seem I will be able to.*

"Perhaps you were wise in your decision to not wear blue, Lady Cecily." Victoria giggled from beside her.

Charlotte was wearing a bright blue dress, while a ribbon of similar colour tied most of her hair back. Savannah had opted for a brown dress, but the fascinator hat and gloves she wore were blue. Wyetta wasn't as obvious, but she wore a blue ribbon around her throat and waist.

"I wonder if he will appreciate the colour once these two weeks are over," Valerie whispered, keeping her face straight.

"That's quite funny! I surely doubt it." Victoria's laughter gained them attention.

"Ah, Lady Cecily, we have been awaiting your arrival," King Bradwick said from his seat in front of the ladies.

"My apologies, your Highness." She gave a small curtsey as she approached. Victoria fell back to no longer be a part of the conversation but remained close by. "When I retired to my room last night, I was so tired from my travels that I did not think to unpack."

His blond hair was tied over his shoulder again, but today's attire was black with golden stitching and red felt buttons.

"Understandable." His brown eyes lit up when he grinned. He tapped the arms of his chair. "Well, now that you are here, we may start the day."

It was only when he leapt to his feet and stepped forward that she noticed his guard moved in reaction, wanting to follow the king.

The suit he wore was dark navy, but she thought it was strange that a simple guard would wear something so extravagant. Although there was a stitched design, the twelve buttons on this coat were attached to chains that ran around his body and fastened at the back.

He was wearing clothing like a lord, and he would likely have needed assistance to be dressed. It didn't match the worn sword belt and scabbard he wore around his hips.

She still didn't know his name, and she wasn't interested in discovering it.

"Come, ladies," Bradwick demanded, while offering each of his arms. "Let us walk around the palace and get to know each other, shall we?"

The three women leapt for his arms, making him chuckle. Wyetta had been lucky enough that she was the closest to his left side and managed to thread her arm through his. Charlotte elbowed poor Savannah out of the way when they both launched for the other.

Valerie patiently waited for the embarrassing show to be over, her hands clasped in front of her waist.

Upset, Savannah walked away from the brown-haired woman to link arms with Wyetta, which meant... She tried not to crinkle her nose and was thankful she'd managed to stop herself. *I will have to walk with Charlotte.*

Geryon walked behind King Bradwick and the four women, listening to them and the people they walked past.

Each of the noblewomen were taking a turn answering the questions asked by Bradwick. Although the conversation was underwhelming, he was following because this is what he always did inside the palace – when he could be bothered.

He was either protecting the king, or he trusted he would be safe while he spent valuable time by himself. With people he didn't know in the palace, Geryon felt more comfortable remaining by his side for now.

"How can you possibly enjoy winter over the other seasons?" Bradwick laughed, shaking his head like he found that bizarre. "I can think of nothing worse than freezing snow. I would much prefer to be warm, so I don't have to worry about having fire, or if I accidentally leave my coat somewhere."

"It's far easier to warm up than to cool down," Cecily answered. "I would much rather seek heat than be desperate to escape it."

"Come now, ladies, you must disagree."

"I much prefer spring," answered Savannah.

Charlotte had already agreed with Bradwick about summer being the best season – she agreed with everything he said.

"Actually, I agree with her," Wyetta grumbled. "The lands of the Haywarde estate are quite high and can be awfully hot in the summer. If given the choice between winter and summer, I would pick winter. Although I must admit, I love spring as well, because of the flowers."

"That's it! I will have to have you both whipped for having such terrible opinions on the weather." Geryon could tell he was jesting, but Wyetta's back stiffened, like she perceived it as a real threat.

When Cecily turned her head to the side to inspect a painting, he could tell she was unbothered. She had worn the same face for most of this stroll: collected and bored.

"Whip me as much as you like, your Highness, but I would much prefer that than to bake in the summer heat with a three-layered dress on."

Bradwick threw his head back with a laugh before he lifted a finger to shake it at her. Geryon knew he'd found humour in what she said, but this conversation was the first time she'd elicited a response from the king at all.

She was more interested in peering at the palace walls. Yet, she never missed a cue in conversation, like she was able to balance both.

"Here, watch this, ladies. I find Baron Cliffard quite hilarious," he whispered. Then he shouted, "Cliffard! You lumbering sod!"

The nobleman started at being called so suddenly. His

hands shook in reaction, throwing some of his ale down the front of his coat.

"Yes, your Royal Highness?" he asked after he coughed to catch his breath. He gave him a bow.

All except Cecily laughed – she didn't even smile. Instead, she turned her head up, seeming irritated. *I also don't find making fun of people entertaining.* Bradwick often teased his subjects because they couldn't retaliate.

"You did not find that humorous, Cecily?" King Bradwick asked with a frown.

"I was so curious about this painting that I did not hear your jest, your Highness. I hope I did not cause offense; it was just so eye catching, I was unable to concentrate on anything else."

Geryon raised his brow. *She is a pretty little liar.*

The king stopped them all so they could admire it as well. The painting they were admiring was one of Geryon's few favourites in the palace.

It was a large image of the fabled Pinnacle of Dragons, a place rumoured to once be their governing location. Dragons of different colours were depicted flying around it, heading over the ocean towards the mountain island.

Humans believed no such thing existed anymore, that the creatures they once thought of as gods were now extinct. Some ventured the seas to find its ruins, only to never return.

"If only the Dragons still existed, right, Geryon?" Bradwick said with a grin, his head turning to him with a certain twinkle in his eyes.

A small growl almost left his chest. He hated it when he made small, knowing jabs of truth towards him. *That mouth of his will unveil me.* Then Geryon would be forced to kill every single person inside this palace.

"They do," Cecily surprised them all by saying.

"No, they don't," Savannah sneered. "Everyone knows

they were hunted into extinction years ago. Anyone who says they have seen one is obviously deranged."

"Yes, and they left us humans to deal with the chaos they bred," Wyetta added. *She speaks of Witches.*

"It's foolish to believe something as magnificent and powerful as the Dragons are extinct. I'm sure they are out there, hiding from us." Then, she turned away from the painting to give the four of them a smile, the first one she'd shared on this stroll. "My apologies. I must sound unhinged to hold such a fantastical opinion."

"No, not at all," Bradwick answered with a frown. "I share the same thoughts."

"Me too. I think they are alive." Charlotte cuddled into his arm so that her bosom pressed tight against it.

Geryon didn't have the mind to roll his eyes at the silly noblewoman. No, he was too busy staring at Cecily. *She believes in Dragons and thinks highly of them... I expected her not to have such childish thoughts of man.*

She'd spoken it confidently, too, like she believed it was the truth. *I'm curious as to why.*

"Well then! Say they really are still alive," Bradwick started with an excited voice, the subject one of deep interest to him. "What would you do if you were able to meet one, ladies?"

"Most likely scream, since it will try to eat me," Cecily answered. Her head turned to the painting one last time before the king dragged them away.

Geryon chuckled to himself. *She has a fair point.*

She peeked over her shoulder at the sound he made. He quietened, raising a brow in her direction since she was staring at him.

Bradwick also laughed. "Say it was like a pet and you could tell it what to do."

"I would ride it and tell it to take me to the sky," Charlotte giggled, putting the arm not connected to the king out. It slammed against Cecily's stomach, and she winced upon the hard impact. "I would tell it to take me all over the world."

It appeared Cecily didn't care that she'd been hit. *Where is her retaliation?* After her words the previous eve, he expected more.

"I think that's everyone's answer," laughed Savannah, for the first time agreeing with the younger female.

"It's not mine," Wyetta interjected, causing his brow to raise. *This one is thoughtful, like Cecily. I wonder what she would do.*

"Well, don't leave us in suspense, Lady Wyetta," Bradwick said, waving his hand in a circle to get her to continue.

"I would try to kill it." This made them all pause, turning their heads to her. She gave a laugh while shaking hers. "I doubt I would be able to, but the glory of winning a battle against such a formidable creature is something I would value very dearly."

"You would like to be called Wyetta the DragonKiller?" Bradwick's eyes lit up further, invested in this conversation now that it was getting interesting. "Perhaps you would have to fight me first at the cave entrance, since I would want such a title for myself."

"Your Highness, I would fear crossing a sword with you more than the Dragon themself."

Bradwick threw his head back in a loud, bellowing laugh. He reached over and patted her arm wrapped around his, almost causing Charlotte to lose her death grip.

"My dear, I would not let the Dragons overhear such a statement. I'm sure they would be infuriated."

She gave a coy smile, while Charlotte and Savannah narrowed their eyes.

"We have yet to hear what you would do, and I'm rather

curious about it," Bradwick said to Cecily, who was facing forward, walking gracefully with her arm wrapped around Charlotte's.

"I thought I already had – I would scream at its fangs."

"No, no." He shook his head. "We have already determined that it's your pet and will obey you."

She turned her head to the king, and it allowed Geryon to see her face. Her lips were twitching, as if trying to suppress the urge to smile in humour.

"Although I highly doubt a Dragon would allow themselves to be a pet, I do believe Wyetta's answer is the most intriguing." There was a long silence. It must have taken her a moment to realise she was upsetting the king by not answering. "I would speak to it."

"You are in the presence of a Dragon that would obey you, and you would don'thing more than converse with it?"

"I have read that they live almost eight hundred years." She looked at the king from the corner of her eye. "Can you imagine how knowledgeable they must be? To be able to speak freely with a creature who would have seen and learned so much would be exhilarating."

"What if the Dragon is a brute rather than an intellectual?"

"With such a long length of life, obtaining incidental knowledge is possible."

"Well, if I ever meet a Dragon, I will send it your way for you to converse with." Then he turned his head to Wyetta. "I will tell it to stay away from you if you hold a sword, though."

Geryon focused on trailing his eyes over the exposed, slender neck of Cecily, feeling a remarkable urge to bite that pale flesh after her words.

*I very much like her answer.* He hadn't expected it. Not only did she understand a Dragon would be something to be feared, not to be controlled by someone like her, she also complimented their obvious mindfulness.

*There is a depth to her that I can see,* and he knew the others didn't.

She wasn't some spoiled, brainless noblewoman.

For most of the stroll, he had thought her boring because she had barely spoken. He realised he had been mistaken.

He had a question, though. If she held such thoughts, why wasn't she trying to use them to get the king to like her, to make the others appear imbecilic in comparison to her?

"Now, what of the gods?" Bradwick asked the ladies, directing them through the main hallways.

There were many areas the king would laze about when he wasn't required to act in his role. He often had moments of ease where he could party and socialise. *He does not have to do much to run the kingdom.*

It helped that he had many advisers and hired help who would organise things for him. He only needed to make the important decisions. Geryon was one of those few people.

Once more, Geryon was following them with abject boredom due to their new topic.

Talk of the gods, fantasizing about them, was one of the more popular conversations among the court. High-born nobles were easy to please, so long as they were allowed to talk as much as they liked.

Opinions on a topic like this could last the entire day if a collection of people were speaking of it. He'd heard such a similar string of words before that he had to tune himself out.

Every species on Earth – human, Dragon, Witch – all believed in their own gods.

He knew it could be true that each had their own set, but no one had seen or heard from the gods for so long, many no longer believed in them. Those that did, who swore they had seen them, were fanatical.

He believed, and he would much rather he did than earn the wrath of a malevolent deity.

They continued to speak, the girls each having their own opinion. They were indirect if their opinion differed from Bradwick's, who shot down their beliefs quickly. They didn't argue back.

He only truly listened when Cecily began to talk in rhymes, the rhythm catching his attention. Instead of giving her opinion, it appeared as though she was reciting poetry that had been born in tribute to them.

*"My lifeblood is shed, steel painted crimson red.*
*Thousands of men shall lay dead,*
*for the battlefield is a place where ravens are fast fed.*
*The all-father calls, we travel to heaven's cavernous halls.*
*Then the pure and guiltless veil falls,*
*when the strike of a life's final bell tolls.*
*When the battle is done, the fight in their names is won.*
*I bow down to the mystical sun,*
*in belief of the truth of my own dear one."*

There was a long silence following the poem she shared, no one understanding why she had.

"Whether the gods are real or not, whether they are gone or not, whether we should love them or not, pray to them or not, we kill for them. Religion and the gods create more hatred. They should be thought of with caution."

"So, you fear the gods, then?" Bradwick asked her.

"Anything that can smite us with nothing more than a thought should be feared. I also don't wish to speak ill of them for that reason." She gave a reassuring smile, pushing her free hand forward. "So please, your Highness. You are welcome to continue the conversation and I will add to it where I see fit."

Bradwick's lips thinned in irritation. "As you wish, Lady Cecily."

*She has upset him greatly.* Geryon was surprised he was continuing to stroll with them. Usually, when one of his subjects angered him, he'd leave to associate with different people for the day.

From his position behind them, he was able to see Charlotte shove her elbow straight into Cecily's ribs before she whispered something. He took a guess that she was telling Cecily not to upset him.

Not even a moment later, the girl went tumbling down, falling so hard and fast that not even King Bradwick's arm saved her. Charlotte's face was one of the first parts of her that hit the ground.

Geryon winced. *That must have hurt.*

Cecily had managed to unthread her arm from the girl just in time. She looked down at her with such a cold stare, even Geryon feared Charlotte would turn to ice.

"Be careful of your footing, Lady Charlotte," Cecily warned. "You could have brought the king down with you, and we don't wish to harm him."

*She tripped her.* He knew it, could tell by the way the two women stared at each other.

Cecily held her hand out, as if she cared for the fallen lady's wellbeing and wanted to help her back to her feet. The action didn't match the bored face she held.

The blush on the young woman's face was a roaring red, one of complete embarrassment.

"But you... you," Charlotte stuttered, making Cecily raise her brow. It was a dare, a blatant threat. "Oh, never mind."

She got up on her own.

"Are you alright, Charlotte?" Bradwick asked, extending his arm so she may take it again – although apprehensively.

"Of course, your Majesty. My apologies. The ground was uneven there."

He turned his head over his shoulder to peek at the ground where she would have tripped. Then he looked up at Geryon while shaking his head, like he couldn't see anything wrong with the floor.

While Bradwick was distracted, Cecily brought her mouth close to Charlotte's ear and whispered something. Whatever it was caused the young woman's back to go so rigid, it appeared as though someone had shoved a plank up her arse.

"I see nothing wrong with the floor," Geryon answered, kicking the toe of his boot over the stone to find this *apparent* tripping hazard. "Perhaps she fell for another reason. Otherwise, we will have to investigate the flooring."

The look Cecily gave him was dull, already bored of his antics when they'd barely begun. Her face appeared gentle, soft even, with her high cheek bones, but her eyes remained ever cold.

"Perhaps it was a tear in her skirt," Cecily retorted. "I'm sure her lady-in-waiting will fix this offense to her clothing."

*She is remorseless, merciless, malicious...* Geryon almost wanted to pant and chase after her skirt.

He ran his tongue over the front of his top teeth beneath his lips before tonguing a canine. It was an action he rarely did; one he only did in deep thought.

*She holds herself with the strength of a Dragoness.* As a Dragon himself, Geryon appreciated a human woman who could make him think this way. *It's a pity she's here for the king.*

Valerie was seated at a round table, with Victoria by her side.

Originally, her lady-in-waiting wanted to stand behind her to serve her and allow her to talk to higher-ranking nobles. She'd forced the woman to sit beside her to act as a buffer. Anyone who tried to insist she move immediately took back their demand at her stern expression.

The chairs and large round tables mainly held women, while the men loitered around the walls and the two balconies of the room.

Wyetta was at the same table as her, while Charlotte and Savannah occupied different ones, sitting with other noble ladies.

Valerie slyly let her eyes fall to the corner of her lids, staring at the young, brown-haired noble at the table furthest from her. She'd not only embarrassed the girl, she'd frightened her.

*I hope she will refrain from speaking with me again.* She was not tolerating the insipid girl very well.

"And what do you think of Lady Charlotte?" Marchioness

Cath asked. *I will never remember all these noble names and their titles.*

"The girl is a wonderful gem. Her beauty is radiant, and she's sweet," Valerie told her, making the woman smile.

There was a twitch though, right underneath her eye. Cath wanted gossip, something she could use against her later. *I'm not so uncontrolled that I would do something so pitiful.*

She lifted her hand to bring the cup of tea to her lips, quietly sipping on it. "Savannah is also lovely. She does not show it, but beneath the surface is a funny and strong girl. I'm fond of her freckles."

"So, you like the other ladies, do you?" Cath asked, swiping a large dollop of butter on top of a muffin. "I watched you all walking with King Bradwick. You were speaking of interesting topics. Is there nothing that could be improved?"

After more conversation and the day fading into afternoon, Bradwick had wanted to eat. She was sure he also wanted a break from them.

Valerie had been instructed to come relax until dinner, where there would be a banquet. She would be required to sit with the king at his table. All the ladies were given the same instructions.

Her feet itched to explore, but until she got the opportunity, she would have to remain close to the court for a few days. *I must be patient.*

"Perhaps how many arms the king had," Valerie said with a forced smile, unhappy at having to be in this room.

"Ah, yes. I noticed you did not get the chance to embrace His Majesty while you walked. The other ladies were forceful in obtaining an arm, I saw."

"We are all very excited for this opportunity. I will get my chance."

"It would have been better if you had, Cecily. You may not have almost dragged the king to the floor." Wyetta giggled behind a scone before nibbling into it.

"Poor thing. I felt terrible for her," Valerie said, before sipping her tea again. "I tried to catch her, but it seems I was too slow."

Wyetta held her gaze knowingly, then casually changed the subject. "I must admit, I appreciated your opinion on the gods and how it leads to war. I have never heard that poem, but I felt deeply when you recited it."

"I found your response to what you would do when faced with a Dragon was rather splendid as well. I don't have the training with a weapon to even consider going toe to toe with anyone." It was a lie. Valerie was a perfect marksman. She could wield a sword and unleash an arrow with accuracy. She could even throw a spear. "Do you know how to wield a weapon to have such grand thoughts?"

*It's a shame I doubt I will ever regain my sword from the real Lady Cecily.* She'd thought carrying it with her would have been far too suspicious. Also, revealing that she was excellent with a sword would cause them to wonder why. Most noblewomen weren't trained to fight.

Wyetta leaned forward to whisper to her. "I begged my brothers to teach me without Father knowing. If I were born a man, I would have been destined to be a soldier."

"Should I be frightened of you, Wyetta?" Valerie teased, finding she was fond of her.

"Only if you cross me."

"Let us make a sweet deal, then," Valerie offered, noting how Wyetta's bright green eyes lit up. "Let us not crawl over each other for this gala."

The darker-skinned woman immediately pouted. "The idea of torturing the other two was to be my main source of entertainment."

"Do as you will with them; they are not a part of this spoken deal."

Her bright grin returned. She reached her hand forward after wiping jam off her thumb, and Valerie grasped it.

They shook hands. "Deal."

*Good, one less person for me to worry about.*

"I'm sick of tea," Wyetta laughed, sliding her chair back to stand. "Would you care to join me for a stroll outside?"

Valerie's gaze fell on the balcony, seeing others already doing something similar.

"Yes, fresh air does sound appealing." She leaned closer to Victoria so no one could overhear. "Please remain here with the other ladies. I'm curious to know what they say while we are gone."

She got to her feet and linked her arm with Wyetta.

The rear of the palace was a vast area of gardens. There was a maze of scrub hedges at the very back that seemed miles away. To the right, there was a thin forest, perfect for men to hunt wild birds. To the left, they grew the food consumed inside by the nobles. She was sure there was more she couldn't see behind those features.

Not too far of a stroll from the balcony exit they used was a tree with a stone bench under it. It faced clear fields and a rectangular lake she was sure the king would keep stocked to fish in.

Wyetta was busy chatting away, reminiscing about their stroll with the king and the controversial opinions they shared.

Valerie had one thought. *How can I use this friendship to my advantage?*

"I think those women are more than I can handle on my own," King Bradwick sighed while collapsing onto a settee.

His head fell back so he could close his eyes.

He appeared truly worn out by the last few hours.

Geryon sat on the settee next to his, placing his feet on the arm of the chair Bradwick sat in. When he finally opened his eyes and sat up, the king almost head butted the bottom of his boots.

"Picked one you like yet?" Geryon asked instead of lowering his feet, even when a brow was raised.

He did have his feet pushed off, though. Bradwick knew telling him what to do would get him nowhere.

"It's far too early to tell. I must admit, I'm thankful I instigated this gala and that I will be able to choose my own wife." Bradwick leaned his face on an enclosed fist, resting both his elbows on the arm rest. "If my parents were still alive, they would have spoken with their fathers and tried to orchestrate the best marriage to strengthen their alliances."

Geryon moved his feet to place them on the long, low table in front of them.

"You have told me this before. Did they not try to force you to marry one of the princesses of the other kingdoms?"

Bradwick cringed, one side of his face crinkling in distaste. "I would rather not be tied to a brash woman of the west or a snow-trotting woman from the south."

"And I know you hate the queen from the east simply because she put a frog down the back of your shirt last time they were permitted to visit."

"I should not have informed you of that." Bradwick pointed his finger at him in anger. "Although Queen Irvette is a great ally and a beautiful woman, she irks me terribly. We broke off the arranged marriage when my parents were killed."

The deceased king and queen had been murdered during their travels from the western kingdom. It was speculated that the king of those lands had orchestrated their deaths, but since there had been no survivors, they were unsure. *Could have been those of the south, since the west has been at war with them for ages.*

"We would much rather tie our kingdoms through the marriage of our children," he continued. "Now, I will have to produce one quickly, since she has already taken a husband and named herself queen. It will not be long before she bears an heir."

"Much could happen in that time for both of you. You may die before you have an heir."

"Then my brother would take my place on the throne. He already has children, and hopefully, he will tie the kingdoms together."

Geryon already knew all this. "So, back to the women. You were informing me you are a yellow-belly secret keeper."

Bradwick looked at Geryon through his lashes, a smirk forming across his face. "Okay, you caught me. I was trying to be respectful."

He leaned his body forward to hush their conversation. He cupped the air in front of his chest, like he was grasping something.

"Did you see the bosom on the younger one? Women who have just come of age should not be so well developed. It makes it hard for men to not fawn over them." He fell back in his chair. "She's submissive, which I appreciate, and I'm hoping she is just nervous. Otherwise, it will be a pity, since it seems she does not have much thought."

Geryon placed his arms behind his head while he listened to Bradwick, hoping to council him like he was supposed to. "As you mentioned, she's young. Perhaps she has not grown into her intellect yet."

"You are defending her?" When he opened his mouth to confirm, Bradwick cut him off with one single word. "*You?*"

"Yes, I'm defending the dim-witted human girl. You

should remain open-minded; each of them will have their positives and negatives. You are only to choose the one you can tolerate the most."

"Although she has yet to win me with any conversation, I do find the redhead pleasant to look at."

"They are all pleasant to look at," Geryon threw at him. "Stop focusing on their beauty. Each of them is appealing. You are lucky none of the dukes bred toads."

"I was sure Duke Grayson would have sent me a deformed ogre."

"And yet he sent you a beauty easy to behold."

"You like his daughter, then?" Bradwick asked, and Geryon had to pause before he answered.

*Yes, she's definitely someone who interests me.*

Still, that wasn't what the king meant by his question.

"I find her wild." *Someone who would not be easy to tame.*

"She has such a pretty face but lacks any real emotion behind it. I don't see how you could find her wild when I think she lacks any form of passion." *Then you are a blind fool.* "She also irritates me with her words."

"It's her words, the confidence in how she speaks, that make her wild," Geryon laughed. "You just don't like that she is not hesitant of you because you are the fucking king."

"Watch it, Dragon," he muttered quietly, so the servant in the far corner of the room wouldn't overhear. Bradwick pointed at him, the softness of his features hardening with a quick show of anger. "Don't be so informal with me."

It was true. King Bradwick knew of Geryon's species and kept it hidden from the rest of the court. He had his reasons for being here after Bradwick was sworn in as the ruler of these lands. He was the only one who knew, although, sometimes, he toed the line in revealing what he was to others, much like how he did earlier.

It was one of the reasons his behaviour was often

overlooked. *He would not dare tell one such as I what to do.* Nor would Geryon threaten him with the sheer power he held in comparison to the weakness of his humanity. *I could burn him to nothing but embers as we speak.*

"Or what?" Geryon grinned, crossing one foot on top of the other instead of laying them both flat on the table. "Must I remind you, once again, that you need me just as much as I need you?"

He sighed, flopping back in the chair as that hardened look fell. "Why must I put up with you?"

"Don't lie. You tolerate me because you genuinely like my company," Geryon quipped, and Bradwick eyed him with a squint. "Now, shut up about me and talk about that black-haired one. You have yet to speak of her."

"Wyetta?" He brought his hand up to cup his chin, thinking for a long moment. "She may appear an all-rounder, but her want to take up arms against a Dragon was rather off-putting." He lifted his hand while he laughed. "I'll admit, it was hilarious that a woman would believe she could slay anything."

"Yes, I found that interesting as well."

He didn't find it funny because she was a woman, but because she was human. *Not even singular men can kill my kind with ease.* Most had to bring an army.

"She could be troublesome if I were to war with the other kingdoms. Women who are interested in topics of war and politics can often be meddlesome during those times." He shook his head while pushing some of the blond hair that had fallen from his ponytail back. "I'm thankful Duke Halmonick's daughters are wed. It relieves me that there is not a fifth one I will have to juggle."

Then Bradwick looked over the back of his chair while clicking his fingers. "Servant, bring us some whiskey. I need to drink."

"Do you not have dinner with the fair ladies this evening?"

Bradwick winced when he sat forward. "Ah, yes, I forgot about the banquet." *How can you forget something so simple?* "It's fine. A few drinks will calm me. You will be joining us, yes?"

"You know I prefer to stay in the shadows and to eat alone."

Geryon didn't like to be a part of court conversations. He found the people boorish in comparison to his own kind. *Then again, we often claw and bite each other.* He just didn't like the verbal backstabbing and gossip. His kind were often up front about their issues.

"But I will be there like I always am."

It was unfortunate for Wyetta and Valerie that, because of their stroll, they were informed about dinner later than some. Since they were his important guests, all four of them were to be seated next to the king on a long banquet table.

Savannah and Charlotte had arrived before them and were already seated – on either side of where he was supposed to sit. He hadn't arrived yet.

"It appears we will not be able to be seated together," Valerie said with a sigh, their arms still interlinked like they had been for most of the afternoon.

She didn't particularly care that she wouldn't be seated next to the king, though.

"Well, that's rather disappointing." Wyetta gave a cute pout. "Alas, I guess it cannot be helped. The early ravens get the best pickings." A giggle fell from the woman. "It seems as though I have the power to torture you or save you, my dear."

"Do what you want. It does not matter who my seating partner is."

Wyetta looked her in the eye, as if she didn't believe her.

With her preferred seating partner not available, Valerie would tolerate whoever she sat with.

*I have three sisters, and we often scratch at each other.* She would handle them with the same finesse she did her younger siblings.

They approached the table and Wyetta crossed her path to sit next to Charlotte, giving her a knowing smile. Valerie took her own place on the other side of the lengthy table, feeling a bout of relief.

"It appears you have become swift friends." Valerie picked up the undertone of a sneer in Savannah's words.

"It's only because we were seated at the same table for tea. I'm sure by the end of this banquet, you and I will be just as harmonious."

"You walk around as though we are beneath you, but we were born of the same title."

"I think you misunderstand me," Valerie answered, placing her hands in her lap. "It's not that I think lowly of anyone. It's that I was raised to not show my emotions so freely. As the eldest, I was told to act and be a certain way for my siblings and those who would visit the manor."

This was true for Valerie, just as for Cecily. *We were both the eldest, and although that girl was brash, she could be calm and collected when she wanted to be.* Valerie had spied on her for just long enough to see her act accordingly.

The king entered, and everyone quickly rose to stand in greeting. Men bowed while women curtsied when he passed by until he made his way to the end of the banquet hall to come to the middle of them.

From the small distance, she could tell he'd been drinking heavily, but he held himself as though he was sober.

"Ladies and Gentlemen of the court," Bradwick said loudly, allowing his voice to be heard through the entire room. "I wish to thank the four dukes who have brought their beautiful daughters, or nieces, to attend my royal gala. The day we shared was stimulating, and I look forward to getting to know them better as the days pass."

He lifted his already-filled chalice to take a swig after the cheers that followed, then he sat down and immediately began eating rudely. The court sat as well.

That's when Valerie noticed his guard was entering the room like he'd been delayed. He swiped a chalice from a noble's table, forced a servant to fill it for him, and walked up to stand behind them.

"Did you enjoy your afternoon, your Highness?" Charlotte asked.

He grunted in response, since she'd caught him in the middle of eating around the bone of an animal. Once his mouth was free, he finally answered her.

Savannah sidled closer to Valerie for a moment while he was distracted.

"The pretty story about your father forcing your expressionless mask is not enough to appease me. You expect me to believe–"

"You are attempting to make an enemy of me. You are painting me as though I'm some sort of villain," she quickly interjected.

"You threatened Charlotte with a knife," she whispered. "I will not tolerate you pretending you are not truly a viper."

Valerie gave a small laugh, not mockingly, but with true humour. "How could I have wielded a weapon with the court watching us on our stroll? I threatened her hair with nothing more than words."

Savannah crinkled her red dusted brows. "You still threatened her. It's the same."

"Did she forget to mention what she had been doing at the time to cause such a reaction from me?"

"She claims you tripped her because you were jealous."

"Gossip is often a terrible habit, but I will rectify the lies with truth. She should have kept her elbows to herself and not altered my hand." Valerie brought her hand above the table. "Perhaps you should check under her nails for my skin."

The girl had been digging her nails into the flesh of her wrist, and the evidence of that was clear as day upon her skin. Little semi-moons bruised her flesh, as well as light scratch marks.

"I don't think she knew she had been cutting my skin, though," Valerie told her truthfully. "She was upset and reacted. Unfortunately, I also acted accordingly."

Savannah pursed her lips together, but Valerie could tell her opinion was changing.

"Mayhap we can restart our dinner conversation and join in on the discussion with the king?" Valerie suggested, wanting to steer away from the conversation before someone overheard.

She ducked her gaze over her shoulder, eyeing the guard behind them. He raised a brow at her, but she could see the peek of a grin on the corner of his lips. *He was listening. Hopefully, he will not tell Bradwick of my and Charlotte's transgressions.*

There was nothing she could do about it. She turned around and began to eat while the war in the west was discussed.

*He's trying to understand how we will assist him in ruling the kingdom.* She wondered why he would while they were in a group rather than on their own – where they would be free to discuss their opinions. *The fact that he cares at all about our opinion is strange. Men don't usually care.*

Then Valerie almost laughed, had to snuff out the urge, especially when she was invited to comment on it.

"War is for men, your Highness, not for ladies. Like everyone, I wish for peace and tranquillity for all, but my opinion is nothing more than a soft-hearted plea – not that of a political warlord."

She knew her response earned his respect because he grinned. *He's testing us, seeing if we will be submissive in the ways that matter.*

*Human men, so easy to understand.* This hierarchy wasn't the same for her kind, for Witches. Status came from the strength of their magic. *Many female Witches are stronger than male Witches.* Male Witches would treat them with respect because of it.

Women were also usually the head of their covens. They were known as the high priestess and would anoint a trusted adviser as a priest. They were usually treated with more respect than mortal human women.

Although, women were not *always* treated gracefully within her species.

Sometimes, powerful Witches were captured and forced into special rituals. They were rituals where death was the result, or where they were raped or even consumed – they were cruel to their own kind. Other times, it was so a certain Witch would be forced to birth a child sired by another powerful Witch, then that child would be taken from her arms and raised elsewhere.

*Only dark Witches commit such terrible sins.*

Thinking of terrible crimes soured her own mood.

As if she'd conjured it with her thoughts, a conversation about her species was ignited.

It wasn't a conversation she felt comfortable with, more so when they began speaking about putting Witches on the stake to be burned, without trial, like they didn't deserve the chance to plead their case.

They all agreed with each other, even Wyetta, who went into far gorier detail than the rest.

Valerie tried not to shudder. *I'm not safe here.* She was one of the most hated species on Earth.

Focusing on her food, she tried her hardest to avoid participating or sharing her opinion.

Often, she thought of Bradwick as warm and light. There was something about the kind treble in his voice, the handsome features of his face, that it made it easy for him to appear this way. Still, there was an air around him when he was angry, like he wouldn't tolerate it. He wouldn't tolerate her not giving her opinion when she very much didn't want to.

"My answer solely depends on if I'm presented with a white or a dark Witch to punish."

"There is often a long-winded answer when you speak. Why would it matter whether they are a dark or a light wielder? They are Witches, and they deserve eternal punishment."

With a sigh, Valerie said, "From what I have been told, white Witches have never caused harm. Keeping them imprisoned is near impossible, since they will escape unless bound correctly. I believe they should be released."

"Unbelievable. What if they turn? You have just allowed a Witch to go who may later turn evil."

"But what if they don't? What if you are killing an innocent person who wants nothing more than to live their life? It's not guaranteed they will become corrupt."

*My family has not. I will be the first.*

Bradwick waved his hand like he was done with that part of the conversation, but she could tell he was not satisfied with her answer. "Fine. What if it's an evil Witch, then? Would you release that creature as well?"

"Not at all," Valerie smiled. "They deserve every lick of flame given to them, since they are rather vile."

"Well, that is an answer I'm much more appreciative of." He turned back to his food.

Valerie was thankful when the conversation became more

relaxed. She could hear flutes, drums, and a guitar being played in the background. It softened the atmosphere when they weren't played as enthusiastically.

"Tomorrow, we will all play games on the lawns with the court," Bradwick told them. "I'm interested to know if you ladies are able to play bowls."

She couldn't think of anything worse. She also didn't want to be in the banquet hall for much longer, but she knew she couldn't be the first one to retire again.

*I will remain until King Bradwick does.*

Her opinion had been forced from her, but now she worried about her connection to the king. *I may need information; perhaps I should have lied.*

Valerie was trying her hardest to be calm and collected, but every minute she wasted not looking for her sister, the more she feared she was running out of time.

*I want to find my sister.* She needed to locate her whereabouts before whoever was holding her unfairly hurt a six-year-old girl. *I miss her.*

Geryon found Cecily laying on one of the many sofa bed lounges in the main library – a place often vacant of courtiers.

She had a small book opened, using her thumb as she lay back with her feet up. Her body was half turned to the side, her knees slightly bent while her free hand was above her head.

*Even alone, she appears composed.* Not once had Geryon seen her act without the appearance of a high lady.

Although he *had* seen her behave with artful jabs of feminine malice towards the other ladies. He didn't believe anyone else had noticed.

*She has even low jabbed the nobles of court.* They didn't seem to realise she'd done such things to them.

For four days, the palace doors had been open to the daughters of the dukes. For four days, he'd been watching them. Well... *her,* really.

The more Cecily interacted with others, forced to attend functions, the more he himself wished to interact with her. *I wonder if I will get to see her devious nature being used against me.*

Geryon grinned. He wanted to banter with her, the kind saturated in spite and cattiness. *She glares at me often with those cold eyes.* She glared even though he'd never uttered a single word to her, or any of the other ladies, for that matter.

He wanted to see her react, wanted to see what kind of emotions he could push from her blank stare. He wanted to see if he could bring her to anger, even embarrassment. *I doubt I would ever be able to make this woman cry.* He wondered if he could get her to share a genuine smile with him.

The only way she would share these things with him was if they were alone.

King Bradwick had been spending time with each female periodically throughout the past four days. He would attend court functions, such as duck racing, or playing games of ball and stick on the palace grounds outside with the ladies.

He would select one to take a stroll with for an hour or two before they returned. Then, he would eventually take a different one for a walk.

It was Geryon who suggested he do this.

Bradwick was feeling overwhelmed trying to entertain the ladies all at once, so this had been a solution.

Geryon would follow them, like he did most of the time.

Usually, he didn't last long when Bradwick was speaking with the other noblewomen. Sometimes, he would leave, and order two guards to take over his position so he could be at court – with *Cecily*.

He was becoming increasingly fascinated with this woman, with her poised face, graceful walk, and unfeeling intellect.

*She has managed to spin the court to like her,* yet he could tell she didn't care about them whatsoever. *She plays as though she enjoys their games and conversations,* but he could tell she was bored of them. *She speaks with logical thought, making the court enjoy speaking with her,* yet she also made them appear stupid without offending them.

It was brilliant to behold such artistry and web spinning.

Instead of being with King Bradwick while he strolled, Geryon had been shadowing her in curiosity. *I like looking at her.* He wanted to play with her, and he wasn't quite sure what that meant to him yet.

It didn't help that he found her beauty easy to admire, with her pale green eyes that caught the light, her glossy brown hair that was always tied back to frame her face. *Such a fierce gaze on a woman who seems as fragile as glass.* She was tall, and yet her frame was so petite; he feared if he grabbed her, he might break her with his strength.

Geryon still hadn't figured this woman out yet. *She's a walking contradiction.*

On this day, Cecily had been the first lady Bradwick took for a stroll.

He'd followed, listening to them converse until they returned to court. Her conversations with the king were far more enticing and thought provoking than the others. *Although that Wyetta female is also quite bright, and the redhead sometimes has her moments.*

He knew he was becoming obsessed with Duke Grayson's daughter.

Geryon had attempted to stop observing her by following Bradwick when he took Savannah for a stroll afterwards. Their conversation had been flirtatious, something he could tell Bradwick enjoyed greatly.

He found it tedious, and eventually abandoned them to be with the court.

No, Geryon wanted to watch someone more entertaining.

Cecily was no longer there.

Instead, he returned at the same time as Victoria, her lady-in-waiting, who was alone.

Wondering what she was up to, Geryon had followed her strange scent into the palace. With his heightened sense of smell in comparison to a measly human, he was able to tell the two women had walked together until they reached the library.

Peeking inside, that's when he saw her laying there.

This was his opportunity to speak with her alone, and he wouldn't dare miss it. He hoped once he spoke with her, his curiosity about her might fade.

She was like a shiny piece of treasure dangled in front of a pixie. And, like a pixie, he hoped once he held the stolen treasure, it would no longer interest him.

He would know after he spoke with her. *I may only like her from afar.*

She didn't notice him approach until he was hoisting himself up onto the waist-high cabinet pressed against the back of her seat, putting himself above her. The wood was sturdy, and the cabinet ran the entire length of her lounging sofa.

The other chairs had been too far, since her spot was in the centre, out in the open. He made his own chair – he needed to be close to her to observe her properly.

He bent his knees and placed the bottom of his boots flat against the surface. The candelabra in the middle had already been kicked off.

The book didn't move from its position against her stomach, but she let her eyes fall to him. "You are awfully close, sir."

It would appear he was. They were almost sitting side by side, except for the fact that he was slightly elevated.

Geryon then pulled an eating knife from his sword belt while taking a pomegranate from his pocket. He'd taken it from the refreshment table in the marquee the court used to shield themselves from the sun.

"I disagree; I could be far closer," he answered before he

began to cut his way through the skin of the fruit.

There was a small silence, and he noted her lips thinned. *She knows I'm right.*

She softened her look. "What do you want from me?" Her eyes refused to leave him, like she was cautious.

"Who said I wanted anything from you? I simply came here to eat my fruit." When he cracked open the pomegranate, the ruby-red seeds began to fall.

They fell from his elevated spot onto her. She used the book to protect herself as they sprinkled down.

"You spilled them on me. Why would you pick something so messy? Most consume these with a bowl beneath them."

"I like things that are difficult. The harder something is, the more it satisfies me." He grinned at the small frown she gave.

"Then you must be easy to bore." *She's perceptive.*

"There is talk between King Bradwick and I that you very much find me unpleasant." He began to pick at his fruit, having to chase the seeds occasionally when they fell on top of the cabinet. *The servants will definitely come here to find a mess.* "I'm interested as to why that is."

"Well, that's most unfortunate," she answered before her eyes finally fell away to look at the book she was reading. "Since you are nothing more than a face."

Geryon raised a brow, pausing his attempt to scoop seeds with his knife. "How do you mean?"

"I cannot hate someone I have never spoken to, heard about, or even know the name of. All I know of you is your face."

*She has never inquired about me?* The court would have informed her of who he was if she asked. Somehow, Geryon was offended at her lack of interest.

He grinned at the terrible emotion she gave him.

"Perhaps we can rectify that, and you may come to despise

me for real." He continued with his messy fruit, bringing some to his mouth. "We would not want to make a liar out of the king."

"We don't need to become acquainted as nemeses. The king can be whatever he wishes."

"Then you would prefer to make a liar out of me? Do you not care that I may be punished for trickery?"

She turned the page of her book slowly, but she didn't skip a beat in answering. "Then you should not have spoken so forwardly with an assumption rather than truth."

"You are a very cold woman."

Geryon pouted, but the humour in his eyes didn't match his lips. He could tell she noticed the conflicting emotions when she peeked up at him.

"I thought you would have already deduced that, since you have been keeping a watchful gaze upon me and the other ladies."

*Her gentle voice...* It never matched the cold-blooded words she spoke.

"You are all quite entertaining, but I find *you* impressive to watch. You spin conversations to your liking and weave opinions of yourself to make the mindless court fancy you, despite your obvious distinction against your companions."

"You attempt to flatter me." She licked her thumb and turned another page. It was like she wasn't interested in his conversation. Yet Geryon was vibrating with excitement from it. "It's unsuccessful. The other ladies are much more... charming."

She let her hands fall backwards slightly, the book going with them as she turned her gaze to him. *Cold, unfeeling, brutal.*

She spoke once more. "Perhaps you should give such dazzling words to those who lack the comprehension to see the truth behind them."

She brazenly kept his eyes, and he couldn't help pausing what he was doing to stare back. It was like he was being controlled against his will.

"And what truth would that be?"

*Why do I feel this?*

He'd felt it occasionally when watching her, admiring her from afar. Usually, it happened whenever he watched her being calculating and blank. He'd felt it the day she tripped Charlotte, and he tried to get her to fumble over her lie about how the girl fell.

The merciless stare she'd given him that day behind those pale eyes reminded him of a cold, unforgiving winter's morning. It was the same one she gave him now, and it stirred in him the same gut-clenching reaction.

"That compliments are nothing but a way to manipulate and control." His tongue darted out to lick at the seam of his lips. *I want her.* "You should speak with the other ladies. You can comment on their large bosoms and darling faces while ignoring the complete lack of thought. They will appreciate such soft words."

*I want to break her.*

Geryon wanted to see that sophisticated face fall by his own hands. Women like this, those who held themselves above others, often held the rawest kind of passion. *I want to see her claw at me with anger.* He thought he could easily get there.

But there was something else he desperately wanted. There was a hidden dark side to women like Cecily – and it was near impossible to obtain. *I want to see her explode in mindless, lust-filled abandon.*

He had to see it, needed a taste of it before the king got his hands on her.

*She will not show me her many secret faces, but there is only one I'm determined to witness.* He feared he didn't have enough time before the gala was over to obtain it for his memories.

The possibility of seeing this woman melt from ice into passionate fire was too much temptation. What he thought would be a conversation that would bore him, instead exhilarated him enough that he felt his cock tingling at the prospect of bedding her.

"Are you often so severe on your own sex?" Geryon retorted while he thought about how to get underneath this mysterious woman's skirts.

*I cannot let King Bradwick know.* Not because it would reflect badly for him – Bradwick would never do anything to him. No, he couldn't let anyone find out for her sake. She would be dishonoured in betraying the king when she was here to win his hand. *But I will have her.*

"That's not what I was insinuating."

"Ah, is it that you hate men?" He already figured as much. Anytime a nobleman attempted to speak with her, she would escape him.

"Your assumption once more is incorrect. They have their uses and are a requirement in a woman's life."

"So, you don't like people in general? I can see you forsaking us, since we can be quite... brazen to the point of stupidity."

He raised his brow when she didn't deny it.

*I often feel the same, but that's because I think lowly of humans. She is one; she should not have such thoughts.*

"Although others are quite bothersome, you should be nice to me. I'm rather close with the king, after all. I can give you inside knowledge the other women will lack."

"I have no care for such games. I will not involve myself in childish play like the other ladies for the king's hand. I find it juvenile." She waved her hand dismissively. "That's something for the court to entertain themselves with."

Geryon pointed his knife at her with a seed on it. It fell onto her shoulder. She watched it, stared at it on her dress, before giving him a bored look.

"I don't think the court will appreciate that you think of them as nothing more than irritating children."

"That's not what I said," she answered, making him frown. "Your words make me think you must make an excellent guard."

*Guards are often seen as unintelligent and low born. What is she getting at?* His eyes widened.

"You attempt to offend me." He chuckled while shaking his head. "It's unfortunate for you I'm difficult to displease. You are welcome to cast indirect insults as much as your stone heart desires. I will warn you, though: you will not gain the emotions you seek from me by doing so."

"I find that hard to believe. People are always the same." It sounded as though she stemmed the desire to roll her eyes... at him!

Done with his fruit and knowing no one was approaching due to his heightened senses, Geryon quickly moved.

He slipped his way from the cabinet onto the sofa bed with her. Straddling her waist, Geryon grabbed her hands when she tried to push him and pinned them against the arm rest with one hand.

*Her bones are so dainty.* The fact he could easily capture both her wrists in one of his large hands pleased him.

"What are you doing? Unhand me."

She looked up towards her trapped hands before relaxing her stretched position to look at him. She wasn't fighting him, didn't squirm, but the glint in her eyes promised retribution for his actions.

"I told you before: I like things that are difficult." Then, he bent over to bring them nose to nose, deeply holding her pale green eyes. "Keep being this callous and unfeeling woman. I do find it rather desirous. The colder you are, the more I will want to eat you." Geryon leaned more forward so he could swipe his tongue up the length of her pale neck to taste a hint of salty sweat. "It helps that you are rather beautiful as well."

He pulled back so that he could run his thumb over her soft jawline and pointed chin. Her eyes narrowed, but he found her lovelier because of it.

"What are you?" she said, causing his eyes to widen and his hand to freeze.

"What do you mean?" *Could she really have discovered that I'm not human already?*

"No simple guard would have the audacity to approach and handle the daughter of a duke in this manner. Tell me what you are so that I may know how to handle this outrageous physical touch. Are you actually a lord?"

"Ah, Lady Cecily, I'm special." He leaned forward to press his unmoving lips to one cheek. "Think of me as someone just as powerful as the king, but without the title." He moved to the other cheek to press his lips there. "Not even he controls me; therefore, neither can you." He brought his lips to her chin.

"I'm here to gain the favour of King Bradwick. You would be so disloyal to him?"

"My loyalty is to myself alone." His lips curved when he placed them against her racing pulse. *She appears so calm, but her heart is fast, her scent saturated with unease.* "And no one will be able to save you from me."

One thing that confused him, though, was that her scent didn't match her. It was flowery.

He took a deeper draw now that he was close.

He expected it to be spicey, something that indicated her personality, the way she acted. *She does not smell how I thought she would.* He was disappointed. *No matter. Her mouth matches her face, and I wish to change them for myself only.*

"And what of me? Do you have no care for how I feel?"

He placed his lips against the underside of her jaw, forcing her head to tilt back and to the side.

"You will enjoy it," he answered her.

What Geryon wanted from her required that she desired him.

Some of it may appear forced, some of it would be confusing to her, but what he wanted was her spreading her legs for him. *Because it's only when she willingly lusts for me that she will allow me to break her.*

Women like Cecily, who were uptight and proper, were not easy to birth desire in. She would have to obtain the power of pleasure before she would allow it to overcome her. *I will make her crave me.*

He now had less than two weeks to steal her passion and take it for himself.

Then, if King Bradwick chose her, he would no longer desire her because she would be taken by another. If she left because she was unsuccessful, then she would no longer be in his sights for him to think of her.

She should feel humbled that a Dragon was interested in bedding her. *I will play with this human.*

He could hear the click of approaching footsteps against the stone ground.

"Be prepared for me, vicious butterfly."

Pulling away from her, he tilted his head so he could let his bottom lip brush against her ear lobe. His voice was soft as he whispered, his breath heavy against her, "Name is Geryon, by the way."

With a grin at her glare, he released her so he could back away. Then he walked to the back of the library and climbed one of the spiralling staircases to the second floor.

Keeping his eyes locked on hers, he walked across to the

other side of the room, opened a door, and left.

Valerie stared dumbfounded in the direction the guard went.

"How are you feeling, Lady Cecily?"

Valerie almost jumped at Victoria's words. She'd been so distracted, she hadn't heard her coming. She'd told the girl earlier that she was feeling a headache and wanted to relax in a quiet location.

It had been a lie, of course. She just wanted some peace and quiet.

"I appear to be much worse," she answered, still eyeing the second floor's exit.

*What shall I do about this?* She couldn't allow him to think he could get away with pursuing her. *He will get in the way.*

Valerie dragged her attention back to her lady-in-waiting. "What is it that you require, Victoria?" She must have come to her for a reason.

"I thought it would be wise to give you an update. King Bradwick has returned with the last lady and has left to complete his royal duties. He will not be available until tonight's dinner."

"Was there any mention of my absence?"

"Yes, Charlotte and Savannah made it plain to the king that you were missing. He did not seem to mind."

"Excellent. He does not care if we are not always with the court."

"As long as you are available for him whenever he wishes for your presence, I don't think he will mind."

"Thank you for the update."

Victoria fidgeted as she spoke. "One more thing. The ladies of the court are having another high tea. I did not wish to leave before I informed you, in case you would prefer to attend."

"No, I'm fine as I am."

When Victoria left, Valerie's eyes found the second floor's exit once more. The last thing Valerie wanted was a man following her around the palace, seeking her.

The question was... how to ward him away?

She could turn her attitude up, go out of her way to be offensive to him. Either he would be turned off by her unpleasant words and behaviour, or he would become more forceful. *Men don't like it when we women act as though we don't find them desirable.*

She thought for long moments on what to do, thinking about all her options. Valerie hadn't expected something like this to happen.

*I could give him what he wants. He may leave me alone afterwards.* She could let him bed her, and once he was satisfied, he may be done being interested in her.

*He said he likes things that are difficult. Perhaps if I play easy, it will sway him to pester someone else.* She touched her neck where he had kissed her. *He could also become more persistent if I play harlot.*

If she opened her thighs freely, he may see it as an invitation to return between them.

Valerie wasn't shy about this, not when her main priority was finding her sister.

*There may be another reason, though...* She may be able to lie to others, but it was impossible for her to be dishonest with herself. *He does have a pretty face for someone I find disconcerting.*

Since he'd been around her so frequently, as he was always with the king, she got to examine Geryon quite often.

With his midnight hair framing his rugged face, from a distance, he was sharp and handsome in his complicated button coats. In the rare opportunities she'd been remotely close, his metallic blue eyes had been captivating, especially when the light hit them.

*Then there is the way he has been looking at me.* She'd observed it was only her he would give this kind of look to.

She noted when he caught the eyes of the other ladies, his expression was dull. With her, he would cock his brow or give a slight grin whenever they caught eyes. She would return it with a bored look, showing him her disinterest. It would make his humorous look grow.

She'd found it rather appealing.

Valerie thought of him like she would a piece of beautiful art: wonderful to look at, but something she definitely shouldn't touch. *Now that painting has grown legs and appears to be chasing me.*

She was here for a reason. The last thing she needed to do was satisfy any curious desires with the guard of the man she planned to steal from.

*If I get caught, the king will never trust me again.* Her plan would fail, and everything she did to get here would be wasted. Then she would have to use other, less savoury, options to find her sister, ones that were precarious.

Valerie placed one of her hands over her lips. *Then again... I could always use the guard to my advantage.* She thought about grinning, but instead, she frowned. *He seems insightful, though.*

Already, he managed to pull apart her antics with the court. There was also that stare of his, a certain look in his eyes, one that screamed predator and all others in the room prey. It was intense, like he could sense things no one else was able to.

With her own observational gaze, mostly under her lashes, she'd seen him listening to the court. His eyes would dart to certain people, like he heard what they said. He would also frequently speak to the king, informing him of court behaviour.

*No, I cannot use him. He's too perceptive. He could uncover that I'm not who I say I am.* Valerie sighed, still unsure. *I will have to see what he does.* Planning for an unknown future seemed impossible.

One thing she did want to know was this: *why did he make his intentions so obvious?*

Valerie sat at the head banquet table next to King Bradwick.

She'd been the first lady to arrive, and she took this as her opportunity to get closer to him. Those who sat directly next to him were the ones who controlled their conversations. That meant she wouldn't be trapped again to answer questions she was not fond of.

Instead, she got him to boast of himself. It made him awfully cheery, and he often placed his hand on her forearm. The other ladies usually talked about themselves to gain his interest.

Valerie knew the true power behind growing a man's confidence, of getting him to talk of himself and complimenting him while he did so.

When he spoke of the battles he'd won, she would tell him that her father, Duke Grayson, could not speak of such triumph. If he spoke of the wealth and peace of his lands, she would tell him she doubted any other kingdom had such prosperity.

Wyetta had taken the other spot next to him, and for the

first time, the conversation with the king had been pleasant to Valerie. Between his boasting, they spoke of stimulating things, things for which one needed to *think*.

"Tonight's conversations are very stimulating, ladies. I must say, I'm enjoying them," King Bradwick said with a broad smile upon his pleasant face.

"Wyetta and I are rather fond of each other, your Highness," Valerie said while cutting into her meat drizzled in some sort of oily herb sauce. "We have resorted to trickery and rehearsed our conversations in order to deceive you with pleasantries."

Bradwick gave a bellowing laugh. "You hear that, ladies and gentlemen?" he shouted to the court, who wouldn't have been able to overhear their conversations. Everyone paused to turn to them. "These women are wicked! They have tricked me into having a good time in my own palace."

While he leaned forward, Wyetta backed up so Valerie could see her and gave her a thumbs up.

"We do so wish to please you, King Bradwick," Savannah said from next to her.

After their discussion about the day Valerie tripped Charlotte, and her version of events, the beautiful redhead had grown to like Valerie, at least enough that she tolerated her.

Charlotte refused to speak to her unless necessary, and Valerie was pleased with that. Often, they were seen on opposing sides, whether that be in a room or beside the king.

"I heard you were not feeling particularly well today, Lady Cecily," he commented.

She nodded. "With my mother so unwell, we at Dyèrie manor have not thrown many parties for quite some time. I have felt overwhelmed with the festivities."

"That's understandable. You will surely adjust in due time." He nodded his head, returning to dig into his plate of food. "I have yet to ask how things are at your manor with your mother unwell. What ails her?"

"Her heart has grown weak, and she must rest often." Valerie only came to know the specifics by asking her version of Duke Vermont what he thought was unwell with Duchess Edrea. "With her guidance, I have managed to keep the house running in the same manner as it had been before."

"I know she has sisters; have they not fallen ill as well?"

"No, they have not. My aunts, who are much older than my mother, come to the manor to visit often."

"What about finances? You surely must pay for the aid of doctors. Does that not burden Duke Grayson?"

Valerie shook her head. "We have a doctor paid to remain at the manor. My father is good at managing his lands."

"I'm pleased the estate can afford to house so many. I worried for your health, but it appears I have nothing to fear." *He wanted to know if what affected Cecily's mother would affect her.*

With their lack of medical knowledge, it was hard to know what sicknesses affected them and what their causes were. Of course, there was too much risk in asking a Witch for aid.

He turned to ask Wyetta about her lands and position in her home, giving Valerie a moment of silence.

When the evening grew late, the first lady to retire was Charlotte, who was obviously unhappy she was barely a part of the conversation.

As these things often lead to, the court began to stand around the banquet hall in disorder. They danced drunkenly in the centre of the room between the tables.

A shiver ran up Valerie's back when the tip of a finger was drawn from her hips to the middle of her shoulder blades. She felt it over each indent of her spine.

"Bradwick, I plan to retire," Geryon said, his head and body closer to her than the king as he leaned in between them.

Her eyes widened, darting across the room. *He touched me*

*so forwardly.*

He continued to do so, placing his entire palm against her back. Even through her clothing, she found it remarkably warm. The guards didn't seem to notice, his body shielding his actions.

"Do as you wish." The king waved his hand to dismiss Geryon, more interested in the party before him.

Once again, a shiver coursed through her as his fingers drew down her spine before he backed away.

Like she often did, Valerie ignored him.

She didn't want to give him the satisfaction that he may have gotten under her skin. She was planning to pretend she found him, and what he had said to her in the library, insignificant.

Valerie was the last to disappear for the night. It put her in the spotlight, and she left quickly after Wyetta.

She sighed when she reached the stairs leading to her living quarters. *I tire already of playing Cecily.*

"It appears the dove has fallen into the spider's web," a deep, husky voice sounded when she rounded the corner.

Valerie spotted the guard leaning against the wall, his back and the bottom of one boot placed against it. He was peering at his nails like he found them of interest.

Turning her chin up slightly, she lifted the skirts of her dress to walk up the curving staircase. He'd been near the bottom and began to follow her.

"Come now. Ignoring the spider will not save the dove."

"It's a fantastical thought that a bird would be trapped by something so minor as the webbing of an insect." She eyed him out of the corner of her lids. "Perhaps the spider should be wary of being eaten."

"What about a bird-eating spider?"

She gave a mocking, snorting laugh as she continued to climb. He continued to follow. "They don't cast webs."

They came to the centre of the staircase curve, a place that couldn't be seen from the bottom or the top.

"True," he answered. Suddenly, he pushed her against the stone wall, pinning her in place with a hand on either side of her head. "They lunge for their fluttering prey."

"You are crowding me. I would prefer you give me space."

Valerie folded her arms, giving him a look that said she was already bored of this. She wasn't, though. This handsome man crowding her was causing her heart to quicken.

Instead of backing away, he leaned forward, so that his elbows were against the wall, rather than his hands. This brought him closer, and he began to lift one of her fallen waves away from her forehead to tuck it behind her ear.

"No. I don't think I will." She noted she was a fraction taller than him. "You are a rather bewitching looking thing."

His eyes were following his hands while he continued to push away the hair that had fallen from her ties. He delicately brushed the strands over her shoulders. There was a gentleness about it, one she didn't expect from a soldier like him.

"Once again, you attempt to flatter me, but your actions are not those of a gentleman."

His metallic blue eyes shot to hers, and she noted the wicked glint in them. "I have never once believed myself to be of man, whether that be gentle or rough."

Valerie couldn't help wondering what he meant, her brow crinkling ever so slightly.

"Your words confuse me." Her look fell back to her normal composure. "Now, I demand you move, before we are caught in this nefarious position."

"Don't fret. I assure you, we will not be seen."

She knew he was right. The only way they would be caught is if Victoria came down the stairs, which she wouldn't, or if Vermont and his lord-in-waiting were to appear, which they wouldn't until the early hours of the morning.

The spot they were hidden in was out of sight, but it wasn't out of ear.

"Perhaps I can show you what I meant." One of his hands lowered to bunch up her skirts.

Before she could answer him, he pressed his lips against hers.

Ever since their interlude in the library, Valerie, sneakily peering through her lashes throughout the day, had noticed him watching her. It wasn't obvious, but it was hard not to think of him when she was so aware of him.

The confidence he'd shown by climbing above her had been titillating. She hadn't found the idea of being pinned again by this man worrisome, which in turn worried her.

Maybe that's why he'd told her his intentions, to get her thinking of him before he continued to play his games. Now, here she was, pinned by him, her heart fluttering, but not with fear.

His lips were forceful, enough so that they moved hers as well. *He smells sweet.* Like sugar. She was tempted to know if he would taste of it.

Rather than kissing him back, she began pushing on his shoulders. *I cannot give into this kind of temptation. It will not bode well for me.* Even though she found this assertive behaviour delicious, and the man behind it even more so.

Geryon broke away from the kiss to lower himself, bringing his lips to her skin just above her collar bone.

Her mind slipped for a moment when she felt the prickle of goosebumps break out over the side of her neck from his tongue. The scrape of his teeth made her want to arch her head to the side to give him more access.

*I could give him what he wants, play easy, and he may leave me alone afterwards.* Then, she remembered that could lead him to wanting to return between her thighs.

His hand slipped under her dress and the skirt of her

undergarment shift. "Wait."

Valerie gave a small breath, a barely noticeable one, when she felt the tickle of his fingertips play at her knee. They were brushing higher, along her inner thigh.

She wouldn't have found the touch so pleasant if his fingers and palm were as rough as his mouth. Instead, he was trailing a careful sweep, the kind of touch that made the muscles in her legs twitch from its lightness.

It caused her abdomen to spasm, telling her it was the perfect stroke to stimulate her body into complying.

"I demand that you stop," she said when she felt desire pooling in the lower part of her belly. She was ashamed of how throaty she sounded, and she tried to push away harder.

How quickly her body was reacting was alarming. It was hard to deny someone with such a pretty face and an even more delightful body. Even with his coat on, she could tell he had rope after rope of muscles that her fingertips would just adore digging into.

He nipped her neck with his teeth, rough and almost hard enough to leave a mark. Then he brought his mouth up to her ear to nip her lobe and whisper, "Why? I can tell your body wants this."

She gave him a dull look when his eyes peeked up at her. He returned it with a grin, and it caused the corners of his metallic blue eyes to crinkle, making him even more attractive.

Dominant, assertive, confident: all the things Valerie usually liked in men. *Yet, he's being light.* The contradiction in his attitude made her mind freeze, unsure of how to proceed.

He lowered his other hand when she refused to part her thighs for him. Geryon did it himself.

Wrapping his arm around her body to grasp one cheek of her bottom, he pulled it to the side to create enough of a gap to slip his other hand in from the front.

"You are softer than you appear." He kneaded her backside at the same time as he pulled her cheeks apart, giving her a loud huff of approval.

*His hands are warm.* With the slow, gentle caresses and grabs, her muscles wanted to melt rather than tighten in tension. Even his breath and dabbling tongue were hard to ignore; warm, wet, yet deliciously mean.

The sharp sting of his teeth made her want to arch her neck so he could do it everywhere. The more he nipped at her, the more she was tempted.

She fought against these wants. "Regardless, we–"

"I created this ache," he said as he gently slipped two fingers between her folds, feeling her wetness for himself.

Valerie flinched from the direct contact before she felt the flush of arousal spread across her chest in reaction to his intimate touch.

He nipped the heated skin of her chest. "I can ease it as well."

Valerie didn't often feel desire, but she'd never been one to deny herself in the past. It had been a long time, though. She stopped being interested in men when she was much younger.

They also never approached her because of her dead expressions. They found her tasteless because of it, boring even. So why had this man snaked his hand under her skirts with exploring fingertips?

She didn't know when she'd stopped pushing him away, her hands halting on his shoulders. *I must stop this.* Yet the moment he pressed against the nub of her clit, she felt the twitch to part her legs for more.

The caring caresses were almost her undoing. *He's being so gentle, it feels like a whisper.* A play of teasing touches, ones designed to get her to ask for more rather than force them upon her.

Unrushed, like he didn't care when he would receive his own pleasure, he moved like he was more interested in hers. *Such a touch is hard to deny.*

Valerie had been in a position like this many times in her life, some rude bastard snaking his hands under her skirt while thrusting his cock against her, like that was some magical way to spur her into wanting it. Those types of men always grunted like pigs, rushing her while trying to combat her into some saliva-filled kiss.

Geryon, on the other hand, was only touching her with his hands, being slow and careful.

His fingers began a lazy circle over her clit while his lips traced a path up her neck and over her jaw, making his destination obvious. If he pressed his lips to hers again, would she want to taste sweetness like she did before?

She found herself turning her face towards him to find out for certain, or if it had been her imagination.

His fingers worked their way down the lips of her folds to greet her pooling entrance. She dug her nails into his shoulders and started pushing away.

"No," she told him when he began to press one of his fingers inside.

*I cannot give in. This is too dangerous.*

She turned her face away from his mouth before she could discover what it tasted like.

He paused, his eyes on her lips lifting to meet hers.

The tip of the finger that entered her core now just rested there. Valerie tried to stop her entrance from contracting around it. It was as though her channel wanted to pull it inside despite herself.

"No?"

She remained silent, unsure of the kind of words that would fall from her lips if she spoke. Then the wonderful pressure of his fingertip disappeared, and his hand came out from underneath her skirts.

"You are pulling away?"

"You told me no. Therefore, no it shall be." Yet, he leaned forward to swipe his tongue from the centre of her throat to her ear, leaving a wet stroke behind it. "But this is not over," he said around a kiss to her skin.

For the first time, she felt something hard, long, and, to her amazement, impossibly thick run over her hip when he slipped his pelvis against hers. He was punctuating his obvious arousal before he gave her a huff of disappointment. He turned from her.

He'd ignored all her attempts to protest, and she thought he would continue to do so. Valerie thought he would take her by force and against her wishes. The fact that he stopped, that she was now watching the back of him descending the stairs to leave her in peace, surprised her. *I expected him to be crude.* It showed her he at least respected her enough to not force the issue.

*Is 'no' simply all I have to say to stop him?* Was it truly that simple?

To her displeasure, she felt herself softening towards him. *Men can often be vile to women; he has shown me he's not.*

The prospect of this happening again wasn't as worrying as it was before. She would be able to have control, and she knew that was what he ultimately wanted.

Unfortunately, the ache between her thighs was currently real and very dissatisfying. *I'm deeply aroused.* It actually grew in strength when he left.

"No matter," she whispered quietly, before she turned to ascend the stairs. She made her way to one of her personal soldiers under her spell. "Were we heard?"

"No, my lady. We heard nothing."

Good. They'd been quiet enough that anyone walking past

the bottom of the stairs may not have heard either.

Victoria was asleep on one of the settees in the seating area in front of her room. She'd fallen asleep upright, her elbow resting on the arm of the chair, her cheek in her open palm.

"Lady Victoria, I have returned."

The woman immediately shot up and got to her feet. "My apologies for this indiscretion, Lady Cecily."

"I said you may do as you please while you wait for me, and the hour is late." Victoria bowed her head in thanks. "Please, help me out of this dress and then you may retire to your own apartment to rest."

They entered Valerie's room, and she began to undo the ties at the back of her dress. She thought about what had just happened and the man behind it.

"You seem rosier in the cheeks than usual, Cecily. Are you not feeling well?" The question made Valerie push the handsome guard from her mind.

Valerie gave a sigh. "I'm hot. Mayhap I had too much wine."

"I often become a beetroot in the face with too much wine," Victoria giggled. "Baron Cole often cradles me back to our room."

Baron Cole was Victoria's husband and was a dashing man. He was polite, and one of the few noblemen Valerie could tolerate speaking to.

Victoria gave a deep yawn – attempting to stifle it to the point that she teared up – once she was done with the ties at the back of her dress.

Valerie turned to her. "I can do the rest; you may leave to return to your husband. I'm sure he wonders where you are."

"Thank you, my lady. Although he's aware of our agreement, he does worry for me when I walk the palace alone at night."

*He fears her walking the castle on her own?* Valerie hadn't thought about the woman's welfare. *Geryon stopped; others may not.*

"Guard!" Valerie yelled, startling the poor woman.

"Yes, Lady Cecily?" one said as he ran in.

He quickly averted his gaze when he saw she was holding the front of her dress up. The back was open and loose.

"From now on, in the mornings, one of you will escort Lady Victoria to me. In the evenings, one of you will escort her to her husband."

"It's okay, my lady. You don't need to worry for me."

"If you wish to have your freedom to commit acts you should not, but I don't care if you participate in, I will rescind my command." Valerie didn't care what the woman did; it was none of her business. "But I'm happy to keep the command if you are truly worried, as it's for your safety. I will not permit you to come to harm in between your care for me."

Victoria nodded. "You are much kinder than you appear. The additional protection would be much appreciated, especially at night, when wine has been involved."

With a nod, Valerie turned her head back to her guard. "You are to issue my command to the others and detail yourselves accordingly."

"Yes, my lady."

**10**

"I have news of the rest of the week's events, Lady Cecily," Victoria said, while she ran a brush through Valerie's wet hair. She'd not long been awake, and she was already having her morning bath. "Each day, King Bradwick will court one of you ladies for the entire day."

Valerie's gaze drifted over her room as she thought on what this meant for her. "So, I will not be with him at all during the week unless it's my day?"

"I know you must be disappointed, but it does mean you will have a whole day to win him without interference."

*No, this is perfect,* Valerie thought. *I can begin to search the palace grounds.*

"Are you informed of which days will be granted to each of us?"

"I am. Today is for Lady Savannah, since she was the first to arrive at the palace. You will be the final lady, since you were the last." *That gives me three days to gather knowledge.* "You will also no longer be dining in the banquet hall. Instead, the formal dining room is being prepared. He will sit at the head with the lady of the day. The other ladies will sit in the middle and converse with the court."

"We will be completely separated from him each day?"

"Somewhat. He may wish to spend part of his time at court with the lady of the day. You may be able to sneak in a conversation with him in those times."

Valerie had no such desires. She was just making sure she understood how far her freedom stretched.

"What will happen after the next four days?"

"There is no news on that. All I know is on the second to last night of the gala, there will be a ball where more visitors will arrive."

After the update, Valerie was dressed in a baby blue dress, low cut and suggestive. She hadn't thought it would be so revealing when she selected it from Cecily's clothing chests.

"What is the court function for today?" Valerie asked when they left her living arrangements.

They were heading there now, so that she could show the court she was interested in them.

"I believe it will be another day of scatter." A scattered court meant they would be spread out over the main lawns and rooms they attended.

"That's perfect. I wish to walk the palace, and it will be easier to not be missed if they are scattered."

"My thoughts exactly. I had a feeling you would want to, since you have not been able to." Victoria gave her a warm smile.

Once they arrived, Valerie spoke with multiple other nobles. She was putting on a show, speaking with as many people as she could before she found the individual she wanted.

She couldn't see Geryon or King Bradwick, much to her relief.

"Lady Wyetta," Valerie greeted as she bowed to her.

"Lady Cecily." She returned the greeting with a bow of her head.

"I wonder if you were rather curious about the palace as well and may wish to take a stroll with me?" Valerie extended her hand in the hopes she would take her up on her offer.

"Since we will not be required, that sounds like a splendid idea. I do so love how clever you can be."

Wyetta took ahold of her arm, and they left court to begin their walk along the lengthy bottom floor of the palace.

The blocks of buildings were connected by two hallways on either side. One could only access the other hallway by walking the long length and entering the room at the other end, before then crossing to the door on the other side of that room to go back.

Each hallway had access to one of the two rooms available in the middle.

The above level was filled with rooms and apartments and was far more confusing. Valerie had yet to touch the third floor.

They were heading to the left side of the palace, and Valerie made sure to check behind every door.

"You are rather curious, are you not?" Wyetta asked, raising a brow at how forward she was with her search.

"Do you not wish to know every nook and cranny of a place you may live in for the rest of your life?" Valerie asked, casually opening another door to peek inside before closing it.

"That's a rather fair point." The woman laughed. "I admit, I agreed to come on this stroll because I want to find the war room."

"It's rather frightful how much you enjoy blood and death. Perhaps you should have been born with a penis so you could have revelled in your bloodlust."

Wyetta put her hand over her heart, sighing like that was the dream she wished for. "Oh, to be a man, to do what I want, say what I want, fuck whoever I want."

"You only speak so forwardly because we are alone."

There was barely even a guard posted in the long hallways. The further they got from court, the less they saw them, until Valerie realised she no longer did.

"Why, of course! Does it not feel good to speak so out of turn without the ears of others?" Then, to Valerie's humour, Wyetta began to shout, "Fuck, shit, piss! See, it's rather uplifting. You must have a go."

"I would much prefer not." Valerie wasn't against such language, she just didn't wish to be caught. "Perhaps we can continue on your daydreams of wishing to be a man."

"That is quite untrue!" Wyetta exclaimed. "I'm fond of men and their dicks. I just don't like the position in which we women are born. We are seen as nothing more than dancing roses and child catapults."

Valerie's eyes crinkled with a surprised laugh. "Your imagery is quite compelling. You should write poetry about the woes of womanhood."

"It will never become famous; men will not appreciate my higher intellect."

The urge to cover the overconfident woman's mouth was too much to bear. She placed both hands over her lips to quiet her, receiving a giggle in return.

"You are just as bad as me," Valerie teased. "Here I thought I was the only one acting in a superior way to my usual self."

"Ha! I knew you had a side to you that may not be all ladyship and poised beauty." She mocked Valerie's constant composure by puckering her lips, holding her fingers out like she was sipping tea, and nodding to nobles who weren't present.

"The only way I can pretend to be you, Lady Wyetta, is if I showered myself in pig's blood."

Wyetta's jaw dropped. "That is rude and vulgar, and I take great offense! Human blood would be a much better way to create such a wonderful portrayal of me. I would wear it with nothing else; a dress made of blood."

Then she gave her a grand smile, which made Valerie's own lips quirk. She was beginning to truly adore Wyetta.

They occasionally passed stairs that would take them to a second floor, cut off from the rest of the upper level, leading them to suites like Valerie's, and they passed hers along the way.

Once they found themselves at the end of the palace and could go no further, they crossed to the other side so they could walk down the hallways they hadn't on their way there. They often stopped to admire certain tapestries, paintings, and sculptures.

Valerie was hoping to find the entrance to the dungeons, but no such luck.

With their unhurried speed, they reached the centre of the palace around mid-afternoon, the court thankfully still spread out.

Against the wall, next to a balcony of nobles chatting, rested Geryon. His arms were folded, his posture relaxed, with one foot crossed in front of the other. She was surprised he wasn't with King Bradwick, but she quickly turned her gaze away from him when he met her eyes. It almost appeared as though he was waiting for something, or someone.

"Come, Lady Wyetta. I'm sure we can stroll the second half of the palace before it's time to eat." They were stopped right in front of the balcony where Geryon was leaning.

"Countess Nicole is holding a tea in the afternoon for the ladies of the court, where we can enjoy needlepoint tapestry. You may venture the palace further, but I wish to attend."

Needlepoint tapestry was where they took different coloured strings and wove them through mesh to create patterns. It was an art for women, something that could be done in a social setting while drinking tea and eating sweets.

Valerie could think of nothing worse. *I wish to continue exploring the grounds.*

For some reason, her eyes found Geryon once more. He quickly looked away, but she could tell by the tapping of his fingers on his muscled biceps that he'd been listening in on their conversation.

"Needlepoint tapestry and tea sounds like a wonderful activity," Valerie answered.

In her peripheral, Geryon's gaze snapped to her, one of his brows raising. He knew she was lying. *He has already unravelled my dislike of court entertainment.* He appeared vexed, his eyes narrowing in her direction.

*She's a sneaky fox, a mischievous weasel.* Geryon was pursuing a woman who very much knew how to keep him away.

*She has not been alone all day.* She'd spent the morning with Lady Wyetta, which in itself had caused his brow to raise. *I thought she would prefer to be alone,* especially since she was often separated from Baroness Victoria.

Then, in the afternoon, she'd remained with the court women. She even persuaded her uncle, Duke Vermont, to walk her back to her room after eating in the grand dining hall.

What he thought would be a day of spending time getting to know her in secret, instead had been him being bored among the people.

*She's purposefully evading me.*

Cecily was playing a dangerous game, one that he would hide his enjoyment of, and one that he would win.

"It appears as though some of the men in my court have become interested in my guests," Bradwick said to Geryon, pulling him from his thoughts.

They were having a small meeting over breakfast, since he often ate his in the king's parlour.

No servant was permitted to enter Geryon's chambers, and therefore, they fed him here instead. He didn't like anyone in his private space.

Geryon also dressed himself every day, working at the complex buttons and designs of his suit coats himself. It was a source of entertainment for him. The harder it was to do by himself, the more he liked it.

"I noticed that as well. They're quite...attentive." Geryon wasn't so obvious in his attempt to know Cecily.

"Yes, especially over dinner. Do you think they wish to take the ones I don't pick?"

"That's a fair deduction. They will become available once you have chosen."

"I'm deciding on whether or not I should be offended and insulted," Bradwick scowled, eating his breakfast with Geryon like he did most mornings.

He used to be fed in bed, but had opted to change his routine so they could discuss things together over a meal. It was the only meal Geryon shared with anyone within the palace, and it was only ever with Bradwick.

"I don't think you should care once you have picked your mate, *urh*, I mean wife. The women are here for you, and I'm sure they'd prefer to wed you. Anyone second is just being fed your scraps."

"That's true. I will be too busy trying to sire an heir to give a damn what the men of my court do with the women I have not chosen." He paused in his eating to scowl. "Unless they attempt anything during the gala. Then I will remove their hands and possibly their cocks, too."

*I would like to see you try to do that to me, dear human king.*

"Savannah worries me for that reason, though," Bradwick

commented, shaking his head. "There is a look about her, one that says, 'Come hither, unsuspecting man, my pussy is ripe for your cock.' As much as I appreciate it towards me, her gaze is always suggestive."

"You are uncertain if she will remain faithful. I'm sure she would not commit such a risk as to betray you. Judging her based on a look she may not even be aware she wears is foolish."

Bradwick pointed his fork at him. "It happens enough that my father beheaded his first wife for it."

"Ah, yes, you often speak of the tale of Queen Larissa. From what I have gathered about your father, he often spent his time between the thighs of women who were not his wife. She may have done so in retaliation."

"As a man, and the royal blood on the throne, he was allowed to do as he wished."

Geryon cringed. "That's something many Dragons cannot understand. It's rare we tolerate sharing a mate, nor will we allow ourselves to be shared. Only a handful will, and that's because there are far fewer females than there are males."

"Don't be so cheeky with me, Geryon. I have never stated I plan to walk in my father's footsteps. I would prefer not to spread my seed where it may grow in places it should not."

Although Bradwick's father was a magnificent king, he was not a faithful husband, nor was he truly a good man. He'd killed many women who claimed to become pregnant with his bastard children, to the point that they stopped coming forward.

Once Bradwick's mother married him after he killed Queen Larissa, she gave birth to Bradwick and his brother. She didn't care who or what he did, so long as he treated her well, which he did.

That was why Bradwick was never surprised when someone stepped forward to say they were an illegitimate child of his father, a half-brother. Most wouldn't live long after announcing their statement, Bradwick making sure to pluck the weeds when they grew. *He must do what he can to remain on the throne.*

"Well, I have given my opinion to *your Lordship*," Geryon sneered mockingly. "You may do with it as you see fit."

*It helps that he's not ugly of face.* Nor were the parts of him that mattered small.

"Who is it you will be with today?" Geryon asked as they stood to leave.

"Wyetta. I'm keen on her, for the same reason I'm keen on Cecily. Their conversations are never dull, both in substance and wit." Then Bradwick snorted. "Although Cecily's humour is prickly, I do very much like it. Wyetta, on the other hand, comes across more sensual."

"You have yet to mention the other brown-haired woman." Geryon just wanted to steer the conversation away from Cecily.

"Charlotte? Her beauty is one of true divinity, and she holds a body I know I would enjoy for years. Unlike the others, her opinions and thoughts are mouldable, but I'm worried about how... intelligent she is. It would work in my favour, since she would never get in the way of politics."

Geryon nodded. "Good. You are looking at them in a way that benefits you, rather than immediately seeing a negative quality as worthless."

"Yes, I was rather arrogant the last time I spoke of them. I never knew women could be so complex."

Geryon chuckled, slapping him on the back. "You are listening to my advice for once, rather than being a fool."

Bradwick scowled, unappreciative of his informal touch. "I have noticed you don't remain as my guard when I'm with the ladies."

"I cannot help it. You all bore me, so much so that I fear I will collapse in sleep where I stand."

Bradwick nodded in understanding, lifting his hand to his chin. "I imagine you are watching the court. What are the current rumours?"

"Many, but none you need worry yourself with."

They arrived downstairs for the day, and Bradwick waited for the arrival of Wyetta. Geryon didn't follow when they left, instead remaining behind.

When it was well into the day, and neither Victoria nor Cecily had made an appearance, Geryon decided to hunt her down. *I will not allow her to evade me today.*

He found her walking with her lady-in-waiting down the right side of the palace, the opposite way he knew she'd gone the previous day.

Now that he had found her, he made his way up the hallway where they couldn't see him.

Rather than coming up from behind her, Geryon appeared in front, opening the door they were heading towards.

"Lady Victoria, Lady Cecily," he exclaimed boisterously, bowing his head in greeting. "What a surprise that I would find you two walking inside on such a lovely day."

A wild grin spread across his features at Cecily's expression, one that told him she knew it wasn't a coincidence he'd come upon them.

"Lord Geryon." Victoria dipped her head in greeting. He was not a lord, but that was what they believed. "Yes, well, Lady Cecily is very interested in the palace and wishes to explore it."

"Is that so?" He raised his brow, subtly licking at the seam of his lips. He rubbed his jaw like he was deep in thought, contemplating an idea, before he waved his hand forward in a casual gesture. "Perhaps I can give her a tour, then?"

"Oh!" Victoria clapped her hands together. "That sounds like a lovely idea, do you not think, Lady Cecily?"

He could see the wheels turning in her head, Cecily trying to find a way out of being alone with him.

"Unfortunately, I must decline your most generous offer. I don't wish to give the king the wrong idea if I was seen walking alone and privately with another man."

"I'm sure King Bradwick would much prefer to know you were guarded while you walked the palace. Is that not right, Victoria?"

"Of course." She smiled brightly, not understanding that the lady she was attending wanted an escape.

*The composed face you hide behind is also your greatest weakness, little fawn.* She wasn't presenting any signs of distress.

"I'm unsure if you have met Lord Geryon, but he's Bradwick's most loyal servant and trusted confidant. He would never think ill of Geryon, so you don't need to fear, my lady. I can return to the court for you."

"Yes, I did notice you had rather cute ears and wide eyes." The woman blushed at being caught in her spying. "It appears as though Cecily was given a lady-in-waiting who is rather useful."

"Yes, well, she does like to know of the events of the day," she mumbled, her blush growing. Her eyes flicked to Cecily, nervous about being caught.

Cecily's expression didn't change, except for squinting ever so slightly. It was a barely noticeable difference, so slight that it wouldn't have been seen if someone wasn't looking for it.

"Is it settled then?" Geryon waited for whatever excuse she attempted to come up with. "Or is there a reason why you are so against my company, Lady Cecily?"

He gave her a charming smile when he noticed that squint deepen into a glare. There was none. She couldn't evade him so openly in front of Victoria without causing suspicion.

She relaxed her features so smoothly that her glare only lasted a second. "No reason at all. Please return to court for me, Victoria. I will walk with Lord Geryon while I explore."

Victoria nodded and turned to walk back the way the ladies came. He held his arm out for her to take it.

"You push your luck." Instead of taking his arm, Cecily walked forward with stiff shoulders. She turned her nose up, staring at the door on the other side of the hallway as they slowly creeped closer. "She called you lord; does that mean I was correct in my assumption that you are not a normal guard? What is your status?"

Geryon walked beside her, placing his arms behind his back to appear casual. "As I said, think of me on par with King Bradwick."

She surprised him when she opened a side door in the hallway to check what was inside. She closed it and continued to walk forward. She refused to look at him.

He, however, hadn't stopped gazing at her. *She looks breathtaking today.* It may have something to do with the pearls in her tied-back hair and her slender neck being exposed. Even her pale shoulders were uncovered.

The make-up she wore was lighter than usual, and he appreciated seeing more of her and less of it. She was also wearing a grey dress that highlighted her skin and made her appear more doll-like.

"Why are you searching the palace?" He had to ask, since she opened the door in the next hallway as well.

"Can I not be curious about such a grand place?"

"Yes, but is there anything in particular you wish to find?" *If I show it to her, she may soften towards me.*

"I'm rather interested in the dungeons," she told him. His brows raised at such an answer. "I'm also interested in the war room; both seem rather glorious."

"The dungeons are the last place a woman should be

searching for, and I can guarantee you, it's far from glorious."

She clasped her hands in front of herself, staring forward with a lift of her chin. He'd offended her. He almost wanted to wince.

"That may be true, but I do wish to see how they differ from Dyèrie manor. The palace is vastly different, and I wish to know all about it." She turned her head slightly to meet his eyes. "Since I may not be the one staying."

*She's right; she may not get another opportunity.* He thought deeply on this for a moment, weighing his options. *How bad could it be?*

"I will have to think on the dungeon, but I most definitely can take you to the war room," he offered.

"If you are expecting a reward, then I will find it on my own."

Geryon smiled awfully cheekily, pulling a ring of keys connected to a lengthy chain from inside his coat. "You may find it at the end of these long halls, but you will not be able to enter it, vicious mouse."

She narrowed her eyes at the keys before her gaze turned away, bored. She didn't seem to care about his endearment.

"You have already made your intentions obvious and will wish for an exchange in revealing the war room."

"Come now, Cecily, you paint me as devious. Perhaps I will unlock it regardless."

Her face remained plain of expression when most women would have pursed their lips in thought or irritation. He found it endearing that she was trying so hard.

"Why are you pursuing me? If you are truly King Bradwick's loyal servant, then should you not act accordingly?"

"I'm loyal to him in the ways that matter. It's not like you are his wife, nor is there certainty that you will be." He frowned for a long moment. "And why would I not want to pursue you? I find you rather... tempting, enough that I would even consider doing so."

The face she gave, and the roll of her eyes, made it obvious she didn't believe him.

"You are trying to make it appear as though I'm the first woman of the court you have tried to play this game with. I'm not so easily swayed, Lord Geryon."

Geryon scowled, having been caught out in his trickery.

"That's not what I insinuated. All I'm saying is that it's a rare occurrence when it does happen. You are welcome to ask Victoria about me. I'm not often part of court and prefer to be on my own."

"That still does not answer my question. There are three other ladies here for King Bradwick, and many more of the court. I find it hard to believe it's I you have singled out when they are far more appealing." When he opened his mouth to disagree, her features dulled to show she wasn't going to hear it. "I'm often told I'm cold and unfeeling."

Geryon chuckled loudly. "But that's exactly what I do so sincerely like about you."

He turned to her, lifting his hand to run it against her cheek. No one was around to see him do it; they were too far away from the centre of the palace to have people loitering here.

"I'm sure under that icy stare, there is a woman who is as hot as an inferno in the throes." He stepped closer, bringing them almost nose to nose. "I'm very much interested in meeting her."

His eyes darted down to her lips. She must have noticed because she stepped back to put space between them.

"Come now," he said with a hint of humour. "You must have realised by now that I'm not an unthinking brute. Someone like Charlotte would never interest me." He brought his hand up to cup his chin when they began walking again. He shuddered in thought. "The way she clings to Bradwick is rather off-putting, even more so than her lack of brains."

She said nothing, but he could tell she was stemming the want to smile. Geryon knocked his elbow gently into her arm.

"Don't pretend you don't despise her every walking step. I have seen you behave with spitefulness towards her. The servants are still trying to find the crack in the floor that tripped her."

"You almost gave me away that day," she grumbled, but her smile started to grow. It was fleeting. "And what of Savannah?"

Geryon gave low a whistle, shaking his head once. "Woman has quite the look, but I would rather not be one of the many men lining up."

"Wyetta is perfect for King Bradwick," she surprised him by saying. "If he chooses anyone else, he will be lessening the quality of his queen."

"It's true, something I have already seen. He will not tolerate your intellect for long, nor your coldness, and the others have their failing qualities. She is most suited for the position." *But no one can tell him this. He's the kind of man who will need to come to such a realisation on his own.* "But what others may think of as a failing quality is perhaps one that I find desirous."

She raised her brow in his direction, causing him to grin. He'd brought them back to the original conversation.

The more she understood his desire, the more she would come to like him. It wasn't about getting his dick wet, but something more, something special that only a woman like her could give him.

"Also, we have arrived at our destination."

He pulled out his key and unlocked the door at the very end of this wing. He ushered her forward by swiping his hand in the direction of the war room while holding the door for her.

It revealed a large room with scrolls and books packed

away into doorless cabinets. In the centre of the room was a large oval table, sunken so figurines could be placed down. It was painted with the closest lands to King Bradwick's kingdom, but painted boards could be placed inside to map further.

They currently weren't planning for an invasion or attack, so Cecily being in this room wouldn't cause any harm.

"Fine, I will allow you to believe that you have convinced me," she said as she walked inside the room, letting her gaze sweep over it in its entirety. "Once this gala is over, I will either be selected, or I will go back to Dyèrie manor."

Geryon remained silent, turning his head to stare out the windows in the hall before he followed her inside. *How deeply do I wish to play this game?* Or rather, how *long* did he wish to play this game?

"Many noblemen have been speaking with you ladies with the intention of courting the ones not chosen by Bradwick."

A sound he'd never heard before filled his ears. Cecily laughed... at him! "You are jesting. You truly cannot be saying that you want me to become your ladyship? You barely know me."

Geryon pouted, disappointed that the first laugh he won from her had been directed at him with sarcasm.

*Why not?* He didn't understand why his words would cause her to laugh at him. *She's a human woman; they usually fawn at these kinds of words or ideals.* He could tell she was human; her scent and lack of magic were obvious.

He'd been hoping his words, although a lie, may soften her.

*I should be the one to laugh at such a notion.* Many Dragons had taken human companions to ease their long years. Dragons could live eight hundred years if they were lucky, and a human life was merely the blink of an eye to them.

They also weren't allowed to breed with them, due to

Dragon law. They didn't want to sire any more Witches that could bring further havoc on his species.

Geryon had considered it for a long time because he thought it would make his life as a human next to King Bradwick more enjoyable. *I'm often bored here, waiting for the reason why I came to this palace to happen.*

Bored enough that he'd instigated his most recent hunt.

"Oh, you were serious." Her laughter died, and he gave her a glare. "I doubt King Bradwick will tolerate it."

"Perhaps not for the other men of his court, but he most likely would for me." He had his arms folded across his broad chest, standing in the middle to be close to her, no matter where she ventured.

"How can you be so sure?"

Her hands were clasped behind her, and Geryon wasn't sure if she was aware that doing so pushed her breasts up. *I wonder if they are soft.* He quickly averted his gaze before she noticed, even though she was too busy looking around the room.

She bent over occasionally to peek inside lower sections of doorless cabinets, inspecting the book titles and unfurled scrolls carelessly put away.

"King Bradwick is annoyingly invested in my state of being. He believes I don't enjoy myself enough, and that deeply offends him." He tapped his fingers against his biceps in irritation. "Quite often, he sends women to my bed in order to cheer me, without understanding I'm already quite merry."

He hated it, because it meant there was someone he didn't know or trust in his private suite. He didn't know where Bradwick kept acquiring keys, since he'd confiscated many.

He tried his best to keep himself happy, since he wasn't able to lose himself in thoughtlessness like most of his kind did. Dragons could go through periods of time with blank thoughts, allowing time to pass quicker for them.

*I can only do that in my lair.* He couldn't with the humans around him. It was a form of rest, one he did in between choosing his hunting grounds.

"He often threatens to whip me for not taking his gifts to bed," Geryon chuckled. "For that reason alone, he does not care what I do."

She'd been walking around the battle planning table, slipping her fingertips over it while she was listening to him speak. Slowly, she was making her way back around.

"Regardless," she said, eyeing him from the corner of her lids. "Such words may work with other women, Lord Geryon, but they are not so effective on me. I'm aware of the games and pretty words men speak to women to lift their skirts. I'm not so silly."

He opened his mouth, but she cut him with a look. It was a warning, and she gave it to him while she stood directly in front of him.

"Don't utter false promises. I don't appreciate them, and they hinder your progress."

Geryon crinkled his nose in irritation and stepped forward. He gripped her jaw, forcing her head to tilt back.

"Currently, what I want is to have you scream for me." He brought her closer with his forceful hold, and her hands reached up to grasp his wrist to pull it away. "But, once I obtain it, you don't know what I may want from you. My words may not be empty, but they most definitely could be." Geryon licked under her jaw to taste the salt of her sweat against his tongue. "But I'm rather fond of your heartlessness."

She hadn't cared if she offended him, hurt him, disappointed him with her words or stares. Cecily was an unsympathetic monster. It made him want to claw at her dress and take her so he could make her feel something. He wanted to know the secrets beneath that blankness.

She stepped back, and there it was, the cold stare that made him want to pant at her like a dog in heat. If a look could kill, hers would have been the sharpest blade skilfully poised at the heart.

"But the question is, Lord Geryon, am I fond of you?" Her tone told him she wasn't and had been purposeful like a snake's fanged strike.

*Insolent wench!* He grabbed the sides of her face and crashed their lips together. He needed to taste that coldness, hoping it was cool enough to freeze his lips.

It wasn't. Instead, his eyes widened when her scent immediately became warm with desire.

She was pushing at his shoulders to force them apart, and he backed up to look at her.

Her stare was the same, but he could see her chest had dotted with the beginning redness of arousal. Her skin even felt warmer under his palm, his fingers across her face.

*Her heart has never beaten this fast.* Not in the library. Not when he'd touched her back in the feasting hall. Not when he had her pressed up against the wall.

He could hear it pounding in her chest with his sensitive ears, picking up speed with each second that passed.

Beaming, Geryon brought their lips back together, kissing her deeply and with force. *Her desire was swift.* She was trying to hide it.

If he were human, he wouldn't have known any better.

Unfortunately for his captured prey, she was in the presence of a Dragon. Geryon could hear it in her heartbeat. Could taste it in her unmoving lips. Could smell it in her scent. Could feel it in the heat of her skin.

Cecily was aroused for him, by him.

He turned them and pushed her back up against a cabinet. Scrolls fell from it when it tilted to hit against the wall.

He left one hand cupping the side of her face, letting his

thumb stroke over the bone of her cheek. He moved his other hand to wrap it around her midsection softly.

*Come on, Cecily.* He could scent that her arousal was deepening. She'd even stopped pushing him away. Something was going on in her mind because she appeared frozen. *Reciprocate.* Once she finally did, at least to return his kisses, he could go somewhere with her.

With a silent growl, he pulled away from her mouth to brush his lips against her neck. He felt her skin prickle against his tongue as he ran it underneath her jaw.

"Why are you so warm?" she said, now that he had freed her mouth. It wasn't a whisper, but it was soft.

"Because my blood is pumping rather hard right now." Geryon thrust his hardening cock against the crook of her thigh and pelvis, giving her an additional explanation as to what he meant. He'd been growing hard from the moment she started uttering callous words to him, her cruel banter in the hallways. "And we are very alone right now."

They were. The shutters in this room were always closed unless it was being used for its intended purpose. This room was at the very end of the palace, meaning not many came here.

Geryon pulled back once more, wondering how he could get her to bend to his will. *She's still fighting me.*

If he didn't get her to break past this first barrier, he knew he would get the same reaction as the last time he tried to reach under her skirt.

*I wonder...*

"Please, let me kiss you," he sweetly begged.

He connected eyes with her, and her stare wasn't as calm as it had been before he asked. Her green irises flickered like the lightning strike of a storm between his own, glittering in the light that peeked in from behind the drapes. *I wonder what she is thinking.*

Was she confused that he asked her? Surprised that he wasn't above begging? Was she caving because he attempted to ask so tenderly? The mystery of her hidden thoughts and emotions was just as titillating.

The tight press of her mouth softened, and he knew he'd won.

Cecily parted her lips for him this time when he dipped his head and brought his down on hers. When he moved them, she moved them in time with his.

Geryon found the perfect moment to tilt his face so he could slip his tongue deeply inside her mouth. She tasted divine, and it felt all the better because she was softening in his arms, twisting his tongue with her own. She twirled it around his, tilting her head the opposite way to deepen the kiss herself.

Geryon's eyes were cracked open so he could watch hers shut. She was quiet, didn't make a sound, but for the first time since he laid eyes on her, her face appeared remarkably gentle.

Slowly, as not to spook his easily skittish prey, he brought his hand up from around her waist. He tried to get her tongue to follow his into his mouth while he did. When he felt it slip past his teeth, he sucked on it, startling her.

While she was distracted, he pulled at the tie on the back of her dress.

Not wanting to pull away from kissing her, in case he broke whatever trance she was under, Geryon began to loosen her dress. It opened for him, and he left it how it was for the moment.

With slow and careful movements, he lifted her skirt. He'd gone unnoticed until he placed his hand on her thigh.

Her eyes peeked open, her brow twitching to show him she was trying not to frown. The gentle expression faded, and Geryon pulled away to kiss along her cheek, his kisses languid but heated.

Now that he'd pulled away, he could hear that her breaths were shallow, as if she was trying to catch them.

"Wait." Her hands pressed on his shoulders.

"Let me touch you," he whispered against her skin, just below her ear. "Part your pretty thighs for me."

They tightened as her head turned up towards the ceiling. He wasn't sure if she was attempting a call for strength, or because the sweeping of his lips down her neck was causing her to arch. He kept his fingertips trailing across her closed legs, up and down to pet her gently.

When too much time had passed, he placed the hand cupping her face behind her head. He forced her head to tilt back down, making her mouth slam against his.

She was still fighting, even though he could tell she wanted it. *Why will she not give in?*

Instead of being patient, he slipped his hand further up between the tight press of her thighs, directly at her pelvis. The moment his middle finger found the nub of her clit, her legs parted.

Her fingers dug into his shoulders as the space allowed him to press harder against that sensitive bundle of nerves.

*Dear heavens... She's very aroused.* He opened his eyes to look at her face. It appeared so calm, and yet he could feel her honey coating his fingers. He hadn't even touched her core yet. Her wetness had pooled and then spread up her folds.

Afraid she would pull away again if he were too slow, he pushed his hand further between her parted thighs. Then he slammed his middle finger inside her and felt her tense at the unexpected intrusion.

Geryon pulled his mouth from hers so he could press his lips against her throat. He didn't want either of them to be distracted by their lips so they both could feel what he was doing to her.

With how easily she'd taken his finger, he didn't think her

body was untried. *But it has definitely been a while.* This didn't bother him in the least. She could have satisfied her desires and then locked them away to become the unfeeling woman she was now. This is what he assumed, at least. *I will bring her back to that woman.*

Geryon began to pump his finger, making sure he collected enough wetness before he added a second. Her body stretched for them, and he kissed at her collarbone in appreciation and praise.

To give her more, he pressed the pad of his thumb against the hard nub of her folds, moving it up and down carefully with his thrusting fingers.

Cecily surprised him by wrapping her arms around his shoulders as she let her head fall back and her breath hitched.

*She will not pull away now.* He reached underneath her dress with his other hand to caress her body. He'd loosened it so that he could touch freely without restriction.

He pulled her bodice down enough that he was able to unveil one of her breasts. He couldn't help dabbing his tongue out at the seam of his lips when he realised she didn't care that he'd exposed her.

He brought his lips to her rosy pink nipple. It grew firm so quickly against his tongue that he knew the sensitive bud enjoyed being inside the heat of his mouth.

Now that Geryon was exactly where he wanted to be – his lips latched onto one of her small breasts while his fingers slowly delved – his behaviour changed.

The gentle touches became rougher. He sucked her breast with determination, lashing it with his tongue before sucking hard. *I want her to feel it later.* He wanted her to have one nipple bruised and swollen from his attention so she wouldn't be able to forget he'd been at it for the rest of the day and night.

His fingers shifted from a slow perusal to a determined

slam. He pumped them in and out of her pussy, feeling her wetness, hearing it swish.

Her legs trembled, and he hated the silence that followed. Her lips were forced shut. She was refusing to allow her moans to escape, quietly breathing through her nose instead. Her brows were twitching, like they wanted to furrow in pleasure, but she was refusing to let them.

Geryon hooked his fingers towards the front of her channel, trying to find her sweet spot. He prodded hard and deep, trying to get her breath to hitch more so he could know where to focus.

She tensed up in his arms, her legs closing as he felt her move to the tips of her toes. Instead of giving him a moan while she came, she finally opened her mouth to give him a squeak on the end of a deep pant, like her lungs had seized.

Her slick dripped, drenching his hand. *There we go.* Geryon had gotten her to come hard with his fingers.

He let out a groan when his cock pulsated, wanting to feel her come around it.

He may not be satisfied with how she'd hidden how much she was enjoying this, but he was very satisfied her body wasn't being so coy. Her core milked his fingers in heavy spasms, wet and quivering around his digits. He wiggled them to get her to continue, and her fingers dug deeper into his shoulders.

She settled. Her head fell forward to stare down at him. Simply because the lax expression in her eyes turned cold again, Geryon started the pound of his fingers once more.

"Wait," she gasped, her palms pressing on his shoulders like she was trying to lift herself away from his touch. "I just came."

"Again," he demanded, before he brought her swollen nipple into his mouth.

He felt bad for it. He'd already been rough with her poor

nipple, so much so that what had once been pink was now red. Instead of being cruel, he circled his tongue around it. He was rewarded with her breast breaking out in prickles of goosebumps.

Keeping with the lighter foray, he was rewarded with more.

His fingers, however, remained an unceasing piston, fast and hard, and he occasionally wiggling them when he thought she might have gotten used to the movement.

To prepare her for when he would eventually try to sink his cock inside this beautifully dripping pussy, he added a third finger.

His eyes darted up when he thought he may have heard the tiniest noise. He didn't spread them, but he pushed them deep, then played.

Her core rippled before he felt her come once more. With the way he was spreading her, stretching her, her orgasm dribbled directly into his palm. He grinned, tonguing her nipple with affection at her reaction.

*I was hoping I could get her to scream for me.* He'd hadn't even gotten her to moan, regardless of how much he'd pleasured her.

When she started to go lax in his arms, he slipped his fingers from her. She seemed dazed, and when she turned her gaze to him, her expression didn't change from its relaxed state.

Her face was rosy, her lips wet like she may have licked at them. Geryon beamed with triumph. *I at least get to see this facet of her.*

He may also be a little thankful he hadn't gotten what he wanted – a writhing and lust-filled screaming woman. He could play with her more, could keep playing this game of cat and mouse he was enjoying.

It didn't take long for her eyes to come back into focus. He expected her look to harden, for her to be angry that he'd gotten himself under her skirt.

His eyes fell over the war room. *I got my reward.*

"You want me to reciprocate?"

Her eyes darted down to his straining erection pressing long and hard against his breeches. *Dear heavens, fuck yes.* She pressed her palm against the material, rubbing the length of it, and his cock excitedly jerked.

"More than anything." He felt a bead of pre-cum rise at the fact she'd even offered, and then stroked his shaft. A shuddering breath fell from him.

She gave it a wonderful squeeze, palming it. When she did it again, he had to brace himself by placing his hand against the wall. He considered bringing the other one to his mouth just to taste the pleasure he'd given her.

Geryon didn't care what she used to bring him to come. Her pussy, her mouth, her hand. With how hard his cock was throbbing, he knew it wouldn't last long and it would be a mind-scrambling orgasm.

"Too bad." She slapped him.

It hadn't been a light slap, either. Cecily had hit him hard enough that his head had snapped to the side. The loudness of it in his ears rang.

Fury filled Geryon, and he lunged for her.

Valerie slapped him.

She slapped him because she was upset with herself that she let him win, gave him his reward when she told him she wouldn't, was upset that he'd managed to control and unravel her to get what he wanted. She was upset because she had enjoyed it so much, she thought about begging for that hard erection obviously straining against his tight breeches.

She slapped him to teach him a lesson, retribution for his actions. It was also a way to hide from him just how much she had liked being in Geryon's embrace.

He was so warm that it melted her, his touches so soft and gentle in the beginning that she'd been helpless to deny such affection. He petted her with his lips, and it took every ounce of her control not to arch into him like a naughty kitten.

Then he had been wild, quickly ramping up her need until she thought her trembling legs would give out and he'd have to hold her up during her second orgasm. Valerie had bitten the sides of her tongue that time, stemming the moan she'd felt in the back of her throat.

Then, she saw the self-assured look in his eye when she'd finally stopped floating and landed back to reality. *He will keep chasing me.* She could see it, and she was confused with herself because she was both afraid yet excited for it.

Valerie flinched when he lunged at her, grabbing the front of her dress and pulling her forward at the same time. She expected him to grasp her hair or strike her in return.

Instead, his lips pressed against her cheek, so softly it felt like a flutter.

Her eyes opened when he gave a deep pant, his lips moving down her cheek to touch at her throat. The hand gripping the front of her dress smoothed over her breasts, the one that was free aching under his caress. His arm wrapped around her torso so they were chest to chest.

"It's like you are begging me to fuck you," he groaned, his tongue darting out. He thrust that straining rod against her, giving her another pant. "I told you, I will not react the way you think when you are callous towards me."

That wasn't the reaction she'd expected.

She pushed at his shoulders. "I wish to leave."

He chuckled beneath her ear, his breath fanning against her. Her skin was so sensitive from the orgasms he'd ripped from her that it prickled in response.

"When you leave, I wonder if it will excite you to know that I will relieve myself with the wetness of your orgasms."

Valerie hated that such words made her gasp – and that he heard it.

"You could always stay and watch, even help me. I'm unsure what will send me over the edge when I come." The shuddering breath he gave her was almost her undoing. He seemed to be thrumming with enjoyment. "The memory of your body coming around my fingers, or you striking me because I made you come."

Then, he brought her earlobe into his mouth. She heard the clank of his teeth against her studded jewellery before he ran his tongue along it. He ended his play with a nip.

He released her completely. Her stomach quivered and her core clenched when she looked at his face. Geryon's cheeks were pink, revealing to her he was deeply aroused and wasn't hiding it whatsoever.

"Make your decision," he said, using one hand to start undoing the buttons of his breeches.

He kept his other hand in the air beside him, not touching anything with it and she blushed, understanding why. It was still dripping with her juices, glistening in the soft light.

Valerie pulled up the front of her dress and swiftly turned from him. She exited the room before she stupidly changed her mind.

"Disappointing," she heard him laugh, before she closed the door.

She needed to leave before he whipped his dick out and she may have tried to climb on top of it. She pressed her fingers into her temples and rubbed them. *Why did I let him succeed?* Her body still thrummed; one of her nipples ached terribly and the other one begged for the same.

She turned her head down to her body in anger at it and gasped. Valerie quickly lifted her dress up to cover her breasts better. *I must look like a mess.*

Going back to court in this state was foolish.

*I let a man touch me when my sister could be close by, hurt.* A pang of guilt lanced her gut, just as much as her heart.

Hurrying down the hallway, Valerie opened the door to the next room so she could feel more private. Then, fumbling with the ties awkwardly, she attempted to lace herself back up as tightly as Victoria had.

She didn't know how long she struggled since her first attempt had been poor. Finding a reflective surface, she gave it her back to try and see what she was doing over her shoulder.

"Would you care for assistance?"

She almost jumped at the deep, rumbling voice and swiftly turned to it. She narrowed her eyes at Geryon.

"Well, you were done rather quickly," she snipped while she continued to fumble with the long strings.

He gave a chuckle, shaking his head before he came up behind her. "I have not come in quite some time." He pushed her hands out of the way to assist her by force. "And I was rather... excited."

She didn't expect him to be so honest. Most men were embarrassed about coming so quickly.

Her breath was stolen with how tight he pulled the ties with his strength. He also managed to secure them neatly and tuck the bow into the back of her dress like it was before. Then, to her surprise, he began to fix her hair by pushing pins back into place.

"There, you once again appear comely." She felt lips at the back of her neck. "Although I did prefer you out of order."

Valerie quickly stepped away from his touches before turning to him. "Why did you follow me?"

His gaze was much softer. He drew it over her, his eyelids heavy. He appeared relaxed and truly satisfied. *He wears such a look well.*

"The last time we spoke to someone, it was Victoria. She's under the impression I'm showing you the palace. It would look suspicious if I did not return with you." He gave her a grin, one that appeared mischievous. "You also did say you wished to see the dungeon, and I do so feel quite magnanimous after that treat."

"Perhaps I wish to no longer spend an extended period of time with you after your *treat.*"

The corner of his eyelids crinkled in humour. "You will not find them any other way, and I may not feel so generous at a later date."

With a deep breath, Valerie allowed her general composure to fall over her like a veil. *Kaeylyn may be there.* If not, she needed to at least know for sure.

"Fine, I will allow you to show me."

"Are you not against seeing people down there?" He cocked a brow, wondering if she would lose her nerve. "It's not a pleasant sight for a lady."

"Not at all. I often accompanied my father to see the criminals we had bound. I'm curious to know how vastly different the king handles such matters."

"Don't say I did not warn you." Then, he began to lead her

there, that look of humour on his face never wavering.

Their walk was long. The war room was at the very end of the palace, and where Geryon was leading her was back towards court.

"You told me your status is similar to King Bradwick," Valerie started, curious now. "Where do you come from? Who are your people?"

*He's shrouded in mystery.* She realised she barely knew anything about him, other than the fact that he had a strange liking for being slapped across the cheek.

She noted his warm skin tone, the light tan of it. His eyes came to hers, and she took in the metallic blue of them. *Such an enchanting colour.* Many believed that one's eyes were the windows to the soul. If that were true, then Valerie very much liked his.

"The hierarchy of my people differs from yours. We do have a king, but he rarely bothers with us. Instead, we have those who govern us equally. Those with a title are often seen as a higher status, and we gain a title through great strengths and feats."

Valerie nodded. "That sounds like the warlord clans between the southern kingdom and the witchlands below it. They scar their bodies with their number of kills, especially since they are so close to the witchlands and enjoy taking the lives of both humans and Witches."

They were often seen as barbaric humans who hated the order of the kingdoms. They came into other lands to kill men, to gain glory. Valerie had read of them in the books she'd stolen from travellers.

"What is your title, then?"

"For you, a person of the northern kingdom, I'm Lord Geryon. You don't need to know of my title."

"Not answering such a simple question is rather worrying, *Lord* Geryon." Valerie took a step away from him.

He chuckled, shaking his head. "We all have secrets to keep. I'm sure there are things you are hiding."

"Not at all," Valerie answered with an upturn of her chin. "I have been told I'm brash and honest. Most doubt that I feel shame, and therefore my secrets are often open to be scrutinised."

"Fine then. Tell me of a deep secret that's the equivalent of mine, and I shall share my title with you." He held a finger up quickly before she could talk. "But I will decide once you have told me if it's worthy of my answer."

"You think me naive. You want me to share about myself and then will deny me your answer. I have no secrets if you know the correct questions to ask."

The words that fell from her mouth were dangerous, every single one of them a lie. Yet, every untruth from her mouth she could see was making him trust her more.

Geryon seemed to think for long moments, eyeing her over as he brought his hand to his chin.

"You don't truly wish to marry King Bradwick," he blatantly told her.

Without thinking about it, Valerie lunged for him to cover his mouth with both her hands. She looked around, thankful there were no guards in the hallway.

"Don't say things so forwardly that will cause me trouble," she said, giving him a small glare.

*It could cause Bradwick to distrust me.* If her sister wasn't in the dungeon, then she needed to figure out a way to ask him, or whoever would know, where she was taken.

"Is it not true?" he whispered behind her hands.

When she didn't move them, he bit her palm.

"Ow! You bit me." She brought it to her chest, cupping her slightly injured hand. It hadn't been a gentle bite. "You are feral, then?"

"I thought you said you had no secrets."

"To those who can find them. If a person does not ask, then how do they know if I hold secrets or not?"

His eyes looked off to the side while he thought on her words, like he wanted to rebuff them. His mouth drew down as he nodded.

"You have a fair point." His eyes came back to her. "You have also yet to affirm my statement."

Valerie lowered her voice, seeing no way of getting out of answering. *He is far too perceptive.* She knew she needed to be careful of him and the things she said, the lies she spun.

"You are correct. I have no true desire to marry King Bradwick," she nearly whispered. "I have no interest in being queen. Duke Grayson pushed for me to attend this gala against my wishes."

"Fathers of noble daughters often do, so I'm not surprised. Do you have no interest in the wealth and power he will grant you?"

"I have no care for pretty things like that. Being someone as wonderous as queen, I will constantly be under supervision and speculation. I imagine that will be tiresome."

Geryon nodded like he understood her words. "If given the option, I would not wish to be a king of hu – these lands," he stuttered, almost causing her to frown. "What will you do if you are selected by Bradwick, then?"

"I will do as I'm instructed and become the queen consort. I would try my hardest to be accommodating and loyal to Bradwick, for that's my role and position."

"But it's not what you want." Geryon seemed oddly perplexed by this conversation. *He's a nobleman. He should be agreeing with this notion, not disagreeing with it.*

"If I may be so bold, Lord Geryon." Valerie's voice became stern, her face hard. "As a woman, it's not my choice. I will do as I'm told by the will of men who control me, because my life has been dictated simply by my sex. Perhaps

I could have denied a lesser person, but he's the king. To deny him is to bring dishonour on my family."

"Perhaps I can assist you then, Lady Cecily." Geryon gave her a grin, one that promised mischief. "I'm King Bradwick's confidant and often his council. I may be able to sway him towards the others."

"You don't need to interfere," she told him calmly. *I may not want to marry King Bradwick, but I do need to get close to him.* She didn't need Geryon getting in the way. He raised his brow in suspicion, so she quickly added, "Unless it appears I'm truly in fear."

That seemed to pacify him, and he nodded.

*Phew,* that had been too close of a call.

Valerie looked at him from under her lashes. *He is kind.* He was willing to assist a woman in wanting to avoid unhappiness. It was all under falsehood, of course, but with the picture she painted, what he believed as truth, he offered to save her from a fate she didn't want.

Although he was forceful with his hands and mouth, he had given her the key to getting him to release her. *He would not take a woman against her will.* So far, his actions had proven this to her.

Her eyes widened when a flush of arousal swept through her. *Perhaps I find this man desirous, not just merely for his face.* She knew enough about him to believe he was a respectable man, one she could trust her body to, at least to some extent.

He also liked her, which was confusing. Her mother always told her no man would want a woman who was unresponsive. To prove her wrong, Valerie had gone to the human towns and lifted her skirt for any man she found attractive.

They had both been right. Some merely wanted her because she had made herself available and knew she was beautiful, in a porcelain doll kind of way. Others didn't, due to the fact they wished to converse with her first and she'd been rather off-putting to them with her dead voice and eyes – she hadn't elicited passion in those men.

Valerie wondered how Geryon seemed to find what others found colourless, exciting.

Her nipple still ached from his sucking, and the other found the lack of attention unfair. Her desire was quickly growing again, since she could still feel the mould of his fingers inside her core, her channel eager to accept them again. It dampened from her thoughts alone, as if in preparation for something bigger.

*From what I felt against my hand, he seemed large.* She'd been shocked at the girth she'd felt.

"Okay, this is the best spot," he said, bringing her out of her thoughts.

If he caught her staring, he made no mention of it. Instead, he walked over to a window to open it, but there seemed to be a hint of wicked humour in his eyes.

"What do you mean?" she asked when he climbed over it and sat on the edge of the windowsill.

"The court will find it strange if I take you to the dungeon. This is the best way to get there from the outside. The room beside us will cover our escape from the palace, and there are no guards that can see us from here."

Then he was gone, jumping down. *So, we are truly doing something troublesome?*

Running forward, she peeked her head out the window to see he landed on his feet. *How did he not hurt himself?* The palace was elevated by stone, so the fall wasn't small.

Looking up to her, he raised his hands.

"I'm not jumping from this window," she said with a shake of her head.

*He survived, but I will likely break an ankle.*

"Come now." He waved his hands, telling her to jump. "I

will catch you."

It felt like she was in the children's tale of Rapunzel, where the prince asked for her to lower her hair from the tower window. Valerie very much felt like telling the prince to go fuck himself.

"I'm sorry, but I don't think I trust you."

She knew he would try; it wasn't that she didn't think he would. She was just worried it wouldn't matter, and she would end up crushing him instead.

She thought she heard a strange sound come from him, something akin to a growl that an angry wolf would make. It was a perplexing sound from a human, one that made her want to shrink away.

"Fine, Lady Cecily. Find your own way to the dungeon without a key or knowledge of its whereabouts."

"Wait," she called, reaching her hand forward when he began to walk away.

He paused, turning back to fold his arms and give her a raise of his brow. She climbed onto the windowsill, her heart tightening in her chest. She sat on the edge, trying to keep her balance with her heels against the outer wall.

One shoe began to slip off.

A gust of wind billowed her hair over her shoulder. "O-okay, I will let you catch me."

"What if I no longer want to?"

Valerie took in two quick breaths. *He will not let me fall; he will not let me be hurt.* Deciding to trust he would catch her regardless of what he said, she closed her eyes and jumped without warning. She hoped he was strong enough to catch her weight from such a height.

Her silent fall ended with her landing within a cradle of strength. He'd caught her with ease, like she weighed nothing more than a pillow.

"See, I told you I would catch you," he grinned.

She quickly turned her head away to snub him, even when her heart gave a tender pang.

He set her down on her feet and grabbed her wrist before ducking down and pulling her along the outer wall of the palace. He walked to the corner of the stone hallway they'd been traversing to the room that extended from the outside.

He peeked his head out to make sure no one was there before dragging her along it to the next hallway. They continued down outside the palace walls, Geryon making sure they wouldn't be spotted.

They came to a wooden door leading from outside, and he slipped a key inside the lock to open it.

"How come you are allowed so many keys?"

"Like it has been mentioned, King Bradwick trusts me. No place within the palace is off limits to me."

Once they were inside, she peered into the inky darkness to no avail.

After moving them to a small perch in the wall, Geryon began striking flint and steel together close to a fabric torch. It eventually lit, and he held it for her as they walked down the narrow, spiralling steps. The further they went, the more a cool chill crept up her spine, the worn stone walls cold and dank.

At the very bottom was another door, unlocked by the same key he'd used to get them into the stairwell.

"Are there two entrances?" she asked when it seemed like they were coming from a strange direction.

"Yes. The one we are using is used to transport the prisoner in and out of the palace without having to go through it. The other is for those inside to visit, like King Bradwick and myself."

He opened one last door, and that's when she saw cells.

They walked for a long time as she looked inside each one, crinkling her nose at the putrid smell. There were no torches lit, no guards, and there was only one reason for that.

"They are all empty," Valerie commented, unable to keep the frown from her voice.

"Did you really think I would bring you here if they were occupied?" Geryon chuckled, folding his arms across his chest with a smug look.

*He tricked me into thinking I would see vile prisoners.* As much as she was relieved there weren't any, because she didn't want to face imprisoned men or women, she wasn't at ease. *Kaeylyn is not here.*

Her heart rate picked up in anxiety. *Where is she?* Where was her sister if she was not here in a cell? *Did they kill her? Did they send her somewhere else?* Is she somewhere else inside the palace, a special place only for Witches?

Panic was beginning to build. *What if I never find her?*

"Hey, what is the matter?" Geryon asked, reaching forward to cup the nape of her neck.

She frowned in his direction at the calming and caring gesture. She wanted to thank him for it, but Valerie also knew she wasn't showing any signs of distress. She didn't understand how he would know she was riddled with it.

"I'm merely upset that you tricked me," she answered, stepping away with a composed face. She settled the quick rhythm of her heartbeat.

Geryon shook his head, the brightness of humour on his features. "I did not think you would be so upset by my game. At least you got to see the dungeon. With it empty, it meant there was no harm in me doing so."

"I guess that's true. It's far more impressive than the one in Dyèrie manor," she said as she pretended to look around with interest. "I wish to leave now."

It was back to what Valerie was originally doing: searching the palace aimlessly. She knew her sister wasn't on the bottom level, since every room besides the war room had been unlocked. Now, she knew she also wasn't inside the dungeons.

There were two more floors to search, and it had taken her two days to search the lower level.

Valerie wasn't sure what would happen after her day with King Bradwick, which was in two days. She may not have the freedom she did now to search. *Am I running out of time?*

She sincerely hoped not.

# 13

"Lady Cecily, please wake up," Valerie heard Victoria plead as she shook her shoulder.

With a grumble, still half asleep, she sat up in her bed. A tray of breakfast was placed in her lap in a rushed manner. Victoria stood beside her bed like she did most mornings, but she was bouncing, seeming to wait for Valerie to wake fully.

This was her seventh day within the palace walls, and not once had the woman ever woken her like this. Valerie waved her hand, irritated by her behaviour. "What is it, Victoria?"

The woman gave a high-pitched squeal of excitement. Kicking her legs forward, she jumped while shaking her hands near her face.

"I heard something rather big from one of the kitchen maids this morning when I asked for your breakfast," she giggled. "I think you will be rather shocked to hear it."

"Out with it," Valerie said, before she put a spoonful of her porridge mixed with fruits into her mouth.

"Lady Charlotte was seen walking the hallways early this morning in a disarray." Pausing with a second spoonful near her lips, her eyes fell on Victoria, whose smile turned into a grin. "She was seen coming from the king's chambers."

"King Bradwick took Charlotte to his bed?"

*She had sex with the king.* If she was seen departing from it in the early hours of the morning, then there was no doubt about it.

"I inquired further," Victoria started, before pausing. She was making her wait, like what she was about to say was worth it. "The guards say she did not walk into it with him. She must have snuck into his chamber when the guards were changing and awaited him."

"Well, that is quite scandalous." Rather than being outraged, it would appear Bradwick had taken the young lady instead. "I did not expect Charlotte to do something so brazen. She very much wishes to be queen."

"It's also her day to spend with the king."

*She did it on a day a different lady was courted by him.*

"I'm curious to know how the other ladies are taking such news." Valerie could care less who was in the king's bed, and if she could help it, she would avoid being there herself.

"I must say, I'm very excited to be with the court today."

Valerie gave a singular laugh. "For once, I actually may feel the same." She finished eating her food and settled the tray near her feet. "Let us prepare so we can take in the action. I wish to beat the other ladies."

With that, Valerie quickly bathed.

The elegant dress she wore was pink with elaborate details. Two layers of frills underneath plumped it out and hid her tiny frame, one of the fanciest dresses she'd taken from Cecily.

She wore it to compensate for the simple make-up she intended to wear, not wanting to spend too much time on it.

With hurried steps, they both made their way downstairs.

Charlotte was already there, and the victorious smirk she wore didn't fade. It was the face of someone who had no remorse for her alleged behaviour.

"She must have remained awake after returning to her own chambers," Victoria whispered to her.

"She may not be the brightest, but she has done something that has worked in her favour," Valerie admitted.

It was obvious that all eyes were on the young woman, everyone wishing to speak with her. No one was brave enough to ask her outright if the rumour was true, but they didn't need to, not with how she was acting.

"I should claw her eyes out," a feminine voice said from the side.

Valerie turned to Wyetta, who very much looked displeased.

"You are upset about this," Valerie accused.

"Are you not?" She folded her arms across her small chest. "I spent the day with the king yesterday."

"I must say, I did think it was villainous that she did not wait for her day. Perhaps you see this as a personal jab?"

"No." Wyetta shook her head. "If she wanted to take a stab at someone, it would have been you."

"This is true."

Wyetta's eyes narrowed in irritation. "I think she just wanted to put herself above the rest of us and get closer to the king."

Valerie leaned in so she could whisper, "She got close enough that she would still be tasting it now."

Wyetta crinkled her nose in wrathful fury. *If the woman had a sword in her hand, she would cut Charlotte to pieces.*

King Bradwick walked into the room then. Geryon stood in the doorway, waiting rather than following behind him. She noticed the hint of humour when his eyes found hers, like he couldn't help searching for her.

She quickly looked away, angry with him.

The bastard had stolen her earring!

She knew when he did. She'd heard his teeth clink around the jewellery when he nipped her earlobe in the war room. He must have taken it then.

The only reason Valerie even knew her earring was missing was because Victoria had commented that it was gone when he finally returned her to court. It was also then that she noticed he was wearing it on his coat for all to see!

He'd walked away when Victoria told her, giving them his back, but Valerie could see his shoulders had been shaking in deep but silenced laughter. When he peeked at her over his shoulder, he wore a roguish expression.

He was displaying her earring now as well!

It was as if he intended to wear it like a badge, one earned by distracting her enough to steal it. *Why would he do something like this?* If anyone noticed it belonged to her, they would both be in trouble.

"Good morning, Lady Charlotte," Bradwick said after he walked into the room, lifting his hand so he could take hers and kiss it. "I do believe today is the day I will be spending with you."

The grin on his face made it clear he was already aware of the rumours circulating and was quite fine with it.

"I will get even," Wyetta sneered when they left.

Geryon was slow to leave, seeming to wait for something.

"I highly doubt that," she answered absentmindedly. *What is he up to?*

When she finally caught his eye again, he tapped his hand over where her pinned earring sat before he gave her a wink. A reminder. Then he fell away from the doorway to leave.

He'd been waiting for her to look at him. *Impish brute!*

When Wyetta cut her a look that said she shouldn't dare underestimate her, Valerie shook her head. "If you are attempting to do the same thing tonight, I doubt that will work in your favour."

"And why is that? If he will go under her skirt, then I see no reason as to why he could not go under mine."

They shouldn't be having this kind of conversation among the court, but Valerie was glad Wyetta at least said it quietly.

She leaned closer once again to keep her voice low.

"Now that she has taken a turn on his dick, she will find herself there again. I imagine he will invite her himself this evening." She turned her head to face the woman, who was now frowning. "The situation that would most likely play out is you would be waiting in his bed while he brought her there."

"That's a fair deduction," Wyetta mumbled, bringing her hand up to tap her lips. "Then I will have to wait until I have a chance."

"My day is tomorrow," Valerie said, taking a cup of tea from a tray that was offered to them. Wyetta took one as well. "I can go out of my way to make sure he goes to his bed chamber alone, and that you are the one who is already there."

"Would you not go there yourself?"

She shook her head. "I have no interest in winning King Bradwick this way."

Wyetta's face flustered in embarrassment. "You think less of me for wanting to take such action?"

"Not at all." Taking a sip of her flowery tea, her eyes swept over the court.

The only person who could overhear was Victoria, who remained silent the entire time. She wouldn't share their conversation; Valerie trusted her in this.

"I'm not willing to give up my virtuous body for someone who may not take that gift and keep me."

"I had not expected you to be pure." Wyetta appeared shocked by her statement.

*I'm definitely not.*

"I know. Women at my age have usually been taken, but I have been waiting for my wedding night. I would prefer to keep it that way. You never know, that may excite King Bradwick when he discovers it." She took another sip of her tea before bringing her eyes back to Wyetta. "So, you are welcome to take my day to get your revenge on Charlotte. I'm fond of you for getting back at the girl."

"You are an absolute devil, Cecily. This may benefit you as much as it benefits me." Then she gave her an accusing finger. "How do I know you are not using me to paint us all as harlots to win the king?"

"Have you ever heard the phrase 'try something before you buy it'? It could also work against me to not participate in this."

"True," the woman grumbled before she gave Valerie a warm smile. "If you help me, I will be forever thankful."

*Before I leave, I do so hope I can help give this woman what she wants.* Valerie wanted Wyetta to be happy, and she was clearly fond of King Bradwick.

They spoke often about him, since that was why they were here. Wyetta would talk about how much she liked him, but not just because he was king. She was genuine. She liked who he was as a man, finding his humour and personality attractive.

Valerie understood her attraction, but she didn't feel desire for him. *Someone else is stealing that.*

She made the decision, then and there, that she would try to direct Bradwick to Wyetta, in the hopes he chose her. *I really do think she will make a wonderful queen.*

Geryon attempted to stay with King Bradwick. Unfortunately, the dim-witted girl was especially flirty with him this day, and Bradwick was as much back.

*One turn with her, and he's a lovesick puppy.* Geryon shuddered at having to witness it and walked away.

He'd been hoping to find Cecily at court so he could figure out how to separate them both from it. When he realised she was gone and Victoria had remained, he knew she was off somewhere else by herself.

Following her scent, it took him to the second floor. *She must be exploring it.* He thought her curiosity about the palace rather cute, although odd. He never expected her to be a wide-eyed woman with an awestruck gaze.

The second floor could often feel maze-like, and it was confusing to those who didn't know it. He'd be happy to help her navigate it.

However, just when he thought he would soon come upon her, he heard tiny scratches. It sounded like a small creature digging their claws into the walls, its body brushing against wooden surfaces. He scented for what it might be.

Geryon paused in his hunt of Lady Cecily.

"What are you doing?" he said to the creature when he made sure that they were alone, wanting to growl. Instead, he gave a sharp tone.

It flew to his shoulder and held onto the back of his coat.

"Don't question me!" it snapped, biting into the back of his neck with sharp little fangs. He winced, but barely paid attention to it. "Obviously, I'm here to speak with you."

*I meant what are you doing here like* this.

With a roll of his eyes, Geryon unbuttoned the front of his coat. "Unless you wish to be seen, crawl into my jacket. I will take us somewhere we will not be disturbed."

The creature climbed into the back of his clothing to hide, and Geryon walked back along the hallway he just came from.

His room was private, but it wouldn't be comfortable. He didn't want to take it there.

Instead, Geryon found his way to the third and final level of the grand building. This floor was similar to the bottom one, with long hallways and rooms in between. At the first corners where the main wall became the arms of the square palace were two level towers.

Geryon walked up the spiralling staircase into a mostly empty room. All that was inside of it was a telescope to see the stars and a table with books and scrolls about the constellations.

"You may get out now."

Both he and the creature shook their bodies, as if with disgust, when they separated. The winged creature glided to the ground, just big enough to fit inside both his hands.

He raised a brow when it glared up at him, like it was irritated, even though it came all this way to speak with him. Without warning, it grew in height, morphing until it was the same size as Geryon. It hadn't appreciated being smaller.

"Why did you enter the palace like this? If someone spotted you, you may have caused havoc," he said to the Dragon in front of him. "You are known to the guards as my companion, and you would have been given access to the grounds. I also sent you an invitation."

"Because I was not going to enter as a feeble human," he responded with a growl. "I would rather not play pretend like you."

"You are on *my* hunting grounds, Rurik. You will adhere to my wishes."

Rurik the WitchSlayer. He had become one of the strongest and most famous Dragons after he killed Strolguil the Vast, the deadliest Witch to ever walk this world, nearly three decades ago. He'd also obtained over a hundred Witch kills – no one else had even come remotely close to that number.

Their heads were mounted on his trophy wall in his cave as proof of his exploits. Many, like Geryon, had ventured to his lair to see them. Most were more interested in seeing Strolguil's head, his long red hair glued to his skull as proof.

"You invited me here!" he snapped, easy to anger with his terribly, *terribly* short temper. "Be lucky I cared to come at all."

The Dragon was ill-mannered, aggressive, and everyone got under his nerves. He wasn't known to be kind or merciful, and he hated being disturbed without good reason.

Rurik was a dark, near black, Dragon, whose scales would turn a brighter shade of purple when exposed to heat. He had a crown of sharp spikes around his head that then ran down his back all the way to the heart-shaped tip of his tail.

Scars heavily marred his body, trophies from his kills, evidence that he was both a warrior and a killer. The more noticeable ones in his Dragon form included the gash that ran across his snout beneath his eyes and the blast scar on his side. They surprisingly remained just as clear in his human form.

His eyes were silver and always held hateful spite and a constant glare. They were usually narrowed, and Geryon knew from experience that Rurik would swipe with his claws if a sharp mood struck him.

"How is your mate?" Geryon knew asking of her would calm him.

"She is well," Rurik answered, eyeing him up and down. "You have yet to meet our son. It's like you wish for me to hate you. You ask me here when he's freshly born but have not come to meet him."

"I would have thought you much rather I did not." Geryon chuckled, folding his arms and leaning his backside against the table to make himself comfortable. "You do so hate visitors, and he has been alive for only five years."

"Which means he's freshly born, and you still have not seen him!"

Dragons grew very slowly. It was believed that ten Dragon

years equalled one human year. They lived to almost eight hundred if they were not killed beforehand, which they often were.

The thing was, Rurik the WitchSlayer's son was part Witch. They had no idea what his human equivalent would be in age yet.

Rurik was the first Dragon to take a Witch as a mate, and after twenty-five years together, they finally birthed a son. Most of their kind were rather curious about the boy, the first DragonWitch ever born.

No one ever thought Rurik would take a Witch as his female. He hated them to such a degree that he would gladly burn the entire planet if it would eradicate the world of them. Yet, somehow, she'd managed to earn his love and deep affection.

After meeting her, Geryon knew why. *She's so soft natured, it's hard to be angry with her.* Rurik couldn't stay mad at the innocent and sweet gaze she always wore.

Geryon waved his hand dismissively. "I have been lazy, but I planned to come soon."

The Dragon huffed, unhappy with his answer. "Will you tell me why I'm here? It took two days to fly here, and I wish to return to Amalia and my spawn."

"Like I mentioned, I plan to come see you soon, but not just for your child." Rurik raised a spiked, scaley brow at his words. "At some point, I will be bringing you a Witch I have captured."

"Why not take care of it yourself? These are *your* hunting grounds, as you pointed out."

Geryon ignored Rurik's subtle jab and let his eyes drift around the room, thinking of how he should answer.

"It's... young." He brought his gaze back to the WitchSlayer. "It's also a white Witch. I'm not like you; I cannot kill something so innocent."

Rurik, on the other hand, had no issue killing Witches, regardless of their gender or age. He'd killed plenty of young children if their parents were dark Witches, which most of the time, they were. He also killed white ones, knowing eventually they would turn.

"So, you wish for me to kill it?" He lifted his paw to his snout, slipping a claw across the scar in thought.

"I don't care what you do with it," Geryon answered in a bored tone.

"Because of Amalia, I don't kill so indiscriminately. If it's a white wielder, then I have been letting them go as of late. If they turn dark, I can just kill them later."

"Then give it to the Elders." The Elders were a group of Dragons comprised of the oldest of their kind who governed over their race. Currently, there were four of them. "It knows of my hunting grounds, my face."

"Do you not want me to take it now?"

Geryon shook his head. "Currently, the child is bait."

Rurik gave him a grin, which exposed his fangs. "You are hoping it will lure other Witches to come for it, those who may have already turned."

"Yes, I currently have it open to scrying. The king is holding a gala, and on the second last night, he will be opening his gates for a large number of nobles."

"You are hoping some will slip inside to find the girl."

Geryon frowned. *How did he know it's a female?*

"And then I will take their heads," Geryon smirked. "Her coven will come. They will not allow what they believe is nothing more than a human king to have one of their own. No one knows a Dragon is here. I present myself as human."

Rurik's silver eyes swept over him. "You are correct. You look and act human so well, it took me a while to find you, what with those human idiots acting like hatchlings on the bottom level."

"Yes, they can be rather foolish. Then again, I do like this king, compared to the others I have shadowed."

This is what Geryon did to hunt Witches. He would take the position of guard for a human king or queen, then present things to cause Witches to come either seeking revenge, or merely just wanting to kill the royal he shadowed.

*Apparently, there is power in royal blood.*

There was one issue, though. He was supposed to move on after a certain number of years, since he wouldn't age like the humans around him. He'd been with King Bradwick now for six years, since the man lost his parents. He had about another fifteen years before his lack of ageing caused suspicion in court.

The king also knew Geryon was a Dragon, knew his human face. By the laws of his kind, he was supposed to kill him. He decided he liked the man enough and trusted that he wouldn't reveal this information.

*I'm breaking Dragon law for a man? I must be unhinged.* He feared he was growing soft on the humans with how much time he spent with them.

"Once I'm done with the young witchling, I can either hand her over to you, or I can give her to the Elders myself if you will not."

There was a pause while Rurik thought, eyeing Geryon intensely. "Bring her to me, and I will decide her fate."

Good. Geryon didn't want the blood of an innocent on his hands. He preferred to kill dark Witches and hadn't realised that the child being offered by human soldiers was pure hearted. *Her coven had not turned her yet.*

"Are you sure none have already infiltrated?" The Dragon looked down to his claws after raising his paw. "Your magic has always been rather unskilled."

Geryon crinkled his nose in response, his upper lip curling back in anger at Rurik's rudeness. "Yes, I'm sure. They are never alone, and they always act out of character for a human. I don't need fancy spells to see their façade."

Although Geryon's magic wasn't as strong as others, his skills with his senses were something to be glorified. He could scent a Witch from a mile away, no matter his form or size. He could also spot them with his eye, could tell they acted differently to humans.

He could use magic; it just wasn't as useful, since he wasn't good with it, wasn't strong at it like his mother. It was one of the reasons why he hunted the way he did.

"My eyes and nose are much better than yours," Geryon continued. "And I can smell through most cloaking spells."

He could smell the witchcraft being used. It lingered on the caster, lingered in their *blood.* They always tried to hide their scent, but he could smell their magic no matter what they did.

"So yes, to confirm, no Witch has made it into the palace halls."

Rurik licked at his maw. "It's true, there are no other Witches here. Since I don't trust in your capabilities, I scouted the palace before I found you and did not find a single trace, except for the one you have shackled."

"You searched my hunting grounds?" Geryon jumped forward to point at him. "You cause offense with such actions, WitchSlayer."

Rurik growled, his anger spiking – he often mirrored others. "Don't shout at me! I simply wanted to make sure the grounds were secure before I made myself known."

Geryon folded his arms with a huff, knowing if he pushed Rurik, he'd start trying to burn the palace down in rage.

"The gates will not open again until the night of the ball. Witches will come that night for her if they plan to at all. They will not be able to get inside any other way without being noticed or causing a fuss. Once the gala is over, and some time has passed to make sure there are no repercussions for the king, I will bring her to you."

"No," Rurik said, shaking his head. "I will meet you at your lair on our decided day. I would much rather not risk my mate and child."

Geryon unfolded his arms with a nod, understanding his apprehension. "Fine, you have a deal."

## 14

After his lengthy conversation with Rurik, Geryon returned to his room. He fell back against his bed and threw his arm over his face. With a heavy sigh, he let his mind roll over the events of the day. Dealing with his kind was always tiring, but Rurik, in particular, could be draining.

They'd gotten into multiple arguments during his visit, to the point that Geryon even had to jump over his tail as it was swiped in his direction.

Once they'd finished speaking about the witchling, Rurik decided he wished to rest. He lived in the middle of the East kingdom, whereas King Bradwick's palace was in the furthest province north, a two-day flight.

The Dragon hadn't wanted to sleep here, but he at least needed to rest his tired wings. Not daring to leave him alone in case he decided to make a meal out of an unsuspecting human who may have stumbled upon him, Geryon stayed by his side.

Lifting his arm to stare at his hand, he pondered a question. *When was the last time I was a Dragon?* Weeks? Months?

*Could it possibly be a year?*

His arm fell to lie back across his face. He couldn't remember.

Being by Bradwick's side often meant he didn't need to shift into his beast form. *I'm a trapper, but have I trapped myself?*

Seeing Rurik's Dragon form had birthed these displeasing thoughts. *I often miss flying the skies.* Was he growing so complacent, parading around as human, that he was losing the most important side of himself?

*I even considered taking a human woman to keep.* Such thoughts were uncommon among his kind these past centuries.

Lady Cecily wasn't the first human woman he'd come across who caught his attention. However, she may be the first who had intrigued him enough to elicit complicated and confusing desires in him, past just playful lust.

*I grow lonely... Yes, that's what it must be.* Geryon had been doing this for over a hundred years. He'd shadowed different kings, queens, and even simple but powerful nobles. Not once had he taken a female companion to help him pass those years.

It often crossed his mind that he should return to his own kind.

Unfortunately, the likelihood of finding a Dragoness to claim was low. There were far too few, and they grew cattier the more males chased them. *They are too aggressive to catch my attention.*

He also tended to prefer something human formed, what with how he'd been living the past century.

Then again, he knew he could visit his own kind to fill that loneliness whenever the mood took him. It rarely did. *I wish to see my brothers and sister, my parents, and yet, I never do.*

Although the humans annoyed and irritated him, Geryon found constant entertainment playing his role as a guard. He would laugh at their silliness, at their gender roles and class that meant nothing to something like him.

Yet, he knew the truth. He found it simpler to be around mortals he could easily frighten and manipulate to get what he wanted. His kind were usually preoccupied with their own issues, and most didn't like long-term companions other than their chosen mates.

*This is why I don't like to see my own kind. They make me feel unsettled.* He wouldn't have had these thoughts if he didn't invite Rurik here.

*I could have been playing with that delectable woman.* Chasing Cecily around the palace was quickly becoming his favourite activity, besides getting under her skirt. *I did enjoy conversing with her yesterday.*

There was something about her that got his blood pumping, made him feel heated. Was it her quick wit? That sharp tongue? *Those green eyes that remind me of a heavy fog in a forest on a cold winter's morning?*

Geryon wanted to unravel her. He didn't want to change her. No, he liked her exactly how she was.

She may have convinced him she didn't hold impenetrable secrets, but she was hiding her emotions.

*What does she look like when she is truly mad?* Her slap had been nothing but foreplay to him. He wanted to hear her shout, wanted to see the stab of fury in her usually expressionless eyes. *I would want to eat her up.*

*What does she look like when she's sad?* Would she cry? Grow rosy in the checks while holding back tears? Geryon wanted to know if seeing such sorrow would make him want to gather her into his arms – when he usually bolted the other way at the sight of a weeping woman.

*What does she look like when she's filled with happiness?* Her smiles were barely noticeable and seemed forced. *I bet her smile would be rather lovely.* A strangeness crept inside his chest at the thought.

His brows grew together, and he pressed his fingertips against his sternum, unsure why his heart suddenly felt... weird. *I'm not growing sick, am I?*

Somehow, Geryon felt if he brought Cecily to face her desires, a place where she went tumbling over the edge and she could no longer hold back, he might get to see them. If she couldn't keep herself together in that situation with him, then she couldn't with the rest of herself, either.

He chuckled to himself. *I'm also making excuses because I'm desperate to bed her.* Even now, just thinking about her put his body in all sorts of disarray.

*Maybe I can chase after her now?* He shot up in his bed, feeling better rested and less depressed, since his mind travelled to more uplifted thoughts.

His mood fell when he realised the day was growing late. The sun was setting, and soon, dinner would be presented.

*My day was wasted.* Not useless, since he finally had Rurik here, but he'd missed his opportunity to do what he really wanted.

*Tomorrow, she will be with King Bradwick.* His nose crinkled at picturing them together. He frowned at himself for his reaction. *Why should I care if she's in his presence? She is here for him, after all.*

With a sigh, he finally got to his feet and headed to the dining hall. He was one of the first to arrive, and he made himself comfortable by leaning against the wall.

This room was different to the banquet hall. There was only one table, and King Bradwick would eventually come to sit at the head of it. Charlotte would be seated next to him on one side, while on his other side would be his most trusted friend.

Count Elric was married to Countess Nicole, and Bradwick was often with him when he was at court. Geryon had already come to trust them with the king, knowing they had his best interests at heart.

Not all at court could be trusted. Geryon eyed those at the table he knew were deceitful.

The table sat nearly thirty people. Those who were here were invited by Elric and Nicole, and each night was a different selection of attendees.

"You did not return," Bradwick said after he helped Charlotte to her seat.

"I had a visitor come to the palace," Geryon answered, choosing to stay in his spot against the wall and forcing Bradwick to stand with him for their conversation.

He raised a blond brow, eyeing him carefully. "Someone you trust?"

Geryon gave him a quiet growl. "They were of my own kind. How dare you insinuate something so impertinent."

"You forget you are in my palace, Geryon. I don't like unknown guests inside it." Bradwick's gaze fell on the people in the room. "There are always mutinous and dangerous thoughts that circle in the minds around me."

"You forget who you speak to." He folded his arms in irritation. "I have no interest in changing who sits on the throne. I have shown you I'm loyal to you while I occupy your lands."

"As king, I must have such caution, even with those who have sworn their loyalty."

Geryon gave a nod, both in understanding and to dismiss him.

He may be the king's trusted servant and confidant, but they often had conversations like this. Bradwick considered him a flame he couldn't control but could wield when he wanted to. That made the king wary of him on the odd occasion. He feared Geryon would turn on him and, with the power he wielded, easily kill him.

They had a special relationship. All the cards had been laid on the table from Bradwick, but Geryon had his secrets. He knew why Geryon was here, but not that he sometimes instigated trouble. He didn't know the lies he'd been told, things that hadn't been shared. *I will protect his life and his place on the throne, but I also endanger him.*

Geryon listened to those seated, his sensitive hearing picking up on their conversations. The dinner had been going for quite some time, but there was one thing missing...

Bradwick waved his hand, eventually calling Geryon to his side. He walked over and leaned down next to his shoulder so he could hear his quiet whisper.

"Lady Cecily is absent."

His eyes drifted up the long length of the table until they fell upon the empty seat near the middle. He'd noticed that, too.

"While you have been otherwise preoccupied, she has taken it upon herself to explore the palace."

Bradwick frowned, showing he didn't know anything about this.

"Although I don't mind what she does when she's not entertaining me, she is not permitted to miss the functions I have demanded she attend." He gave a huff of annoyance before a short paused followed. Then he gave a sigh. "As much as I know you hate it when I give you demands, I fear she may be lost." He eyed him through the corner of his lids. "Sniff her out."

Geryon crinkled his nose and rolled his eyes. "Must I? Chasing after your ladies is not appealing."

Except for this one.

"Are you truly to let me believe you are so insensitive to a woman who could be lost and scared?"

*I highly doubt she's frightened.* Still, she could be lost.

"Fine. I will go find her."

With another wave of his hand, Bradwick dismissed him, and Geryon turned from the room.

Once he was out of eyesight, a wicked grin crossed his features. *I will get to play after all.*

Geryon followed Cecily's scent, even though it was faint and trampled on by others. With his keen sense of smell, he was able to track it with ease. *Here, kitty kitty kitty.*

Valerie walked the halls of the second floor with her hands clasped in front of her. They bounced with each step forward as she noted the walls next to her. She appeared like a calm and composed woman merely going for a stroll. However...

*I'm absolutely freaking lost!* Night was already upon them. *I'm supposed to be in the dining hall. It will not reflect well that I'm not there.*

She truly had no idea where she was going. At some point, she had gotten herself turned around. She no longer knew if she was travelling towards the centre of the palace or the arms of the building.

It was maze-like, with halls that led nowhere, rooms with locked doors, and everything appeared similar in every direction. She walked into a room to see the windows were dark, while a noble appeared confused that she'd opened the door to their suite.

Not everyone's living arrangements were as grand as hers. Coming across that noble didn't stop her from opening other doors, merely issuing the same apology to all.

Valerie had only become horribly confused about her whereabouts when she got to the end and needed to turn back. The way she came looked different. Stumbling across stairs that led to grander living places that didn't touch the bottom or top levels made it even more confusing.

*Have I been going in circles?* She thought she may be coming upon the corner of the palace, only to realise it was just another strange hallway. *Shit,* she cursed.

"It appears the curious kitten has gotten herself lost," a delectable, gruff voice said from around the corner she was about to turn.

"Lord Geryon." Valerie tried to keep the relief from her voice. *He will know the way back.* "It appears the palace floors wish to lead me astray."

Like he'd been there the entire time, his arms were folded across his chest while his back was leaning against the wall.

Two wall drapes hid him partially from view. They were there to make the long hallways look less bleak, and Valerie had seen them in each hallway on this floor. It gave a warm and cosy vibe compared to the wooden panel walls.

"Have you not been told that curiosity killed the cat?" he asked coyly.

"I do believe the ending to that saying is, 'but satisfaction brought it back.'"

"Satisfaction, huh?" He raised a brow, the corner of his lips forming into a naughty grin that told her he was being mischievous, or, at least, was about to be. "You should be careful wandering these halls. There are predators afoot, and a disoriented bunny could be seen as an easy meal."

Valerie's brow twitched with the urge to raise it when his head turned to her. There was an impish hint to his lips, to the crinkle of his eye. His tongue darting out to dabble at the seam of his lips only made his face appear more devilish.

*Yes, he's definitely up to no good.*

With an upturn of her chin, she walked past him.

"You often compare me to meek creatures. Perhaps the predators should be wary of those they think of as prey."

A warm and light chuckle fell from him. "Where are you going, my lady? The centre of the palace is the other way."

She frowned slightly. She thought he'd come from this way since he was leaning against the wall. *I have been walking away from the centre this entire time?*

"Did King Bradwick send you to help me?" she asked, her arms folding across her chest. "Wait, how did you know where I was?"

"Yes, he did." Then he shook his head, like his answer to her second question was obvious. "The last anyone saw you, they said you were walking the second floor. I knew if I searched these halls, I would eventually find you."

"Thank you for your help. I would appreciate it if you were to take me to the dining hall," she said before she walked past him again, going back the way she came.

Geryon grabbed her wrist and pulled until she slammed against his chest. He wrapped his arm around her midsection to hold her to him.

"I missed you today," he grumbled with his lips against her jaw.

Valerie didn't like how such words could make her stomach quiver, nor how his lips could so quickly cause her skin to prickle.

She'd been trying to tell herself all day that she hadn't wanted to see him. Yet, she spent most of her day ducking her head around corners, expecting to find him watching her. Her chest may have tightened in excitement the first few times, only to find herself disappointed in his absence each time.

*I should not be having such reactions. I'm here in this palace for a reason.*

"Yes, well, you were otherwise preoccupied with more important things." Her voice was calm, her tone non-lethal, but even she could hear the trail of something in it.

She clenched her hands when his palm slid down her back

to grasp her backside, pushing her hips against his.

"I was on my way to find you when I was called away – to my great disappointment."

A flush of arousal lifted to the skin of her chest when she felt something hard push against her. Then, his tongue darted out in a wet stroke just below her ear, making her even hotter.

"Unhand me, Lord Geryon. You should exercise more caution with your hands and mouth," she said in a lowered voice.

The hallways they were in were short, only a few feet long, and she thought it may lead around the back of a room. If someone came upon them...

"We are rather deep in the palace." He used his index and middle fingers to lift her chin, exposing her neck more. His mouth became rougher when he lowered it, his lips trailing faster over her flesh. "Nobody comes this way, and those who do are already asleep or in the dining hall."

Valerie tried once more to push against his chest to separate them, feeling like a cornered woman in his large embrace. Her palms found warmth and the wonderful press of strong muscles.

"Were you not sent to find me?" She heard the slight tremble in her own voice and frowned at herself for it.

She wasn't fretting to get out of his arms as much as before. *Am I really so easily swayed by this man?* She feared she knew the answer to that question.

Valerie may appear an unfeeling woman, and though usually that was quite true, she wasn't impervious to tempting attention, especially not from a man she found sinfully attractive.

*He's someone who does not appear gentle but is remarkably so.*

His lips were teasing, but they were careful, seeking the right places. It was like he was trying to find the spots that would make her breath catch, even if she tried to hide it.

He was attentive in all the ways she didn't want him to be... and it was perfect.

It didn't help that she could still remember his fingers inside her pussy, playing with her most sensitive places. She found it hard to ignore those memories when Geryon's hands and mouth were upon her, forcing them to resurface. Wetness pooled between her thighs.

"It does not matter how long we take. They will think it took me a while to find you."

"I'm still angry at you for stealing my earring. Don't think such a theft will be forgiven."

Before she could utter another word of protest, he moved his hand to the back of her head so he could lower it. Then his lips were upon hers.

There was a rush of heat from the impact that spread throughout her body. Desire flipped in the lowest part of her belly, making her gasp into his open mouth. Then, like she was unable to stop herself, Valerie kissed him back, almost moaning at the decadent taste.

*His mouth tastes like sugar.* His tongue was firm as he slipped it into her welcoming mouth, and, wanting more of him, she swirled her tongue around his. *I could taste his mouth forever.* She'd thought the same thing last time.

The press of his mouth was deep, passionate, but not suffocating. It was the kind of kiss that ignited the need to return it with the same fire, and Valerie tried to, not realising she was getting swept up by Geryon.

She didn't know when he turned them. She only became aware that her back was against the wall when he slipped his hips against hers, and the action squeezed her between him and the hard surface.

Like he was unhappy with the way his shaft slipped against her, he darted his hand out to lift her leg before thrusting once more. A pant came from him, forcing her to swallow the delicious sound with the tight press of their mouths.

"I want inside you," he whispered in between kisses.

He thrust again, and she answered his pant this time with her own. The hard length of him was grinding against her folds, pressing deep and hard against her clit through their clothing. Her nipples budded, tight against the material of her dress. What once felt soft now scraped over the sensitive points.

He continued to grind, and it almost felt like they were having sex without actually doing so. He was pressing against her hard, her body bouncing against the wall.

*I cannot do this.* She really, truly wanted to. It posed too much of a risk. Not just in getting caught, but in other things, in ways that could risk why she was here. *I should not want him. We should not be doing this.*

Valerie turned her head to the side to break away from the kiss, finding the sweet taste of him lingering in her mouth. It made her want to return to him. She even licked at the seam of her lips for just another taste.

"Wait," she begged, feeling how shallow her breath was becoming. She tried to catch it, tried to bring herself back to her usual composure.

Lifting her leg away from his hip, she forced him to let go so she could stand.

Instead of pulling away, his mouth once more found the soft, sensitive section of skin right over her jugular. She noticed he often liked to lick and nip at her skin, but she worried he'd notice how quick her pulse was fluttering. *He's always affectionate with his mouth.*

His breaths were so laboured, they hit against her, hard and loud in her ear, so deafening, they made the hairs on the back of her neck stand on end.

"I don't think I can wait any longer." He groaned so

hauntingly, her core quivered in reaction. His hand found the back of her head while the other gripped her backside. His hands were rougher, like he was losing the control to be gentle. It called to her; she wanted him rougher. "My cock is unbearably hard, and I'm desperate to have it inside of you."

"We cannot do this," she answered, trying to get away by turning her body in his arms. "We may be seen."

"I'm glad that's your only issue with this," he huffed, his lips finding the back of her shoulder.

She was now facing the wall, but what she thought would help stop him, didn't. Instead, Geryon lifted the back of her skirt so that he could thrust his clothing-clad cock right against her bare backside.

Valerie realised she'd put herself into a position that was harder for her to fight in. She pushed against the wall. *I must escape.* There was a slight pause before he squished her against it again.

"I don't know if it was intentional or not." His voice was so deep and pleasant to her senses, she found herself always desperate to hear his words with care.

She halted now, just so she could listen.

*He's too close.* With his breath fanning over the shell of her ear before it rolled down the side of her neck, her flush of arousal deepened.

"You have yet to tell me 'no'," he whispered, and her jaw fell a little in realisation.

He was right. Not once did she say that particular word. Did she truly not want to stop him? She was no longer sure. There was a moment of unmoving silence while she took in this realisation.

Even now... she still couldn't say it, even when she felt his freed cock slipping against her slit and backside. Instead, she found herself backing onto it, only for his hips to retreat. When she didn't move to reject him, even though he'd given her ample time to do so, Geryon slammed his cock inside her core, forcing her to take all of him in one go.

With her mouth open, she accidentally let out a loud, guttural breath. Valerie moved to the tips of her toes as her legs tightened, everything going rigid as her knees knocked inwards in tension.

Fighting the quick, burning stretch, her body tried to adjust to something of his size. *He's so big.* She didn't think she'd felt something this thick inside her before. There was a sharp sting at first, an uncomfortable feeling of being spread, and her body struggled with it. Valerie eased her breathing, tried to get her body to relax as she bit her lip.

She knew her tension wouldn't last.

"Whoa." He shuddered in reaction to being buried deep.

He snaked his hands around her, one cupping a breast, while the other crept under her lifted skirt to cup her folds. Pressing his fingers against her clit, he moved in a lazy circle just once, like he wanted to soothe her and help her loosen.

"You feel exquisite," he whispered softly, pressing his forehead against her shoulder. His shudder, the way his breath came out shaken, made her insides flutter against her will. "I did not think you would take the whole length of me."

As if to punctuate his words, he cupped his sac to push it against her sex, showing her through touch that they were just at her entrance.

His words, his actions as he began to pet her clit again, caused her body to soften. Her squeezing channel stopped gripping so tight as she got used to the feeling of Geryon spreading her pussy.

"Now that you have felt me and I have felt you, do you want me to stop?"

Her eyes crinkled at him giving her another chance to back out of this if she wanted to. He had already gained entry, and yet he was *still* being considerate. Who was this man?

He pressed lavish kisses against the nape of her neck. The sound of it was right at her ear, begging for her attention. His hand began to knead her breast through the constriction of her dress, thumbing her nipple while the touch against her clit deepened.

He didn't start thrusting, didn't move, even though she was relaxing. All she could feel between her legs was her core thrumming around him in a desperate ache of need.

*He feels good.* She finally gave a pant when she realised how good he really *did* feel. The pressure she felt was everywhere, the head of his cock sitting somewhere that had her skin rolling with a rush.

Valerie couldn't deny it anymore. *I want him.* She'd wanted him since she first spoke to him in the library. She just hadn't wanted him to know it.

It was hard to deny it to him now, when her pussy was wet, warm, and throbbing. She could feel his heartbeat inside her, how hard and erect he was while he was buried all the way to the hilt.

"Say the word and I will take myself away." He ground his shaft deeper, making her feel the tip of him squish softly against her cervix. "Tell me you don't want me, tell me no."

Instead of answering, Valerie clenched her eyes shut and pressed her forehead against the wall. She hoped the curtains on either side of them were enough to hide them, because she knew she didn't want him to stop.

She gritted her teeth to hide her moan when he ground his hips again, making her feel like he was trying to get impossibly deeper. She considered pushing her hips back so he could be.

They were nearly the same height, so she wasn't straining on her toes to reach him, and he didn't have to bend around her to grind his cock inside. She also didn't have to lean forward to lower her hips, like she often did for shorter men.

"Say it," he growled quietly.

*I cannot.* She shook her head in response.

For the first time, Geryon drew his shaft back and her body refused to let go of it. Her hips moved with him, and he had to push her forward so he could withdraw. She felt the loss of him when he pulled back, to the point where all that was nestled inside her was his broad head.

She wanted to spread her legs in welcome, but his were on the outside of hers and kept them together. A loud, broken breath fell past her lips when he surged forward, hitting the end of her in a quick slam. Her fingertips dug into the wall as a rush of wetness dampened her core.

She'd felt it. The head of his shaft in this position had ridden right against the sensitive ridge inside her channel when he thrust in. While he was seated deep, it put constant pressure against it.

Valerie understood with that one single stroke that she was going to feel everything.

Geryon pulled back and didn't wait this time; it was a swift exit and shove inside. Each time he thrust, he gained pace in his rhythm. It was slow at first, hard, the power of his thrusts knocking her front against the wall she was practically melting into. *It has been so long.*

Valerie tried her hardest to hide how much she was enjoying this, but it was difficult to think past his cock beginning to pound in mind-scrambling thrusts.

*He's so deep.* She was so full of Geryon, she feared she'd never recover. *Feels so good.* Her body contracted around his shaft every time he prodded against her G-spot. *I need more.* She started pushing her hips back so she could make him hit harder.

Nothing stopped him from lapping his tongue against her neck. His body shoved her to the point he was massaging her against the wall, and he held her like he didn't want to let her go, squeezing tighter and tighter. The pressure of his large, muscular embrace was surprisingly comforting.

Geryon's breath was so shallow, she thought he'd cease breathing at any moment. *He sounds so turned on.* She could hear it in the depth of it, in his unhidden groans that whispered to her.

For a moment, she almost considered joining in. To let herself fall into carelessness. To drown in the feeling that overcame her body at each wonderful glide of his cock. Prodding. Sliding. His muscles jolted each time, making her fall deeper.

"I'm sorry," he moaned, shaking his head against her. His breath fanned against her flesh, making the hairs on her scalp lift. "I cannot hold back anymore."

Valerie disappointedly thought he was about to come.

Instead, he pulled his body back to give them space. It allowed her to turn her head to the side so she could look at him.

*He has turned pink.* A deep flush of desire and lust was heating his face, making his usually sharp metallic eyes appear exponentially soft. Their eyes met, and his nose crinkled as he panted from the exertion.

He placed his hands on her hips, and the easy rhythm of his thrusts suddenly picked up in speed.

His head fell back. "Dear heavens," he groaned.

Valerie was forced to turn her head forward to brace herself. Geryon started pounding so fast, it violently pushed her over the edge. In only a few sharp strokes, Valerie started coming around his thick, plunging shaft. Every muscle in her body bunched, her vision blurring as she clenched him.

Her orgasm rushed forward, and she didn't know what else to hold on to when she reached for the curtains beside her. She needed to hold something, to let out the intensity of her reaction somehow. Her knuckles went white.

It only occurred to her she'd lost the ability to keep her usual silence when Geryon slipped two of his fingers into her mouth to take the worst of her pants. She thought she may have even moaned for the first time for him.

"More. I will quieten you."

Even though her eyes crinkled in pleasure. Even though her legs and hands began to shake wildly out of her control. Even though she couldn't stop her core from clamping down around his beautifully pistoning cock. She didn't allow herself to be louder.

She couldn't lose herself. Not here, not in this hallway, not in this palace, not with this person. As hard as her orgasm was rippling through her, making her want nothing more than to scream out to the sky, she couldn't.

But dear heavens, did she want to.

When she finally came down, her pussy no longer spasming, she started sucking on his fingers still in her mouth. When he realised what she was doing, he pressed them in further. A deep huff came from him, and he even groaned when she swirled her tongue around them, between them.

"I *knew* you had a naughty side to you," he almost chuckled. His hips moved faster, like he was becoming more desperate, like her mouth was spurring him on.

It was exactly what she wanted.

She could feel him shuddering, could feel his legs were quaking next to hers.

His grip on her waist tightened, and he started to move with such speed, she could barely breathe. He was deep, the pound hard. Every thrust spread her wetness so that it dripped down her thighs.

It was hard to keep sucking his fingers, showing him she could tease him back, when she started coming again. That seemed to throw him over the edge.

"You are squeezing me so tight." Geryon shot forward to

be closer, burying his head into the crook of her neck. "Don't stop." His voice was deep, husky, and filled with such intense ecstasy, he almost sounded frenzied. "Just like that."

She clenched him harder, her orgasm so powerful, her own body trembled from it. Her legs were unsteady, and he had to hold her up when they threatened to buckle.

*He's going so fast.* He'd picked up speed, mindlessly thrusting while his face rubbed against her like a cat. Valerie wanted so badly to moan, to scream, to let out the sweltering intensity of this moment while he drove her through her orgasm like a mindless beast.

He muffled his shuddering groan with her skin, his mouth open wide against her. Then he pulled his cock from her, shoving it between her closed thighs as it pulsated against the lips of her folds. She could feel each burst of his seed climbing the length of him before it released.

Some of it hit the skirt of her undergarment dress, but most of it spread between her thighs when he pulled back to thrust forward, bursting between the tight press of them.

Her thighs were wet, not just from him, but from her own juices trailing down. *I have not come like that in a long time.* She also hadn't realised just how much she needed to feel it, to feel sweet, sweet utopia at the hands and body of a wicked man.

They both fought to catch their breaths, Geryon twitching at the aftershocks while Valerie tried to calm her racing heart. Valerie wanted more. Her core clenched at nothingness, now remarkably empty after having him inside her. She wanted to turn around and climb his body. She wanted him delving between her thighs while her legs wrapped around him.

"We must go to the dining hall," Valerie whispered, despite her own desires.

He tucked his shaft away, turned her around in his arms, and slammed his mouth against hers. It was like it was his own way of saying he wanted nothing more than to stay how they were. With the tiniest sound of bliss, Valerie returned it, taking his mouth just as deeply as he was taking hers.

He broke away to look at her, his eyes searching her face. "So lovely. Next time, I wish to see your beautiful face while you come around my cock, Lady Cecily."

Hearing him call her a name that didn't belong to her right after they were intimate was hollowing.

She ignored it. *It does not matter. I must do what is necessary to find my sister. I can enjoy anyone I like in the meantime, so long as it does not get in the way.*

However, it did douse her heated thoughts.

"Next time?" Valerie stepped away from him, her satisfied state falling away, replaced by her mask of cold indifference. Unfortunately for her, she could hide desire from him, but not herself. Her body was thrumming with it. "There should not have even been a this time."

She looked up and down the hallway, praying they hadn't been heard or seen.

"Oh yes, my fair lady." He gave her a grin, one of pure determination. "I'm going to ravish you again, and next time, I don't want to be disturbed by duties."

*Duties...* she thought solemnly.

Geryon was a human guard, and there would never be a promise between them. She knew what he felt for her was nothing more than lust, so her disappearance would only be disappointing. She wouldn't care either way once she was holding Kaeylyn safely in her arms.

This is what she told herself, knowing that nothing good could come from falling for Geryon, or anyone in this palace.

"I don't think that's wise. You have gotten what you wanted. I see no reason as to why this should be a repeat offence."

Geryon's nose crinkled while his teeth gritted in irritation.

He gripped her jaw, squishing her cheeks in with his fingertips.

"You can pretend you did not love the feel of me inside you, but I will not pretend I did not thoroughly enjoy your pussy wrapped around me. I will have you again." Then he leaned forward with his eyes narrowed. "Especially since you did not give me everything I want."

*What more could he want from me?* She frowned, having no idea what game he was playing, but more so because his words made desire flip in her stomach to pool between her legs, priming itself so she could take him again.

Geryon's glare softened into a grin, his eyes ducking down momentarily. His tongue even darted out. If it wasn't for the fact that she knew he was human and couldn't sense her increasing desire, she could have sworn that look said otherwise.

"Don't deny me any longer," he whispered, releasing her face so he could gently cup the side of her cheek, stroking it with a careful touch. "I want to touch you more, pleasure you more. I want to experience you for the irresistible woman you are. Let me do so freely."

*Such pretty words.* They were designed to soften her, to make her cave and give him what he desired, designed to manipulate.

"I fear if we are missing from dinner for much longer, it will raise suspicion." She waved her hand forward, hoping Geryon would take the lead.

Her heart panged at the crestfallen face he gave her. With a shake of his head, he began to lead her to the dining hall.

Along the way, she tried to figure out how to get her nipples to calm, since they were obvious as they pressed against her dress. She cursed him for making her feel this way with a glare at his back.

Every footfall made her now-tender sex remember just

what happened, aching further for this man. *When did I become such a needy woman?*

"How are you feeling? You are not hurt, are you?"

She would have ignored him if he didn't appear so sincere as he slowed to walk beside her. *He genuinely cares about my wellbeing?* Considering his size, it was actually sweet that he was concerned.

It made her feel less... used? Then again, she hadn't really put in much effort to stop him. Perhaps *she* was the one to take advantage of *him*.

"I'm well." She averted her gaze. "Thank you for asking."

Even though her body somehow wanted more of him, she was more sated than she could remember being in a long time.

*When was the last time I came?* With three sisters around constantly, it was difficult to masturbate, so she often didn't. Then, one day, she'd just stopped feeling the want to at all. Desire wasn't an emotion she'd experienced in an exceedingly long time.

After her apology to King Bradwick, explaining to him she'd gotten lost, she took her seat. No one cared they were gone for quite some time.

Her eyes constantly ducked up to Geryon through her lashes. He was watching the court, but she could tell he was merry. His lips occasionally twitched into a grin, and then his eyes would find her. *He's obviously satisfied.*

Sitting there among the court while she could still feel the imprint of his cock inside her, his seed still slicking her thighs, was titillating, to say the least.

15

Valerie walked through the palace grounds with her arm linked with King Bradwick's. They had been strolling throughout the morning and into the afternoon, occasionally stopping to sit somewhere nice among the grounds.

She'd been apprehensive of her day with the king, but she found she was rather enjoying herself.

Bradwick was being charming. There was a relaxed aura about him this day. She figured Charlotte must have satisfied him enough to hand him over in an elated mood. He no longer appeared worn or stressed – quite the opposite, in fact.

He was being more tolerant and gentlemanly. He let her speak freely, although she was careful of their conflicting opinions on certain topics. If he disagreed, she wouldn't push, but her opinions were not met with the same arrogance they were before.

He was being so considerate of her, he'd even brought along a small book of poetry from his collection.

"I thought perhaps you may appreciate this author's work, considering the poem you recited to us on the first day of the gala." He gave it to her to read through, but she got the impression it was not hers to keep. "Will you read some of it out loud? The only person who read to me was my mother, and I do miss it."

"It would please me greatly, your Highness, to read poetry for you."

With a warm smile, he pointed to the shade not too far away to escape the sun, and their stroll eventually led them through the maze at the back of his grounds.

It wasn't much of a maze, since the neatly carved square hedges came to their waist, but it still gave them an interesting path to follow. Flowers were sprinkled all throughout, and the grass and hedges were so healthy, they were a lush, vibrant green.

When they made it to their destination, he held his hand out to help her kneel on the grass before joining her.

Valerie eyed Geryon behind them as she made herself comfortable. He maintained a large distance, but he'd been with them for most of the day. She was unsure how he wasn't unsettled by this. She was currently being courted by a different man after she'd spent an intimate moment with him the previous night.

*Then again, King Bradwick was with Charlotte.*

His hand rarely left the hilt of his sword attached to his hip.

*Usually, he's so expressive.* She expected him to wink or have a gloating grin if she ever met eyes with him. Instead, he was blank, but she could see he was still wearing the earring he'd stolen from her. *I really must get that back before someone notices.*

Averting her eyes before the king caught her attentive gaze on someone else, she opened the book and began to flick through the pages. She eventually came across one of interest to her.

"'A Hymn to the Moon', by Mary Wortley Montagu," she

said.

*"Thou silver deity of secret night,*
*Direct my footsteps through the woodland shade;*
*Thou conscious witness of unknown delight,*
*The lover's guardian, and the Muse's aid.*

*By thy pale beams I solitary rove,*
*To thee my tender grief confide;*
*Serenely sweet you gild the silent grove,*
*My friend, my goddess, and my guide.*

*E'en thee, fair queen, from thy amazing height,*
*The charms of young Endymion drew;*
*Veil'd with the mantle of concealing night;*
*With all thy greatness and thy coldness too."*

"A very good selection. What do you think the poet was writing about?" There was a crinkle of humour in Bradwick's eyes.

"You put me on the spot. I have never read this poem to have a thought on it." He gave her the time to read over it by herself. "Hmm, well, the moon has a special kind of magic, a guider of those at night in the darkest of time. She's the oldest goddess and a companion to all, and she gives her light to all. The poem is a tribute to it."

He pointed to the third and fourth verses. "Witness of unknown delight? The lover's guardian? My mother used to tell me it's of a woman who was using the cover of night to warm the bed of a secret lover."

*I mistakenly read the wrong poem.* She gave a small smile and handed the book back to him. He took it, periodically giving it back throughout the day for her to read. Along with him being chivalrous, there was a playfulness about him.

It was when Bradwick started flirting lightly that she felt she was out of her depth. It took every ounce of her control not to look towards Geryon, but she knew he'd left them when the king began to touch her rather affectionately.

Valerie managed to direct him away from this kind of attention with ease. It continued to happen, and she figured he must be enjoying her company enough to be so open and forward with her.

If he touched her, she would point to something in the distance, like she was curious. There was nothing she could do about his cheeky humour. She concluded he was expecting her to blush, or was, at least, trying to make it his goal.

She would merely laugh with him and call him silly, then she would subtly change the subject.

There was one moment in which he attempted to kiss her, and she pretended to fall before he got too close, so it wouldn't appear obvious she'd avoided it. He laughed at her apparent clumsiness.

"My my, Cecily. Here I thought you were a lady of constant poise and grace, but it appears as though you can be inelegant upon closer inspection."

He held his hand out to help her back to her feet. "My apologies, your Highness. I often think pixies follow me to play tricks upon me."

He gave a bellowing laugh. "I heard they are mischievous creatures. If you like, I can have a guard follow you with a bow and arrow to ward them off if such things are true."

"That may be wise. I fear I have unwittingly brought a plague of them upon your castle."

His smile widened at her jest. "Perhaps I will have to have you spanked if disorder occurs."

She placed her hand up as a ward. "Please, your Majesty." She began to rub her bottom like it hurt from her fall. "I believe I'm punished enough for my unsteadiness."

"Very true." His face turned to the sky, since it was starting to darken.

Valerie had managed to keep them both outside for the entire day – sticking to the shade if she could. With Charlotte showing the king that the ladies could be available to him in an intimate way, she didn't want to be alone with him.

"Dinner will be served soon. We can wander back to the palace while we converse." She unfortunately had to take his arm, but she did go with him. "I will be open with you; I was unsure of how our day would progress, but I must say, I have rather enjoyed myself today, Cecily. Your humour and conversations are strange but quite wonderful."

"Thank you. I do try my best to be entertaining."

"Yes," he said in a thoughtful tone, placing his hand on his chin. "You do seem to know how to play your part in every situation. You mix well with the court. I have not heard a single unpleasantry about you from them." He gave her a chuckle with a roll of his eyes. "And rumours do circulate so fast."

"I have noticed gossip is a quick topic. If you will permit me to be so forward, your Highness, I'm cautious of your court."

"With good reason. You have chosen well to keep your distance." Then he eyed her through the corner of his lids, his brown eyes striking even from this angle. "You have given me much to think on."

"I'm pleased." *Think on what?* She didn't know if that was a good thing or not.

Once they reached the palace walls, he guided her to the dining hall and sat her down.

They were the last to arrive, as Bradwick and his companion usually were, and he helped her to sit. Only when he started to eat did the dinner begin. The conversation was mild and often shared with his other guests seated around them. She wondered if it was to see how she interacted with those he considered close to him.

Geryon appeared unhappy, leaning against the wall with his arms folded. His gaze was elsewhere, and she shrugged.

*He knew I was here for the king. He has no one to blame but himself.* She hadn't instigated their relationship.

Actually, she'd been very much against it from the beginning.

*It's a shame I like him.* There was something about Geryon that made her feel weak. *If there was a chance I could return to this palace without being beheaded or put on the stake, I would have happily allowed him to try and win me.*

She thought she would have enjoyed the game.

Not many men made Valerie feel this way. She usually avoided them because she was a Witch, but there were a handful of men who had grabbed her attention.

*I do like it when they look rough around the edges.* When she tried to be spiteful and prove something to her mother, she'd been fond of human soldiers, strong, meaty men who could lift her like she wasn't some tall, giant woman. *Hardened muscles, rough, calloused hands.*

Valerie looked at King Bradwick while he ate.

He was a pretty type of handsome, a man who looked kind and gentle with his sparkling light brown eyes, long blond hair, and soft features. She often thought men who looked as beautiful as women wouldn't be strong enough to demand her pleasure and desire, and would be meek and cowardly in bed.

*Bradwick would definitely not be.* Now that she'd spoken to one such man, she realised they, too, could be self-assured and assertive. She knew he would be rough. *Yet... I don't find him as appealing as Geryon.*

With his metallic blue eyes, midnight-coloured hair, and brutish stalk, he was absolutely gorgeous. The man was tall, with strong muscles that pressed into his dress coats. His broad jaw was soft, yet his high cheek bones made him appear rugged, like he would prefer to bite rather than kiss.

Valerie had been curious to know if her feelings would change after she spent the day with Bradwick. She found both as attractive as each other.

She was drawn to Geryon's domineering, menacing, and lustful personality. Rather than being frightened of him chasing her, she melted for him. He aimed straight for her without hesitation, with brutal honesty while keeping her will intact.

She wondered if Bradwick would spark any vigorous desire from her. She'd tried to be open to it, to see if it was possible. He hadn't.

In just one moment, Geryon struck a flicker of something inside her. Then, when she'd been trying to snuff it out, just like a master and god of fire, he made it grow rapidly and uncontrollably. He reminded her of wildfire. She could picture him dancing around her with a wicked glint in his eyes, trying to get the spark to grow.

*I have known the man for little under a week, and already he tries to scald me.*

"Are you alright, Cecily? You seem flushed," Bradwick said when she'd been playing with her food rather than truly eating it.

Valerie blinked a few times, only realising now that she was becoming aroused by her own thoughts. She wanted to rub her eyes with her fingers, disappointed in herself. *There you go, Mother. Your unfeeling daughter has unwittingly become horny for a man who may be helping the king hide her sister.*

It wasn't his fault.

As Bradwick's servant, he would have to do what he was told. *With how he has been with me, I don't think he would have the heart to hurt her.* King Bradwick, on the other hand, came across so high born, he wouldn't care that she was a child.

"Yes. I'm just warm from the day."

"I see. Your skin is snowy. No wonder you said you prefer

the wintry months." Then he leaned back in his chair and placed his hand over the flat plane of his stomach. "Well, I'm done, and I consider retiring early this evening."

He gave a large smile, his eyes perusing over her.

Valerie placed her hand on his forearm, still resting on top of the table. "Are you sure? There is still much enjoyment to be had."

In her peripheral, she saw someone get up and leave the dining table. Valerie kept her eyes forward, kept them focused on Bradwick as a small smile pestered her lips. She retracted her hand.

It had been a pre-organised signal.

"Yes, I'm sure." He paused, thinking on something.

"Would you mind if I accompanied you through the halls before I retire?" she asked, and his thoughtful look quickly disappeared into a beaming grin. *He was wondering how to get me to leave with him.* "I'm rather tired myself."

"Why, of course." He got to his feet and helped her to hers.

She took his arm with a smile. It fell when they walked next to Geryon, who was giving her a squinted glare. She ignored him; she wouldn't allow him to get in the way of her villainous plans.

They weren't followed as they walked to the main stairs of the palace – the ones that ran up to the second floor before they eventually turned so the third level could be reached.

She made him pause at the bottom.

"Goodnight, your Highness." She bowed her head and removed her arm from him.

"You don't wish to accompany me further?" He frowned, seeming perplexed.

Valerie gave a small, forced giggle.

"I'm not sure where you wanted to take me, but I'm suddenly feeling hot. I think I have had too much fun with you today, and you did mention I appeared flushed."

*He handed me the perfect excuse to escape.*

She could see he wanted to argue, but didn't. "Perhaps another time then, Lady Cecily." The cheerfulness in his tone faded, replaced by a disgruntled one.

She waited until she knew he was going to climb the stairs the entire way to his bedchamber before turning away towards her own apartment.

*Enjoy Lady Wyetta, your Highness.*

**16**

Valerie was one of the first people to attend court in the morning.

Already, news about Wyetta was beginning to circulate, and Valerie was thankful any mention of her possibly being in the king's bedchamber was being corrected.

When she didn't see Wyetta, unsure when she would attend since she may have been awake rather late, Valerie decided to start exploring the other half of the second level. *Today may be my last day to have such freedom.*

King Bradwick was taking a break from the ladies to perform his royal duties for a day. She figured he'd been putting them off until he had spent personal time with each of them.

Valerie had the day to herself, and with how complicated the second floor was, it meant she could get as lost as she pleased – as long as she attended the dinner.

She had just stepped onto the second floor when she saw a certain dazzling guard coming from the direction she was heading.

She bowed her head in greeting, since she was feeling cheery this morning. "Good morning, Lord Geryon."

"Morning," he huffed, his narrowed eyes finding anywhere else to look but her. "How was your night?" She couldn't help noticing the sneer in his words.

"It was rather enjoyable," she answered with a small, cruel smile. "Have you not seen King Bradwick yet?"

His nose crinkled in obvious distaste. "No, I did not rise and approach him early this morning, unsure if I would appreciate what debauchery I would find."

She came to the realisation that he was not aware of the true details of the events of the evening. She hadn't appreciated the tone, nor the disgusted hint to it. He also was no longer wearing her earring proudly, and she was disappointed.

Valerie may understand that he was feeling a certain way because he believed a certain thing, but it didn't permit him to treat her so coarsely. He had no proof she'd gone to bed with Bradwick, nor had he spoken to the man to have such a confirmation. *Nor has he asked me.*

She'd told him she wasn't interested in the king. *He should not have thought the worst of me.*

"I'm sure King Bradwick will have a joyful tale to tell you." His eyes widened at her brazen words, taking deep offense to them. His bottom jaw even lowered slightly in shock. "Your impolite and insolent tone has been noted, Lord Geryon. I hope you don't come to regret your words, for they can have a lasting effect." She gave him a bow before she started to walk away. "Enjoy your day."

Valerie didn't even care to turn her head back to know if she wounded him or not.

She pursed her lips together with agitation. It was only now that he deeply upset her to the point where she sincerely no longer wanted to see him again, she knew how badly she had wanted to. *I will not allow a man to treat me in this manner and then reward them with my body.*

During dinner, she'd grown excited at the idea of him touching her again. Instead, now the word 'no' sat at the tip of her tongue.

Valerie searched the confusing second level. *I think I'm starting to recognise the pattern.* Everything on this floor was built in a specific gridlock pattern. There were four living areas only accessible from the bottom floor that held the four ladies and their dukes, whether they be uncle or father.

The second floor had to compensate for them and house the rest of court. The way it was designed created the largest spaces for rooms while having small hallways. They were split so rooms and apartments were not side by side, giving them some privacy.

"Good morning, Lady Cecily." A cheery, masculine voice said from behind her. "You appear to be lost again."

"Baron Daerk." She turned and nodded in greeting.

Baron Daerk was a tall, dark, and very handsome man. He had a charm about him she had witnessed make most woman blush or run an appraising eye over him. He was an easy conversationalist and attracted both men and women to his side.

Valerie hadn't minded speaking with him in the past in a large group. However, she'd never been alone with him before.

"No, I believe I have started to decipher the walls," she continued.

"Surely not," he laughed. "Please, allow me to accompany you. It would be dreadful if you were not to attend dinner again. I doubt King Bradwick will tolerate it a second time."

Valerie eyed Baron Daerk. He'd been a nice enough gentleman to her in the very few times she spoke with him. She also didn't mind his wife, a quiet yet sweet woman.

"I assure you, I'm quite fine on my own. I appreciate the care, though. Your chivalry has been seen."

"Come now, Lady Cecily." He gave her a large smile. "I will walk with you."

He placed his hand on her lower back. Her eyes darted down his body as he gently pushed her along. He always carried a sword, which she'd only seen a handful of men do so in court. She knew he was a war official, someone who would help guide the king should a war begin, or if he wished to incite one.

They were getting further away from the centre of the castle, and an unease grew within Valerie. They had been walking down the outer arm for quite some time, and she knew they hadn't come across anyone for a while.

He was also pushing her forward so fast. she wasn't able to truly search.

"Thank you, Baron Daerk. I believe I have seen all I wish to." She tried to give him a smile before she turned around.

Without warning, Valerie was pushed against the wall with her back to him. She quickly turned around and pushed against his chest.

"Excuse me, but I do believe you are too close."

He grabbed both her hands and pinned them next to her head. Then he leaned forward until his chest rubbed against hers. "You are quite lovely. I have been captivated by you since you entered the palace."

Then, to her horror, he slammed his mouth against hers. He squeezed her hands tightly, forcing her fingers to remain straight while crushing her knuckles.

Valerie fought him. Her struggle was met with a tongue being forced inside her mouth and a hardening shaft thrust against her.

He only pulled back when she bit his lip hard enough to draw blood.

"Get off me, Lord Daerk. Not only do you have a wife, but I'm here for King Bradwick. If he were to hear of such actions between us, we could be seen as traitorous." She yanked her arms again but continued to keep a level head, to keep her calm composure. "Now, I *demand* that you unhand me."

Valerie now understood why he'd pulled them close to the end of the palace, where it was scarce of people. No one was going to come across them to save her. *He was intending to trap me.*

The smirk that crossed his features was unsettling. It made his handsome face turn bitter.

"I believe you are no stranger to risk." He leaned forward to kiss at her jaw and throat, and her skin crawled. "You will accept me, my lady, just as you accepted Lord Geryon."

Her eyelids fluttered in shock. "Pardon?"

He continued to bump his hips against her, like it would spur her on when it did nothing but make her grow colder.

"You could only imagine my surprise at what I discovered two nights ago. A female companion and I had ventured to a deeper part of the palace, an area with a few vacant rooms where we could... be alone and unseen." His tongue darted out to lick across her throat, and Valerie tried to get his mouth to cease by pressing her ear to her shoulder, hoping to deter him. "Of course, my companion left before me, so we would not be discovered together. So, once I tied her dress and sent her on her way, I waited until I thought it was safe. Just as I opened the door to leave, I heard odd noises like the ones I just shared in."

The more he spoke, the more a sense of dread crept along her spine.

"Not wanting to be questioned about why I was where I was, I waited for it to end. Then, I peeked through the crack in the door to see you and Lord Geryon, walking familiarly with each other."

He brought his mouth back to hers and she froze. Valerie tried to think of a way out of this.

Against her lips, he said, "If you were willing to take that unsociable brute, then you will take me as well."

"No," she told him, turning her head to the side.

"I wonder how King Bradwick would feel if I told him of what I saw and heard? I don't think he will appreciate learning one of his ladies was taken like a bitch by his guard dog." The words were curt, dripping with menace.

*He's threatening me. If I don't do what he wants, then he will tell the king.* She stopped fighting and eyed his body. *I don't have a choice.*

"Do what you will." She let a rush of calmness wash over her.

"I promise I will be better than him." There was a chortle of excitement before he released one of her hands so he could free his shaft.

He began to pull up her skirt. There would be no preparation for her. This bastard intended to make this short by slamming inside her without even a gentle caress to make her wet or wanting for it.

Now that her hand was free, Valerie quickly darted it to his sword belt to grab a dagger. She pressed the tip to the underside of his jaw.

"Move and I will jam this into your jugular," she threatened. "We are alone, and it will take everyone a long time to notice you are dead."

He froze, his eyes widening. When he started to back away, she pressed the tip more firmly into his jaw, to the point blood began to well.

"I told you not to move. Do you not believe I will kill you? You would not be the first."

He stopped retreating and froze completely, realising she was serious. How quickly she'd turned the tables was pitiful.

*He should be ashamed of himself.* Not just because of that, but because he truly intended to take her against her will, just because she had allowed someone else to touch her. *Disgusting pig.*

"You will understand, Lord Daerk, that I'm not some feeble, helpless woman." She nodded her head to his pants. "Now, put your unimpressive penis away before I cut it off."

When he went to release her other hand, she made a jarring movement that caused his head to tilt up and back, so she didn't cut him further.

"Slowly."

He released the tight squeeze of her hand at a snail's pace and lowered his hands. She threaded one of her own through his short hair to keep him in place while he put himself away.

He buttoned his trousers with both hands.

"You will keep what you witnessed the other night to yourself, or I will tell King Bradwick you raped me. If you share my secrets, then I will share lies." She gave a glare, one filled with determination to maim and hurt. She pulled his head closer and pressed the blade deeper, until that ball of blood became a slow stream down the sharp edge of it. "I wonder how Lord Geryon will respond to you blackmailing him."

"I did no such thing!" He wore a face of deep-seated regret.

He'd appeared so confident before. *Just how many women have you been vile to? Your poor wife.* She had an unfaithful demon for a husband.

"Did you not? In threatening me, did you not also threaten him? If you told King Bradwick of the truth, it would harm us both." She tapped his neck with the blade when she knew he wouldn't dare move away. "I think I will tell him, regardless; he will be so pleased to hear of this."

"Please, no," he whined, and she gripped his hair tighter.

"Don't make demands of me when you had no intention of

retreating when I told you no. Feel lucky I will not tell the king of your transgression, for it's far worse than what Lord Geryon and I participated in. At least both parties had been *willing*."

Valerie pushed at his chest to get him away from her. She took his sword from its sheath at the same time, so he couldn't attempt to use it against her. She pointed it at him as well.

"You will find your sword here tonight when I'm no longer at risk of being cut by it. The dagger I will be keeping as a gift, in case another idiot like you tries to commit a heinous act against me." She nodded her head forward at his wide-eyed stare. "Now go, before I change my mind about bleeding you dry."

There was no apology, no words uttered before Baron Daerk fled. *For a war official, he is rather cowardly.*

Valerie leaned the sword against the wall for him to find later. Then, she cut the dagger into the skirt of her beautiful dress, twisting into the layers beneath it to hold it in place.

She could feel the cold blade pressing against the material of her undergarment shift, and she hoped it was enough to stop her from getting cut.

*I was almost taken against my will.* Valerie placed her head in her hands, taking the time while she was truly alone to process it. *If he had not had a dagger in his weapons belt, I would not have been able to escape.*

She wouldn't have been able to draw his sword, not with how close he was. With how much pushing against him hadn't aided her, she knew he was stronger than her. Usually, she would use magic in a situation like this, but she currently was unable to.

*I'm too reliant on my magic.*

Like Geryon had told her, there were predators afoot, and someone lost was an easy target. She thought he was speaking of them in a playful manner.

*I'm not safe on this floor.* No longer knowing where she was, Valerie turned the way she saw the bastard come from. She kept her hand close to where her new dagger sat, ready to use it again if he showed up.

*I don't think Kaeylyn is in the palace any longer.* She would search the top level just in case, but she knew she needed to enact the next phase of her plan. *I need to figure out a way to get the king to reveal where she has been taken.*

She was hoping she could get him to tell her on accident.

*Otherwise, I will have to use other measures.* Ones she did not want to take.

Valerie wanted nothing more than to retire to her room, losing her enthusiasm for her task.

# 17

Geryon growled quietly as he walked towards Bradwick's chambers on the third floor. *To say such things to me!* He wasn't pleased with his conversation with Cecily. *To rub her actions so callously in my face.*

He was a male who was very interested in this woman. There was a deep gash of jealousy he hadn't expected. *I thought I would not care if she were to bed Bradwick.* Instead, he was offended.

*I was not done playing with her.* There were four days left of the gala. He thought he would have more time with her.

*I will not bed a woman who has taken another while I'm chasing her.* Geryon was not the type of Dragon who liked to share.

There may be another reason as well, one he was angry with himself for.

*I considered courting her once the gala was over, if she was not chosen.* He hadn't made any decisions, but there was something about her that made thoughts like this grow.

He could have taken his time with her then. He could have

sniffed around her when she was no longer inside the palace to find out who she really was – and if it made her someone of interest to him in the long term.

It would have been cruel, because he would have had to fake his own death when her life was creeping towards its end. He would have given her enough wealth and her own manor to be widowed in, to grow old in. Since he wouldn't have allowed them to breed a Witch, he would have convinced her to take in an orphan if she sought a child.

*Other Dragons have done this.* It wasn't uncommon. Sometimes, they took a human to live in their lairs, sometimes they lived as a human among their kind.

Geryon no longer wanted to be alone when he'd found someone so tantalizing.

*Perhaps this was a blessing. I cannot grow fonder of her now.* Yes, that was what he decided.

With a calm resolve, Geryon opened the door to Bradwick's bed chamber without hesitation. No guards stopped him, nor was the man shocked.

"You are very late," Bradwick stated while a servant was helping him dress. "I ate breakfast on my own."

"I did not want to disturb you, in case you still had your bed guest," he answered, before walking forward to take a seat in one of the lounges.

He made himself comfortable, like he always did. He placed one ankle on the opposing knee, his jaw and cheek in his palm, and rested his elbow on the arm of the sofa.

"What a woman," Bradwick laughed, lifting his arms back so a servant could put his coat on. "She knows how to please a man. With the way she screamed, I would not be surprised if the entire palace heard her."

The grin he gave to the ceiling while he reflected on his night caused Geryon to curl his upper lip back.

His nose crinkled tight. *And yet she remained quiet with*

*me. Did she allow Bradwick to break her?* Why did that make seething rage build under his skin and boil his blood?

"It seems you thoroughly enjoyed yourself," Geryon bit out.

"It was exciting. She obviously wishes to become my queen consort, since she kept me up for most of the night. I grow hard just thinking of it."

Geryon averted his eyes to the side, wishing to concentrate on something other than the man in front of him, who was pleased with the female he'd been desperate for.

"And yet you once said you thought she lacked passion."

Bradwick turned his head to him with a frown. "I don't believe I said that about Lady Wyetta. I always thought she would have passion inside of her."

"Lady Wyetta?" His head came away from his palm in surprise. "Did you not bring Lady Cecily to your bed chamber?"

"I tried to, but she had not been feeling well, something to do with the heat and sun." He gave a laugh while shaking his head. "That worked in my favour. I was disappointed until I came to my bed chamber to find Lady Wyetta laying on my bed... naked."

Geryon fell back in the chair. *She did not take a turn on his cock.* He grinned, realising he could still chase after the woman. *I can continue to try to catch my vicious butterfly.*

Then he winced before running his hand down his face. Now he understood her behaviour towards him this morning. *I was rude to her.* She told him he would regret his tone.

*She could have told me. Instead, she chose to keep the truth hidden.* It reminded him of the quick strike of a scorpion, attacking without care with its venom. It made him dabble his tongue at the seam of his lips, thrumming with want.

*She retaliates with cunning lethality when angered.* Like her slap, it made him want to fuck her even more.

Now that he knew it wasn't Cecily the king was speaking of, Geryon had no issue allowing him to talk on this subject for as long as he pleased. *The more he speaks of Wyetta like this, the higher the likelihood he will select her over Cecily.*

When the conversation finally ended, Geryon followed him while he performed his tasks as king.

For a week, he'd been ignoring letters, and there was much to speak of in the terms of the kingdom. Bradwick had a personal scribe write for him, whether that be notes or letters.

Some of the court was with them, those required for the discussions. Some involved taxes, others major crimes they'd received letters on. They also discussed the ball that was to happen in three nights, and the extra security measures required.

As one of his councils, Geryon stayed by his side until there was an intermission. King Bradwick wished to eat his lunch in private while he thought on the morning's events.

Geryon had an hour to check his room, something he did once a day to make sure none of the court had tried to enter it. It was locked, but he'd seen and smelt a few trying to be nosy. His apartment was in a corner of the palace, one of the largest on this floor, as well as one of the grandest.

There was no parlour or drawing room in front of it, like some of the more special apartments. Instead, everything he wanted was furnished in one long area with plenty of room to walk about.

It held a bed, tub, mirror, sofa, and chairs around a table, in case he wanted to entertain guests, which he never did. There was a writing desk as well, something he used frequently.

One of his favourite spots was a settee he lounged across with his leg over the arm. His side of the palace was above where the court played, and he often watched them by positioning the chair to face the window.

The only time servants were permitted to enter this room was when he was inside it. It was only ever to fill his tub or bring him food if he wanted it.

Before he could make it to his destination, he turned the final corner and was surprised to find Lady Cecily walking towards him down the hallway.

*Why did I not scent her approaching?* Usually, he could.

There was a note to her eyes, one that told him she wasn't pleased to see him. Like a young Dragon chasing after a female's tail for the first time, he wanted to huff with eagerness at the defiant look she gave him.

It may cause others to back away and avert their gaze, but it only made Geryon boldly stare her down to take up the challenge.

She didn't say anything to him when she went to walk past, her head tilted up with the intention of snubbing him.

He ducked in front of her path. "You are quite the delinquent, my lady."

"Please move out of the way, Lord Geryon." His brow twitched at her tone. It was like steel, cold and sharp.

"You could have told me the truth, but instead, you attempted to wound me with my own beliefs."

She went to step around him, but he followed her, unwilling to let her pass.

Geryon frowned when she wouldn't meet his eye directly, like she usually would. Although she was her usual calm and controlled self, she wasn't as forceful with her stare now that they were face to face.

"It's not my fault if you carelessly injure yourself. I told you, actions can have lasting effects. Now, would you be so kind as to be a gentleman and let me pass?"

*She's not going toe to toe with me like she usually does.* The special kind of foreplay he liked between them was absent. *Something is different.*

He could tell she genuinely wanted to flee.

Had his foolishness this morning done major and lasting damage to her feelings? She desired him at one point; was it so quickly extinguished?

He was just about to let her pass when something caught his attention. *Why can I scent Lord Daerk when he's not near?*

His eyes swept over Cecily, who had the audacity to push him out of the way. It wasn't something the poised and lady-like woman would usually do.

With a silent snarl, he grabbed her wrist and pulled her forward to sniff her in a closer inspection. *She smells of him!* Geryon could smell him on her face, her body, her hands.

He lifted her arm higher to bring her face closer, to inspect it while she was nose to nose with him. There was a slight redness to her lips, like they were kiss swollen.

"Let go of me," she demanded in a quiet yet fierce tone.

"You smell of another man," he said in a lowered voice, trying to hide the growl in it. He didn't care that he'd just told her something that could reveal he may not be human.

Instead of answering him or denying it, she kicked him in the shin. *Wretched little snake!* He let her go to hold his bruising shin bone, hopping on one leg. She made sure to boot him hard.

"I will not discuss this with you when it's your fault."

*My fault?*

Geryon chased after her when she walked away, grabbing her wrist again. He pulled her along the hallway while she tugged to get free, bashing on his fist.

He wouldn't have this kind of conversation out in the open, but he would be damned if they didn't speak.

Pulling out a key clipped to his coat by a lengthy chain, Geryon opened the door at the end of the hall and threw her inside the room. Then he turned and locked the door behind him so she couldn't escape.

"You have the gall to blame me for your own heinous actions?" He threw the words at her, anger crawling beneath his skin. "You betray King Bradwick with nothing more than a noble?"

Cecily folded her arms across her chest with defiance.

"That's not why the idea of another bothers you, Lord Geryon, and pretending otherwise when the real reason is obvious is ludicrous."

"So, what? You take my cock and that gave you the freedom to take others?" He shook his head with a dark laugh. "And here I thought you set up Bradwick and Wyetta with cunning brilliance. Would you have gone to his bed chamber if you had not been feeling unwell?"

"You may wish to believe what you want, but I don't have to explain myself to you. I have no reason to."

He opened his mouth to rebuff her, but then closed it.

*It's true. There is no promise between us.* He still couldn't help feeling something, an emotion he didn't particularly like. He was even more furious than he'd been at the idea of her being in Bradwick's bed.

"You would let a married man touch you?" he sneered, disgusted at the deceitful act.

Geryon knew the man cheated on his wife regularly from the mixture of women's scents on him, and Valerie was aware he was married.

*Do I feel... betrayed?* He grew aghast at himself. *By a fucking human woman?*

"How do you know he's married? I don't believe I told you who it's."

His eyes widened. *Shit!*

"Lord Daerk is the only one who wears that disgusting, pungent cologne anyone can smell from a mile away."

Accepting his explanation, Cecily walked around him to get to the door. She pushed the handle down, only to tug on it when she realised it was locked.

"Release me. I desire to go to my apartment."

"Tell me why, at least," he said with a frown, feeling hurt when he shouldn't. She eyed him with that blank and unfeeling mask. *There is no apologetic face, no shame at doing it or being caught.* "Or are you actually a slag in disguise?"

"I will not answer such an offensive statement." *Show me something other than that blank stare for once.* Because currently, it was having the opposite effect on him than it usually did. "I don't wish to be in your presence."

"Do you truly not care for how your words cut me? Are you truly unsympathetic towards a man who has been rather intrigued by your nature?" She opened her mouth to say something behind narrowed eyes, but closed it at the disappointed face he gave her. "King Bradwick, I understood, but anyone lower than his status is nothing but an insult."

"You will release me, Geryon. Now."

He stepped forward with a stomp, while swiping one of his arms to the side. "Not until you tell me why!"

Not until he understood why this woman was more villainous than he thought. *Why am I so angry over this?*

She pulled a dagger from the layers of her dress and pointed it like she would truly cut him.

"I'm in no mood to hear your cries when this is all your fault. You have no one else to blame for how you feel, and it's deserved."

*Where did she get a dagger?* He growled at it before circling her, not appreciating a human threatening him – regardless of their gender.

She mirrored his movements.

"You dare say I deserve to feel this way when I have done nothing but be tender with you?" His nose crinkled in anger. "You don't get to cast blame on me for your devious behaviour. You cannot be mad at me for it!"

He stepped forward so he could grab her wrist, but she slashed the dagger forward, warding him back. She finally frowned, her brows creasing heavily. Her eyes crinkled, as though she felt something, like his words finally pushed her over the edge.

He blinked when he realised her mask had partially come down, and he was unsure if it was a face of hurt or fury.

"We were discovered!" she snapped, now holding her dagger with both hands. There was a slight tremble to her bottom lip before she skilfully stilled it. "We were heard and then seen walking away together. I was almost taken against my will by Lord Daerk because of it. He threatened to reveal what happened between us to King Bradwick if I did not comply." She stepped forward with her eyes squinted, threatening him more boldly with her weapon. "Instead, I stole his dagger when he was not looking. Even now, his blood coats the blade."

It was true. He'd thought it was a trick of the light, but he could see dried red liquid on it. Geryon's eyes widened, realising she was telling the truth. *How dare he!*

"I told you I was hesitant about being out in the open, and you convinced me otherwise. So yes, Lord Geryon, this is your fault. I have every reason to be furious at you for it." She stepped forward, poised like a tiger about to strike. "Especially when you cast such nastiness at me."

"I did not know." Geryon's anger quickly faded and was instead replaced by guilt. She was right; this was his fault. *I took her in a hallway, had thought there was no one around.* He'd been desperate to be inside her, had damned the consequences just so he could have her. *She suffered for it.* "Why did you not tell me rather than play catty? You said you did not keep secrets."

He had a great sense of smell, but even he could be

confused by doors. What he thought were old scents were just faint because of barriers.

"Because you did not ask me. You only assumed the worst and threw insults. Why should I have corrected your stupidity?"

*I'm finally seeing her unhidden anger.* He wasn't as proud of himself for it as he wanted to be. He'd been hoping he would witness her anger over something that wasn't so unpleasant.

"Because I was enraged," he huffed. "And confused."

"That does not excuse you," she answered, her tone dulling. She was calming. "I thought you would have learned your lesson this morning."

Geryon winced. *I'm not used to feeling this way because of another.* He was handling it with the skills he had – with inexperience.

He tried to pick his next words carefully.

"Perhaps you will forgive my impudence if you learn that I'm fond of you? That mayhap I want you for myself if King Bradwick does not choose you?" He let his eyes fall over the walls of the room as he thought. "That I may have acted in a certain way because of these things."

"Once again, you speak pretty words to manipulate me into getting your way."

His eyes narrowed. *She thinks I'm lying like a cad.* He stormed forward, ignoring when she raised that dagger higher.

With a swiftness, he smacked her hands up to separate them, and then he grabbed the wrist that continued to hold the dagger. He squeezed it tightly to make her let go.

She threw it at his face when she knew she wouldn't be able to hold it for much longer, nicking the side of his jaw.

"I was being rather sincere," he said when she struggled to be free of him. He held her closer by wrapping his arm around her waist, keeping her wrist in his grasp. "I'm also sorry."

He watched her brows furrow slightly, her movements halting. "You are apologising?"

*Why does she seem so confused?* "Is that not something I should do if I have done wrong?"

"Do you even know what you are apologising for?"

*Incredible. She will not let me escape so easily.* Why did he think otherwise? *I should have known.*

"I have committed many indiscretions this day. Shall I start from the beginning?" *I must rectify my mistakes with her.*

For a creature who had never needed to do so before, he wasn't sure on how to really do that. He often didn't care how his actions affected others. *I don't want her to leave this room feeling the way she does.*

He now understood her lack of banter before was because she was hiding her unease. She'd been touched by a man she didn't want; how could Geryon make her feel better?

He also didn't want her to be angry with him anymore.

Valerie watched as Geryon lowered her captured hand to bring it closer to his face. She hadn't expected him to apologise. Men don't usually think they are required to. It took her by surprise.

Then, there was his talk about why he'd been angry, the depth of his feelings. She didn't want to believe his words, didn't want to soften towards this man. *Not when I will have to abandon him anyway.*

If he was being sincere, then his words and actions had come from jealousy, from hurt and betrayal rather than just disgust. It would mean he cared about her.

*Do all men act so strangely when they are wounded in this*

*way?* Geryon, who usually acted with thought around her, had been impulsive.

"I'm sorry for my assumption that you had gone to bed with Bradwick, and for how I treated you so poorly afterwards when I had no proof."

He held her eyes with his blue metallic ones, lined with undoubtable softness. Then, with the intensity of his stare, he leaned forward to lick up her palm. It tickled, and she had to stop herself from frowning at what he was doing.

"I'm sorry I assumed the worst from you when you had actually been treated with great and terrible unkindness." He licked over her thumb before he brought it into his mouth for a moment. "And that it was caused by my carelessness."

His tongue ran under her fingers before coming back to kiss each knuckle.

"I'm sorry my actions put you in a position of danger, and that I shouted at you for the consequences of those actions."

"What are you doing?" she softly asked when he began to bring each finger into his mouth to suck on for a moment.

"I'm removing his unwanted touch from you," he answered, and her stomach clenched in reaction to his tenderness.

Geryon reached up to grab her other hand from his shoulder, releasing the first so he could begin to play with this one using his tongue and lips.

*I should be pulling away.* He was rude to her. He didn't deserve her forgiveness. Yet, she was surprised at how sensitive her palms and fingers were to his touch. Desire pooled subtly between her legs from the wetness of his tongue, the caring and sweet strokes of it.

"And I'm most sorry for upsetting you when you were not deserving of my anger."

"You did not apologise for doing it," she told him, a small breath leaving her when he licked over the sensitive nerves in her wrist.

His touches were more sensual this time, more playful, while his eyes darted between looking at what he was doing, to looking at her face.

"I should not have taken you so out in the open." He leaned forward to swipe his tongue against her throat, right where Daerk had tried to kiss at her neck. "But I will not apologise for taking you, not when I enjoyed it so much."

A rush of prickling goosebumps washed over her skin from her neck down to her chest. They made a shiver tickle down her spine, caused her nipples to bud. She wasn't sure if the reaction was from his touch or his words.

Valerie was torn, wanting to tell him to stop because he deserved to be punished, the logical side of her demanding it. Yet the rest of her wanted him to keep touching her in the gentle way he was.

There was no heat to it, no rough passion like usual, but it set her body aflame all the same.

Right now, she needed someone to not be forceful and overpowering. For some reason, she wanted to allow him to comfort her and help her forget what just happened.

"What if someone tries to come in?" she asked, not needing another person to discover them.

"No one will come into this room, for it's mine," he told her before he began to trail deep, slow kisses against her skin.

Her eyes darted around the room, taking in the masculine details. *I'm in his chambers?*

He brushed his lips up her jaw until he took her lips with his own.

*So soft.* His kisses were light, barely caving her lips under his. *So slow.* It made her feel every drawing movement, allowed her to simply feel the firmness and shape of his mouth. *So gentle.* Even his tongue seemed shy, only just lapping at the seam of her lips rather than slipping inside her mouth.

*So sweet.* She couldn't help deepening the kiss herself, slipping her tongue into his mouth just so she could have a taste of him.

He slowly pushed her backwards until her backside felt something hard. Reaching back with her free hand, she touched what she thought was a desk behind her.

Geryon pulled away from the kiss with a deep pant. "Where else did he touch you?" He swept his fingertips very gently over one of her breasts. "Did he touch you here?"

She shook her head. "He did not touch me anywhere else."

"Are you sure?"

He lowered his head to kiss at the pale skin of her chest. She felt her dress being pinched up by both his hands, the skirt of it crawling against her skin and making her shiver.

"No, stop," she whispered.

He immediately paused and looked up, his lips still pressed against the mound of one of her breasts.

She averted her gaze from his frown. "I don't wish to have sex with anyone right now."

"I had no intention of entering you," he said against her breast, dropping the skirt of her dress. "I only intended to touch you with my hands and mouth."

Then, he knelt and pressed his face against her hip bone while wrapping his arms around her legs to bring her closer.

"I'm not good with apologies. I only intended to gift rather than take." He turned his head up to her with a sincere look. "I wish to erase what happened with my own touch."

"You have already done that."

Valerie bit the inside of her cheek. She wasn't completely averse to him touching her with his hands.

"Are you sure?" he asked again with such a disappointed tone, it was almost cute. He buried his face against her pubic mound, rubbing his cheek against it like he wished to pet it. "I wish to make you feel good."

That's when Valerie understood what game he was playing at. He wanted her to say that she'd been grabbed simply so he could remove that touch with his mouth as well.

"I'm sure."

She wouldn't admit to something like that, not for any reason.

Instead, she lifted her skirt until it reached her knees. He must have understood what she meant with her actions, because he gave her a grin, his tongue coming out to dabble at the seam of his lips.

Valerie rested back against the writing desk to perch herself better. Geryon was the one to lift her leg so that her foot was placed on the chair in front of it.

"I cannot wait to taste you." He pushed her skirt up further and began to lay slow, wet kisses against her raised thigh. "I have been wanting to since the moment I first touched you."

She watched him nestle in closer between her legs. His movements were jerkier, like he was vibrating with excitement when only a moment before, he'd been careful.

When his head disappeared beneath the crumpled layers of her dress gathered around her hips, she didn't know where she would first feel his lips. Her mound, her clit, even the crook of her thigh?

His tongue dipped inside her entrance, spreading her with it. Her core contracted as she let out a gasp, not expecting him to go right for the honey pot on the first move.

A rich and loud groan left him as he retracted his tongue so he could swipe it up her folds in a long, deep stroke. She felt the pant of his breath against the sensitive apex of her clit. It forced her to answer it with one of her own.

He wrapped his hands around each leg before he gave her another one of those clit-tingling strokes. Her thighs twitched as the flat plane of his tongue ran over the hard bud, making her breath catch. Then, he began to lash at it, twisting his head in different directions to see which way she preferred it.

*Dear heavens, his tongue feels delectably sinful.* Valerie's head fell forward when he started to swirl it around.

Leaning one hand behind her on the table, the other pet her own breasts, her nipples aching for attention. She was surprised by how hard she found them, wishing she could touch them directly.

Her mouth fell open on a hidden moan when he sucked on her clit. Then, he swirled his tongue only to suck again, and an actual moan broke.

"More," he demanded before the movements of his mouth became rougher.

He lowered his head to twirl his tongue at the entrance of her pussy, and her hands flew down to grab at the back of his head through her skirt. A flush of arousal hit her, sending a wave of heat through her body all the way to her empty core.

"You got wetter," he told her before he slipped his tongue inside as far as he could. She felt his words hit her tender flesh when he said, while licking at his own lips, "You taste so fucking good."

Another rush came, and he began to prod her with it. Her breath hitched, a moan caught on a breath going in rather than coming out.

*I'm so close.* She was at a point where she was standing right on the cliff of bliss, and just needed an extra push to go crashing into the waves.

She didn't know when she started rocking her hips back and forth, trying to get him to go deeper, faster, anything to make her fall. Her head fell back, and she found she couldn't lift it anymore.

Not when she was concentrating on his wicked mouth, trying not to cry out. She was subtly grinding against his face while pushing his head firmly against her. She bucked harder.

His movements became more erratic underneath her skirt, his mouth darting up and down. His teeth joined the foray to nip at the lips of her labia before he lashed at her folds. He played there, making the muscles in her thighs twitch, her leg bouncing on the chair.

Then, he sucked her clit while tonguing it with snorted groan, and Valerie came undone. Her eyes snapped open. Her mouth fell wide as she tried to concentrate on breathing through her orgasm. Valerie could feel her core quivering around nothing, could feel that she grew damper in a scorching rush.

Geryon lapped it up. He shook his head like that would spur her to give him more, his tongue and mouth slurping.

His fingertips were digging into her thighs to pull her so he could bury his face deeper. He was savage, like he was so thirsty for the taste of her he would happily drown against her pussy.

She didn't think, when she finally stopped coming, that she would feel more desperate than she had before. She'd come around nothing. *My body is hungry to be filled.*

When he tried to go in for more, a whimper quivered past her lips. She pushed at him. Ducking his head out from under her skirt, Geryon lifted himself until he was facing her. He placed his hands on either side of her hips on the writing desk, his eyes focused on her.

He blatantly licked his glistening lips with a look that told her he thoroughly enjoyed himself.

Then, he leaned forward swiftly and kissed her with obvious pent-up lust and need. The press of his mouth was deep, the speed of his lips eating at her like he was desperate to sate his hunger.

Geryon groaned when he came closer so he could thrust his hips against her. His cock felt incredibly hard as it slipped against her hip.

"Your mouth tastes awful," she whispered when she broke away, knowing if she let him continue, she wouldn't stop him.

"I disagree," he answered between panted breaths. "I think it tastes wonderfully delicious. Mouth-watering, even."

Then, he brought their lips back together, forcing her to taste her own orgasm. The taste of it mixed with his sweet saliva caused her body to tingle. It didn't last long before he was the one to pull away.

Geryon lifted her chin so she was forced to look into his spellbinding blue eyes. They caught the light from outside the window, making them almost appear to have glimmers of silver in them.

She often lost herself trying to spot a glimpse of that metallic shimmer.

"I promised I would not take you now, but return to my room tonight. I swear, we will not be discovered; I will make sure of it. There are hidden tunnels." His eyes darted between hers. "Spend the night with me."

It wasn't a question but a demand, and Valerie was tempted to follow it.

**18**

Valerie spent the remainder of her day socialising with the court, since she felt better after her intimate moment with Geryon.

Baron Daerk had been taken by the scruff by Geryon, and his pale face being dragged away brought Valerie an immense amount of pleasure.

She also spoke to Wyetta, who was in a cheery mood. When she realised Valerie had no issue hearing about her night with King Bradwick, they strolled together while she spoke of it. She thought her companion needed to vent.

She understood the need.

*I wish I could speak of my interactions with Geryon.* It would help her understand what she was feeling, and uncover why she couldn't stop herself from wanting him or constantly letting him get under her skirt.

*I was terribly upset with him.* Yet it had turned into a sizzling kiss between her legs. His apologies helped in his favour.

Valerie had made no promise about returning to him after

dinner. He just seemed pleased she didn't forwardly say no. She guessed she would consider it.

She wished to. *I know what will happen if I do.* Thinking about it caused that ache between her legs to grow, to the point of becoming unbearable.

All four ladies were to dine in the dining hall with Bradwick tonight. Since he'd been absent for the entire day, they were to sit with him while he ate.

There had been a race to be seated next to him, and once again, Wyetta and herself lucked out, as they had been strolling. She sat next to Savannah, Wyetta across from her.

There had also been a competition as to who would leave with the king when he told them he wished to retire.

Valerie saw the look of humour on his face. He was aware of what the females wanted, and he was all too happy to comply. Wyetta ended up being escorted out of the dining hall by Bradwick.

When Charlotte left in a huff, Savannah sighed loudly and rested back in her chair while she pushed food around on her plate.

"Is there something you wish to talk about?" Valerie asked with a soft voice.

"Does it not bother you?" She leaned closer to keep her voice low. "They fight to go to his bedchamber this eve, but neither you nor I have been there."

Valerie took a sip of wine before resting her wrist against her chest. "You wish to go to his chambers?"

"Yes," she answered. "And no."

"Well, you are welcome to speak openly of your reasonings, if you wish." Valerie took another sip of wine before frowning into her chalice. "You don't usually speak to me about such matters. Why now?"

"Because you are in the same boat as I am." Savannah continued to push food around her plate before looking at her through the corner of her eye. "I'm unsure if I should trust you, and yet I admire you. I would not be willing to speak of my reasonings with the other ladies."

"Then you must either gather the courage or allow me to retire to my room."

Savannah nibbled at the corner of her lips. "Would you be willing to allow me to speak with you privately?"

Valerie was surprised by her request.

Usually, Savannah could be quite rude, and she often gave the other ladies the cold shoulder. Not just Wyetta, Charlotte, or herself, but also the other women of the court. She preferred the company of men.

*She has no one to speak to about her thoughts.*

Now that she knew this woman felt alone, she couldn't help wanting to listen. Valerie often gave her guidance to her sisters.

She nodded, then slid her chair back and waited for Savannah to do the same.

They left the dining hall side by side.

After they had walked for quite some time and the woman didn't say anything, Valerie tried to open the dialogue. "If you wish to go to the king's chambers, why have you not tried?"

"I don't have any sisters, Lady Cecily." Savannah looked to the ground. "I have never been with a man, and I don't know what it's I am to expect."

Valerie's eyes widened in shock – how could they not? This woman, who had one of the most flirtatious, provocative stares she'd ever seen, was a virgin? *I can barely believe my ears.*

"Is that why you are hesitant?"

"Yes. I'm inexperienced, and I would not know what to do. I don't want his Highness to catch me stumbling my way through it, not when it appears Lady Charlotte and Lady Wyetta may have experience." She turned her eyes to Valerie.

"Even if they don't, they were confident enough to go there."

Out of all the ladies, Valerie wanted Wyetta to be the one joined with King Bradwick. *But I cannot stand by while a woman does not do what she wants because she is afraid.*

"Are you not concerned that even if you give your 'purity' to him, he may not choose you, regardless?"

Savannah laughed. "If I'm not successful, would any man really think less of me if I tell them my first time was with the king? I could spin a tale that I felt pressured because of his status."

"That's very true." Valerie tried not to smile at her words. *She can be quite cunning.*

"Why have *you* not?"

*Do I tell her the same lie I told Wyetta, or do I change my answer so I may help her?* Valerie looked forward as they walked, trying to make up her mind.

"I will tell you if you swear not to speak of it with another."

"I would much rather my secret not be shared," Savannah said. "I took a risk telling you of my hesitation. I may never find myself in his chamber, even after this conversation."

"I don't wish to go to his bed," Valerie admitted. "My reasons are my own."

"I see. No wonder you did not wish to share this with me."

"Exactly, but" – Valerie turned to her – "I'm experienced, and I'm able to explain it to you, in rather great depth, if you would permit me to do so."

A spark lit in Savannah's honey-brown eyes. "You would do that for me?"

"Yes. No woman should be in the dark about what they should expect."

With a squeal, Savannah interlocked their arms. "You must come to my room. We can speak of this there."

Valerie was dragged through the halls of the bottom level until she was climbing the stairs to Savannah's apartment. It was so similar to her own, the only notable difference being the colours. Hers were green rather than purple.

Geryon followed behind King Bradwick and the four ladies attached to him as they strolled in a group.

*She did not return to me.* Cecily didn't come to his chambers like he'd asked of her. There had also been talk of her walking the palace late at night by herself.

He wasn't given the chance to know why.

He hadn't realised when he set out to pursue her that she would be this difficult.

There had been a look in her eye the last time he'd been with her, after he tasted her. He shuddered at just the memory of the sweet vision. She had wanted him, desired him. If he hadn't promised her he wouldn't, he would have taken her then.

*To take her with the taste of her pussy on my tongue?* He shuddered again.

Yet she didn't come to him to slake her lust like he asked. Geryon had wanted to take her relentlessly. Then, in between bouts of sex, he wanted to get to know her. He craved to learn more, show her he wanted more than just her body.

*I want to peek behind her mask and see all her hidden faces.* Most of them wouldn't require sex.

Instead of waking up this morning satisfied and elated, he realised he'd fallen asleep on his bed, alone.

His mood was sour, and the only reason he was still with the group of ladies and the king was because he was waiting to speak with Cecily alone.

He was sorely mistaken that he would get the chance. Not once did she have a moment to herself. There she was, right in front of him, yet so out of reach.

Never had Geryon felt so trapped. He'd never felt so frustrated at not getting what he wanted. *I must constantly dance around Bradwick and the court.* He couldn't just grab the female.

*I cannot even speak to her without prying eyes and ears about. Apparently, just getting in proximity is near impossible.* He barely got the chance, and it was often fleeting. *Does she do this on purpose?* She even left the dining hall accompanied this night.

At his place against the wall, listening in on the conversations of the court, he'd watched her. There was one thing that made his eyebrows raise when dinner came.

She had chosen to sit next to Charlotte.

That in itself was strange, and it got stranger over the course of their meal. She often tried to speak to the girl, like she wished to be friendly. Then, when Bradwick told them he wished to retire, before any of them could do or say anything, he watched Cecily purposely knock her wine straight into the girl's lap.

When the girl gasped and Cecily was trying to apologise, Savannah cut in to ask Bradwick to accompany him. Geryon noticed Wyetta sitting there without speaking, a smile upon her face.

Bradwick took Savannah from the room, and there was a

slightly pink hue to her cheeks. *She intends to go to his chambers.*

Charlotte stormed from the room in a huff, much like she did the previous night, her lady-in-waiting fawning over her to help remove the stain with a napkin.

Wyetta began to silently laugh behind her hand while Cecily's lips twitched into a smile. It seemed this was a planned affair between all three women, which left him internally scratching his head. Wyetta leaned forward across the table to touch her hand.

"You really are a fiend." Even though Wyetta said it softly, he was still able to hear her. "Your plan was brilliant. Come, I wish to play a game."

With a growl, realising he wasn't going to get her alone this night either, he'd exited the hall.

Geryon woke the next morning, not long after the sun rose, and eventually made his way to Bradwick's suite. Food had been laid out for them both, but Bradwick wasn't already eating like he normally would be.

He was also still in his bed clothes.

He held a singular gold coin, twirling it across the back of his knuckles, deep in thought.

"I can smell Lady Savannah was here, but you don't look as pleased as you have the last few mornings," Geryon said before he took a seat and grabbed his plate of food.

He ate with his fingers, not bothering to be neat. He hated eating with proper etiquette; it was one of the reasons he refused to eat with the court. It was also because Dragons were notoriously defensive of their food; they preferred to eat in private.

"She was lovely. I'm tremendously pleased with her," he answered, his eyes narrowing at nothing.

He cocked his eyebrow. He expected Bradwick to tell him the girl was wild, not lovely.

"Are you going to reveal your thoughts, or should I perhaps marry you and that wall you seem to be so enchanted by?"

"She bled," he finally said, making Geryon pause.

"She was a virgin?" He shrugged. "I'm surprised, but why does that bother you?"

"It does not. It just made me realise you were right about her."

"I did tell you her gaze may be empty," he chuckled, digging his fingers into the eggs on his plate.

"Knowing she was pure has eased my concerns with her," he answered, still twirling that coin, still looking at the wall. "It has made me re-think my stance on the ladies. So far, you have been correct about them, whereas I was wrong. I don't appreciate it."

"What else has this made you think on?"

"Lady Cecily, for one." That made Geryon pause. "You told me she has passion in her. Maybe you are right, but I'm yet to know." He looked at the coin. "She's also the queenliest. The way she holds herself is how I always pictured my queen. Someone who will know when and when not to step out of line. There are also her imaginative thoughts. She believes such things as pixies and fairies would follow her. She even believes your kind are still alive."

Geryon thought that was strange. Most humans honestly thought his kind died out long ago, since they hid themselves from the world. *A known Dragon is a dead Dragon.*

"You like her?" Geryon's mouth went dry. "I did not think you would."

"I'm unsure if she would make me happy yet, but maybe I should select her for the people." Then Bradwick went back to staring at the wall. "I like Wyetta and Savannah as much as each other. Savannah's hair is bright, and I like looking at it. I also like the dark complexion of Wyetta's skin. Cecily and Wyetta are both smart, but Cecily's constant composure is what fascinates me the most about her. Savannah has her fierceness, and she would not shy away from responsibility."

"You have yet to speak of Charlotte."

"I have made my decision on her." Bradwick sighed. "She's much too young for me, and I need someone who will be able to handle their duties. She would be nothing more than a pretty face, one I would have to spoil."

"You did not think this of her yesterday." Geryon placed his plate down, now that he was done with it, before eyeing Bradwick's. "If you don't eat your food, you know you risk me eating it."

Bradwick grabbed his two-pronged fork to spear the two thick sausages on his plate and began to nibble on them. He nodded to the rest, silently telling Geryon he could eat it.

"There are four days left. I must start thinking about my decision. I am thoughtful this morning because I don't know how to select from the other three." He took a big bite from his fork, chewing loudly. "They each have their merits, and I like each of them for varied reasons. I don't know how to select one without coming to regret it. Who would you pick?"

Once again, Geryon was brought to a halt, this time halfway through Bradwick's food.

"If I tell you, it may sway you to pick her merely out of spite." Geryon pointed his food-coated fingers at him. "You are a selfish, human man."

This made Bradwick raise his brow. "I don't believe it; one has taken your interest. I thought you hated them."

"Just because one has swayed me from thinking she's not completely irritating, does not mean I like her."

"You must tell me!" Bradwick laughed, the coin stopping on his knuckles so he could clasp it in his fist. "Perhaps I will let you have her. You are sometimes a bore, and I know you don't always enjoy my palace. A woman driving you mad may be just what you need."

*She is already driving me mad.* He was still angry with her. *I'm not used to humans not heeding my demands.* He'd never had this much of an issue getting a woman into his bed.

"I don't plan to tell you who it's, because it's of little significance."

"Like I mentioned, you are a bore. You are of no help to me."

"I disagree." Geryon once again pointed his fingers at him, this time circling them in Bradwick's direction. "Your ill-minded brain would have selected the one with the biggest tits, like a cock-hard teenager. At least I made you consider them with deeper thought."

"You are a Dragon; I did not think you would be so thoughtful about human women."

"Shows what you know of me," Geryon said with a shake of his head. "I have spent many years with humans, and I have been watching your kind for centuries."

"Fine. Who do you think is the best fit for me?"

"If I tell you that, you may not pick her in spite of me. You don't like being told what to do, Bradwick, and I will not have you make the wrong decision because you are being an imbecile."

He fell back in his chair defeatedly. "Fine. I will figure it out on my own."

"What are your plans for the day?" *Will there be an opportunity for me to get Lady Cecily alone?*

"I spent the day with the girls as a group yesterday, to see how they react now that they have come to know each other. Today, I plan to take them away from the court one by one, like I did those first days."

*Excellent.* He pushed the plate away now that he was done. He placed his hand on his stomach, overfull but very much satisfied.

"I think that's wise, considering tomorrow night is the ball.

You will not be available, since we will have much to plan to keep you and the people safe."

The king raised his blond brow in concern. "Why? Do you expect something to happen?"

Geryon let his face fall to one of casual boredom. "We do have a witchling here. Some may come to try and take it."

"I thought you intended to be rid of it by now," Bradwick said, raising his brow.

"I have no plans on killing it, but the Dragon I sought to take it has not come. I don't trust giving it to someone else."

It was a lie; he was just not done with it. Geryon hadn't told Bradwick of his true plans. *It's much easier to kill a Witch if I have an army behind me.* Even a human one.

It was one of the reasons Geryon's hunting grounds were always in a well-guarded place. Rurik was right; his magic wasn't strong. It meant he could hunt without having his head removed from his shoulders.

He didn't care if humans died for him to complete his hunt. He would continue to put Bradwick at risk in the future.

Geryon had already killed five Witches, ones who tried to gain a place of power by becoming a council member to Bradwick, where they would weave their magic to manipulate him. Either that, or they had come to kill him to take his place.

They hadn't expected Geryon.

"Have you not considered how this may put all those who attend at risk? Or myself? I cannot retract my invites this late. The ball must happen, but I would have preferred not to have one if I knew it could become dangerous."

It was all according to Geryon's plan. "It's fine. You have me by your side."

"You are mighty arrogant for just one Dragon. What if you have brought an entire coven down upon my walls?"

*That could pose an issue.* "It would not be the first time I have fought a coven. Your soldiers will assist me. The sheer number will be enough to take them."

The child refused to speak to him, so he couldn't gain any information on where it came from. Geryon had no idea the number of Witches in its coven, if they were strong or weak, if they were dark or white. *It's likely they are corrupted.* Every coven he'd ever heard of was.

One Witch would turn evil, and it would poison those around it. It was like a virus, a contagious disease that spread quickly among their vile kind.

He was set on killing every single one of them.

Valerie returned to court after visiting the library so she could obtain a poetry book. There was a poem she was sure the king would like.

*I must gain his trust before the gala is over.* She needed to get him alone. *I don't wish to go to his bedchamber; there must be another way.*

The poem was one of killing Witches, a gleeful tale for humans, a dreadful one for her kind. She was hoping to get him to gloat and tell her where her sister was.

She was running out of time.

She couldn't search the third level of the palace. It was filled with guards because it was the king's floor. It was where his apartment was, where he held hobby rooms of interest to him.

Getting caught lurking in those areas was dangerous.

Valerie considered trying to get Geryon to reveal what he knew. *He holds his own secrets, ones I don't know. He also will not betray the king.* Getting under her skirts was one thing, treason was another. She knew it would cause far more suspicion if she tried to use him.

*No, it must be King Bradwick. He's arrogant; he will be less guarded.*

The court was outside this day.

"I will get you a shade umbrella, my lady," Victoria said before she rushed to find one, leaving her on her own.

The day was blistering hot, and most of the ladies were using one to protect their skin during the worst of it.

As much as Valerie hated the heat, she adored the sun.

If she was able to use her magic, she would've shielded herself from the worst while allowing her to soak up its power. Witches were able to derive energy from most nature sources. Even the grass against her bare feet made her feel more energetic.

*I have not felt mud between my toes since I came here.* She already missed the little things of her usual, simple life.

There were a few people around, flitting in and out of the palace. She thought they would keep her safe while Victoria obtained a sun umbrella. She was mistaken.

One minute, she was walking down a hallway in the direction of the balcony that would take her outside. The next, she was being dragged into a room by her upper arm.

She stumbled slightly as she was tossed forward while the person locked the door behind them.

"Good afternoon, Lady Cecily," a familiar, sinfully rich voice greeted. Her heart practically skipped a beat in joy.

"Lord Geryon," she answered, folding her arms across her chest. "Us meeting like this is too risky." They were on the bottom floor of the palace, near the court no less!

She walked around him to the door.

Just as she was about to turn the key still in the lock, he turned her, pushing her back against the wall.

Before she knew it, his hands were on either side of her face to hold her still. He brought his lips down on hers in a hungry kiss, filled with so much longing, it made her heart ache for him.

A surprised gasp left her lips, and he used that moment to slip his tongue into her mouth. She almost moaned at the sweet taste of him, at the feel of his lips against her own. Lost, Valerie kissed back readily, unable to keep herself from melting under his swirling tongue.

There was something about the way Geryon kissed her that unravelled her thoughts. It was always filled with hunger, like he was so starved he needed to eat her lips to quench himself.

Every time, it awakened her own need, and she found herself trying to match its depth, its passion, her own hunger rising. Everywhere throbbed; even her skin tingled, like it was desperate to be touched.

There was a more present sensation, though, one that was between her thighs. It would start as a subtle pulse before it became an ache she could barely ignore.

She wished it was her who had the thought to break away, since they could easily be caught. Instead, it was he who drew back, placing his hands beside her shoulders, his breaths coming out as pants. He stared at her with narrowed eyes.

If he asked her to go to his chambers right now, Valerie would agree. *Have I missed him?* Her clenching inner walls answered her with an excited yes.

"You have been avoiding me," he accused.

"I most certainly have not." Her eyes trailed across the room they were in rather than focusing on him as she tried to calm her own breaths. She wasn't interested in having this conversation, especially when she was now deeply aroused. "Once again, you have made an incorrect assumption, and I begin to tire of them."

"Have you not?" He gently directed her face by placing one knuckle under her chin to make her look at him. "At every turn, when you could have had a moment to yourself, you have made sure to be accompanied. You even took Lady Victoria to the library today, when you usually go by yourself."

She folded her arms over her chest, her desire beginning to fade. "I may do as I like."

If he asked her directly, she would tell him the truth, but she would much rather she didn't have to. *I worry about being on my own now.*

After being attacked by Lord Daerk, Valerie didn't want to be caught in a position that could lead to the same situation. Unfortunately, that meant Geryon wasn't able to approach her. She'd felt the loss, but she would much prefer to feel safe.

"What else would you have me believe?" he bit, his nose crinkling. "You did not return to my room as promised."

Valerie blinked rapidly. "Excuse me?" She gave him a single laugh while keeping her usual expressionless composure. "I said I would consider it. I became preoccupied."

The high-handedness of this male could sometimes be quite infuriating. Valerie liked a man with this kind of confidence, but not when they thought it meant they could command her.

"Where did you go instead?" She didn't like the squint in his eye, one of distrust. "You were seen walking the palace late into the night, when you should have been with me."

"I was with Lady Savannah." She threw her hand up to stop him before he could talk. *The nerve!* "I should have been wherever I wish to be. I may do as I please. You are acting rather impolite."

"Because I'm angry," he said, and she thought she could hear a growl in his voice. "I waited for you, and instead, you decided I was not worth your time in comparison to another? A female I'm aware you don't genuinely care for? You know I'm fond of you, and yet you play games with me."

Valerie had to stem the urge to puff her cheeks in anger.

He was beginning to get under her skin, and she fought to keep her cold face she preferred to wear.

"I don't toy with you, but perhaps I should," she answered before she pushed him hard enough that he backed away. "I wish to leave."

"I'm not done speaking with you."

Just a moment before, Valerie had felt warm and soft for this man. Now, she was just annoyed and feeling spiteful. *I will truly play a game with him, and he can come to learn the difference in my actions.*

"If you had asked me directly, Lord Geryon, rather than command me" – she narrowed her eyes in his direction, giving him a cruel glare – "I would have come to your bedchamber."

His head reared back at her admission, his anger fading. His brows furrowed, his lips ever so slightly pouting.

"Instead, I don't know whose I will end up in, but it will definitely not be yours."

His eyes widened in shock as Valerie swiftly unlocked the door. She left before he could get the chance to stop her.

She'd always believed in retaliation for actions and words. *Karma is a wonderful medicine for those who are deserving of it.* She would teach Geryon she wasn't some submissive woman. No, she was a vicious one. He often referred to her as a soft creature. She would show him she was not prey, but rather, a predator of her own.

*I'm a wolf among sheep.*

She wished she was in private so she could kick something. *Why must I feel desire for such an arrogant man?* Even now, she was tempted to go back on her words, to go to him this eve.

*His cock had felt good.* Perhaps he knew once she felt it, she would be partial to feeling it again.

*And then there are those lips.* Those firm, wicked lips that she couldn't resist kissing back. *What power do they have over me?* She feared if he were to kiss her out in the open, where others could see, she would lose her senses and kiss him back.

*Ugh! He's too handsome for his own good!*

"Lady Cecily!" she heard Victoria exclaim as she ran down the hall. "I have been searching for you."

"My apologies. I realised I grabbed the wrong book and quickly ran back to the library. I was afraid to keep King Bradwick waiting by delaying myself for your return."

"That was a good idea," she nodded, then handed her a white lacy umbrella. "I was just outside, and he's returning now with Lady Savannah."

Either she or Wyetta would be taken from court next to go on a stroll for a few hours.

She was surprised to see Geryon walking with the king when he returned. He gave her a glare, and she turned her chin up at him.

"I hope you don't believe I think less of you by selecting you last," Bradwick said as she held his arm.

They were walking the grounds when he directed her into the shade of the forest. Geryon was following behind them, and she made it a point to ignore him completely.

"Not at all. I'm sure it must be difficult to make such choices."

He shook his head. "No, I did not find the choice difficult." He patted her hand in a caring gesture. "I did not want to make you stroll in the heat again. Your skin is rather pale. I did not realise the sun would overcome you so easily."

"Well, that's rather sweet of you, your Highness." She held his arm tighter, giving him a large, warm smile – one she had to force. "Not all men are so... considerate. Not only are you handsome, but you are chivalrous as well."

He gave a laugh. "No, many of us can be quite brutish!"

She'd been complimenting the king regularly, more so than usual. She was also forcing more pleasant emotions to incite the king to be more affectionate.

Not far away, Valerie could see a blanket and basket laid out just on the outskirts of the forest. They could see the grounds and the palace with ease in the shadow of a large willow tree.

"I organised a picnic for us," he told her, gesturing his hand to it.

"What a lovely place for a picnic. Did you choose it?" He helped her kneel on the blanket, holding out his hand. "If so, you have quite the taste for a view."

Unfortunately, their seats put Geryon directly in her line of sight. He leaned up against a tree with his arms folded, staring at the grounds rather than at them.

*He appears irritated.* Good, that's what she wanted. *I need to get rid of him. I need Bradwick alone.*

"I have been informed you like things that taste sweet." He began to pull cakes and sweets from the basket, laying them out for her.

She almost frowned. "How did you–?"

Bradwick gave a laugh. "I must be truthful. The court has been watching each of you, to inform me of things like this. You have been noticed eating sugar cakes at the high teas."

He took it upon himself to feed them to her. She didn't giggle, knowing it wouldn't be convincing, but she tried to keep her smile. *My face tires of such antics.*

Then, something happened. King Bradwick leaned forward to cup her chin softly.

"It appears you have icing on your face."

She knew it had been a ruse when he leaned forward to kiss her. The moment his lips touched hers, she froze. She hadn't been intending to let him get so close, had no interest in kissing him.

His face was turned, and he made sure hers was as well.

Her eyes found Geryon over the king's shoulder in her

frozen moment. His eyes were wide, like he couldn't believe he was witnessing this.

If he hadn't reacted the way he had, she may have tried to find a way out of it. Instead, she squinted her eyes to give him a glare. She kissed King Bradwick back eagerly. She even gave a loud moan while placing her hand gently on his cheek.

Geryon's nose crinkled as his hands clenched into fists. His teeth were gritted, a muscle in his jaw popping visibly.

Now she was deserving of his anger. She could see he was quite envious, and she broke away quickly.

"Why, your Highness, I do believe that was one of the most pleasing kisses I have ever had." She wiped at the corner of her lips lightly with her fingertips.

Bradwick beamed at her compliment, just as Geryon stormed away.

*Good, he's gone.* Now she could finally read her poem to Bradwick in the hopes he would foolishly reveal where her sister was. *All I hope is that she is alive.*

Wherever she may be, Valerie was determined to find her.

# 20

With much frustration, Valerie sat in the dining hall with Bradwick, the other ladies, and the court. No matter how hard she tried, she hadn't managed to get him to speak on the whereabouts of her sister.

She read her poem to him, as well as another she thought may help. They were gory ones, ones that would show her apparent hatred of Witches, especially corrupted ones.

Although it started a conversation about her kind, there had been no mention of her sister – even when she indirectly pushed.

Frustration bubbled inside of her. Valerie considered grabbing Bradwick by his shoulders to shake him while screaming to tell her where he was keeping her.

*I have three days left, and tomorrow night is the ball.*

She wouldn't be able to speak with him tomorrow, and she wouldn't be able to have such a conversation while they were surrounded by people in the ballroom.

Geryon was surprisingly absent during dinner. She barely noticed while she thought on her sister.

She didn't feel unsettled. Valerie had other options to get what she wanted from him. They required the use of her magic, but she was becoming less concerned about that. *I can access it anytime I wish.* She would just no longer be cloaked.

Her eyes fell upon those in the dining room with her. *Then again, it does not seem like anyone within the palace walls would be able to sense my witchcraft.*

She'd assessed them enough to know they were all human, or at least she thought so. No one seemed suspicious to her.

*It may not matter if I reveal my magic.*

The idea made her smile to herself.

King Bradwick didn't retire early this eve, not like the last few nights. She felt like he was awaiting something. *I have not gained enough of his trust.* He eyed her, only to eventually sigh and excuse himself.

She thought it odd that he refused any of the ladies from accompanying him. *He's intending to go to his chambers alone?*

Deep in thought, Valerie made her way back to her apartment, knowing Victoria would be waiting for her in her parlour room. *She will have fallen asleep.*

She fell asleep often there, usually by accident.

Climbing the stairs, she turned around the curve. That's when she heard quick bootsteps thundering behind her, echoing against the walls.

*It must be Vermont.* As time crept on, she realised he wasn't a liability. She should have asked him to walk her. *I walked the halls alone in the dark.*

She'd been too busy thinking about her sister to feel fear for herself.

She turned to greet Vermont before she froze, her eyes widening.

"Lord Ger–" Valerie didn't get to finish.

Geryon barged her stomach with his shoulder, forcing her

to flip forward until she was resting over it. Without interrupting his stride, he began to carry her up the stairs. Valerie beat at his back with her fists while she kicked her knees into his chest.

"What are you doing? Lady Victoria is awaiting me in my chambers," she said with a hushed whisper.

"Tell them to assist you, and they will regret doing so," he threatened. His voice held a deep rumble of fury, like it had been building and was soon to explode.

"Lady Cecily," the two guards gasped.

They ran forward when they saw Geryon emerge with her at the top of the stairs. She was thankful they were hers and not the king's men.

"It's fine," she answered, throwing her hands up to ward them back.

They'd been standing near the centre, and Geryon walked her between them. He paused. "Speak of this to anyone, and I will remove both your tongues."

Then he continued to walk forward. There was a door here, one she'd only opened once.

It sat in the middle of the long, wide hallway separating hers and Vermont's chambers. It was a simple bedroom, small but still fairly grand. It was furnished beautifully, since it had no extension like a parlour room for guests to be seated.

There was a large bed resting against the back wall, but the only other furniture in the room was a writing desk, a vanity table, two picture frames, and a long, backless chair at the foot of the bed.

Geryon slammed the door behind him and promptly walked her further inside.

"What are you thinking, Geryon?" she loudly snapped now that they were somewhere they wouldn't be overheard. "If someone were to–"

"Other than your guards, I made sure we would not have

been seen," he bit before he tossed her down onto the bed.

Valerie bounced high, the wind knocked out of her from the strength of his throw. The mattress squeaked when her body thudded against it.

Before she could say anything, do anything, Geryon grabbed her leg and pulled her towards the edge of the bed. Then, he was kneeling above her on one knee and hand, kissing her.

Valerie pushed at his chest, fought against him even as she kissed him back. *So sweet.* She had to stop herself from making a sound of enjoyment at the taste, the feel of his firm lips.

"Stop pretending you don't want this!" he finally broke away to shout. "I can see it in the redness of your chest and cheeks, can feel it in the warmth of your skin." He brought his mouth against hers with force, moving his lips in time with hers. He broke away again. "In the kisses you return."

"Wait," she begged.

He was more determined than usual, more forceful, as he began to kiss at her neck and lift the skirts of her dress.

Valerie tried to turn away from his mouth that was making her pant. Already, prickles trailed up and over her scalp. When he realised she'd turned to her side to get away, Geryon rolled her over so her front was against the bed.

"You played a dangerous game with me today." There was a heaviness in his voice, one that told her he was filled with rage. "You used Bradwick as a way to incite jealousy in me out of spite."

It appeared he was at the end of his apparently unflappable patience.

It was true; she knew she'd been teasing him with the king. He deserved it, since he'd been demanding and controlling, but she didn't think he would do something as bold as this!

Her legs dangled off the edge as he moved back to stand

so he could prepare himself. He pulled her skirt over her rear while his other hand pushed her back so she was pressed against the bed, stopping her from moving.

"Geryon."

"Tell me no!" It was another shout, his anger causing him to be louder. It made her want to roll her hips against him in welcome rather than away, the fierceness of it calling to her. "Tell me you don't want me, and I will leave."

"I–" she started, but found she couldn't continue.

She wanted to tell him no, that she didn't want him at all.

She knew it would be a lie.

*What do I want to do?*

*I came here for my sister, not for this man to enchant me.* Valerie didn't know what she wanted to do or say to him, not when truths and lies were so blurred inside her.

She wanted to say no, her mind demanding her to, but every inch of her body screamed for him to fill her. He'd sparked a fire in her, one she couldn't seem to put out no matter how hard she tried.

"You cannot say it, can you?"

Her brows furrowed deeply in confusion.

*I want him.* Even though he made her angry and she thought him foolishly arrogant, she had wounded him in return. *He was so angry and jealous, he threw me over his shoulder where others might have seen.*

She should be frightened of him. He had her in a position where she couldn't fight him, couldn't get away, could don'thing but be exposed and taken.

Instead, she was *aroused,* and could feel it in the ways he'd described. She was flushed and heated, and there was wetness between her legs. Even her heart rate was quick with excitement.

It was because she knew she was safe. If she really wanted him gone, she knew how to get him to leave.

Even now, he was giving her the chance to say it. He was waiting for it. It was her last chance to deny him, and Valerie shook her head.

*I want Geryon inside me.* Even just the thought of it made her channel quiver, made that pool at the entrance to her core grow.

"Then don't deny me any longer!" With her thighs pressed together, her legs dangling off the bed, he shoved his cock inside her from behind.

Valerie gasped at the swiftness of his body filling hers. She palmed the bed beneath her as she lost all her breath, trying to adjust to the size of him inside her pussy.

He was so hard that if it wasn't pumping with heat, she would have thought it was made of steel. He filled her all the way to the hilt, and she could feel the head of him pressing deep against her cervix, pushing at it like he wanted to bury himself impossibly deeper.

She felt spread and filled, so much so, she doubted there was a place inside her he wasn't touching.

"Fuck!" He shouted the word like he hadn't expected the tight feel of her body wrapped around his.

She could feel him shuddering. The hand that had been pressing her down slipped back, and eventually, he held her hips with his palms.

Geryon groaned, holding her steady as he slowly drew back, only to shove forward a moment later.

Her core clenched around him when he slammed back in, tightening against the impact. Then he was pounding inside her, his thrusts filled with such strength, her breaths were stolen from her every time he moved. She tried to catch them when he drew back, but he was taking her with a speed that only gave her a second to breathe in.

His meaty hands dug into her skin so deeply, she feared he was bruising her hips with his fingertips. Panted grunts came from him every time he hit the end of her, and she knew he would be feeling it on the tip of his shaft.

It was a savage taking. Aggressive. One filled with pent-up lust, need, desperation. It was also filled with anger, like he wanted to punish her.

He was taking his emotions out on her, and Valerie could don'thing but take it. She felt her lungs squeezing. *Cannot breathe, cannot breathe.*

Even if she wanted to moan, she couldn't. Instead, her mouth hung open, her chin resting firmly against the bed. All that came from her were shallow puffs of breath while she stared at the wall.

It felt primal. The guttural, ferocious sounds that speared past his lips only added to it.

He was being brutal, but she could feel her body growing wetter with each inward slide of his cock. She tried to back onto him every time he pulled back, wanting to keep him within her.

Valerie clawed at the bedding, her hands clenching and unclenching the blanket beneath her. She loosened her grip as she relaxed ever so slightly when he pulled back, then gripped the fabric when she felt the wonderful slide of his cockhead run over that swelling ridge on the wall of her channel.

"The next time you decide to use the king against me" – Valerie's eyes widened when she felt him grow impossibly harder – "remember whose cock it's you currently have inside you."

Her legs began to shake in reaction, trembling wildly at being taken like this. She was thankful he was holding her hips in place against the bed, because she was barely able to stand. Her toes skimmed against the ground as her feet slipped.

She would never say it, but her mind begged him. *Yes!* A mangled moan squeezed its way from her lungs. *More!* She quietened herself once more, even as she thought, *right there.*

*Don't stop.*

She was almost there... not much further...

A harsh, broken sound came from him as her body swelled around his cock.

Her features furrowed in deep pleasure, needing to give herself something as she orgasmed against this stunning man's lust-crazed movements. She knew she came hard when it trickled down her thighs, when she could hear the wet slapping sounds as he drove in and out.

Her eyes were hopelessly dazed as her vision split in two, as she lost all control. Her hands were gripping the sheets so tightly, she feared she may rip them, but her entire body was tense, shaking as prodding bliss made her arch her backside.

It was only once she stopped squeezing him, stopped coming, that he finally spoke again.

"Next time you wish to toy with me by using Bradwick, knowing I cannot do anything," he started, his thrusts slowing.

He didn't soften his pounds, didn't take her any less mercilessly, but it wasn't as fast. It gave her the chance to feel how violently he was starting to shake, his hands unsteady on her hips.

She thought she could even feel his nails digging into her flesh.

"Remember whose seed you are filled with."

Valerie's eyes widened as she buried her face against the bed. *So warm.* She could feel him coming against her cervix, hot liquid bursting against it.

She should be trying to get away, to stop him from filling her body. She found herself pressing against him harder, to feel it more as it spread inside her. *How can it feel so good?*

The shuddering groan he gave, while he remained seated deep but pumped against her, made her stomach clench. *Such a delicious sound.* He sounded like he was strangled by ecstasy.

Then, Valerie gave a cry, not one of pleasure, but of pain.

Geryon didn't know what emotion struck him when he finished coming inside this irresistible woman after he ravished her like an uncontrollable beast, but something had caused him to lean over and bite her.

He bit her hard enough on the side of her nape that he cut through skin, and blood welled in his mouth.

His eyes rolled into the back of his head when he did, like some deep-seated need had been accomplished. His softening shaft twitched, his arms bunching to squeeze her against him.

A bite from a Dragon could mean many things. Usually, it was aggression, some angry emotion that caused them to lash out. Geryon knew the truth. *I bit her with affection.* Possessive, unyielding affection. Maybe it was also in jealousy.

He only released his bite when he needed to finish withdrawing from her pussy. Then he slipped his hand between her torso and the bed.

Pressing his middle finger low on her stomach, just below her navel, he mentally chanted. She didn't react to the spell, one she wouldn't know he used.

His magic may be weak, but most Dragons were fond of this spell. It was one that prevented the wearer from becoming pregnant with their seed in particular. If a Dragoness did it to herself, it prevented all.

Geryon had never intended to come inside Cecily; usually, he wouldn't take such a risk.

*I was unable to stop myself.* The closer he got to coming, the more he knew he needed to pull out, the more crazed he became not to. He had wanted to know what it was like to come while the heat of her body gloved him.

He was so filled with rage and unbridled jealousy, he may have wanted to use it as a way to mark her. Dragon males often did this with a female they wanted to deter other males from bedding.

*But humans would not be able to sense such things.*

"You came inside me," she said when he finally pulled back to stand, tucking his shaft away.

Time to think of a lie. He had time to come up with one while she turned over to face him.

"I told you I'm not from these lands. I wear a rare enchantment I stole from a Witch that prevents me from getting another pregnant."

He watched her brows twitch for a moment. "I did not know something like that was possible."

*It's not.* A human wouldn't know that. Witches had their own form of preventatives, at least from what he heard; teas and concoctions they could make.

Before she could think much longer on it, he cut into her thoughts.

"If you believe we are done, then you are mistaken." Geryon's chest was heaving, his breaths still coming out in deep huffs. "Take off your dress," he demanded.

His nose crinkled at the cold look she gave him, one of clear defiance.

*She still wishes to deny this? Even when I scent her orgasm, her lingering arousal?* If only he could tell her he could sense it, tell her she couldn't hide it from him.

He wasn't satisfied. He wasn't done with her body this evening.

He expected her to hit him like she did in the war room, was waiting for her to give him some rebuff. The moment she did, he knew he would take her in the same way he just did, with unyielding force.

If he had to teach her just how much she wanted him, he would, but... *I don't want her to deny me anymore.* Geryon wanted to enjoy her, to coax her to truly let go.

She was beginning to moan, was beginning to show him more emotions, small though they were. *The mask is beginning to slip.* Still, he didn't want a peek. No, he wanted to violently rip it from her.

He wanted her to explode with abandon.

"No," she told him, denying his request to unclothe herself.

His heart began to beat erratically, frustration boiling in his veins. *I cannot rip it from her.* Not after that word. Oh, how he longed to see this beautiful woman naked. Here, in this room, they were private, and he wanted to unveil her.

He may not get another chance like this.

His fists clenched tightly, averting his gaze from her to calm himself. He hadn't felt anger and disappointment like this in a long time. It tickled the back of his neck, a warning that he was a hair-trigger away from losing his control to those terrible emotions.

Then, stepping forward with that expressionless mask, she came up to him, and he was unsure of what she would do.

*Will she strike me? Point that dagger of hers at my chest? Kick me in the shin again?* He feared his own reaction to any of those possibilities.

The closer she got, the worse he felt.

Pressing her fingertips underneath his jaw to gently caress it, she pressed her lips next to his to kiss the corner. "But you can remove it."

He didn't even know he was holding in a breath, not until her words knocked it out of him.

*I can remove it?* Dumbfounded, since her words weren't what he anticipated, he stared at her rather than moved.

She pressed her lips to his softly, giving him fluttering little kisses. They were so gentle in comparison to the way he took her mouth that he was unsure if he truly felt them.

He could barely believe she was instigating this kiss. She had never reached to kiss him before.

He thought she would be angry with the way he took her. He hadn't been kind to her while he released his pent-up emotions. *Is this another trick?*

It was only when she wrapped her arms around his shoulders and began to lightly pull on his hair, playing with it, that he kissed her back. He stayed with her lightness, enjoying this playful dance.

It was one that dripped with womanly, sensual desire, rather than his aggressive, masculine lust.

There was a rush from the crown of his head that flowed all the way down to his feet. Rather than be filled with anger, it was like she was slowly changing how he felt to pure yearning. It cooled his anger but made him burn in other ways.

With a deep sigh against her lips, his eyelids drooped. *She's showing she wants me.*

Geryon slipped his hands behind her to undo the ties of her dress. Being gentle with the delicate fabric, he pulled.

She lowered her arms for him, and he could scent her arousal deepening, a mouth-watering swirl of it. Pushing her dress down her body slowly, his hands followed by sliding against her sides, just so he could caress her.

She continued to kiss him as she stepped from it. Yet, she wouldn't let him remove her undergarment dress.

Rather than letting him, he felt her hands reach around him to undo the special clips at the back of his coat. He was wearing one of his elaborate coats today, one with many chains winding around him for design.

He could tell she was struggling to fumble with something she'd never tried to undo, and she pulled away from the kiss to concentrate.

"Perhaps you should turn around?"

Geryon brushed his lips against the side of her neck, lowering his hands so he could place them against her backside.

"No. This is turning me on," he answered before he pulled her hips towards him to thrust his already growing cock against her.

"How is that possible?" She shook her head like she couldn't believe him.

"For four days, I have wanted nothing more than to be buried inside you. The anticipation of doing so again while you are finally naked is enough to excite me." He pressed against her again while drawing his tongue against her skin, tasting the salt of her flesh. "Take your time."

The wait would just draw out more desperation from him, make him yearn for it harder. It also meant he could play with her, grow her desire while he teased her with his mouth and, hopefully, by sliding himself against her. He even twirled his tongue into the shell of her ear.

The fact she wanted him naked as well, to look at and touch him, was deeply satisfying.

*I will get to spend the night with her.* He knew that's what this meant. *She wishes to remain with me.*

Geryon began to remove the pins and clips from her hair, wanting to see it free for the first time. He wanted to see how the rich, long length of her brown hair waved around her shoulders and back. He wanted to watch it halo around her head, wanted to be able to freely fist it if he wished.

When she finally removed his coat, she made short work of the white tunic that laid underneath. The moment it was gone, she began to press feather-light kisses against the top of his chest.

Her lips travelled up the side of his neck as she pulled down his breeches. He'd removed his boots before she'd even finished with his coat. With his vision wavering, his head tilted back to give her better access to his neck as he felt her hand wrap around his cock. A quiet groan broke from his lips when she stroked him, petting his shaft with her delicate palm.

"You are rather impressive," she said softly near his ear.

The compliment made him pulsate in her hand.

She ran her other palm up his torso, over his muscled chest. He wondered if she purposely ran it over his nipple before she brought it over his shoulder. It drifted down his back, like she wanted to rub her palm over all the muscles that happily leapt to her soft touch.

Geryon shuddered against the overwhelming sensations she was trying to feed him all at once. She even grabbed his arse, like she was admiring his body.

He didn't want to come like this. The fact she was reciprocating was already bringing him closer.

He lowered his head so he could see as he grabbed the shift still covering her. As he pulled it up, she was forced to release him so she could raise her arms.

There was no blush, not a shred of bashfulness.

She was confident, and she revealed just how much so by stepping away to lower herself against the bed once she was fully unclothed. She crawled backwards until she was completely laying on her elbows.

While she kept one leg straight, she bent the other and pulled it to the side, revealing the pink of her folds and core to him. She didn't even seem to mind that a dribble of thick, milky-white liquid dripped from her, proof that he'd already filled that warm channel with his seed. *Such boldness is my undoing.*

Pre-cum welled on the tip of his shaft at her blatantly showing her body like this.

"Your body is just as lovely as your face," he told her, his voice husky and coarse.

*So comely.* He fell to his knees on the bed, each one beside her straightened leg.

He ran his hands up her bent leg, up her inner and outer thigh to circle it completely with both his hands. His lips followed in the middle between his thumbs. When he ran them over her hips, his tongue licked over one of her hip bones that became prominent when her pelvis arched to his wet stroke.

As his hands ran up her sides, he nipped up the flat plane of her stomach. He even trailed the tip of his nose over her sternum.

Her skin was pale, but he could see a handful of beauty marks dotting one leg, a hip, a shoulder. He licked the one over her left breast as he brought his hands back down to caress her body.

Her hips were not wide, her waist didn't tuck in, but she still had just enough womanly curve that he could feel it under his palms. She was slender, but she didn't appear weak or fragile.

Her skin was smooth and felt like silk under his hands. He hoped she liked the rough feel of his tough and calloused skin caressing her body.

He'd noticed her bottom was round when he had her bent over and exposed. He ran his hands under her so he could knead her firm cheeks now, needing to feel them better.

*Her breasts are small.* They were perfect for him. He liked that he could bring most of one into his mouth, her nipple deep and easier for his tongue to flick. Her nipples were such a soft pink, he feared hurting them. The colour made them appear delicate.

*She likes them played with.* He moved to the other, sucking on it when she gave him a deep pant.

She didn't moan often, but he had started to notice the weight behind her breaths. Small ones told him she was getting close, big ones told him she really liked what he was doing.

"Tell me what you want." He let his eyes rise to her face as he began to slip his mouth up her chest.

She pursed her lips, her relaxed face turning hard. *Perhaps I pushed too far.* Geryon crawled up her body so he could take her mouth to distract her.

The welcome return made him thrum, and he lowered his body to lie on top of her.

Now that she was no longer fighting him, she was allowing him to do whatever he wanted, be exploring and slow. Her body was open for him, and she hadn't rejected a single touch.

He spread his knees, forcing his body lower, to take the worst of his weight. When he laid his forearms around her head, she wrapped her arms around his shoulders and snaked her fingers through his midnight hair.

Their naked bodies were close enough that he could feel the heat growing between them already. *Have to be inside her again, need to be buried while she is like this.*

Her mask hadn't come down, but she was welcoming him, accepting him. Naked, panting, compliant. *Want her soft for me.*

He gripped his already throbbing cock, giving it a stroke to feel just how hard it was for himself. He tucked the head against her entrance, and he groaned at the dripping pool that greeted him. *She's so wet.* Wetter than any other time he had touched her.

Holding the base while still kissing her, he pumped his hips forward once, just so he could collect her juices over the broad head before he pulled back. Then, he pressed the wetted tip of his shaft up her folds. Her legs twitched when he ran over the hard nub of her clit before she wrapped them over his thighs.

When he returned to her entrance, he found the wetness he had stolen had been replaced with more. He shuddered as he slowly began to push inside her core. She gave a shivering noise against his lips while he fed her body inch by slow inch of his cock.

They both sighed when he was gently pressing up against her cervix, a place where she couldn't take anymore, and he couldn't give anymore.

*She feels wonderful.* Around his shaft, beneath his hard and muscled body, wrapped around him in every way.

She was dripping, easy to feel when he began to withdraw. She was warm, her body giving him a gloving heat to bask in. She was tight, his girth not giving her much room, and he knew she would only grow tighter the more he took her this eve. Her body would adjust to his size but would swell from his thrusting, swollen and tender.

*She's trembling.* He could feel it in her legs as he increased his speed ever so slightly, in her arms wrapped around his neck. Even her core was quivering around his shaft. To feel it made his jaw fall, his lips separating against her mouth so he could give a shaking groan.

He finally broke away from the kiss, and she seemed disappointed that he did, as she tried to follow his lips.

He wanted to stare down at her when he felt her pussy beginning to spasm. She was about to come, and he wanted to watch her, wanted to see what would slip from her mask.

*I have yet to watch her while she wrings my cock.* His tongue fell to rest between his teeth while he panted like the beast he was at the possibility.

"Come for me," he demanded when it was taking longer than he wanted. Fuck, he just wanted her to constantly come on him.

She peered up at him, those wintry pale eyes dazed. Her lips were parted just enough to allow her shallow breaths to dance past them. He increased his speed, and her back arched, causing her chest to rub against him.

Knowing she needed more, he separated their bodies just

enough so he could go faster.

Her head fell back when he felt it, her body contracting around him. It rippled – wet, warm, gripping up and down his cock. Watching her orgasm, watching her fight to keep her mask in place while she did, was delightful.

Her brow twitched, her mouth falling open just enough to let out a moan he knew she wanted to keep hidden. There was a crinkle in the corner of her eyes, one he knew would have been prominent if she would just let herself go.

"Do I feel good pumping inside you while you come?" he said while she tried to milk him. She somehow clenched harder, her body answering him even if she wouldn't. "Do you like my cock inside you?"

When this woman finally broke and lost control, he couldn't wait to force those answers out of her. *For her to tell me yes?* A tremor rolled through Geryon.

He began to move faster when the clutch of her body wasn't so tight, wasn't forcing him to slow down at the gripping intensity.

"Your body feels so fucking good. Your pussy is so hot."

Blasted, Geryon wanted to tell her she smelt amazing, that he could feel and scent her orgasm coating his hips, his thighs, his body, but he couldn't.

To stop himself from foolishly rambling, he started kissing, nipping, sucking at her neck – as well as just to spur her on. She turned her head to allow him more surface to play with.

His own orgasm was swiftly approaching, and he wanted to bring her over the edge again before he did. He could feel her bouncing beneath him, his chest massaging hers, the muscled plane of his abdomen slipping against her stomach.

Her hands moved to cross over his back, trailing down it as she dug in her fingertips. Her nails were long, but she didn't dig them into his skin like he wanted her to. She wasn't clinging to him in desperation, and yet her core was gripping him like it was on the cusp of milking him for his seed again. Her body told him she should be out of control while he pumped, but she still held back.

He had to back away from her when he felt his spine tingling, needed to give himself space when his back started to arch.

He raised above her on straight arms as his head fell forward to watch himself thrust. Her lips were spread around his cock as it dipped in and out of her body. Her breasts jiggled, and they tantalised him, making him pout that he couldn't bring them into his mouth while he moved.

*Her body is wonderful to behold.* He wanted to sink his teeth into each inch of her wintry skin, wanted to lick it, taste it like he always did.

*Feels so good around me.* His nose crinkled when he felt his seed rising. His shaft felt engorged, thickening by the second. Desperate to get her to fall back over the edge so she would come with him, Geryon thrust his hips with frenzied force and speed. A sudden change of slow to fast.

He worsened his own ache by doing it.

He thought he failed, thought he lost.

Then, he felt her squeezing him just as the first burst came. Just as it started, she shot forward and bit into his pectoral muscle with such strength, he feared she'd broken through skin. She was doing it to hide the loudness of her moan while her nails scored his back. He revelled in it.

His thrusts became uncontrolled, slamming so deeply, he thought he'd break her. He shook above her, his mouth falling open as he gave a haunting, shuddering groan, feeling it squeezing its way out of his lungs. He moved one hand to grip the back of her head, forcing her closer in the hopes she would bite harder.

He was coming inside her, filling her pussy while it

spasmed with gripping wetness. *Nothing has felt better!* He couldn't stop moving, couldn't stop from trying to draw it out for them both.

Then she surprised him, squirming against his hips, her knees digging into his sides. She relinquished her bite to speak.

"Why is it so warm?" He couldn't believe how breathless she sounded, like she couldn't hide how much she enjoyed the feeling of him spreading inside her.

*Because you have a Dragon between your thighs.* His body would always be better, hotter.

"Because you turn my body aflame with wicked passion," he answered with a chuckling puff when his shaft finally ceased filling her.

They shared in a moment of tranquil calmness, and it gave him time to feel her body throbbing around him, gave him the chance to hear how erratic her heartbeat was, how laboured and sharp her breaths were.

"You bit me." He touched his chest, finding blood. It was also smeared across her lips.

*It's a good thing she is not a Witch. Such an act would be seen as a crime against my kind.* Then again, he would never bed something so vulgar.

"It was in retaliation." She reached behind her neck to touch her own bite wound. "How will I hide this from Lady Victoria?" The inflection in her voice told him she was angry.

"Shhh, shhh, shhh," he cooed, hoping to calm her. "Your hair is long, and you are astonishingly clever." She narrowed her eyes at his compliment. "I'm sure you will come up with an acceptable excuse."

When that didn't appease her, he worried she would try and storm from the room. Geryon still wasn't ready to allow his captured prey to escape.

He chuckled while he lowered himself to kiss her neck in

hopes of distracting her.

"Will it not be exciting to know you wear a lover's bite while trying to hide it from others?" He thrust his soft cock inside her, trying to get himself to harden once more. "I know it will bring me great enjoyment to feel it on my chest while you dance in a pretty ballgown tomorrow night."

Geryon's jealousy and possessiveness towards this woman, which he didn't quite understand, would be tempered knowing she wore his teeth marks and was filled with his seed.

*Especially since she will be forced to dance with King Bradwick.*

He squinted his eyes and his nose crinkled, while his lips curled back. Rage was threatening to surface. He buried his face against her throat to hide the growl that suddenly began to emerge from his chest at the thought of another male touching her.

*Why does she elicit such a reaction from me?* He'd never been this way with others.

Valerie didn't know what time it was when she finally managed to crawl away from Geryon.

The man was relentless. She lost count of how many times he took her, giving her orgasm after orgasm, but she was utterly exhausted by the end of it.

To her surprise, when he finally did release her, he hadn't clothed himself and run away. Instead, he put his breeches on and helped her with the ties at the back of her dress so she could make her way back to her suite.

She was in a state of complete disarray, and his assistance barely helped. Still, the gesture meant much to her.

He'd given her a sweet kiss goodbye, but it was his words that made a strange emotion flutter in her stomach.

At the end of it, when he broke away, he placed his palm against the side of her face and said, "I'm sure you will look beautiful, and I know I will wish I could dance with you."

Then, he let her out of the room like freeing a bird from its cage.

Valerie then promptly woke Victoria and ushered her back

to her husband.

Once she was alone, she wandered over to the window to find the sky was still night, but it wasn't as dark as it should be.

Every time she had tried to escape Geryon, he would pull her back by her hips and make her forget why she wanted to leave in the first place. *Now I'm exhausted, and the sun will rise soon.* She wished she could say she was truly cranky about it, but she wasn't.

Valerie had enjoyed herself. Deep down inside, she knew she would cherish her memory of this night forever. She would think back fondly on every single second of the sweet passion she'd shared with Geryon when she finally left this palace.

*After the ball, there are two days left.* Valerie needed to be gone by the end of the last day, in case the real Lady Cecily turned up.

A terrible emotion crawled its way inside her chest at the thought of leaving. *I feel something for Geryon.* Something small, a tiny piece she'd given to the man who made her feel light under his heavy body.

*What a silly notion.* The fact she'd allowed herself to feel something like this was idiotic, but she was happy to silently gift him this. It wasn't love or anything truly deep, but it was a tenderness.

It was care for the man who saw Valerie was wearing lies upon her face rather than believing she was truly lifeless, a fondness for the person who had forced her to feel unimaginable desire. For the first time in her life, she had felt it deeply.

Knowing her time here was almost over, Valerie fell asleep with a sad smile upon her lips.

She didn't rise when she was given her breakfast by Victoria. Instead, she spent the day sleeping and lazing about in her room, allowing herself this quietness. Soon, she would have to face the complexities of the party she was about to attend.

Then, night began to fall.

Victoria returned with a handful of servants in tow after finding Valerie awake and ready to be attended to. They filled her bath and set out a tea with food and cakes. After eating, she bathed in the cloudy liquid, a perfumed solution added to it to make her smell like lavender.

"Are you excited?" Victoria asked, brushing her wet hair for her.

Valerie used the rim of the tub to hide the noticeable bite mark on her neck; she was enjoying the sting it constantly gave.

"Excited would not be the word I would use," Valerie answered, allowing her skin to soften and soak up the perfumed water. "I'm curious to see what a ball thrown by the king will be like."

"It will be spectacular. It always is." Once her hair was clean and brushed, Victoria rose to her feet and stood in front of her. "I mean no offense, since the dresses you have brought with you are lovely, but they are not extravagant enough for this event."

Valerie scoffed lightly. "What would you have me do about it?"

"If you would permit me, I have brought a dress I have never worn but I can assure will fit you." Victoria nibbled at her lips while rubbing the back of her neck, a blush rising on her cheeks. "I wish to gift it to you."

"Should I not be the one giving you gifts?" Valerie eyed her curiously. "You have been my attending lady and have done a wonderful job."

"Mayhap, but please allow me to do this for you." She averted her gaze for a moment before it returned to Valerie, a bright smile forming across her features. "When I went through my outfits to see if I had anything that may be of your taste, I knew I must have bought it to one day give to you."

A silent sigh fell from Valerie as she waved her hand. "Fine. Show it to me."

With a squeal, Victoria ran to the seating parlour before bringing in an elegant yet expensive looking dress.

The design was two layered, but the skirt wasn't wide like she feared it would be, like some puffy thing.

It was two pieces: a plain white bodice attached to a pleated skirt underneath. However, it was the dress coat that drew Valerie's eye. It appeared like someone had dipped it in quicksilver, shiny yet still faint – a trick from the meshy material over the top of it. Dark grey stitching embellished the edges, even around the buttons that would sit against her wrists, since the dress didn't drape like most did.

"Lady Victoria," Valerie gasped while gently running her fingertips over the coat's material, worried she'd damage it with even the barest touch. "You cannot give me something this stunning."

"Please. This ball is for you and the other ladies. I want you to look breathtaking. You are trying to win King Bradwick's heart. I'm sure he would not resist you in such a fine dress."

Valerie eyed it. Although it was far too glamorous for her, she did find it beautiful, and she knew she would feel so if she wore it. *It looks like something an angel would wear.*

Despite her lack of expression, Valerie's heart swelled at the idea of wearing it, that Victoria cared enough about her to want to give it to her.

"Fine, I will wear it," Valerie conceded. "Only if you allow me to choose the style of my hair and an additional accessory, one you cannot question."

Victoria gave her a sheepish smile. "Only if you wear the

shoes I brought."

She placed a pair of lacey, silver-beaded, heeled slippers in front of the dress.

Valerie rolled her eyes but couldn't suppress her own small smile. "You twist my arm and have succeeded in getting your way."

She emerged from the tub, agreeing to her terms, and could tell the woman was excited. Somehow, Valerie found the childish manner oddly endearing, as well as contagious.

Victoria helped to dress her and then styled her hair into a sweeping cascade over one shoulder like she asked – to hide her bite. It also allowed the long subtle waves of her hair to be seen.

Once one side was all pinned back with pearls, Victoria paid careful attention to the make-up she insisted must be painted on Valerie's face. Like usual, her skin had little powder, but her eyes were darkened with mascara and liner. Silver was the theme for her this eve because even her eyelids were painted the colour with a smoke of dark grey.

"I don't look like myself." Valerie sighed, showing the woman she was unsure of her appearance, while also hiding her nervousness.

"Well, you look radiant." Victoria forced her to turn away from the long mirror. "If King Bradwick does not become captivated by you, then it will mean he is blind."

Valerie wanted to roll her eyes again. She didn't need encouragement; she could see she looked beautiful. It was just dismaying she had to play some rich noblewoman that she wasn't – not to this extent.

There was a reason she never took Lady Cecily's elaborate gowns. She never wanted things to get to this point. *I feel as though I have strayed as far as I possibly can from who I truly am in this outfit.*

It was a costume, and it felt like a betrayal. It also made

her miss home terribly.

She quickly dismissed her darkening thoughts. "Let us go."

Vermont was waiting for her at the top of the stairs to be her male guest.

Already, Valerie could hear the bustling of people and the sounds of music as they walked closer. They hadn't even made it to the ballroom, but it was so loud, it carried through the palace.

Valerie entered the same ballroom she had when she'd first arrived, and once more found herself admiring the beautiful glass dome above.

The other ladies had already arrived, and most guests were there as well, although some were still filing in from outside. A line of carriages awaited their turn at the palace doors to empty their passengers.

Everyone was in their loveliest outfits, creating a sea of colourful people. Men wore suits of the finest quality, bright and colourful to match the ladies who walked on their arms. People were already dancing, laughing, drinking.

"You are frozen, my dear," Vermont said, tightening his arm around hers in comfort.

Yes, she had stopped moving once she entered the grand hall. "I'm just admiring the general splendour. Let us continue."

She may be a little dazzled by the shining light of the crystal chandelier sparkling above in the middle of the dome. She felt a little choked by the different perfumes that clogged the air, but it didn't necessarily make it unpleasant.

The sheer amount of people was staggering, and she wasn't prepared for such a vast amount.

There was also an issue. She hadn't thought on if these additional guests knew the real Lady Cecily. Duke Vermont's glamour should be enough. *Hopefully, with this many people, no one will think too deeply on me.*

They did look similar, after all.

King Bradwick was seated so he could watch his guests. Periodically, he would get up and move around the room to walk and converse with the people. Geryon stood stationed beside him wherever he went, his eyes narrowed and hyper focused. Not once did his hand leave the hilt of his sword, like he was prepared to draw it at a moment's notice.

Even with the distance between them, she could tell he looked impeccably handsome. He was dressed in a dark-navy suit with buttons and buckles that would send her cross-eyed if she ever tried to undo them herself. His hair was even swept back with some sort of gel.

*He really should not look so nice with such an intense gaze* – one that made it appear as though he'd run his sword through anyone who came near.

Each lady eventually took a turn dancing with King Bradwick, who was gentle and smooth. She'd been controlled in her movements, the dance intending to be close. His arm wrapped around her waist while he held her hand delicately. His body pressed up against hers while they swayed before he would twirl or dip her.

The waltz and closeness were the same with all of them.

"You look enchanting this evening, Cecily," he complimented her with a beaming smile.

*I grow tired of being complimented so regularly.* It had been incessant this night, people constantly at her with pretty words.

"To hear you say such words, your Highness, is rather heart fluttering." She dipped her head with a forced smile. "I must say, you look rather dashing as well."

Valerie was relieved when he finally let her go, so he could dance with Wyetta. They each got one song while the night continued to creep on.

A small part of her wished Geryon could dance with her,

and she had to stop herself from wistfully gazing upon him.

Vermont eventually offered his hand, and she enthusiastically took the chance to flee from conversation. It put her once again in the middle of the ballroom. A ring of people watched them, but someone caught her eye.

She'd obviously already caught theirs. *Wait... do I know that person?*

Vermont turned her so her back was towards them. When she finally forced them to turn back, the person was gone. *Did I imagine it?*

With the number of people here, it wasn't hard to believe she may mistake someone for another.

Unfortunately, it caused her heart to squeeze. She kept her blank expression while her eyes darted over people. *I should not have put myself in the light like this. I must shadow myself.*

Dancing with King Bradwick had been enough. Doing so with Vermont was just asking for trouble, to be caught and seen.

She quickly ended their dance, giving him a smile as a show for the people. Valerie used a spiralling pillar and Vermont to shield her while she tried to settle herself. *I'm merely paranoid.* She took a deep, calming breath through her mouth, feeling it shudder silently. Her cheeks were warm, and her increased heart rate wasn't helping.

*The night is almost over.* She took in another calming breath.

"Valerie?"

Everything inside her froze.

Her lungs caught in her chest, her heart squeezing so tightly she feared it would explode. A spike of dread so thick speared her, she thought she'd collapse.

She ignored her *real* name, knowing she couldn't respond to it.

"Uncle," Valerie said, gaining attention while turning

away from the voice. "Do you think Father will be disappointed that he was unable to come to the palace? I would have liked to dance with him."

She needed to keep Vermont with her, needed to use him as further cover. *Please go away.*

"Valerie? Is that you?" A hand grabbed her shoulder from behind, and a chill crept up her spine.

She turned to the man's voice with a cold and unfeeling face, forcing her to hide her complete and utter panic.

"Excuse me?" Valerie met the eyes of the person she knew without a shred of doubt and asked, "Who are you?"

"I know it's you," Eldaeric whispered, coming closer to keep his voice low. "Helvette sent me to find you and Kaeylyn."

Hearing her mother's name, Helvette, made anxiety thicken in her throat. There was nothing she could do to settle her racing heart, not when she was so close to being discovered because of his stupidity.

"I'm Lady Cecily of house Dyèrie," she said before she gave a curtsey. "It's a pleasure to meet you."

He grabbed her wrist and pulled her closer while looking for a way out of the crowd. She eyed the people around them, thankful no one appeared to notice, not with Vermont and the pillar mostly blocking their view.

She'd known this man for most of her life. She knew him well enough to know he wouldn't leave her be.

"Don't play games with me," Eldaeric bit. His eyes found the balcony attached to the ballroom, one that would take them outside into the privacy of night. "Come with me."

"Unhand me," she hissed quietly, wringing her wrist to free herself, but to no avail. "Please."

He would give her away if they were caught speaking! *I need to escape. I need a way out of the ballroom.* Vermont came to her side and placed himself between her and Eldaeric, who refused to release her.

"Cecily, are you okay?" Vermont narrowed his eyes at Eldaeric, who looked at Valerie with utter confusion. "Unhand her. Immediately."

Then, before her very eyes, she watched an arm thread around his throat from behind. Eldaeric immediately let go of her to fight against that arm. It was only when he was being dragged to the centre of the ballroom, forcing dancers out of the way, did she know who had him.

Geryon was holding him in a headlock while he had the point of his sword pressed against his spine. The pointed tip of steel forced his back to arch in a submissive position.

A swift hush fell over the crowd as they watched Geryon and Eldaeric struggle against each other. Music abruptly stopped, and gasps rang out as people almost tripped over each other, scattering to get away.

Valerie thought Geryon interfered because he'd been grabbing her with the intention of dragging her somewhere. She thought it was to protect her.

She knew she was wrong by the words that came out of his mouth.

"Come now, Witch, give us a show," Geryon grinned, humour lighting his eyes. He spoke loudly, making sure everyone could hear his accusation.

Valerie was just close enough to hear Eldaeric's soft words. He was still struggling against the arm, but he wasn't panicked as he tried to look over his shoulder at Geryon.

"How did you know?"

Geryon buried his head next to his ear and whispered something. No one was able to hear what he said. It didn't matter. Whatever it was made Eldaeric's eyes widen in fear. *He plans to fight him.*

Valerie wanted to step forward to stop them, but she knew she couldn't. Then Eldaeric looked to Valerie to mouth just one single word. *'Run.'*

He dropped his arms so he could tighten his hands near his torso and clenched his eyes tight as he spoke a single chant. Two fireballs exploded from his tension-filled fingers.

Whatever he planned to do was swiftly ended by Geryon slamming that sword through him.

He'd been waiting for him to reveal his magic, to prove to all he was a Witch before Geryon killed him. Eldaeric hadn't stood a chance, not with the way he'd been grabbed.

It had been a perfect trap, one that was obviously planned – there had been no taunting. *This isn't the first instance.*

Geryon twisted his sword in Eldaeric's chest as the man fell to his knees, making sure he would feel an extra bite of pain before he died. He cleanly sliced his blade back, and blood squirted from his torso before dribbling down the front of his tattered brown clothes.

Before Eldaeric could attempt a final retaliation, Geryon cut into his neck with a quick sideway slice of his sword, embedding it halfway and making sure he was truly dead.

There was a ringing sound of gasps and chatter around the ballroom. People either looked horrified and shocked or pleased by watching the kill.

Valerie couldn't stop her eyes from widening at what she just witnessed. She just watched someone she had known since she was a child, her friend, murdered right before her eyes.

*How did he know Eldaeric was a Witch?* How could Geryon have known when he hadn't initially used his magic? *How?!*

Geryon was satisfied with his kill, pleased with the Witch's blood that coated his body. She could see it in his grin as he stared down triumphantly at the corpse currently bleeding out.

A singular pair of hands began clapping from the end of the room. It came from King Bradwick, who stood from his throne with a radiating smile.

"And that's why, ladies and gentlemen," he laughed, continuing to clap for the performance of a swift kill, "Lord Geryon is my most prized guard and treasure."

*Could he be a Witch working for King Bradwick?* It wouldn't be uncommon. *Yet he killed Eldaeric without speaking to him, did not find out why he was here.*

She also thought she would have figured out if a Witch was so close to her. *My powers are locked away. I cannot perceive others' magic like I could before.* Still, she should have been able to recognise another of her kind.

She feared she knew the answer when Geryon's eyes found hers with a predatory deadliness. It was a look she'd never seen in a human before.

And she feared it... because it was directed at her.

Before Geryon had killed the Witch, he'd been watching the partygoers enjoy themselves while he stood guard.

The overwhelming amount of chatter mixed with the sound of music was enough to disorientate his sensitive hearing. He had to use a simple spell, a sound dampener. It softened the worst of the noise, otherwise he wouldn't have been able to cope, not with how alert his senses were. It put him at a disadvantage to hear conversations, but that wasn't what he needed right now.

No, Geryon needed his sight and impeccable sense of smell.

For someone who was mentally prepared to fight this eve but apprehensive of doing so, he was in an awfully good mood.

His elated mood had to do with Lady Cecily.

His observational gaze had caught sight of her when she first entered the room, and he'd nearly lost his breath.

*She looks like a wintry princess.* A beautiful maiden who belonged in the snow. If she had worn wings, he may have mistaken her for an angel.

Still, it wasn't the way she looked that put him in a grand mood.

It was the thick red ribbon that had been tied around her throat. It almost ran up the entire length of her slender neck that he was awfully fond of licking and kissing. It was bright and stark against the softness of the silver and white she wore.

She wore it for him.

*She asked me if I had a preferred colour.* Last night, after they were done being wonderfully intimate, he hadn't thought much on her question. To see it wrapped around her throat when it didn't match her outfit made his eyelids droop with heavy satisfaction.

Not even when Bradwick danced with her did he feel a shred of anger or jealousy, not when that brazen display of possession was staring the king in the face. Instead, he'd just pictured Cecily as a swan, merely gliding gracefully along the top of a lake – something he could watch all day and night with much pleasure.

His eyes were riveted to her every time she danced, and he let himself be enchanted when he should be focused on his surroundings.

However, the subtle breeze from outside pushed in fresh air. It also pushed the mingle of smells of all the people towards him, and a snarl overtook him when he scented it: the smell of a Witch. *There is only one.*

He filled his skull with magic, changing what his eyes saw so he could track the tendrils of magic to home in on that power.

Everything went darker, allowing him to see the waft of energy from anything that had a magical essence.

*Uck!* He cringed at a glaring bright light that pierced his eyes. He swiftly closed them. *Someone is using a glamour; one I don't have the power to see through.* Whoever cast the spell would have to be a strong Witch.

Like shining a bright light against a mirror, instead of his magic assisting him, it was reflected. It blinded him until the spell he used faded. He needed to use his sense of smell instead, since the changing of his sight failed him.

He left his place next to Bradwick to stalk it. He kept his back to the wall, trying to remain out of sight from most as he attempted to figure out who and where it was coming from. It eventually led him to the back of a man. He wasn't sure if he was correct until he heard the conversation the Witch was having with another.

He only heard the end of it, since his hearing had been dampened.

"Come with me," the Witch demanded, and that's when Geryon noticed Cecily had been grabbed. *She's in danger.* His chest tightened in worry and anger.

"Unhand me." Even now, her composed face was exactly as it always was, not understanding what kind of danger she was in. "Please."

Before things could escalate and she was at serious risk, Geryon grabbed the man.

He would have preferred to drag him to the shadows, but he decided against it because of her. He wouldn't risk her. She was the one person here the Witch had found who Geryon didn't want harmed – besides Bradwick.

He didn't care about the rest of the humans; they could be unfortunate collateral.

"How did you know?" the Witch asked when Geryon had his sword poised at his back.

He brought his mouth closer to his ear so he could whisper. "Because you have found yourself on a Dragon's hunting grounds."

Then, once this Witch proved what he was to all, Geryon made sure his death was swift so he couldn't unleash his magic against the humans. He didn't risk drawing it out, in case the Witch got free of him. If he'd managed to somehow overcome him with his witchcraft, he would have killed many.

After Bradwick complimented him, people began to clap like it had been nothing but a theatrical show. The festivities would continue, and it would be nothing more than an interesting conversation. No one cared for the lives of Witches.

Eventually, soldiers would come to remove the body while servants would clean the blood.

His eyes fell on Cecily, concerned for her wellbeing, as well as why this Witch wanted her.

Her mask had slipped enough that he could see she was shocked. Shocked enough that she didn't react when he grabbed her wrist and pulled her along until they were in a hallway.

He could justify his actions easily.

"What do you want?" Her voice was higher pitched than usual.

"Are you alright?" He released her wrist and took a step back, so they didn't appear so informal. Yet, he wanted nothing more than to reach forward and cup her face gently, to stroke her cheek with his thumb soothingly. "What did he want?"

"He–" she stumbled, averting her gaze before it quickly darted back to him. "He knew I was here for King Bradwick. I think he wanted to use me against him."

Geryon's nose crinkled, an uncontrolled growl slipping from him that made her flinch. Sometimes, he forgot he couldn't make such noises in front of humans.

Since they were in a relatively quiet space, only a handful of people loitering the hallway, he could hear her heart rate spiking.

"Are you alright?" he asked again, beginning to frown

when he saw her hands were shaking wildly. "Cecily?"

Suddenly, he scented a reek of fear. It was growing by the second as she stood there with him. *Is she frightened of me?* He stepped forward to grab her gently, unable to resist doing so, but she quickly shuffled back, her heart beginning to pound. The scent worsened.

Her eyes darted down his body, at the blood covering him. He winced when he realised it was no image for a noble lady like herself to see.

"How did you know he was a Witch?"

His head reared back. That was a strange question to ask him.

He cooled his expression. "I have keen senses. I have come across them before and have learned to spot them."

"But you were so far away." Her breaths came out strangled. "You killed him so quickly."

He hadn't expected this reaction from her.

"I thought you were quite comfortable with death and blood, since you said you've been to the prison cells at your family estate," he pointed out, his confusion growing. "You know I'm a guard. This is something I have been trained to do."

Then... her mask fell completely.

Her eyes were stark, her brows furrowed deeply. She wasn't just simply afraid; no, she was completely petrified. She stepped further back until her back knocked against the wall.

*I don't understand.* He stepped forward, lowering his voice since no one was walking past at this moment. He didn't dare touch her with his blood-coated hands.

"I was hoping to come to you this evening."

He wanted to spend time with her while she was dressed like this, court her like he could extend the ball in her rooms. He wanted to dance with her while she looked like a magical snowy princess, wearing a bright red ribbon around her throat for him.

Geryon wanted to woo her before he played with her.

"No," she said without hesitation, her eyes widening further. "Don't come to me."

Then she fled, and she didn't return to the ballroom.

*I should not have asked her.* He could have snuck into her rooms after she calmed down. He was fresh from a kill; he was sure he was frightening. *Now I cannot. She has told me no.*

Geryon was deeply disappointed as he made his way back inside the ballroom to take his place next to Bradwick. He couldn't leave him unprotected in case more of their vile kind appeared.

"What did you want with her?" Bradwick asked, eyeing him cautiously.

"I noticed the Witch grabbed her," he answered, leaning his head down to hush their conversation. "Wanted to know why."

"Oh." Bradwick's suspicious eye fell as he frowned. "Well?"

"She thinks he wanted to use her against us as a shield or a bargaining chip."

He raised his brow at Geryon. "Would it have worked?"

"No." It was the truth.

Even if Cecily had been in direct danger and he didn't want to risk her, she was a human. Her life was fleeting in comparison to his own, and he wouldn't allow a Witch to kill Bradwick or roam free.

Bradwick clenched his fist in anger. "Although one of my ladies was put at risk, you have proven to me I should not have been worried, nor doubted you."

Geryon folded his arms with a nod of his head. Usually, he would grin at the king admitting to his idiocy. Instead, his sour mood refused to lift.

He wasn't happy that she was targeted. *I wished to be with Cecily this eve.*

Uncaring of who saw her, Valerie fled.

*He killed Eldaeric.* She continued to run, her heart pounding so heavily, she worried it would give out.

*No matter where I went in the palace, he was able to find me.* He could sense where she was, track her, *smell* where she had gone.

Her breaths were short as she climbed the stairs to her apartment, almost stumbling up them. Valerie could barely breathe, her knees wobbling like they would buckle at any moment.

*He told me he could tell when I was aroused.* He'd told her it was because he could see it in her flushed chest. He'd even blatantly told her she desired him.

He wasn't from these lands. He was a soldier from an unknown place, with unknown origins.

*He could smell Baron Daerk on me.*

Once she made it to her rooms and closed the door behind her, she fell to her knees. Her blood ran cold. Her hands were trembling when she placed them both against her mouth.

Valerie finally understood.

She understood why he could find her, could sense things others couldn't. *He's a Dragon.*

Barely muffled by her hands, a loud sob fell from her lips. The man she had been kissing, had been touching, had spent a wonderful night being intimate with, was actually a creature.

*One that obviously wants my kind dead.* She had been

bedding her worst fears. *I'm on his hunting grounds.* Now that she had seen him kill, and he had known what Eldaeric was when a mere human couldn't have, she knew.

That predatory look he always wore was because he was the apex creature of this world. He told her to think of him on par with King Bradwick, that his status was the same.

Technically, he was above them all. *He could rip this palace apart with claw and fire.*

*I need to escape before he figures out what I am.* She couldn't do that without finding her sister.

Valerie's eyes widened, her heart spasming. *If I find her, he will hunt for me.* He would think she tricked him, had tried to use him. *He will seek revenge.*

*I had someone inside me who would have killed me if they knew I was a Witch.* Would still try to kill her if he found out. *Geryon does not know.* She wouldn't be alive if he did.

The spell she had cast on Vermont would have blinded him if he tried to sense it, unless his magic was stronger than hers. The real Cecily's blood was hiding her scent, her magic, everything that made her a Witch.

Now that she was aware of what he was, she understood what she had to do. *I must control myself; he will be able to scent my fear.* He would know something was amiss with her.

She'd acted strangely before, but she could pretend it was because of what she witnessed.

Her eyes fell upon the room. *I'm out of time.*

She realised she'd been out of time since he set his dangerous sights on her. Valerie spent the night reining in her fears, her apprehension, her worry.

*I know what I must do.*

23

Geryon spent the day by Bradwick's side while he remained with the court.

This was his final day with the ladies before he had to decide which one he would offer his hand in marriage to. At the end of tomorrow, he would have to tell them of his decision, and those he hadn't selected would leave.

Bradwick was still uncertain. He would spend time in court with the ladies before taking each one on a stroll like he had been for most of their stay.

It meant Geryon could be near Lady Cecily, and he'd been watching her.

When she arrived with Lady Victoria, she appeared worn, like she hadn't slept much, but she hadn't been out of sorts like when he last saw her. A heaviness had been weighing in his chest throughout the night. He hadn't liked her fear of him.

Geryon felt terrible about frightening her.

Like she often did, she surprised him. Rather than the averted gaze he expected, she nodded her head in greeting with a small smile from a distance.

Because they were not able to speak, she showed him her apprehension of him was short-lived. *She still wears the ribbon.* She hadn't removed it, and that heaviness in his chest lifted. He'd grinned, looking away from her so that others wouldn't know she was the cause.

He'd received further explanation when he followed her and Bradwick strolling.

"You did not return to the ball last night," Bradwick said with a look of concern.

"My apologies, your Highness. I was caught off-guard by witnessing such a sight." She gave him a reassuring pat on the arm. "I have never seen anyone be killed before."

*She had wanted to see the dungeon, so I thought she was used to seeing things not for the faint of heart.*

"Do you wish for me to send Geryon away?" They looked behind them at him.

She gave a shake of her head when they turned their gazes forward once more. "No, he's fine. I'm actually rather thankful for him; he protected me."

His chest swelled proudly. *Does she think I did it to save her?* Was that why she was wearing the red ribbon again?

Bradwick nodded while he brought his hand up to cup his chin. "Yes, he did mention to me he questioned you because he saw you were grabbed."

"I was really frazzled at the time. I think I may have given him a fright with my behaviour." There was a forced laugh, but he knew Cecily often did that with Bradwick. "Once I had time to process, I felt rather ashamed of my behaviour."

"A woman's heart can be quite fragile." This time, he patted her arm. "I have had to comfort the other ladies as well."

"I thought as much," she sighed, turning her gaze to look at the grounds of the palace. "I don't know if you are aware, your Highness, but I adore Lady Wyetta. I wanted to visit her chambers once I calmed."

"Why did you not then? She has told me you two are fast friends. I'm sure she would have appreciated your comfort."

She shook her head. "I cannot just invite myself to someone else's chambers. It's not respectful."

Bradwick gave a frown, not understanding, since he often did what he pleased. "How so?"

"I have been taught I must be invited to such places. It's why sometimes I don't attend the court functions when I feel I have not been personally invited. They hold teas, but I'm unsure if they are open to all, in the same way we feast only with those at night who have been invited to dinner."

There was a long silence while Bradwick thought hard on this. "I did not know you felt this way."

"Of course. I spent an evening with Savannah when she invited me to her suite to play games and speak of some feminine things, but I would not have done so if she had not invited me." She looked down to watch their feet. "My mother taught me all the ways of being a proper lady. I'm also private and have been taught to be discreet with my actions. It's why some people are often confused by me. I don't like the gossip here. I would prefer to keep my actions hidden." She gave a smile. "Except for Lady Victoria. She really is a lovely lady-in-waiting. I trust her implicitly."

"It appears your mother has taught you too well," Bradwick grumbled with a shake of his head. "I'm relieved you are feeling much better after the night's events."

"It was exciting. I enjoyed the ball until the Witch appeared." She turned her head to Bradwick. "I have never seen one before. They look just like us."

He nodded as he spoke. "I have seen a handful. They do try to take over my palace, which is one of the reasons I have hired Geryon as my guard." Geryon crinkled his nose, not liking the risky subject. He was once again being too open and honest about it, when Geryon was trying to parade around as a human. "He has also killed human assassins. He has an eye for those who wish to commit evil against me."

"You are lucky to have such a strong and cunning guard, then. Otherwise, I fear I would not be strolling with you this day."

Geryon grinned, liking her openly complimenting him.

Bradwick laughed. "You are quite right." Then the king turned to face him. "You must be enjoying this conversation, Geryon."

"Enormously," he chuckled back. "Please, continue. I do so like having my ego stroked."

"No, this is supposed to be about me." Bradwick gave a pout.

Geryon rolled his eyes at him for it. *Selfish man.*

Their stroll didn't last much longer, and they returned to the court, where Bradwick eventually took another for a walk. Geryon stayed behind, since it was Charlotte he'd taken this time, and Bradwick was aware he couldn't stand their conversations. He'd been hoping to get a chance to corner Cecily, but she remained with the court.

"It's sad we will have to separate tomorrow," Wyetta said while Geryon listened in from a small distance away. "Someone will be chosen to stay to be courted further, and the rest of us will have to leave. As much as I'm hoping it will be me, I have grown attached to you."

"Yes, there are people I will miss here," Cecily answered with her calm composure, not actually showing such care. "You and Lady Victoria have been kind to me. I have enjoyed my time here."

*She may leave tomorrow eve,* Geryon thought, not realising her possible departure was so close. She may also be selected. *No. I will convince Bradwick otherwise.*

Geryon had finally decided what he wanted.

After the night they'd shared, Geryon knew he wanted to keep this female while he was pretending to be human in this palace. He would never reveal what he was to her, but he could give her twenty years, maybe more, if he was able to push his luck with lies about his lack of ageing.

At some point before she left, Geryon needed to speak with her. He would ask her if she would allow him to court her, visit her at her family's manor.

*She may reject me.* If she told him 'no,' he would let it die and leave her be. He hoped she didn't.

It bothered him she didn't separate from the court whatsoever, as though she wanted to spend time with them before they were forced to say goodbye.

*Humans are strange. If they wish to see each other, can they not visit one another?* He hadn't expected this sombre display from them. *It's because they are females.* Not only did he not feel like a human, he was also a male. *I'm the last thing that would be able to understand the oddness of human women.*

He noticed when Bradwick returned right before the last dinner they would all share together, he pulled Lady Victoria to the side to speak privately with her. They were done talking by the time he managed to approach, and their hushed conversation had been drowned out by the loudness of the court.

He'd been unable to hear, but if it was important, Bradwick would tell him of it. Otherwise, Geryon didn't care.

"Quickly, Lady Cecily," Victoria chirped as she pulled Valerie along to her living arrangements. "There is something

I must tell you."

Victoria was giggling from a little too much wine, but she was quite charming when intoxicated.

Valerie had a feeling she knew what it was, since she had planted the seed earlier in the day. If the king didn't take her planted thought, she had another plan up her sleeve – one that would cause a fuss with the creature she'd been tip toeing around this day.

Geryon had been like a lurking watch dog around her. Valerie had done everything possible to avoid him without being suspicious.

*I think I succeeded.* She touched at her throat. *Wearing the ribbon helped.* She saw him smile at her, delighted in the fact she had chosen to wear it.

Instead of wearing it as a show of affection, an unspoken secret between them, she had used it to collar him. He didn't lash out in untempered anger, didn't pull her into any rooms to speak with her.

Now, she just needed to survive this evening without seeing him.

Once they finally made it to her rooms, Victoria quickly shut the door and squealed while running on the spot.

"Lady Cecily!" The high-pitched tone that came from her was ear piercing, and Valerie stifled her wince. Victoria clapped her hands like a giddy child. "King Bradwick has demanded your presence in his chambers this eve! He told me to invite you when you were in the privacy of your rooms, and that I'm not permitted to share this news with anyone."

*Good, my plan succeeded.* She felt no joy in hearing the words, but she tried her hardest to appear pleasantly surprised.

"Oh my! That's shocking news."

"You know what this means, my lady?" Victoria was embarrassed for Valerie, since she started fanning her blushing red cheeks. "He will want to spend the night with you in his bed."

Valerie knew Bradwick had already retired to his apartment. *He's expecting me.*

Her only other option would have been to sneak to his chambers this night to catch him off-guard. *If Geryon caught me doing this, I don't know how things would work out for me.* That had been the next plan.

"Then I must freshen up and leave presently."

Victoria helped wipe her body with a wet cloth and made sure she smelt pleasant. Then, Valerie made the woman leave her chambers and wait in the parlour room so she could collect the items she needed to take with her. *I don't know what I will do if I fail.*

She clutched the small vial she had in her hand, something she'd been carrying with her amongst Cecily's chests in a hidden pocket. Valerie had stored various kinds of potions she might need in preparation for coming here.

*There is a possibility I will die this night.* Valerie narrowed her gaze into one of determination. *I will do whatever it takes to save Kaeylyn, even if it costs me my life.*

Valerie spoke in hushed whispers to a guard before she and Victoria began to walk together through the palace. They stopped at the second level.

"Before you go, I wish to thank you for everything you have done for me," Valerie said genuinely. "You have been a guardian angel for me in a place I did not truly understand. I know I will never be able to repay you for your kindness. You are truly a wonderful woman, Victoria."

With a blush, she flapped her hand dismissively.

"You don't need to thank me. I have been more than happy to assist you. Like I once mentioned, others have not been so kind to me." Then, she made a shooing motion, as if to usher her away. "Now go, he's waiting. We will speak of such heavy words tomorrow."

Valerie watched her walk down the hallway on the second level, waiting until she was out of sight before she began to climb the stairs. *I feel the same apprehension I felt the first night I arrived.*

Valerie swallowed a chunk of fear when the person she was desperate to avoid came around the corner. The stairs at this high of a climb began to turn around to the other side of the palace, compensating in space to fit every step.

With a skill she'd been taught by her mother in the same way she had been taught how to wield a sword, Valerie erased her fear.

With a deep breath, she calmed her suddenly spasming lungs. Within a second, she quietened her stuttering heartbeat to a tranquil calm. Clenching every muscle in her body all at once, the tension that filled them was released as she relaxed.

With her posture calm, her face composed, she met Geryon's gaze directly. *He must have come from visiting Bradwick.* She wondered if he knew.

He didn't seem upset or angry, but he did frown when he saw her.

"Cecily?" Geryon's eyes fell over her, trailing down her body. He stepped down the stairs while she climbed them. "What are you doing, walking the palace at this hour?"

She walked past him when she spoke. "I have been invited to the king's bedchamber."

His feet immediately froze, and he grabbed her wrist gently to stop her from walking. She allowed him to halt her and turned to face him.

"What?" His eyes widened, appalled by the idea.

Now that she knew what he was, she couldn't believe she hadn't seen it before.

Those metallic eyes weren't human, and she'd been too busy being enchanted by them rather than observing them for what they were. His hair was black, but blue haloed it – she knew it must be how his scales appeared when he was in his Dragon form.

Valerie had never met a Dragon before, but she'd read about them, had been taught about them from the moment she was born. Every Witch was told about the origins of where they came from.

They were meant to be beautiful but deadly creatures. As a Witch, to meet one meant death was certain and close.

"Bradwick called you to his bed?" She could hear the frown in his voice, could see it in his face. He climbed a step to be closer when she pulled her arm free from his grasp. "And you are freely going?"

"I have been called by the king, Lord Geryon. No matter the insinuation behind the request, I must go to him."

She expected anger – that was not what she received. Instead, he looked deeply troubled.

His eyes drifted around them, making sure they were alone before he grabbed a pleat of her dress. He pulled it lightly. "If you take Bradwick, I will no longer seek you, Cecily. You must understand this."

Valerie had been worried about what she would do if she came across Geryon. She realised a situation had presented itself, one that could work in her favour. *I must remove him from the picture.*

She let her fingertips trail over his knuckles tenderly as she gave him a smile – one that was genuine simply because she'd figured out a way to potentially escape safely.

"I never said I planned to spend the night in his bed," she told him. When his frowned deepened, she cupped her hand over his. "It's unfortunate, but I will have to inform him that the reason I have not come to his chambers while the other ladies have is because I have my blood."

"But you don't have your–" Geryon grinned. "Once again, you are rather clever."

Valerie stepped down a step to be closer, knowing no one would be able to see them behind the curve. She caught the surprise on his face when she pressed against him.

"I don't plan to stay in his chambers, but perhaps I will not be spending the night alone in my own." She looked around like she wanted to appear mischievous. "I have already sent Lady Victoria to her own suite. I will attempt to get myself out of this, Lord Geryon, but you should know not all men are as considerate as you. If you wait for me in my chambers and I have not returned to them in an hour, you are welcome to hate me until your heart is content, but know this is not what I wanted."

He gave her a crinkle of his nose, even a dissatisfied huff, but he nodded like he understood. *I have given myself an hour of freedom within the palace.*

Valerie had an hour to find where her sister was and then flee.

She turned away and climbed the stairs. She didn't look back; she didn't think she could bear to.

*I don't wish to hurt him.* That piece of her heart she'd given him was still lost, no matter what he was. Valerie may fear him now, but she didn't hate him.

When she made it to Bradwick's chamber door, she knocked on it softly. She wondered if he purposely had no guard posted.

"Enter," he commanded, and she opened the door to let herself in. "Lady Cecily," he grinned, laying against his bed like he'd been waiting for her.

"Your Highness." She bowed her head in greeting. "You asked for me?"

"I was hoping I could convince you to spend the evening with me, since you are the only one who has yet to do so." He wanted to try her on before he decided which woman he would pick. The idea made her internally cringe.

Valerie approached, and he sat on the edge of the bed, preparing to stand. *I do this for my sister. I do this for Kaeylyn.*

She pushed on his shoulders to force him to lie back and crawled on top of him. She brought her lips over his to kiss him deeply. There was a grunt of surprise before he lifted his hand to press it into the back of her head to bring them closer. He responded, kissing her back with warmth and passion that did nothing to light her body.

Valerie closed her eyes as she began to unbutton his coat, allowing him to lick the inside of her mouth and trying to match him as best as she could. He lifted his arms to help her remove it, their mouths only separating for a moment.

Bradwick pulled on the ties of her dress to loosen it, and she immediately felt his palm against her breast through her shift. She tried not to cringe when he pressed his hips against hers, forcing her to feel his hardening shaft. She ground into it, causing a small groan to fall from his lips.

Slowly, sensually, she began to lift his tunic.

Their mouths separated when she pulled it over his head, revealing his lean but slightly muscled torso. She pushed it up his biceps slowly as she leaned back in to kiss his welcoming mouth.

Then, she let it go so she could run her hands over the material to grab his wrists, like she was intending to grab his hands to lovingly hold them.

With both his arms above his head, she broke from the kiss to quickly reach up and tie his wrists together with the sleeves of his own tunic.

He tugged on them, but she'd already knotted them before he noticed what was happening. "What is the meaning of this?"

Bradwick tried to sit up as he attempted to free himself, but to no avail. In the time it took him to sit up with her still straddling his waist, Valerie unsheathed her dagger from the layers of her dress. She pointed the tip of it against his jugular, and his head turned up to avoid the sharpness cutting into him.

Anger was clear in his features. "What the fuck do you think you are doing, Lady Cecily?"

*Ego me dimittere vinculum Ceciliae Dyèrie.* Valerie felt a swirl of magic release as she chanted the words that would no longer tie her to the real Cecily.

Valerie released her witchcraft.

*Spiritus ignis.* A ball of fire came to life above the palm of her hand, and it felt wonderful to finally have her magic coursing freely again.

She briefly closed her eyes in relief, stifling the urge to moan in bliss.

When she opened them again to stare down at Bradwick, his eyes were wide at her show of magic. She pressed the tip of her dagger more firmly against his throat, forcing him to lie back down.

"Move, and I will make sure you die this very night," she threatened, keeping her flame lit and the dagger at his neck.

His eyes flittered to the door, expecting to be saved at any moment. "You are a Witch?"

She rolled her eyes. *Obviously.* She let the formality with which she'd been acting fall away.

"It's unfortunate for Lady Cecily Dyèrie that she happened across me on her travels to the palace. It was not hard to take over the minds of their entire travelling party with my magic." She turned the fireball in her palm, showing him the depth of her control. "My poor Duke Vermont is nothing but a soldier I entranced to think he is my uncle. The man will be confused when I release him from my spell."

"Who are you really, then?" He squinted his eyes into a glare, and she could see the hate in them, the spite.

"Where is the witchling?" she asked instead. When he opened his mouth to speak, she knew the words would be a lie. She pressed her blade in harder until a drop of blood welled on the tip. "I know you had her at some point. Where is she?"

He smirked cruelly. "You will not reach her."

Valerie's cold stare barely flickered during their entire conversation, but she did raise the blade of her dagger. She tapped the point against his cheek.

"You speak of the Dragon." His smug face fell. "Currently, I have him chasing his own tail. He will be quite upset when he discovers what has happened, I'm sure of it."

"How did you escape detection?"

"Easy. There is a spell that locks my witchcraft from being detected by Witches and Dragons. It makes me appear human to all senses. I was lucky I used it. I took Cecily's blood to mask my own." Valerie tickled the point of her blade over his face, bringing her flame closer to threaten him with it. "Now, tell me where the witchling has been taken."

He pursed his lips in silence.

"I have many options here. I could scar that handsome face of yours." She brought the flame closer until he winced from its heat and turned his face away. "I could pluck an eye." She tapped the dagger right below an orb.

Then, she lowered it down their bodies as she lifted herself. She tapped it dangerously low on his body. "I could make you a eunuch. Would be a shame if you could not sire heirs."

She brought that blade back up to press it against his bare chest, causing blood to well where his heart was. "Or I could just kill you. I have you bound, at my mercy, and your Dragon is not around to save you."

"She's in the dungeons," he bit with gritted teeth.

"Don't lie to me. I have searched this palace. I have been to the dungeons. If you lie to me and force me to return to your chambers, I will make sure you regret it."

"How do I know you don't plan to kill me either way?"

"Please don't make me hurt you. I actually don't want to."
She sighed, leaning back to give him space. "I have no desire
to kill you, King Bradwick. That's why I have not attacked
you until now. I was hoping to find her quietly and leave
before anyone noticed. As you can see, I have been most
unsuccessful and have needed to resort to more drastic
measures."

Some of his anger dissipated, but he still didn't look
trustful. "You will release me if I tell you?"

"No." She gave him a deadened laugh. "Someone else can
free you. I don't trust you will not send guards to apprehend
me before I get the chance to leave. You are a good king, and
I can see you are not a terrible man. Tell me where the child
is so I can take her. That's all I seek. No death. No blood. No
pain. I promise you this."

He seemed to think for long moments, eyeing the fireball
floating above her hand. She waved it, showing him her magic
in hopes of convincing him he couldn't fight her. Then she
brought it closer when he stared for too long.

"In Geryon's room, on the second floor to the right, there
is a secret door. It's to the left of his bed. The Witch child is
behind it."

Her eyes widened slightly, showing her surprise. *Of
course! It makes sense he would be the one keeping her.*

Her heart shrivelled inside her chest. *I could hate him for
this.*

"Thank you."

Valerie backed away from the bed before extinguishing her
fire. She quickly pulled a vial from the sleeve of her dress.
Bradwick stood from the bed, but before he could do anything,
she thumbed off the cork lid and threw the powdered contents
in his face.

Within a few seconds, he hit the ground like a limp sack of
potatoes, fast asleep. She sprinted around his room, finding

material to tie his legs together with. She hog-tied him by wrapping his ankles in the sleeve of another tunic, forcing his feet and wrists to touch behind his back and tying them together as well.

*He will not be able to escape that, even if he wakes from my sleeping powder.*

Valerie sprinted down the hallway on the second level of the palace. *I don't have much time.* It was lucky she'd been to Geryon's apartment before and remembered its location.

When she got to the door she knew to be his, she twisted the handle and pushed. Her body slammed against it. It was locked, and she looked up and down the hallway to make sure it was clear.

*Vis aeris,* she mentally chanted as she placed her hand over the lock. A powerful force of magic blasted from her palm, blowing the lock apart. The door swung open.

Worried someone would come to investigate the noise, she ran inside.

Valerie went to the empty wall to the left of his bed and ran her hands over it. She found the edge of the door, but she couldn't find a handle with which to open it. She beat it with the bottom of her fist in frustration and it clicked.

The door revealed a small, thin corridor that led to another door at the end. Once more, she had to use her magic to force it to unlock. She dug her fingers into the hole she created and pulled it open.

"Valerie!" Kaeylyn squealed when she saw her.

Her hands were bound together by metal shackles, her fingers interlocked by frayed rope so she couldn't weave her magic without harming her own hands. Wearing the white pyjamas she'd disappeared in, she looked like a ragged prisoner – although it was obvious she'd managed to bathe at some point. There was a chamber pot, but what surprised Valerie were the children's toys she could see littered around the room.

Paying little mind to them, knowing she couldn't delay their escape, Valerie sprinted forward. She expected to run into a ward that prevented a Witch from approaching, or Kaeylyn from escaping, but she didn't.

There wasn't even a shield.

With her dagger, she cut the rope to free Kaeylyn's fingers so she could use her hands. *I will have to sacrifice the blade.* It was the only way she could give her sister true freedom.

She chanted while holding it, a difficult spell that required a substantial amount of power. The blade of her dagger turned white, and she used it to cut through the metal links of the shackle. As she cut, the blade melted away. For Valerie to cut through steel, she had to sacrifice steel.

"Valerie!" Kaeylyn squealed again, this time jumping into her arms to hug her.

"Come, we don't have much time. We must go." She couldn't stop to feel triumphant or proud. She couldn't even allow herself to feel relief that her baby sister was still alive and with her, or that she didn't seem to be injured. They were in grave danger. "Don't make a sound."

Pulling Kaeylyn along with her, Valerie took her from Geryon's room and led her down the hallway. At any moment while they travelled the maze of the palace, she feared they would come face to face with the Dragon.

They didn't, even when they ran down the steps of the palace to the bottom level. *Not much further.* Just as they were about to hit the bottom level and turn the corner, Valerie ran into another person.

All of them went tumbling to the ground from the hard impact. She scrambled up, dragging Kaeylyn to her feet.

"Lady Cecily?" Wyetta groaned, rubbing her rear before she got to her own feet. "What are you doing up so late?" Then she blinked at the young girl Valerie was currently holding hands with. "And who is this?"

*I really like this woman.* Valerie had truly come to admire her.

She let go of her sister's hand to grab her shoulders. "Lady Wyetta, you wish to be queen, do you not? You have fallen for King Bradwick?"

Her dark brows furrowed. "Of course."

"Then tell them you tried to stop me. Tell them you thought I was suspicious."

"Wait, what is going–" Before she could finish, Valerie clenched her hand into a tight fist and slammed it into her cheek as hard as she could.

Wyetta fell to the ground with a cry, and Valerie got on top of her to straddle her waist. She wrapped her hands around her throat and began to squeeze. The betrayal in her eyes was obvious and immediate, Wyetta slamming her fists into Valerie's arms with desperation to get her off.

She kept her expressionless stare while she strangled the woman. *I befriended her; they will not trust her.* In using this woman to cover her tracks, by being so friendly with her, Wyetta may be seen as a traitor. *They may think she helped me.*

Valerie wanted to undo this wrong. She knew this was the only way to help Wyetta get what she wanted, since she hadn't thought about the consequences until she saw her while fleeing.

Wyetta eventually stopped moving, her eyes rolling into the back of her skull. Valerie held on until she was truly unconscious and then released her. After checking she still had a pulse, she nodded, then swiftly grabbed Kaeylyn's hand again.

Kaeylyn said nothing. She may not understand why Valerie had strangled Wyetta, but her sister was old enough to know Valerie needed to do whatever she could to save them.

Knowing it would be less suspicious if they walked, she kept their pace brisk.

Cool air rushed over them as they moved through the main front entrance and out into the palace grounds. Valerie headed to the right, in the direction of the stable path. There was a small tunnel that ran underneath the palace, used to ferry horses and carriages to the back.

In the shadow of that tunnel was a guard, holding onto the reins of a horse.

Before she'd left her chambers, she'd commanded he bring her a horse to this spot. She was relieved he had managed to meet them.

"Your horse, Lady Cecily." He handed her the reins as the horse neighed and bucked its head.

She took them after she placed Kaeylyn in the saddle. He even helped her, giving her a boost so she could climb onto the back of the large stallion behind her younger sister.

There was no point in thanking him. Once she released them from her spell when she was a safe distance away, her guards wouldn't remember anything of the last two weeks.

*We are almost free.* She'd managed to get this far without being caught. *But we are still not safe.*

No, Valerie knew they had a long distance to travel to return to their home, to the safety it would provide. She knew Geryon would come after them.

The darkness of night would cover them.

Kicking her heels in, she whipped the reins and forced the horse into a gallop. It whinnied as they headed straight for the palace exit and the gate that would let them off these fenced lands. She pulled on the reins when they got to the closed wooden bridge gate. The horse turned in a circle, neighing at being abruptly stopped.

"Who goes there?" a soldier yelled.

"Open the gate," she demanded.

She could see the crank to the right, but the second guard began to draw his sword instead of doing as she asked. "There has been no mention of anyone leaving the palace grounds."

A decision made in haste, Valerie launched two fireballs, each one slamming into their chests and knocking them back. They patted at their bodies to rid themselves of the flames while rolling in the dirt.

It gave Valerie enough time to focus her magic on the crank while she chanted. Her brow crinkled in concentration as she directed both her palms to it. She felt tension in her fingers, like something was pushing back against her. Struggling against it, she tried to close her hands into fists, even as pain radiated up her fingers, the back of her hands, up her forearms.

There was a grinding sound, the noise of something solid groaning under an immense amount of pressure.

Right before the guards were almost upon them, the crank broke apart. The gate bridge suddenly fell.

With a whooping call, she kicked her heels in and grabbed the reins again. The horse sprinted forward, shooting them through the open gate and knocking the guards away.

"Hold on tight, Kaeylyn!"

Valerie made sure her arm was around her sister's torso, the horse moving at an impossible speed.

When they were a small distance down the field path that

would eventually become forest, the sound of alarm bells rung behind them.

*Now, we run.*

The sound of a bell ringing broke Geryon from his impatient and worried thoughts. Laying on Cecily's bed, he sat forward. *Is that... the alarm bells?* Quickly getting to his feet, Geryon wasted no time leaving Cecily's apartment. *It could be another Witch.*

Pumping his arms while he sprinted, he descended the stairs before making his way to the front of the palace. A guard was running across the grounds, heading towards the main building. With a snarl, he took in the scent that had recently passed through. *It's definitely a Witch.* One he'd never smelt before.

However, his eyes widened when he picked up a second odour trail. *They have the witchling.*

"Lord Geryon, we have been attacked by a Witch." The guard pointed to the gates, huffing as he came to a stop in front of him. "It has left the castle grounds."

Soldiers were already preparing themselves for whatever demands he issued, their heavy boot steps echoing as they ran.

*How? How did one get inside the palace without me knowing?* Why was there only one track – a track of it leaving? *It must have entered a different way.*

Something didn't seem right.

*How did it know where the child was?* It hadn't needed to search the palace. It had known where to go.

There was no point in going to his chambers. He could smell the Witch child was with it, knew it was gone.

*Bradwick!* He was the only other person who knew Geryon had the child.

Turning from the guard, he sprinted towards Bradwick's chambers.

He passed a servant trying to wake Wyetta, unconscious against the ground. Seeing her made him worry as to what he might find in Bradwick's chambers. *He's most likely dead.* Geryon had to know, had to check before he went after the Witches.

*My hunting grounds have been infiltrated while I was awaiting a woman in her chambers!* The shame! Suddenly, he remembered who had been with the king. *Shit! Cecily was in danger!* No wonder she hadn't returned to him!

A feral growl broke from his throat, his heart clenching in fear for both of them. He bounded up the stairs two at a time. *Depending on their wounds, I might be able to save them.*

As he expected, more guards had come to this floor to protect the king, who was still in his chambers. They didn't enter, not having permission. They wouldn't know.

*Idiots! Damn these humans and their strange rules.* Their leader could be bleeding out, and they were doing nothing more than standing there. They tried to prevent him from entering, unsure of what was truly going on, considering everyone a threat.

"Move!" He shoved them out of the way. "King Bradwick may have been attacked!"

*What will I find?* The door slammed against the wall with a distinct thud as he swiftly opened it. *Are they alive?*

He expected to find the scent of blood. He didn't. At first, he couldn't see either one of the people he knew should be in this room. Sniffing the air, he walked forward, and that's when he saw him: Bradwick tied with his hands and legs behind his back like a pig on a spit.

Bradwick was alive, awake, and struggling. His mouth was

covered to stop him from calling out for help. Relief sailed through him.

"Where is Lady Cecily?" She wasn't in the room.

*She could have been taken.*

Pulling his great sword from its sheath, Geryon cut him free. Bradwick pulled out the cloth that had been shoved against his face. Although Geryon was relieved to find the human king alive, he still worried for the pretty woman he was growing attached to.

*She's still in danger.* He needed to be calm to think, but his fear for her was making his thoughts race. *I like this one. I don't want her to come to harm.*

"She is a Witch!" Bradwick yelled, narrowing his eyes at Geryon.

"Who?" He turned his head to look around the room.

He could smell the scents of three different people: Cecily, Bradwick, and the Witch, each of their smells different.

"She was not the real Cecily Dyèrie, Geryon." He stood and held one of his shoulders as he rotated it. "She told me she used a spell to mask her witchcraft and blood."

*No.* He couldn't believe Cecily wasn't who she said she was. Geryon didn't want to believe the woman he'd been fond of was actually something he hated more than anything in this world.

"You are mistaken. She smelt human. They could have used a false face to get close to you." They could use glamours to trick those around them. He'd been blinded by one during the ball. "She could be tied somewhere."

"She told me herself!" Bradwick pointed at him with a glare. "Where the hell were you? She said she had you chasing your own tail, whatever that means. She knew what you were, Geryon."

Geryon stumbled back in shock. *If it's true...* He didn't know what emotion was slowly rising its way up his chest, but it was a dangerous, treacherous feeling.

He could feel his nose crinkling.

"No wonder she was exploring the palace." Bradwick threw his hands up with exasperation. "She has been searching for the child this entire time. She even knew it was not in the dungeons."

*Because I took her there!* King Bradwick was right; he could see the signs now that he was aware. *Blasted!*

*She sent me to her room to get me out of the way.* His eyes widened while bile rose in the back of his throat. *I bedded a Witch!* The shudder that crawled through him was one of utter disgust. *I fell for her trap!*

He'd kissed it, touched it, had it beneath him. *I even fucking liked her!* Geryon wanted to rip his own skin off, knowing what he'd done, wishing nothing more than to shed her from him.

With a deep, guttural sound from his chest, he turned to Bradwick. "I will get that witchling back, and then I will make sure the Witch pays for what she has done."

The look he wore must have been horrifying because Bradwick's tanned complexion paled, and he stepped back in fright. *I will make her regret this.*

Geryon took himself from the room, storming towards the stairwell that would take him to the roof. The area was large and flat, perfect for what he was about to do.

He felt toyed with. *How did I not see it?* How did he not see through her magic cloaking her? Why didn't he scent she wasn't human?

Geryon was filled with anger towards her, filled with disappointment at himself. He was also filled with a loss he didn't understand. *What of her was real?* He'd felt tenderness for this woman because of what he'd been able to see of her.

Now, all he felt was disgust and hate.

When he finally made it to the roof of the palace, he stood

facing the only road leading away. It was the only way she could have gone, and he glared when he saw the path was empty – she'd already managed to get far.

His hands were shaking with fury, his fists closed so tightly, his knuckles were white. After a deep, drawing breath, he released a ring of fire from his lungs into the air. It floated, holding its shape for a moment.

Then, he chanted the singular word he needed for the spell. He couldn't remember the last time he'd done this.

"SHIFT!" He yelled the word, unable to keep the rage from his voice.

The ring of fire blew back over his body, encasing him in flame, disintegrating his clothes until he was naked. His body began to change as ancient magic swirled around him to create a new shape.

Where nails once were, claws grew. Where human teeth once sat, sharp rows of fangs cut through. A tail sprouted from the base of his spine as wings jutted from his back. As this happened, his body grew, scales pushing up through his skin. It had been too long since he'd shifted; it was both painful and euphoric at the same time.

When the flames disappeared, Geryon was a Dragon.

Without hesitation, he lifted off from the stone bricks beneath him, his large, weighty wings flapping dust and dirt from the roof. Even after so long, his body moved with ease, like it was only yesterday he'd been in this form.

Geryon immediately flew in the only direction they would have gone. *I will fucking burn you to ashes, Witch.*

*I hear wings constantly.* They flapped from a distance. Most would assume it was merely a bird flying directly overhead, but Valerie knew it wasn't that close, knew it wasn't a bird.

"Why did we have to get rid of the horse again?" Kaeylyn whined.

They were running through the forest on foot. She didn't tell her young sister what they were running from, only that they needed to flee.

The canopy of leaves would give them cover, and as long as they didn't use their witchcraft, they wouldn't be seen. Only if the Dragon used his special sight directly where they were would he be able to see them.

"Because a horse would have been easier to track," Valerie answered.

She'd set it free a day ago.

The clomping of hooves would have been easy to hear in comparison to their light footfalls. *He can smell a horse from the air.* Their human-shaped bodies were harder to follow.

Every few hundred metres, Valerie rubbed their skin with

pine needles, leaves, and bark to hide their scents. He would be tracking Kaeylyn more than anything.

*He did not take my scent directly, so he will not be able to remember it well.* She just had to make sure she kept him from smelling either of them.

She was praying the horse confused him. She sent it through the forest in the opposite direction they needed to run. While he chased after it, they had been heading the other way.

"I'm tired, Valerie." Kaeylyn's feet were dragging while she pulled her along.

*We are both tired.* Instead of complaining, she crouched down so her sister could climb onto her back. The child clung to her torso while she continued to run as best she could. She constantly had to slow to a walk so that she could catch her breath, then she would sprint again.

Sparingly, Valerie used her magic.

The only spell she used was one that would direct them home. With a small chant against the back of her hand, a white beam of light would show her which direction she needed to go.

She had to stop to do it, making sure a tree covered her from above. She would wait for it to fade, shaking her hand like that would help, before she took them forward again.

*It will be days before we are home.* Already, a day had passed, and she knew they had many more to go. They often stopped if she passed food, like fruit and nuts, knowing what was safe to eat and what wasn't.

Valerie wasn't scared. She was determined, using that to give her strength. Her heart was only rushed because of her exhaustion, her lungs tight because they fought for breath.

Valerie was adamant about getting Kaeylyn home, even if she had to carry the girl the entire way.

*I don't care what happens to me after.* Once they were there, the likelihood of her being found was low.

There were protections in place, spells that made it near impossible for them to be found. Her family and ancestors had lived in their large cottage in the woods, undisturbed for centuries, for good reason.

Until then, she knew they wouldn't be able to escape the Dragon for too long. He would search the skies, and eventually, he would pick up on them. It was only a matter of time, and Valerie was planning to beat it.

*Once we are on our lands, he will not find us.*

The sun was beginning to set on the second day, and she was thankful for it. With the cover of night, she would be able to rest for a few hours. *I'm exhausted.*

She put Kaeylyn down so they could walk side by side for a little while. *I cannot keep running, or I will burn out.* Pain radiated up her legs already, her feet aching, and the beautiful dress she wore was heavy and often tangled around her legs.

She wanted to stop constantly, wanted to rest, but she knew she couldn't. The previous night, she'd walked without rest so Kaeylyn could sleep against her back.

Valerie thought keeping them away from the road would stop them from coming across potential travellers.

She was wrong.

As they walked, she eventually heard a small camp just ahead of them, echoing through the trees. In the last light of the sun, she saw four men setting up camp for the night.

Valerie ducked down to hide and took them around the group of men, who looked like rogues or bandits.

"Keep quiet," she whispered. "Don't say anything."

Kaeylyn slapped a hand over her mouth with a nod and followed behind, keeping a hold of Valerie's hand. *I don't trust them.* Then again, she wouldn't have trusted anyone. *We must avoid being seen.*

The camp was to their left when Valerie heard a stick snapping under a heavy foot to the right. A man emerged from the tree line, buttoning his pants like he had just finished using nature as his bathroom.

He smiled when he caught sight of them. "Well, hello there. What are a couple of lambs doing out in the woods by themselves?"

*Shit!* Valerie cursed to herself.

"Just passing through," Valerie answered, stepping away to put space between them.

She didn't like the assessing eye he gave them, one of his brows raising. He was silent as he watched her continuing to walk around him while skulking low.

"That's unsafe. Why not travel with us? We have plenty of bedding and food."

The man brought his thumb and middle finger to his mouth, producing a loud, ear-piercing whistle from his lips. He gave them a dazzling smile afterwards. His face appeared kind, but there was a devious glint to his eye. The fact that he hadn't hesitated put Valerie on edge.

"No, we don't need any help. We know where we are going."

The appreciative gaze he slid down and then back up her body made her spine crawl. "Are you sure, little ladies? We can protect you, keep you safe."

Valerie held her sister's hand tighter. "We don't need your protection."

"I must insist." He stalked forward. "You don't understand how dangerous these woods can be for a woman like yourself."

"Come closer, and I promise you will regret it," Valerie threatened, ready to use her magic.

She would rather not fight him. Any large amount of magic she used could bring Geryon on top of them. *The smell of blood could attract him.*

"Will he now?" someone said from behind her, and Valerie

turned at the new voice.

The four men she'd seen at the camp were now behind her. *He called for them.*

"Young lady said she did not need our help when I so willingly offered," the first man said, shaking his head in disbelief with a laugh. He placed his hands on his hips, the glint in his eyes deepening.

"That's rather rude. Such kindness is not often found," another said.

They were beginning to circle them.

"They appear to be all alone." One of the newer men came forward to make the circle smaller. "A beautiful woman walking by herself without anyone to protect her... Seems she's asking for trouble."

"It's lonely out in the forest. We can promise you a warm bed to lie in."

"Leave us alone. We are merely travelling through." She pushed Kaeylyn against the back of her legs to protect her, and the girl clung to her dress.

"Come willingly" – the one that spoke this time was more direct, uninterested in the game the others were playing – "so the little one does not have to hear your screaming."

*Screaming?* Before she knew it, Kaeylyn was ripped from her. She turned around to face the one who grabbed her.

"Ah, ah," he laughed, raising the edge of a dagger to her sister's throat. "Be good, or the girl gets it."

"Give her back."

Her face didn't change. She refused to reveal her worry and fear to these men. *Sickening animals.*

"Looks like she's not afraid of us. She will be fun; I like the feisty ones."

Valerie lunged forwards just as two sets of hands grabbed her waist. She kicked her legs out when they started pulling her back, trying to force her to the ground.

"Let go of me!"

She opened her mouth to chant, but one of them shoved material against it. She struggled harder against their hold when one knelt in front of her and began pulling up her skirt.

With her hands free, she was still able to cast her magic if she mentally chanted the spells. Valerie's magic was strong, and she long ago developed the skill of wordless spells.

Thinking of the chant she needed, she directed one hand towards a shrub and felt her hand grab resistance. She shot it towards the man currently fumbling with the button of his pants.

Vines shot from the shrub to grab him by his neck. She pulled her arm, and it sent him flying. She directed her other hand towards a stone on the ground, using her magic to grab it. It went sailing through the air towards another, pelting him in the head and sending him hurtling to the ground.

This was light magic. She could manipulate things already present in her environment at the cost of her essence. Fire was the only one she didn't need to find; no Witch struggled to create it. Their Dragon ancestors could wield it from within and had passed that power down to them.

She wouldn't be able to kill with her magic, not unless she strangled them with vines, but they could easily be ripped if they grabbed at them. However, it was enough that she could throw stones and prevent people from grabbing her. If she had herbs and spices, she could have done more powerful spells.

"She's a Witch! Kill her!"

Valerie turned her head up to face the two men still holding her back and directed her hands towards them. Two fireballs burst against their faces, and they screamed as they fell back.

Once free, she ripped the material from her mouth so she could breathe properly.

"The young one must be as well." A bandit pointed at her sister from across the clearing.

Quickly turning towards one of the men whose faces she'd burned, she ripped his sword from his sheath. She no longer cared about spilling their blood or how much magical essence she left behind; Kaeylyn was in danger.

She spun around to face the one who had her sister, the sword poised and ready, only to watch him push her forward so he could shove his dagger into her midsection.

*Kaeylyn!* The horrible clench to her heart made it feel like the tendons holding it in place might rip free and tear it to shreds.

Her baby sister cupped her stab wound as blood pooled in her hands. Tears instantly pooled in her eyes and quickly fell.

*You bastard!* What kind of sick person injures an innocent child?

Valerie charged before he had the chance to notice she was coming for him. She slashed her stolen short sword across his neck, opening the front of his throat. Blood sprayed from his jugular as he died.

Then she turned to the other four men who had drawn their swords, preparing to fight her. *I will kill every one of you.* She would put all her sword training to use.

Being white Witches, their magic could rarely be used to kill. They could harm, but it was rare they came across a spell that could take a life. Because of this, her mother had taught each of her four daughters how to use a bow and arrow.

*But right now, I hold a sword.* Their mother had taught them how to wield one just as wonderfully as their witchcraft.

Valerie made quick work of them, not hesitating as she lashed out with swiftness. She was angry, filled with hate and a need for vengeance.

She used her magic to wrap vines around their ankles to distract one while she cut into the body of another. She stabbed one in the stomach before she pulled it back and slashed it across his torso. He gasped as he fell to his knees, trying to prevent his entrails from spilling out.

Valerie was fast and lethal. She used the fact that her body was slender, flexible, and lighter to fight the men, their slow bodies weighed down by their muscles and leather armour.

She cut the throat of another, then rammed her sword into the chest of a different one.

She barely had enough time to block with her blade when the final one tried to cut her with a downwards swing.

She scrunched her nose in disgust at the human. It was the only thing that showed through her indifferent façade. She did it purposely, wanting to show just how putrid she found him.

"I will kill you for this!" He motioned with his head towards the death and carnage she'd caused. "These were good men."

He swung downwards again. Valerie was forced to back away from him to compensate for the brute force behind his swings, her arms threatening to cave. She even had to use her other hand to hold the flat edge of the blade to help her block.

Stepping sideways to evade the last downwards swing, she sliced his leg across his thigh. It crumbled immediately, forcing him to one knee.

He lifted his head to find her, but it was too late; she was behind him. Valerie shoved the blade through the back of his throat until it came out the other side.

Not all of them were dead yet, but it wouldn't be long before they bled out. There was no point in ending them quicker, not when she had more important things to attend to.

Dropping her weapon, she ran over to Kaeylyn. She was sitting on the ground, staring down at her midsection.

The bandit had cut her side. Nowhere vital, but the wound was deep enough that if Valerie didn't act quickly, she'd bleed out.

Scooping Kaeylyn into her arms, Valerie searched for herbs, anything she could use to heal her.

Unfortunately, the darkness of night had crept in, and searching was near impossible. She even unleashed a ball of fire to swirl around her body to help her light the area. It did little to help.

Valerie's heart raced. She feared for her sister's life, feared being discovered by the Dragon. She'd never been this choked with it.

Seeing her free-flowing magic used to create light caused her anxiety to spike every time it passed her face. *I cannot see properly.* Kaeylyn was growing paler. She was going faint, her eyes drooping.

"Stay awake, Kae. Don't fall asleep," she told her, tapping her face gently while still trying to search.

Panic began to set in. *It cannot end like this.*

Valerie laid her gently down on the ground so she could search in their immediate vicinity. She moved shrubs with her hands while crouching low, trying to find something, anything, that would either heal her sister, or at least stem the bleeding so she could wait until daylight.

Dirt collected under her cracking nails as they broke from her digging at the ground and stones. It was after the third time she checked on her sister to make sure she was still conscious, only to find she no longer was, that Valerie's face began to twist. Her own heart was erratic, and her eyes crinkled with deep sorrow.

She couldn't find what she needed here. *She will not make it to morning.*

Without the help of herbs, Valerie couldn't heal Kaeylyn's wounds. Something had to be sacrificed for wound mending and regrowth, and white wielders used natural means to do it.

*I took her from the palace only to get her killed in this stupid forest.* She scooped her into her arms, clutching her tightly while she knelt next to her body. She embraced her, unsure of what else to do.

*I should not have hesitated in killing those men.* She'd been hoping to convince them to let them leave so Geryon wouldn't find them. *Instead, I gave them time to grab her.*

*What do I do?* Valerie began rocking her. How could she fix this? How could she save her when her magic couldn't? *I cannot call upon fairies; they will no longer listen to my call.* They would have been able to heal such a small yet deadly wound on a child.

Something began to tickle her face, an emotion that she hadn't felt this deeply for an exceptionally long time.

*I'm so sorry.* Something thick built in her throat, like she was suffocating.

Valerie helped raise Kaeylyn. She was dear to her, just like all her sisters were. They were the only people she cared for.

*I love her.* Valerie had taught her about witchcraft, had been a guiding light for her until she was taken. *The people I love are not allowed to betray me by leaving.*

Cold, unfeeling Valerie couldn't handle such a thing.

*Please...* Valerie's lungs were starting to squeeze every time she took a shaking breath. She could feel the crack in her mask, could feel her façade breaking. *Please! I don't want you to die.*

Staring down at the sweet girl's face, she knew the answer. She bit at her bottom lip tightly. It was dangerous. It also may not work. It would put them directly into the clutches of something terrifying. *I have no other choice.*

*I hope I don't regret this.* With a deep, haunting breath, holding Kaeylyn across her knees and against her chest, Valerie raised one of her hands to the night sky.

She sent forth a beam of white light.

*I will bargain my life for hers.*

Geryon flew across the skies, searching relentlessly, when a great beam of light shot towards the stars. It was far in the distance, shining out from the ground through the trees.

He narrowed his eyes, unsure of what it was. That did little to stop him from heading in that direction.

*Where is that sea snake?* The slippery woman he hadn't managed to find. *She's clever. She will have found other ways than magic to hide their tracks.*

Much could be done to throw off and obscure the senses of a Dragon.

A person rubbing themselves with strong scents could dilute their own, or jumping into water would wash it away temporarily. The fact he'd chased down their horse and found no rider meant she knew he'd follow it. Only another tracker would know these things, would be able to evade him with this aptitude of skill.

*Her kind usually does not have this type of knowledge.* Witches often just relied on their magic without learning anything beyond it.

She'd known human etiquette, so much so that she convinced him completely. Geryon didn't see through her disguise whatsoever. She hadn't been a fumbling, uneducated, unknowledgeable Witch, someone easy to catch playing pretend.

Instead, she'd known which fork to use when eating, how to hold herself, how to speak with those of noble blood. Now to discover she also had knowledge of tracking? The fact that she was able to evade him meant she knew of his kind, their strengths and weaknesses.

*She used a spell that hid herself from me.* She'd masked herself completely in the palace and must understand Dragons to do so.

It was only when Geryon came close to that beam of light did he know he'd come upon the Witches. *Finally, I found them.* He could smell them, even from the air, but he also smelt blood, a deep, air saturating amount of it.

He paused in his descent. *This appears too obvious. She knows I'm hunting them. She would not be so careless with her witchcraft.*

Geryon could see this for what it was: a trap.

Trap or not, they were stationary and unmoving. *She's one Witch.* The child wasn't much of a threat. *I have killed many of her kind.* One woman wasn't frightening.

Geryon thought about the spell that would morph his size smaller. He changed to the same size Rurik had been inside the palace when he heard him climbing the walls, the same size as a common house cat.

Flying between branches, he attached himself to a tree trunk so he could observe them carefully from above.

The Witch was kneeling, her body crossed over the torso of the child, who was lying on her back. Her arms were snug against the child's side, folded while her head rested against them.

*She's bowing like a frog.* That was strange.

Neither were moving, but he could smell her magic, could scent the essence of it, the power of it. He allowed his own to fill his skull so he could see the tendrils of her essence, what she was doing.

*She created a shield.* One to protect them.

Now that he could see them, he noticed she was covered in blood. The smell of human men was strong in the air, and it was the same blood coming from a direction not far from them. It was a confusing mix.

Either they were attacked, or she attacked them. *She managed to kill multiple people?* One woman had killed what he could smell was at least four or five men?

"I know you are there," she shouted. Her hands were clenched, and he frowned at the tremor in her voice, one he'd never heard from her before.

He wasn't surprised she knew he was there; she would have heard his large wings flapping when he first approached. He, however, was too small to reply, not with the distance between them.

"Please. I don't intend to attack you."

He eyed the way she was sitting. *She placed herself in a submissive position to show she does not intend harm.* It could be a ruse, though.

Geryon flew forward, once again chanting the spell that would change his size. It brought him to his full, terrifying height.

He landed in front of them in the clearing.

"You called me here." That light had been purposeful. She wanted him to see it, had wanted him to come to her. His snout crinkled as he lifted one of his scaly paws and bashed it against her shield. "You think this will save you from me?"

"I did not trust you would not try to kill me before I got the chance to speak with you."

"And what should we talk of?" He laughed darkly. "I will kill you for what you have done, and–"

"Save her." Her voice was small, soft, as she backed up slowly. She revealed the child to him, one he could see was injured. "I cannot find the items I need to do it myself."

He listened to the tiny flutter of the girl's heart, how weak and laboured her breaths were. It was hard to make out over the deafening roar of the Witch's heart next to her, but it was there all the same.

Once she backed away enough to reveal the child, she put herself back in the same submissive position. Her arms were folded against the ground, her forehead against them. Not once did she lift her head to face him.

This situation felt bizarre.

"Why would I do that?" he bit out. Him? Saving a Witch instead of killing it? "I would much rather it dead."

"Please, Geryon." He growled at her speaking his name. The fact a Witch knew it at all was an offense! "I know you can heal her with fire. There is little time left; she will not last much longer. If you heal her and let me take her home, I will do whatever you say."

"You don't have any power here. I can take you now, as my prisoner," he sneered.

"Please!" Her shout was a loud, desperate plea as she reached forward to clutch the child's dress with trembling hands. "Please save her. I'm begging you."

Then she finally lifted her face, and he reared his head back at what he saw.

This woman, who always wore a mask of indifference, was crying. It was ugly, deep red blotches marring her pale face, but it was how he knew her tears were real.

"She's my sister!" She moved to be over the child, cupping her cheek. Even he could see the love she held for it. "Everything I have done was to save my family."

Her shoulders shook. She heaved through shuddering, unhidden sobs. They were as loud as her tears were heavy. She even placed her cheek against the child's, nuzzling it as she rocked her back and forth.

Geryon hated her, yet he was uncomfortable seeing such intense emotions from her. *This is a face of grief, of deep sorrow.*

He should be relieved at seeing her pain, should be revelling in it. So why wasn't he? Why was he staring in shock rather than laughing at her misfortune? *It should please me the child is dying.* He didn't have to kill it, nor worry about giving it to Rurik to deal with.

"I don't care what happens to me," she said against the child's cheek. "I know I don't deserve such kindness from you. I know that as a Witch, I should not be asking a Dragon this, but I cannot live knowing she's gone." She placed her head in her hands and shook it against her palms. "I have done things I have never dreamed I would do, have hurt people who did not deserve it, touched evil magic when I was a white wielder before she was taken. To do all of this just to have her die is too much to bear."

Geryon knew this woman was a dark Witch by everything she had done to hide from him in the palace. *Yet, she does not have the lingering smell of one. She has not fully turned corrupt yet.* She still smelt pure.

"She's dying because I hesitated to kill those men. It's all my fault." Her voice broke an octave at the last word. She heavily sobbed over her sister currently dying in her arms.

He couldn't help silently staring at her. *She was a white Witch?* There was often a delay, a small period before it began to fester.

"Back away," he bit, lowering his head. He let out a snarl when he took a slow step forward.

"What?" she gasped in surprise.

He couldn't stand watching this female, who appeared a maiden of unfeeling grace, be torn down the way she was – not when he'd admired her for the way she had been, not when it was the reason he'd originally felt so tender for her.

He could be angry later, could get his revenge after this.

"I will not change form with you so close!"

Geryon no longer trusted her with his human body. He didn't trust her with something so squishy and weak.

An explosion of glittering essence sprayed out as she released her shield. The Witch backed away, putting a large amount of distance between them. Only when he felt like it was enough for him to quickly escape if she tried to attack did Geryon shift.

He blew a ring of fire above him before chanting the singular word he needed. "Shift."

After those flames came back to encase him, he emerged human, naked. He didn't care about his nudity; none of his kind did, since they were rarely seen clothed. Then, with a quiet warning growl, eyeing her cautiously, he approached the child. Unfortunately, he had to lift the skirt of her dress to see her wound, but he kept his eyes on only it.

*It was a small weapon, probably a thin dagger.* The girl was so young and small, it had caused severe damage.

He filled his index finger with magic and eventually blew fire on it. Then he shoved that flaming finger into her wound, cauterising it and changing it to one he could save.

Dragons couldn't heal deep cuts like this without the assistance of other items, in the same way Witches couldn't. However, they could heal wounds of fire, as it was in their essence. They lived it, breathed it, worshipped it.

Changing a stab this terrible into a deep burn meant that Geryon could then reverse the damage.

Once he felt he'd burned the child enough, he placed his hand over the wound and began a very lengthy chant. The spell he was doing required strong magic, and because he was weaker than most, he had to concentrate heavily on his task.

This was the moment the Witch could kill him. Right now, he could not hear, could not smell, could not see. He was hyper focused on saving this child.

The spell would reverse the burns by forcing the girl to relive every lick of flame that had created it. She was unconscious and unaware she was currently going through excruciating pain. Only when he could no longer feel warmth and magic radiating under his palm did he remove his hand. He opened his eyes to see she was healed, that not even a scar marred her side. He leaned forward so he could hear if her heart was still beating.

It was faint and weak, but she would live.

Geryon backed away so he could shift into his Dragon form, something he was more comfortable being in with the Witch nearby. Then, he dug his claws into the dirt around the child to carry her in his paw, holding onto his bargaining chip.

"You may approach." His scales puffed as she came into the clearing, and he licked his mouth in agitation. "I have saved her."

He still couldn't believe he saved one of her kind.

Geryon had to avert his gaze at the bright, unhidden smile she gave him. Her eyes watered with tears of relief, of joy. *She is an ugly crier; I hate it.* His eyes darted back cautiously to check on her, to wait for her to settle.

He'd told himself he wanted to peek beneath her expressionless façade, but it appeared as though he'd been averse to seeing anything negative. *I hated her anger when I saw it.*

"Thank you," she said once she finally calmed.

When he did finally bring his stare to her, her face wasn't as cold as he knew it to be. It appeared as though she was still fighting her emotions, trying to rein them in. She didn't ask for him to return her sister, likely knowing he wouldn't.

"I want to make a deal with you," she said when the silence bled between them for far too long.

He curled his upper lip back over his sharp, pointed fangs. "I will make no deal with you." He lifted the child. "And I currently have you at my mercy."

She lowered herself to sit on her heels while she spoke with him. It was casual, like she expected their conversation to be lengthy.

"I'm aware." Her mask began to slip back into place. "I still wish to offer a deal, in the hopes you will accept it."

Her cheeks were still stained with tears, and a pink hue showed they were swollen from crying, but that unfeeling coldness had returned to her eyes. He could hear her heart was beating regularly again.

It hadn't taken long, like her emotions were fleeting.

She didn't feel fear, even though he currently had her sister in his paw. He couldn't scent, taste, or see it. To witness her shift from a sobbing woman to this was daunting and oddly... confusing. *She must genuinely care for her sister.*

"No. I have no intention of giving you anything more than what I have done to save this child. You tricked me, played me like some fool!"

He watched her lift her chin dismissively. He narrowed his eyes at her for it.

"You tricked yourself."

*What?*

"How dare you say such an insolent thing to me!" He stamped his front paw down against the ground. "I did not deceive myself!"

"I did not ask for you to chase after me," she blatantly retorted, raising a brow, as if to punctuate her point. "I believe I tried to prevent you from doing so."

"And yet you gave in because you knew you could

manipulate me. Admit it."

"You were rather persuasive," she conceded, shaking her head. "You were more of a distraction, one I was constantly torn with."

He scrunched his face in confusion. "What do you mean?"

"I was trying to find my sister, and instead, I kept finding myself in your presence. I had no intention of trying to manipulate anyone except for King Bradwick. As his guard, I knew you would not reveal her whereabouts, so I did not try." She let her eyes trail over the length of his Dragon form. He was sure she wouldn't be able to see his true colouring or shaping in the dark. "The only night I truly tricked you was the night I went to Bradwick's chambers."

"You expect me to believe such lies?"

She shrugged. "I did not know you were a Dragon until the night of the ball, Geryon. After I watched you kill that Witch, I realised what you were. I knew then that I had to leave." She averted her gaze, looking down at her hands. "I believed you were human, just as you believed I was a human. The reality of the situation is: we tricked each other."

He thought back on that night. A quiet gasp of realisation left him. "You were afraid of me."

Only once she realised what he was did her fear set in. He'd never scented it from her before that moment.

"Yes, because I understood what you were. Once I did, I realised I should have seen the signs earlier." She brought her gaze back up. "You would always find me, like you knew where I was. You were following my scent."

*Could it be true?* Had she really not tried to trick him?

He thought she knew what he was from the beginning, that she had been using her wiles against him, since it was obvious he'd been intrigued. He thought her desire had been false, a way to manipulate him.

*Was it a lie?* Or had she actually felt lust for him? Did it matter? The fact she was a Witch still made him shudder with distaste.

But if this was the truth, then it dissipated some of his anger. *What would I have done to save my own kin?* Geryon would do anything to save his family, just as they would for him.

"Not your scent; someone else's." The woman in front of him didn't smell soft anymore. Her scent changed to one of a rich musk, one that suited her.

"Lady Cecily was very useful to me."

He snorted. "Who are you really?"

"My name is Valerie Faerydae, the Heartless – named by my mother." With her mask firmly in place once more, he could see why she would have such a title.

He frowned deeply, tilting his head in thought. "Faerydae? That name no longer exists." A snarl rumbled from his chest. "To wear this stolen name is a disgrace to its owner!"

She folded her hands in her lap as she gazed around the clearing. She looked like a delicate lady, just like in the palace, but it didn't suit the woman when she was covered in blood from head to toe.

"No, I speak the truth. Our ancestors are those of the first Dragon and human mating. My family and coven come from the first Witch, born over a thousand years ago." She didn't look at him while she spoke, too busy studying the trees like they were of more interest. "We have been hiding since Strolguil the Vast began to turn Witches corrupt. We have been continuing our line in secret so we may follow the old ways."

Finally, she looked back to him.

"I don't care if you believe me. You merely asked me who I am, and I'm telling you what I have been taught since I was a girl. I live with my mother and three sisters, including Kaeylyn, who you have in your hand. That's my coven."

His eyes narrowed. "If what you tell me is true, then your bloodline is special. Faerydae was a great Dragon, and although he started the unfortunate plague that is your kind, he's still respected."

"Faerydae did not start the plague. Strolguil's Dragon parent was careless and caused him to go astray. If we have remained white Witches for a thousand years, it means our incorruptibility comes from the strength of our blood and will of mind. If even now we remain pure, it cannot be his fault."

He couldn't help but sneer. "You say this, but you have used dark magic."

"Yes, and I don't regret it." When he snarled in her direction at her brazen words, she looked away, as though she were bored by his display of anger. It only angered him further! "Which is why I wish to make a deal with you. You could say it's more of a favour."

"Why should I help you?"

"You don't have to, but I can still fight you for my sister." His head reared back in a response. He gave a laugh, but she spoke before he could give an offensive retort. "Let me take my sister home. She does not deserve to be punished, and I believe she has suffered enough."

"What a ridiculous suggestion. I cannot free her."

"She does not know what you are. When I asked her about her time in the palace, she made no mention of a Dragon. It means she does not know of you. All she knew was that human soldiers took her. By Dragon law, I know I'm not permitted to be free, since I have seen your human face and know what lies beneath it. She, on the other hand, still has a chance. She's a white Witch. My entire family is, and they have been for centuries. Let her go home to her family."

*She knows the laws of Dragonkind.* That was puzzling; few Witches knew so much about them. There were only a handful of Dragon laws, and they were not to be broken unless one was prepared for punishment from the Elders.

Regardless, it was true; he never revealed to the child what he was. He also wasn't the one who captured her. She'd been brought to Bradwick as a gift by some of his foot soldiers, who wished to gain favour with the king.

Geryon ended up being the one to take her instead.

"And what do I get in return?"

"I will allow you to permanently bind my witchcraft so that I cannot wield it."

"There is no such magic," he scoffed, waving his claws dismissively at her.

"Yes, there is, and I can help you do it. There are only three ways to break the spell: the holder of the magical key must unlock it, the caster must undo it, or I must be cleansed of magic."

"And who would be the holder of this apparent key?"

"You would be."

Geryon frowned at her suggestion. "You want me to have this power over you? Why would you allow your magic to be sealed away?"

"I want to take my sister home. I know you will not let me do so if you think I have the power to escape you. In giving you this power, it will guarantee that I'm at your mercy." Then she looked him directly in the eyes as she said, "Once that's done, you may kill me."

*She does not care if she dies?* He eyed her curiously. *She would truly let herself be powerless just to take this child home?*

He would have to accompany them for the duration of their travel. He couldn't fly them there, since the child would see him.

"How am I to trust what you tell me is true?"

"You will not need to approach me, nor change your form, but I will need your help in doing the spell. You may hold onto my sister until its completion and see its evidence for yourself."

"And doing this as well as promising me your compliance is in exchange for me allowing your sister to return home? You must understand I find this peculiar."

"Peculiar or not, it's what I'm offering." She slowly rose to stand. "It's either that, or you and I may fight for her."

She rolled her shoulders back with confidence while staring ahead with determination. She was daring him to deny her request.

*She will really try to fight me!*

The Witch was giving him the cold glare he'd come to desire in the first place. There had always been something about the defiance of it and, despite what she was and how much he detested her for it, that look gave him the same reaction.

He wanted to break it, and doing so could be accomplished in many ways. He almost wanted to fight her because of it.

"Fine. I will allow you to take her home once I have seen for myself that you cannot use your magic."

*I'm curious to see this coven of Faerydaes.* He also didn't mind letting the child go free in exchange for the guarantee of Valerie's will and life to be his to do with as he pleased.

*The child has done nothing to warrant my wrath.* Valerie, on the other hand, had.

Valerie knelt once more in front of the Dragon, knowing it would be less threatening if she did.

"I need you to repeat my song, but you must imbue your voice with magic."

Geryon raised his brow from his position of safety. She was thankful she didn't have to fight him, since she doubted she would have survived, and the idea of harming him brought her little joy.

"What will it do?" He was sceptical and hesitant – she understood why.

"It will call pixies to you." Valerie looked to the tree line. A spike of shame hit her, but she made sure she hid the emotion in her features. "I have harmed them; they will no longer answer my call."

"You wish to call upon mischievous pixies?"

He shook his head in disbelief, but he let her teach him the song.

One arrived quickly, every block of forest having their own collection of pixies and fairies. They lived amongst the trees, mushrooms, and shrubs, sharing the land with the animals that lived in their woods.

Fairies were sweet creatures. Pixies, on the other hand, were considered vermin. Both were no larger than her hand, and they tried to remain hidden from the outside world.

A male pixie hissed at her before turning to Geryon with his own sharp little fangs. "You bring me to a Witch?"

"I need your assistance," Valerie told the pixie before he could flutter away. "We need you to perform a binding hex on my witchcraft."

He paused to squint his little eyes at her. "That's old magic, a kind we don't use anymore."

"I know. Witches tried to rid the world of your kind because we discovered you could bind our powers away. It has all been forgotten but... I know you still can do it."

The little creature fluttered its tiny wings while bringing its hand up to tap his fingers against his sharp, shark-like teeth. He grinned at Valerie, joyful at the idea of binding her magic.

"This will require lots of magic." The pixie turned to

Geryon. "Instead of one of us holding the key, do you intend the Dragon to be the holder?"

"Yes," she answered.

"Do you give your permission to act as the keeper of her magic? I will require the use of your blood."

Many believed pixies were the reason Strolguil the Vast discovered he could increase his magic with blood. Valerie could tell Geryon wasn't pleased his essence would be required, but he accepted it.

The pixie left and returned with two others.

Valerie knelt inside the circle they carved into the grass and dirt. Special symbols were drawn on the outside of it before they drew a second circle to encase them. They untied the back of her dress to reveal the skin between her shoulder blades.

One asked Geryon to dig his claw into his scales so it could collect his blood and use it to draw a final symbol on her back.

Their magic glittered with greens and blues while they flew in a circle around her body, chanting in unison. The symbols on the ground lit up as tiny beams of light shot up around her body. Without warning, Valerie felt her witchcraft being taken away. It felt like a sucking sensation, starting from the tips of her toes and fingers, pulling up her limbs to draw it away.

It was painful, almost cold, but she didn't make a noise nor any movement in reaction. That icy, sucking sensation flowed backwards until it burned like frost against her spine – right where they had drawn the symbol in blood.

Valerie gave a sigh, feeling the tension in her muscles fade when the worst of the pain was gone.

"There. The spell is done." They turned to the Dragon. "If you wish to unlock her witchcraft, you must place your hand on the mark on her back and say 'release'."

They immediately left, unwilling to linger.

Valerie looked down at her hands, clenching and

unclenching them. *I feel so strange.* She could tell it was gone, like a part of her soul was missing. It was different from what she'd done with Cecily, as she'd been able to feel the nagging desire to release her magic. Now, there was nothing at all. *I already miss the feeling.*

"It's true." Geryon sounded surprised. "I cannot see free witchcraft in you. It's localised to the symbol between your shoulders."

It burned, constantly reminding her it was there. She figured it was the concentrated power of her magic causing her pain, since it was no longer equally dispersed. Valerie attempted to create a ball of fire, but there wasn't even a tingle to inform her she'd tried.

"I feel human." She looked between her pale hands. "Such a weak sensation."

"You still smell like a Witch."

Valerie turned her head up to Geryon. "Now that it's proven I'm powerless, may I have my sister returned to me?"

"I'm considering snatching you as you are and taking you both as my prisoners." He said this, but he lowered his paw to place Kaeylyn gently on the ground in front of her. "However, I will not break my word."

27

Only when the child regained consciousness did the Witch finally set out on their journey.

Geryon followed them.

He morphed to be no bigger than a common housecat, so that he wouldn't be seen.

He either walked along the ground beside them or behind them some safe distance away from the child's sight. He also jumped from tree branch to tree branch, flapping his wings and using them to glide.

Valerie was carrying her sister on her back since she was weak. Geryon had healed her wounds, but she'd still lost a lot of blood. As much as he wanted to help, there was little he could do for her.

However, he was learning much about them, just by watching and listening.

The first thing Valerie did was take them to the men who currently lay dead.

He was surprised she would take her young sister right through the middle of such carnage until she removed a weapons belt from one of them so she could strap it around her own waist. She was making sure she had the ability to protect them on their travels. *She told me they would not need my help should trouble occur.*

Valerie began to go through the personal items the bandits had in their campsite. The first thing she did was give food to her sister so she could restore her strength. She sat on the ground while Valerie searched. She took a drawstring bag and filled it with a blanket, food, and a water sack.

It wasn't long before they set off again, finally making their journey through the forest.

"Are you okay, Valerie?" Kaeylyn asked with crinkled, sad eyes.

Valerie looked over her shoulder at the girl hugging her back, like she was surprised by the question. Geryon was as well, since she wasn't showing any signs of distress.

"Of course. Why would I not be?"

"I know what those men were going to do to you," she whispered. "I saw them lifting your skirt."

"It's not the first time something like this has happened to me." *This was why they were attacked?* "You should be more concerned with what happened to you."

"No, I barely remember it." She patted Valerie's hair like the woman needed comforting. "Do you hate men now, like Aldora?"

"No. I cannot hate men when they are not all evil. What happened to Aldora was terrible, and far worse than what any human men can do to me. She has every reason to reject men, in any form."

"But you saved her from those dark Witches who tried to use her in a ritual."

Valerie shook her head. "I did not arrive in time, and I was not alone." She turned her head back to her. "You forget that Mother and Carwyn helped me."

Geryon imagined Aldora and Carwyn were her other two sisters.

"But you were the one who healed her of her wounds." Kaeylyn hugged her neck tighter. "It's always you who comes to save us. You always fight for us."

"I'm the eldest; it's my job to protect you. I will always come for you."

A small silence was shared between them before the girl pressed her face against Valerie's shoulder and let out a wail.

"I'm so sorry!" Geryon reared his head at the sudden change in the girl's emotions. She burst into tears, clinging so tightly, he could tell she was gripping Valerie's throat in a suffocating squeeze. "I did not mean to venture so close to the road. I was playing with the fairies when you and Mother told me not to. I-I did not mean to be seen, I promise."

*They play with fairies rather than pull them apart?* The idea was foreign to Geryon. Since Witches turned on other creatures, used them to fuel strong, dark magic, pixies and fairies avoided them out of fear.

"Kaeylyn, it's fine. Don't worry yourself. You are safe now."

"B-but," the girl blubbered. "You had to come save me. I knew you would come for me, but I was so scared you would be hurt because of me."

"I saw you had toys in your confinement," Valerie commented, obviously trying to change the subject.

Kaeylyn nodded with a sniffle, bringing her arm back to wipe her snotty nose on the back of her sleeve. "Mhm. The man gave them to me to play with."

Geryon imagined the child would have been bored without them. *I'm a hunter, not a monster.* He wanted to kill evil Witches, and he'd known the child was pure.

"Was he nice to you?"

Her tears began to slow as she became thoughtful. As a

child, her emotions were fleeting.

"No, but he did not hurt me." Geryon wanted to laugh. He was as kind as he could be to a witchling he hadn't wanted to harm but still despised. "How did you know where I was in the palace?"

"There was a ball the previous night. I snuck into the palace in a beautiful dress and searched for you."

"I bet you looked pretty!" *She had been captivating.* He quickly turned his gaze away, not knowing why such a thought came to him. "You always have men follow you when we go through the town."

The child was bouncing on her back, giddy with their new conversation. He crinkled his snout at hearing this. Was that a spike of anger he felt? Jealousy, even? Ridiculous! He hated Valerie for what she was, now that he knew. He wouldn't, shouldn't, be jealous of some faceless men.

"Yes, well, they come to realise a pretty face does not mean I have a pretty heart."

"It's because you never smile." The girl dug her index fingers into Valerie's mouth and pulled the corners up, forcing her to grin. "Mother says it's because you are broken."

"Mother says a lot of things," she retorted, her lips and cheeks stretched like she was unbothered by the child doing it. She put the girl down to take her hand so they could walk together. "You are obviously well enough to irritate me, so you may walk on your own."

They walked silently through the forest, the constant shade keeping the worst of the summer sun's heat away. Geryon could hear a few buzzing insects that quietened when their crunchy footsteps approached. The air smelt muggy, but for a reptilian creature such as himself, he thrived in the heat.

He noticed the light sweat dotting down the Witches' foreheads and neck, and they occasionally swiped their brows. It wasn't too deep into summer yet, but he imagined their constant movement was keeping them warm.

The child spoke again after having a thoughtful look upon her face. "When we return home, can you teach me how to fight? I don't want Mother to teach me. I want it to be you."

"I thought you did not want to learn how to fight."

Kaeylyn looked away with a grumpy pout. "I changed my mind. I don't want to be taken again." Then she held her hand out like she was holding an imaginary sword. "I want to do what you did when those men tried to hurt us."

"I'm glad you wish to learn to fight. Our magic is not used to harm, so you must know how to protect yourself," Valerie said, as she looked down at her. "But Mother will have to be the one who teaches you."

"She's not like you, Valerie. She will be upset if I get hurt, so she will not do it properly. She never lets me learn anything fun."

Valerie let out a small sigh. "Who do you think taught me? Mother is a wonderful teacher. Give her a chance."

"No!" The child stamped her foot. "I want you to be the one who teaches me."

"What you want, and what you can have, are two different things, Kaeylyn." The girl folded her arms, pouted, and stopped walking, forcing Valerie to stop as well. "Don't act like a spoilt child."

She booted Valerie in the shin, who gave no response to the kick except for a tiny twitch on her brow.

"Kick me again and I will push you."

The girl pulled her leg back and kicked even harder, before launching forward to start smacking her in the torso. Valerie shoved her little sister so hard into the ground, she rolled back. Geryon was surprised she did it.

"I will not tolerate your childishness. You may be able to get away with hitting because Mother spoils you, but I will not stand here and let you hurt me because you are not getting your way."

Valerie turned and stormed through the forest, as if to leave her. Kaeylyn ran after her, in fear of being left behind.

"You pushed me!" She started crying again, this time wailing into the air with her head tilted back as heavy tears streamed down her red, blotchy face. "Why are you always so mean to me, Valerie? I'm going to tell on you!"

The loud, squealing shrieks irritated his sensitive ears, so much so that he waited until they were further ahead. He squinted his eyes as he watched them from his perch on a branch. *This will be a long journey.*

Already, he grew impatient with the child.

"You speak as if you are a singled-out target. I was given my title for a reason." Valerie rolled her eyes as Kaeylyn grabbed her skirt and pulled. "Don't pretend Aldora and Carwyn would not have done the same."

One thing Geryon was learning from all of this was that the woman he met in the palace had not been false. That cold, unfeeling personality he'd liked in her was real, and he was able to bear witness to it now.

The only things that were different were her name and her scent.

If he hadn't seen her cry for her sister with his own eyes, hadn't seen her sadness at her possible death and then relief when she was healed, Geryon would have figured she hated her.

*She wears that mask tight, even with her family.* What a strange thought.

Valerie piled rocks into a circle before she collected a large bundle of dead branches from the ground and placed them in the middle. Kaeylyn was collecting smaller ones as they searched. They were mostly useless sticks, but she didn't tell her otherwise – Valerie was just happy her sister was feeling better. She didn't want to invalidate her when she was trying to help.

"Kaeylyn, I want to see how well you are able to cast your magic," she told her before motioning her hand towards what she crafted. "I want you to light this campfire."

"No."

Valerie wondered if she fought her just to be defiant, but as she turned, she couldn't help noticing Kaeylyn looked away from her, as if she was ashamed.

"Why not? We must stay warm throughout the night, and we need to be able to see."

*I cannot light it myself.*

She no longer had the power to do so. From this point forward, Kaeylyn would have to be the Witch for them both. It was unfortunate she would have to rely on a six-year-old, one who had recently been harmed, but there was nothing Valerie could do about it.

Kaeylyn gripped the sides of her skirt and pulled, as though she wanted to make herself smaller. "I don't want to use my magic anymore."

"Excuse me?" Valerie tilted her head before she knelt in front of her sister. "What do you mean, you don't want to use your magic?"

She rubbed her arm, still looking away. "I don't want to use my witchcraft again."

"Kaeylyn..." Valerie shook her head at the silliness of her statement. She raised her hand and gently lifted Kaeylyn's chin so she would face her, tenderly stroking her cheek with her thumb. "You are supposed to use your magic. If you don't, it will fester inside of you. If you don't train it, it will grow chaotic."

"I'm scared to be taken again." Then, like she had many times this day, she began to cry.

The girl had always been quick to tears, but she'd never been this unstable. Valerie hadn't realised she was so traumatised. *It has affected her more than I thought.* She brought her in for a comforting hug, wishing there was more she could do to ease her little sister.

"If you do the right thing, you will be fine." Then Valerie turned her towards the campfire, rubbing her back soothingly. "I'm here with you. I will protect you. Use your magic."

"No!" Kaeylyn pushed her, forcing her to sit back on her heels before running into the forest by herself. "I don't want to be a Witch anymore!"

Valerie watched her go, knowing she would be back.

The campfire suddenly burst to life, sparking quickly from a large impact. She eyed the area, knowing where it came from. *Geryon is still with us.*

It bothered her she had a witness to their conversations, some of which had been private. They'd spoken of their sisters, their mother, parts of Valerie's life Kaeylyn unwittingly shared.

It couldn't be helped. She couldn't let her sister know they were being followed. She also knew whatever he discovered wouldn't matter in the end. There was nothing truly damaging Kaeylyn could reveal, only small, embarrassing things.

The child was bored while they travelled. She was entertaining herself the only way she could: with her irritating mouth.

After a short while, Kaeylyn came back with tear-covered pink cheeks and a heavy pout.

"I'm sorry I pushed you," she grumbled when she came closer. "You lit the fire."

She put her hands out to the warmth it provided.

The air was warm because of the summer heat, but they needed the light to see.

"You were upset. You often act irrationally when you are." Valerie sat on her bottom and stretched her legs forward. Lifting her hand, she offered it to Kaeylyn while patting the ground between her legs with the other. "Come. I wish to teach you something."

Valerie was often the teacher for her sisters. She was the oldest and felt it was her responsibility, especially as their mother grew older and more forgetful. She was even more knowledgeable than their mother now, since Valerie also shared knowledge with other Witches. She traded spells if they happened to come through the towns she often visited.

She didn't care if they were dark or white Witches, as long as they taught her more spells. Their mother was against learning from the corrupted, but Valerie was aware that sometimes, one had to learn of evil in order to shelter themself from it.

The girl sat between her legs with her back to Valerie's front. They both watched the fire while she hugged her midsection tightly.

"Where do you think this fire came from?" She pointed to it.

"From you?"

Valerie shook her head. "The magic we wield comes from our Dragon ancestor. All witchcraft comes from them, and, while we remain pure, it pays homage to them every time we use it." She leaned forward so they were closer, where they could feel its heat. "Do you know what colour pure fire is? When it's at its hottest and most cleansing?"

"Orange?"

"It's white, Kaeylyn. That's why our magic is white when we wield it." Valerie lifted both her hands, swirling them towards the flames. "Dragons are beautiful creatures, and to deny your magic is to deny the one you came from. Do you wish to deny Faerydae while he watches over us?" Valerie lifted her hand to the stars above them, and Kaeylyn lifted her gaze to follow it. "Do you wish to no longer honour him when he has bestowed upon you such a wonderous gift?"

"Well, no. I love Faerydae!" Kaeylyn turned to her with bright eyes, full of love for their Dragon parent.

Valerie eyed the forest around them.

She knew Geryon would find this conversation rather odd. He must be cringing or scoffing at what she told her sister, but it's what her family believed. These were the teachings of the old ways, the ways Witches used to believe in their magic and its source.

*I cannot let her turn her back on her witchcraft.*

Regardless of him and how he may feel, however he decided to perceive this, she needed to help Kaeylyn heal.

"Then don't deny your magic. Breathe it through your body in the way they breathe fire through theirs. Understand that while it's white, it's wonderful and should be cherished." Valerie tucked a strand of Kaeylyn's red hair behind her ear. "If you grab a piece of the fire, I will show you."

There was a long pause while Kaeylyn waited to decide if she wanted to use her magic again. *She is afraid.* She shouldn't be.

Valerie grabbed her hands gently and rubbed them with her fingers. "I'm with you, Kaeylyn. Know that I will protect you from anyone or anything that might come."

Tentatively, she leaned forward and used her magic to suck a tendril of flame into the palm of her hand. It floated, and she used her other hand to concentrate, so she didn't lose it while it settled.

Even her tongue came out while she concentrated.

Once it was tamed, Valerie cupped Kaeylyn's hand wielding that flame.

"As you know, witchcraft comes from dragoncraft. At the base of all our magic is dragonfire. That's what you carry with you, and although we cannot breathe it, we can express it."

"Like love?"

"No, but it spreads like love. It leaves a mark behind every time we use it."

She moved Kaeylyn's hands for her, forcing her to cup it, knowing she would protect herself from it. When she pulled her hand away, she was cupping two flames, smaller now that they were split.

"Fire can mean many things. It can mean the burning passion of love and desire. It can be the smoulder of a broken heart as it burns with sorrow. It can be the jealous rage of a scorned lover. It can be the fiery hate behind being wronged. It's the brightness of happiness, the warmth of comfort. Fire is the symbol for life, for death. It's everything, in everything. It's essence, Kaeylyn, just like our souls and our witchcraft."

"So, it's inside me, whether or not I use it?" She stared at the fire she was holding, almost with awe.

"Yes. It can also be chaotic and cruel, eating and burning everything it touches. It can even eat you from the inside out." She brought her hands back together to create one flame again. "It's dangerous, Kaeylyn. Mix your magic with the wrong things, and it will have everlasting damage, like a sickness. Once you start mixing other essences with it, it changes colours, becomes green, blue, red, yellow."

"You are talking of dark magic."

She tried to close her hand to get rid of the magic she was wielding, now worried. Valerie forced her to keep it by keeping her fingers straight.

"You cannot be afraid of it. You cannot be afraid of your magic for this reason. If you fear the world, that might make you seek to strengthen it, to change it. This is the risk you take in denying yourself." Valerie looked down to Kaeylyn who was now frowning with distress. She merely stared back with coldness, even though she knew her sister deeply hated it. "You cannot fear the world and its dangers. Fight it with your sword, fight it however you can with your white magic, but you must never turn your back on who and what you are."

Kaeylyn squirmed enough that she fell from Valerie's grasp, rolling to the side to crawl backwards on her hands and bottom.

"You invite darkness inside you by holding onto your fear of what has happened to you. If that happens, everything I have done to save you will be for nothing."

"But I don't want to be unfeeling like you!"

"I'm not unfeeling, Kaeylyn. I have just learned to not let the things that have hurt me linger." Valerie averted her gaze to look at the crackling fire, hating the way her sister picked on her coldness – as if it was something she could control when she couldn't. "Embrace what has happened to you as the lesson it was. Grow your magic and let it be beautiful. Then, pass it on to your children because you are the only one left who can."

"Why does it have to be me? Is that why you truly saved me? So that it did not have to be you who continues our line?"

With a sigh, Valerie folded her legs and reached into the supply bag she'd stolen to grab a roll of bread. She'd taken a lot of food from the bandits and was now rather thankful she'd come across them, considering everything worked out in the end.

"I saved you because you are my baby sister, and you know that," she answered before she broke the bread apart. "Don't throw accusations at me simply because you are upset and wish to hurt me. It... it's not fair."

Then she leaned forward with the second half to give it to Kaeylyn. "Eat. You must gain your strength. We still have another day or two of walking before we are home."

With a huff and a deep pout, Kaeylyn ate by shoving the bread into her face. Then she eventually curled up next to the fire on the left-hand side of it. She'd chosen to lie there because she wanted to be close to Valerie. She made her feel safe, but she also didn't want to cuddle up to her because she was upset.

She leaned against the trunk of a fallen tree, some ways away from the heat of the flames. It meant she could look out for those who might stumble towards the light.

A shadowy figure headed towards her, and she placed her hand on the hilt of the sword she'd taken.

"Come, I wish to speak with you," Geryon said quietly, and she relaxed.

"There is no need." She motioned her hand towards Kaeylyn. "She sleeps like the dead. She will not awaken for any reason." To demonstrate this, she yelled the girl's name as loudly as she could. She made no move in reaction. "See? Useless when asleep."

He stepped forward into the light of the fire, letting it dance over his scales just enough so she could see him on the other side. He was the same size as her: not small, but not large.

"Your scales are dark blue."

This was the first time she'd seen him with any form of light in his Dragon form.

The longer he stood with the heat of the flames reaching him, the lighter his scales appeared. They began to turn a brighter shade of blue, and she couldn't help looking in wonder as they reflected the light and almost sparkled.

He had a crown of spikes jutting up around his head, with smaller ones coming up from his shoulders all the way down to his tail. She eyed it tapping against the ground, noting his tail was crudely missing its tip, like someone had severed it – a stump. His wings rested tightly against his body.

He also had tiny spikes jutting from his snout up to his

forehead and across what she thought might be his brows. They made the metallic blue of his eyes seem fiercer, but she noticed the light made them appear more silver.

"I'm sure we have caused you offense with our lesson."

Valerie drew her knee up so that she could rest her forearm against it while she laid back against the trunk. He eyed her sister laying down cautiously before he sat to make himself comfortable.

"No. Quite the opposite, in fact."

She felt the twitch of a frown on her brow before it settled. She expected anger and disgust, and his response caused surprise to fill her. "How so?"

"It sounds as though you worship my kind and honour where you came from." He looked to the fire before flicking his eyes towards her once more. "I have never heard a Witch speak like this. I found it peculiar, but not offensive."

"Have you spoken to many, then?" She raised a brow in question.

"No. I often kill first and ask questions never."

"I don't particularly blame you," she answered. "There are more evil Witches than there are good. It's safer to be rid of one before it has the chance to kill you."

"You have killed some, have you not?"

He was asking this because of her conversations throughout the day with Kaeylyn.

"Yes. A small group of dark Witches stole one of my sisters when she and I had been walking through the town closest to our home. I saw them take her, knew who and what they were, and went home to get my mother's help to rescue her. I killed them because they deserved to die." She clenched her fist tightly. "Especially since I had been too late to save her from their perverted ritual of sex and blood."

This had been ten years ago. It was a disgusting and cruel act, and Valerie made sure to get redemption for her sister by murdering all those who hurt her.

"I'm curious to know what you did to the real Lady Cecily."

Valerie pursed her lips. "She's off somewhere in the forest with her real uncle and two soldiers."

"I doubt that would be safe for her if you took over her mind. Are you truly so callous that you would let a human woman be harmed just for your sister's safety?"

She didn't understand the emotion behind the raise of one of his spiked brows. There was a long pause shared between them, while Valerie decided on whether she would tell him the truth or not.

"Lady Cecily would have been a terrible queen," she told him. "She was also in love with another."

"What does that have to do with anything?"

"In order to do the spell that allowed me to mask both my scent and my witchcraft, she had to willingly give me her blood. That's the price for the spell."

"Are you telling me you struck a deal with her to take her place?" He twisted his head, a frown forming across his features.

"Yes, that's correct."

He stomped his foot forward with a soft growl. "Then she betrayed King Bradwick! She assisted a Witch in entering the palace."

She waved her hand forward.

"Is King Bradwick not alive? I never had any intention of harming him, and I told them this. I told them something was taken from me and all I wanted was it back. It gave me the ability to go there, and she will now be able to marry her darling soldier lover. Sometimes, we must take risks for the things we care for."

*I definitely have over the past two weeks,* she thought with a grumble.

He gave a huff of irritation, the lips of his snout puffing. "You truly believe your Dragon parent is Faerydae?"

"Yes. It was what I was taught from an early age, and much ancient magic has been passed down to me, long forgotten spells. I have no reason not to believe it."

"It seems as though you admire him."

"Not just him, but all Dragons." She met his eyes directly as she spoke, folding her arms. "Believe whatever you want from this conversation, but my family and coven respect your kind and think highly of you." She let her eyes move over his body in a sweep. "Even now, I feel honoured to be able to meet one, speak to one, see one for my own eyes, since my family has not done so in five hundred years because of Strolguil's actions. As I always imagined, it's quite a magnificent sight to behold."

The scales around his face became exceedingly brighter for a moment, almost like he blushed at her compliment. She just took it as a trick of the light.

"You tried to teach your sister to embrace her magic so that it will not turn into something evil, but you have done just that. You have corrupted yourself."

Valerie turned to stare at the fire rather than at him.

"I did what I needed to save her. I needed a dark spell to see who took her so I could bring her back. By that point, it was too late, and when I saw where I needed to go, I knew it would be dangerous. White magic would not have been enough to help me." She gave a snort, a single laugh without humour. "Your kind of hunting is not uncommon, Geryon. Although I never knew what you were until the night of the ball, when I was making my way to the palace, I knew I could find myself against a Dragon or another Witch. If I had not known, I would have tried to do this without the use of dark spells. But I did, and therefore, I prepared myself for any possibility."

He nodded his snout towards Kaeylyn, still asleep on the ground. Even from the short distance, Valerie could hear her snoring.

"What did she mean by 'continuing our line'?"

"It's complicated," she answered, turning her head up dismissively. "It's not something you will understand."

A low, grumbling growl sounded. "I have agreed to let you release this child when it's against my usual conduct. The least you can do is humour me with truthful answers to my questions."

She wished she had the capabilities to growl in return. *Fine!*

"Our family has only ever given birth to one child, a daughter, every generation. It's believed there is some form of a curse or a spell Faerydae placed upon our bloodline. All boys are stillborn." Valerie picked a leaf off the ground and began to slowly break the leaf-blades off its stems as she spoke, giving herself something to fiddle with. "After I was born and my mother discovered how I was, she decided I was not fit to be a mother. She told me I'm not allowed to continue the family line. So, even though she was only meant to have one child, she gave birth to Carwyn."

Valerie looked towards her hands. "She's unable to hold a child. She has additional powers, and those powers often come with a sacrifice. That's hers. So, then came along Aldora, who was then brutalised, raped, and stabbed by men. You can see why she would be unfit, since she has sworn herself to celibacy."

"This child is your last hope?" He frowned in her direction, and she knew he couldn't understand the ways of her family.

"No, I could still have been the one to do it." His head snapped to her, and she didn't understand why he gave her a wide-eyed expression. "But that was before. I have now made sure I cannot by allowing darkness into my heart. I'm the first in my family line to do so, and now I cannot continue it. It's up to Kaeylyn."

"You must understand, I find this all hard to believe. You speak as though your family is pure, but I have never met any other Witches who are this way."

"That's why I said I don't care if you believe me. You are welcome to take from this what you will, but I will not sit here and attempt to convince you. I'm merely answering your questions."

"Fine," he bit, turning his head away from her with a huff. As if he couldn't stop himself, he turned back to look at her. "Why were you given the title 'the Heartless'?"

"If you think it's because of my personality, you would be very wrong." He gave a scowl, and she knew that was what he'd been thinking. "My mother gave me that name after I stabbed a dark Witch in the heart when he tried to take me from her. I was twelve at the time. It was only after she told me I killed my own father, and I did not care, that she told me I was truly a monster who lacked compassion."

She watched his snout crinkle. "You did not know who your own father was?"

"No. My mother made sure she got pregnant, then left him so she could raise me alone in our family cottage. It's what has always been done, daughters raised by single mothers and unknown fathers. When he discovered us together in the town near our home, he knew I was his. He tried to take me to raise me in his coven, and I attacked someone who tried to steal me."

"You truly did not care that you had murdered your own father?"

Valerie gave a shrug. "He was a stranger to me. I saw him as nothing."

There was a long pause as the Dragon tapped his tail against the ground. "You have given me much to think on."

"I have my own question for you." She eyed him cautiously, and he raised his brow when she folded her arms over her chest. "Were you the one who stole Kaeylyn?"

Was Geryon the reason this all happened? She wanted a reason to hate him.

"No." He lifted a paw to inspect the points of his claws. "She was brought to Bradwick as an offering, and I took her instead. I knew someone would come for her."

"You used her as bait?" Valerie attempted to hide her disgust.

"Yes. It's why I told Bradwick she gave a foretelling that he would find his future queen if he opened his gates for a gala."

"Wait..." Valerie frowned as her arms loosened. "You lied to the king about Kaeylyn revealing a prophecy?"

He grinned, revealing all his fangs. "He was easy to convince. I needed him busied by taking a wife, since he was beginning to irritate me. This also got him to open his gates so Witches would come freely."

"That's awfully manipulative." Valerie couldn't believe how devious he truly was!

He was still looking at his claws as he said, "Don't be so surprised by my wit. I have duped many kings into doing what I want." He finally brought his eyes to her. "You look tired. I will allow you to rest."

She thought he was just done talking to her.

"I can rest when my sister is home safe," she answered, turning her head to look at the dark forest.

"Are you insinuating I will not protect you both while you sleep?" His snout curled in anger. "Rest. I will keep guard."

Stemming the want to roll her eyes and knowing there was no way she could convince him otherwise, Valerie got to her feet and walked over to Kaeylyn. She said nothing to Geryon as she lay down behind her and pulled her closer, cuddling her sister as she closed her eyes.

Regardless of what he said, she felt better about holding her in case danger came.

Geryon watched as Kaeylyn pointed to the sky and shouted, "Valerie, look! The moon is full!"

She gave a loud, high-pitched squeal as she ran around the campfire she'd helped create on the second night of their travels. He was still in his Dragon form, smaller so he could perch on the branch of a tree.

He watched over them carefully. He was unintentionally growing protective of them the more he learned. The child was a constant source of information since she spoke so freely, and often merrily, while she ran around her older sister.

She was adjusting to using her witchcraft again, with much pushing from Valerie. She was easy to convince. Geryon could tell she wanted to use it, but was just hesitant.

"Is that your way of saying you wish to do the dance of the white snake?"

"Can we? Pleeease?" Kaeylyn bolted to Valerie and began to tug on her dress wildly.

Geryon was intrigued by this dance and what it meant. The child was obviously excited about it, and he was growing increasingly more curious about them and their witchcraft.

"You can, but I'm feeling tired." Valerie waved her hand dismissively.

"No! I cannot do it on my own. We must do it together." She nibbled at her bottom lip. "I promise I will be good from now on."

He cocked his head when he noticed Valerie avert her gaze before giving a nod.

They positioned themselves on either side of the fire, their backs slightly turned to each other. Then Valerie began to sing, and they danced around the fire with mirrored movements.

*Her voice is filled with life when she sings.* It was melodic and gentle. He expected a dead, expressionless song, not something that would make his eyes droop like a lullaby. His tail even began to sway, as if it wanted to join in on their dance.

They stretched their arms out beside their bodies before they both pushed in one direction, slowly making their way around the fire. Their hands would go up, then down, then separate as they spun and twirled.

The fire in the centre began to spiral in the direction they were dancing.

Kaeylyn was giggling as she tried to copy Valerie's movements, sometimes offbeat, like she didn't know the next move. Valerie's face didn't look as hard as it usually did, instead appearing remarkably soft while she sang.

*She looks like she might be enjoying herself.*

At the very end, they both threw their hands up. Geryon felt a wave of wind energy come from them right before a smoky snake-like creature with wings formed.

It shot upwards, exploding into a cascade of glitter when it hit the tree canopy.

"I did not see your moon Dragon, Valerie!" Kaeylyn

frowned when they both calmed, her small torso wildly huffing.

Valerie's chest was pumping a little harder than it usually did, but it was barely noticeable.

"It's because yours was so bright that it shadowed mine."

*It's because she does not have access to her magic.* He wondered if that was the real reason she didn't want to do the dance.

Kaeylyn put her hands on her hips in disbelief. "You have the strongest magic I have ever seen. It's even stronger than Mother's."

"Exactly. You should be proud you shadowed it."

Valerie clapped for her, and she went so bright red in the face with joy, Geryon feared she'd pass out. Her hands shot to the sky as she spun in a circle.

"Do you think Faerydae saw it?"

"He's always watching over us, so yes, and I'm sure he's proud." She turned her face up to the moon. "It's why we do the dance on the full moon, to honour him. He would not miss his own celebration."

It was such a wild concept to Geryon that these two Witches would go out of their way to waste magic just to honour their Dragon ancestor.

They sat by the fire, Kaeylyn choosing to sit between Valerie's legs. She accepted it like she wasn't bothered by her sister climbing over her, restless and constantly moving. She even braided her hair.

*She can be feminine like this?* He never thought he would see her willingly plait the hair of another. She even tried to comb it with her fingers first.

"Do you think I will get to meet a Dragon one day?" Kaeylyn turned her head up to Valerie as they spoke.

"I most certainly hope you don't."

The girl gave a pout, folding her arms across her chest

when she looked down at the fire. She gave a sigh.

"I know they hate evil Witches, but I'm not evil. Why can I not see them?"

"Because they have been hunted by our kind. We don't deserve such kindness from them. If you are to meet one, it will most likely bite you in half."

Valerie began to tickle her sister's sides to punctuate her words, and the girl squealed. Her lips quirked ever so slightly.

"I would much rather die by the mouth of a Dragon than of old age," the girl giggled. "At least then, my death would be useful!"

"That's only because you don't know how sharp their teeth are. They will chomp you." She lifted Kaeylyn's arm and bit into it.

"But would that not follow the old ways? Why can a Witch not be a sacrifice for a Dragon?"

Geryon knew what she spoke of.

How their kind came to be was by accident. Humans used to give a sacrifice to the Dragons, thinking they were gods. His kind allowed them to think this foolishness so they could get an easy meal.

One Dragon decided he liked the human he'd been given. Rather than eat her, he bedded the woman, not knowing it would create a Witch – a creature that was human but could use magic, like them. This was none other than the great Dragon Faerydae.

"Because there was usually a ceremony."

"Okay, then. Well, how would you want to die?"

There was a long pause as Valerie's eyes moved from the girl sitting with her to the flames dancing in front of them.

She spoke so softly that Geryon could barely hear her from the distance. "I want to be cleansed in dragonfire."

Geryon reared his head back at her admission.

*She wishes to be burned?* His spiked brows furrowed

deeply. It didn't matter if it was a Witch or a human; it was awfully alarming to hear. It would be one of the most painful ways to go. If he knew it, then she knew it. He couldn't understand why she would seek her death this way.

Geryon hated Witches because they were evil, vile, and monstrous.

They pulled the wings from innocent fairies for spells, killed them, and took their blood. They shook pixies to take the dust their magic emits while also stealing their teeth and bones.

They hunted Dragons just to take from them. No part of his kind was left unused. Their fangs, bones, scales, wings, tail, even their eyes and tongue were not spared from defilement.

They took from humans. They even took from their own kind, were cruel towards their own species.

They smelt putrid, like their magic was toxic and odorous. They smelt unclean, tainted from the inside out.

He should hate the two he was watching. He once had. In the beginning, he'd wanted nothing more than to chase after them and kill them.

Now, with a safe distance between them so the younger one couldn't see him, he realised he no longer did.

Watching them interact with each other over the past two days made him see them for what they were. They were harmless in the ways that mattered.

He knew Valerie had used dark magic, but she didn't smell corrupted. Her scent was still pure, and he was realising he actually...liked the rich, deep scent. *It suits her much better.*

Although she had used dark magic, with the hex locking her magic in, she was of no danger to anyone. *Except for that sword she has strapped around her waist.* Still, anyone who died from the fairness of a sword deserved it.

It wasn't Valerie's lack of abilities that caused him to no longer hate them. It was what he learned of them as they spoke with each other freely, like he wasn't there. The conversations weren't being used to manipulate him, since it was the child who instigated most of it.

Valerie seemed relentless in teaching her different things about witchcraft, and she would often direct their conversations to it. Throughout the day, she even collected different herbs for the child to play with, telling her to experiment with what she had in her hands.

Kaeylyn had begun to open up about her magic again after the previous night. She used a spell to show them they were travelling in the right direction, and she respected her sister enough to take all her advice and teachings.

*She called my kind beautiful...* She also called him, directly, magnificent. Words and praise like this could make any Dragon puff their scales out in appreciation. His cheeks grew warm, susceptible to it.

They spoke often of Dragons. It should bother him they were speaking of his kind with him so close. It didn't, though, not when most of it had been of wonder from the child.

It was obvious their coven thought them sacred.

It should also bother him to see witchcraft being used so easily in front of him. Yet, it was soft and light, and it smelt wonderful. It wasn't harsh and filled with blood and malice. Instead, it was pure, and his nostrils found that satisfying.

There weren't many pure-hearted Witches left in the world, and not only had he found two, but there was an entire coven of them. *They honour us with their words.*

Geryon hated dark Witches for what they did. He couldn't hate what he couldn't see in these two.

No, instead he heard Valerie tell the child about the sanctity of life, how it must be cherished and protected at all costs. She was teaching this child to remain in the light when she herself had walked a path of darkness.

*She has not been corrupted yet.* He wondered if she ever

would, if her heart would turn black, if she would seek to destroy rather than protect.

It was hard to imagine after observing her as she was now. She seemed to have such hard-set opinions about her beliefs, was headstrong about them. She spoke of the right path in what seemed like unwavering resolution.

*Can someone who has beliefs this strong still turn?* Or was she able to beat the power of corruption with the power of will?

Geryon hoped so.

Not just for her sake, but... because he had once liked this woman. Watching her as she was now, it was hard to not be reminded of the female he'd constantly wanted beneath him, especially since she had worn her mask heavily and with unfaltering persistence since she cried in front of him.

He understood why Valerie did what she had, even though it happened to be on his hunting grounds.

She'd gotten herself into the palace he'd been guarding and using as a luring trap for her kind, and paraded around it like a vicious butterfly. Without meaning to, she'd captivated the Dragon rather than ending up in its claws.

She tricked the king he was currently serving. She had even tricked him. *But it's I who really lured her.*

Geryon managed to seduce the Witch, who should have been trying to entrance him instead.

*What of her desire, then?* Had she truly felt something as strong as passion for Geryon when she'd thought of him as a human? What did she think of him now that she knew he was a Dragon?

She told him she hadn't tried to fool him. He knew he'd been persistent, forceful even, coaxing her to melt for him. *Was I truly unwrapping that mask from her face?*

Her wintry green eyes still caught his attention, especially when her cold, sweeping gaze crossed over where he was hiding. He knew her pale skin was soft and easy to bite through. Her long, wavy brown hair fluttered when she moved, and he realised he'd never grabbed it in his fist.

Geryon still wanted to unravel this beauty, but he was also deeply against it, simply because of what she was. Once more, she had become a thing he could look upon but could not touch, like when she first arrived at King Bradwick's palace.

When the child was fast asleep, Geryon emerged from the shadows the same size as Valerie. He made himself this size so his voice would be easier to hear, but not loud enough that it was booming.

It also meant he wasn't small and vulnerable, either.

"I'm hoping we will be able to return her home tomorrow," Valerie said without facing him.

Like she often did, she stared at the fire. It was as if she were wishing for something from it. It was an intense gaze, like she wished to take it into her soul.

"I will warn you. Since you are not of our family, you will find when we get closer that you will not like it. If it's too much for you, you may stay outside of the magic there."

"What kind of magic is it?" he asked when he sat down, looking over her body.

She changed her position to kneel in front of the fire. "There are wards, ones that have been on those lands for centuries. Every year, we replace them, and our magic mixes with the lingering magic to refuel them. It's off-putting to most, and since I cannot place a passing spell on you because my magic is bound, you will find it uncomfortable."

Geryon couldn't create wards. They required strong, focused magic, and he didn't have the kind of power to make anything long lasting. It was why she'd been able to steal her sister from him so easily.

"Also, if you intend to follow all the way to the house, you will need to stay close, or you will get lost. There are other spells that confuse travellers." She turned her head to him. "You will keep your claws to yourself when we arrive?"

"Are you asking if I intend to harm your family?" His nose crinkled in agitation, a light growl coming from him.

"This is the perfect opportunity for you to wipe out an entire coven. I'm like the sheep leading the wolf to others. I have no idea as to the real reason why you have allowed me to take her home."

"I have no intention of harming your family, unless I smell darkness and malicious intent. Only then would I kill them."

"Try to," she corrected. "You would not be successful, but they would not harm you." She turned back to look at the fire. "Our family has sworn an oath to never kill your kind."

"Your family is truly odd." He nodded his snout towards the child. "She's often whimsical with her magic."

"Kaeylyn is six, not old enough to understand her magic is not just about fun. She plays with it like it's a toy." Valerie tilted her head at her younger sister. "I do hope she never loses her playfulness."

"You love her dearly, do you not?"

She nodded. "Yes. I know I don't often show it. Sometimes I cannot and sometimes I don't wish to, but I love my sisters and mother more than anything in the world. I have chosen to sacrifice myself for Kaeylyn for that reason alone."

Geryon was surprised she would admit to such a deep emotion.

"Why do you do it? Why do you hide?"

She gave a shrug. "Most of the time, it's not conscious. Sometimes, I simply don't wish to burden the world with how I feel. Other times, I just don't wish to honour it with my emotions. Mostly, it's because I cannot feel. I'm often numb." She looked to him. "I have always been this way. My mother told me I'm wrong, that I'm broken, but I'm happy with the way I am."

Geryon eyed her, unsure of why his heart stammered when he asked, "And what did you feel in the palace?"

"Determination," she answered. "Often confusion. Getting lost in what I was supposed to be doing and where I was going. I was a Witch pretending to be human. I was taught enough about the etiquette, but there was much I did not know."

His claws gouged the earth in tension. "What of me? I often think you used an enchantment against me."

Her brow quirked slightly. Even her ears twitched back, like she was surprised or shocked by his question.

"No. The spell I used to hide what I was did not allow me to use magic after it was cast, or I would break it. I did not use magic against you."

Surprisingly, he believed her. "You did not answer my question."

"You were a source of confusion. I did not understand why you were interested in me." She looked to the flames like she often did, but this time, she also nibbled at her lips. "I also did not understand why I could not seem to resist you."

She lifted her hands to the fire, dangerously close to it, until her palms and wrists turned bright pink. He wondered why she would purposely bring her hands to the heat of flames. That was, until he caught the change in her scent in the air and his eyes widened.

*She's becoming aroused.* She'd used the painful burn of the fire to stop herself. He cooled his expression before her eyes found him. *She does not want me to know she still holds desire for me.* Or at least, what human Geryon had been to her.

It was the answer to his question. Geryon had wanted to know if she truly felt something for him, or if it had been lies. He had his answer, but he just hadn't thought she would still hold desire for him.

*She's not averse to the idea of me now that she knows what I am.* Not like how he was with her because of her true species.

"I punched Wyetta in the face."

"Yes, I did see that she was unconscious. I thought you were friends with her."

"I was. That was why I did it." When he tilted his head questioningly, she 'tsked' at him. "I realised my befriending her and then threatening King Bradwick would reflect terribly on her. I decided to make it appear as though she tried to stop me, to spare her any possible suspicion. She had no idea what I was or what I was doing, and I do honestly think she would be the best queen for him."

He nodded his head in agreement.

"I believe you are correct." He brought his paw up to tap a claw against his snout in thought. "When I realised your sister had been taken, I thought I would find Bradwick dead."

"Like I said, I had no intention of harming anyone within that palace." She paused, then rolled her eyes. "Except for Lord Daerk. He would have deserved a good neutering."

Geryon snorted a dark laugh. *I still must punish that man.*

Even now, Geryon still wished to claw Lord Daerk's face for his actions; not just because he attacked and attempted to blackmail a woman he'd been interested in, but because he would even do such a heinous act at all.

"What would you have done if you knew what I was from the beginning?" The question had been on the forefront of his mind since they'd begun their journey.

"Refused you without hesitation," she answered, turning down to stare at her hands. "I cannot imagine how you must feel, knowing what you have done with a Witch. I know how much your kind hates mine. It must be a violating thought." She turned her eyes to him, and he saw a hint of something in them – something he didn't like. "I apologise for it and have come to regret it."

Geryon averted his gaze to look at the forest, his claw gouging deeper into the dirt. *She regrets it?*

"I'm sure even a human would be against bedding a Witch, so I should have just focused on my task and left. I was selfish."

At one point, he'd regretted it. *Do I still?* Every time he looked back on those memories, something strange stirred inside him. *I enjoyed it thoroughly.* He couldn't remember the last time he'd had that much fun.

Chasing this woman around the palace, forcing her to give him peeks of her true self, coaxing her body to feel desire and reaping the rewards of it around his fingers and cock...

It was a game he'd become smitten with.

Seeing she was different to what he usually hated meant... *I don't regret my actions.* Actually, when he thought back on them, they made him want to pant.

*I still have not gotten what I wanted from her.* He didn't know if he ever would.

"That was not what I meant," he finally answered, turning back to look at her. He was changing the subject, since he was finding this one unpleasant and confusing. "Would you have targeted me rather than Bradwick, had you known you were on my hunting grounds?"

"No. Bradwick was always the easier person to manipulate. I would not have stayed around for so long, though. I wanted to do it silently, find her and slip out without anyone noticing or being harmed."

*In doing so, you saved yourself from me.* If she had acted rashly, he may have sniffed her magic out and killed her on the spot. *I would not have discovered what a tantalising creature you could be.*

Late into the following afternoon, Geryon understood what Valerie meant when she said he might find approaching her home uncomfortable.

The air was cloying and thick with magic, making it hard to breathe. The magic told him to turn around, but not in fear. No, more like it was telling him there was nothing for him here, that there was no need to go this way.

He even forgot why he was going through the forest, constantly shaking his head to rid himself of the dizzying haze. He found no relief.

More than once, his body turned away of its own volition. He even slowed, occasionally having to force himself to catch up. The only thing keeping his paws moving forward was Valerie and her sister, a beacon through the confusion.

He couldn't look away, even for a second, or he would lose them. He couldn't smell them over the magic, and their voices were distant, no matter how close he got.

*I smell dozens of different magical essences.* It was as though he was walking into an area heavily filled with

Witches. He feared she was luring him to his death with just the number of different energies hitting his senses.

He knew she wasn't. *She warned me.* It was good she had. He may not have tolerated it if he didn't have prior knowledge. He would have just picked them both up and fled with them in his hands.

It was a brilliant defence. She said they'd managed to live here for centuries. With so many kinds of spells and wards in place, telling him different reasons why he didn't want to go this way, it was no wonder they felt protected.

It eventually lifted, right before they came to a large clearing with a cute stone-and-wood cottage in the centre. There was a chimney, but the smoke he could smell was softer, near clear, as though to hide it from a distance.

There was glamour above it where the trees were, but this tree in particular shading them looked far too tall in comparison to the others surrounding it.

*They must have an illusion in place so it cannot be seen from above.* How else would Dragons have missed it?

He was thankful the ring of spells and magic had lifted, so he could focus without his thoughts being pulled astray. It was like they were in the eye of a storm.

Making himself comfortable by laying across a branch, he stuck his head through the leaves so he could watch while remaining hidden.

"Mamma!" Kaeylyn shouted, accidentally yanking on Valerie's arm when she ran towards the house.

A woman hanging out washing turned her head. Her hair was white with subtle streaks of red, and her skin was tanned with freckles dotting her shoulders and face. She looked more like the child than Valerie, who seemed to look nothing like either of them.

"Kaeylyn?" she gasped, before hiking up her dress so she could run as well. "Kaeylyn!"

With obvious relief and happiness written on her face, she met the child in the middle of the clearing and scooped her into her arms. She even began to cry.

Geryon frowned at Valerie, who stopped moving just past the trees, like she didn't want to step closer. *Why isn't she joining them?*

At the commotion, two other women appeared.

A girl with blonde hair and pale skin walked out of the house cautiously. The younger one that followed nearly pushed her over and stumbled as she ran down the pebble walkway. She had darker skin than the rest, and her long brown hair fluttered behind her head.

*They all smell similar.* He examined all their differences as he thought, *Do they have different fathers?*

"I was so worried about you, my dear little Kae."

Their mother was much older than the rest of them. Geryon could tell she was near the end of her life cycle for a Witch.

There were tears, lots of hugging, but none of it involved Valerie, who stood off to the side.

"Aldora, take her inside." She turned her head to the blonde as she pushed Kaeylyn towards her. "Feed her well and give her a bath."

The pale one, who he guessed was Aldora, nodded, but glared in Valerie's direction. She even turned her nose up at her before taking Kaeylyn's hand. He figured the other woman was her sister Carwyn, and her eyes crinkled like she felt sorry for Valerie before she took Kaeylyn's other hand.

Geryon didn't understand why they weren't embracing her as well. *She brought their sister home. I expected to see a grand reunion.*

Once they were gone, their mother approached Valerie.

"You brought your sister home, Valerie. I knew you would, I knew you would save her." There was a spark in her face. It was easy to see the gratitude in it, the relief.

"Yes. I could not bear to know she was taken."

She clasped her hands in front of her waist and stared her mother directly in the eyes.

"You stupid girl!" Disbelief soared through him when he watched as Valerie was slapped across the face, the smack radiating through the air. "How dare you!"

She slapped her other cheek.

Valerie didn't react, but she was slapped hard enough that her face turned to the side each time. Already, redness began to swell in her cheeks.

"You accursed child!" Another smack; it sounded as though they were getting harder, louder. The woman was beginning to cry as she hit her own daughter. "You took blood from fairies! You used dark magic!" Slap. "I could not believe my ears when they told me!"

Her lips were twisted, her eyes filled with tears and pain at what she was doing.

"You were the best of us all. Your magic was so strong, and now you have poisoned it." Another slap rang out before she hesitated momentarily.

Geryon was shocked at what he was witnessing, surprised that Valerie would allow this kind of punishment.

*The child would still be in my clutches if it was not for her!* He didn't understand them, her mother, why Valerie wasn't retaliating.

"You are a disgrace. You no longer belong here. You don't deserve to call yourself a Faerydae."

*She's not even trying to defend herself.* She was allowing it, like she thought she deserved to be punished. Geryon got to his feet to intervene, but paused when he understood the significance of it.

If he revealed himself, he would have to imprison them. What if they turned on him? *I made her a promise I would not attack her family.* His lips curled back over his fangs. *Blasted!*

His claws dug into the branch, resisting the urge to retaliate on Valerie's behalf.

"I would much rather Kaeylyn not come home at all if this was the cost!"

His head reared back, and his claws lessened their bite when Valerie backhanded her own mother hard enough that she hit the ground. After delivering blow after blow, she hadn't expected to be hit in return.

"Never say that again." There was a dangerous glint to her usually cold eyes – which only made them appear icier. "Such words make what I did pointless. I saved her at the cost of my own soul, and I did it knowingly." She leaned forward to tower over her. "I would do it again if I knew there was no other way."

"You cold, unfeeling, wretched child," she sneered back.

Carwyn came running out of the cottage to their screaming and yelling mother. She helped her to her feet and led the crazed woman inside. She sniffled and cried, so many emotions torn across her features, but Geryon no longer found pleasure or pity in her relief. He sneered at her instead.

"Please." Carwyn held her hand out with a plea. "Stay there. Don't leave. I will return in a moment."

Valerie gave a nod and they both went inside.

She brought her hands up so she could press the back of her fingers against her cheeks. They looked swollen and sore, but she made no face of discomfort. *Such control.* She didn't even flinch when being hit.

Eventually, Carwyn came outside. She reached forward to cup Valerie's cheeks to inspect them, but Valerie knocked her away, smacking both her wrists.

"Don't touch me with your empathetic hands."

She withdrew them from the air. "You look terrible, Valerie."

Her eyes must have taken in the blood and grime covering

her. Valerie's hair was a tangled mess, her skin paler than normal, which brought out the dark circles under her eyes. Her hands were caked in dirt, and there were smudges of it over her dress and exposed skin.

"Carwyn, I would like you to grant me a few things."

"Of course, whatever it's you need."

"Bring me a bucket with water, a rag, a dagger, a brush, and one of my dresses. I would also like my heirloom. I don't care if Mother says I cannot have it; it's mine and I wish to wear it."

With a nod, the woman went to collect the items. Valerie waited where she stood, staring at the cottage in the centre of the clearing. *What is she thinking?* What was going through this woman's mind?

Not too much later, all the items she asked for were laid out on the ground. The other female was wearing gloves now, whereas before, her hands had been bare.

"Thank you."

Valerie then took that dagger to her own chest and cut through her dress, like she couldn't be bothered with the ties. She was stripping, pulling it from herself without a care for her sister in front of her or the fact that she knew Geryon was watching.

"Valerie! What are you doing? If you wished to bathe, you should have come inside. You know Mother often has odd guests."

She rolled her eyes and shook her head, not seeming to find an issue with stripping.

"She will not permit me to enter the cottage, and I don't care. If someone wishes to stare at me in a lecherous manner, while I want nothing more than to remove the blood of men I sincerely no longer wish to have upon me, that's their prerogative."

*So brash!* There was a possibility Geryon was looking at

her naked form in such a manner. *I knew she was not shy, but this just makes me realise how much so.*

She knelt next to the bucket of water to wipe down her skin, washing the blood, dirt, and grime away.

"My heavens!" Geryon's brows raised in shock. *Only my kind says this.* Carwyn knelt next to her, shaking her head in disbelief. "You are bleeding."

The back of her ankles and sides of her toes were covered in blisters and cuts, along with cuts on the soles.

Valerie paused to note her feet before shrugging. "It does not matter."

He'd seen her throw her shoes to the side this day, but she'd never grimaced, or even limped – even when she'd been carrying Kaeylyn on her back. *She's injured.*

Why did knowing she was injured and in a tired state make his stomach knot? *I'm sure we could have found something to heal her.* He and Valerie wouldn't have been able to do so, but he was sure Valerie could have showed Kaeylyn how.

"You must be in so much pain. Please, let me heal them."

Valerie paused in wiping herself down. She eventually sighed. "As long as you promise not to touch me directly, you may do what you wish."

Carwyn ran inside and came back moments later with an ointment. Valerie rubbed it on her feet for her, then Carwyn lifted her hands above her feet and began to chant.

Once she was done, she knelt while Valerie resumed her bathing.

"What you did, Valerie–"

"Leave me be. I know what I have done."

"I'm surprised Eldaeric is not with you. He told us he scried for Kaeylyn and saw she was at the northern king's palace. Did you not see him?"

She eyed her sister before she scrubbed her arm downwards. "Eldaeric is dead."

Carwyn's eyes crinkled. "I'm so sorry, Valerie. I know he was your friend."

Geryon's eyes widened. He hadn't thought she may have known the Witch he'd killed. *Is that why he grabbed her?*

"I hardly counted that dark Witch a friend. He was an idiot, always had been. He should not have come for me, should not have tried to save Kaeylyn when he knew his magic was weak." She shook her head before she knelt to wipe her midsection, rubbing her stomach and breasts without care. "For his stupidity alone, he deserved what happened to him."

*Such a cold-hearted response to a friend being killed.*

"How did you do it when he could not? Who killed him?"

"He tried to take on King Bradwick during a ball and was overcome by human soldiers." She paused for a moment. "He almost uncovered my identity. He could have gotten us both killed and Kaeylyn would still be imprisoned."

Once her body was clean enough, she dunked her head into the bucket of water so she could wash the blood from her hair. She wiped at her face quickly, rubbed her neck to clean it, and then stopped to finger the ribbon around her throat.

It seemed she'd forgotten about it. Geryon had barely stopped staring at it. The ends were so frayed, when she tried to untie it with her wet hands, she was unable to. She reached for the dagger, and Carwyn shot forward.

"Stop, you will cut yourself. Let me help you." She stood behind her, only to pause. Her voice turned into a breathless whisper as she said, "Is... Is that the Witch's curse mark on your back?"

"Yes."

Instead of untying the ribbon, the woman pressed her gloved fingers into her back to inspect it. "How did you manage to get pixies to come to you for this?"

"Easy. They were fond of the idea of binding my magic."

"It's so cold; I can feel it through my gloves. It must be

painful, especially with how much magic you have."

Geryon didn't know she would experience pain from the mark, or why that made his stomach tighten. He noticed Valerie lied so easily and convincingly that Carwyn didn't realise it. *How often has she done that to me?*

"The longer I wear it, the less I will notice it." She shrugged in answer.

"I know why you have done this. You think that if you cannot access your magic, then you may be able to stop yourself from being corrupted."

"There are many reasons as to why I did it. Yes, that was one of them. I have others."

*She is trying to stop herself from turning?* She was going out of her way to avoid it. Geryon should be angry that she'd tricked him, but he wasn't, not when it had a noble reason behind it.

*She said she could not call the pixies on her own.* She'd needed his help to do it. *She said it was more like a favour than an offer.*

"As always, you are calculating." Carwyn shook her head and began to untie the ribbon. "I'm surprised you are wearing red when you hate the colour."

*She hates my preferred colour?* Yet she had worn it... for him?

"I wore it as a sign of affection for someone," she answered truthfully. "Before I then used it to manipulate them the following day."

Carwyn giggled freely. "I find it hard to believe you would wear anything for another, but manipulation sounds exactly like what you would do."

Valerie began to brush her wet hair in long, rough strokes. It was knotted and matted, and she struggled with the length of it. Carwyn untied the ribbon and Valerie swept her hair to the side to brush it with more ease.

Then, the woman slapped her own sister on the back of the head to push her forward, her lips parting.

"What are you doing?"

"You wear a lover's bite!" She grabbed her hair and violently yanked Valerie's head back, forcing her to look at her. It forced her into a deep arch, pushing her naked chest up. "Why do you have this?"

"Perhaps I was attacked."

The woman pouted, squinting her eyes. She came closer.

"You would not allow a man to attack you in this way. I have seen you threaten plenty of men with a dagger to their balls." She squinted further, like she was assessing Valerie's empty face, as if she could read it. "It was willing!"

The woman gave a squeal while running on the spot with joy. Geryon was stumped, trying to figure out how she knew that.

"Valerie has a boyfriend!" She danced around her and the bucket while Valerie shook her head, still brushing her wet hair. "Valerie has a boyfriend," she repeated.

"I most certainly don't." The yanks in her hair became rougher, like she wanted to speed up the process. "And regardless, it does not matter. They were someone from the palace."

"Oh, but it does to me! You had sex with someone, and you let them bite you. People only bite another during sex when they are enjoying themselves. It looks like he enjoyed himself."

*She's rather perceptive.* He couldn't help the grin forming across his face. *I did rather enjoy myself that night.* Even now, his cock jerked at the memory.

"You say this to tease and embarrass me. You have no idea about the situation, and you are making assumptions based on your own hypothesis."

*She's trying to spoil the fun.* He was enjoying this

conversation. It was revealing much, which is why he knew she wanted it to end. He couldn't help but chuckle.

Carwyn got down to her knees to be level with Valerie and stared at her with squinted eyes.

"Did you moan?" Valerie said nothing, and to Geryon, it appeared as though she didn't react at all. The woman went rolling to her back as she kicked her legs, squealing all the while. "You moaned! You, who did not even care that her feet were bleeding, moaned because of a man!"

His grin grew. He'd gotten her to moan only a handful of times, but it was true. Apparently, that was something he should be proud of, with how this woman was reacting.

"Cease speaking. You don't understand the repercussions of your words."

The woman rolled back to sit on her bottom, staring once more at her sister. "Did you like him?"

"I will not dignify that with a response," she answered smoothly while lifting her chin up.

Carwyn tilted her head and frowned. "Did you like him?"

*Yes, do tell.* Geryon wanted to know the answer more than he cared to admit.

"You did!" The girl laughed, her head thrown back. "You cared for another outside our–"

"Do you wish to pester me with such a trivial conversation out of intrigue because you are useless as a woman?" There was a cold bite to the words, her tone. "To annoying me because I'm not, and you are jealous?"

The cheer in the woman's face dropped into a crestfallen one. Tears watered her eyes.

"You are such a heartless person sometimes."

She ran off, leaving Valerie by herself. She shook her head as she watched her sister go, then continued with her hair.

He remembered what Valerie had told him of her family, how one of them was not able to carry a child. She wounded her sister on purpose to end the conversation. *I have always known she can be callous.*

She'd been occasionally cruel to Lady Charlotte.

It was while Valerie was placing a dress over her clean body that Carwyn returned. She was pouting, but she came to stand with her again.

"Are you going to continue the same conversation?"

"No." She turned her head away dismissively. "You only hurt me like that because you yourself are hurting."

"You know I must leave."

Valerie used the long point of a needle clip to twine her hair until it was a loose, messy bun. She threaded the needle into her waves until all he could see was a raven with its wings spread out across the back of her head. It was silver, and he figured this was the heirloom she'd spoken of.

"You are lying. You would not hurt me so directly if that was the cause." Carwyn removed her gloves, dropping them to the ground so she could raise her bare hands. "I want to know, Valerie."

She stepped forward with the intention of cupping Valerie's face.

"No. You will not feel anything worth noting. It's pointless."

"Let me do this." She continued to walk forward, and Valerie immediately retreated from her with a spark of certainty lighting in her eyes. "Let me be the one person who truly understands you, one last time."

Valerie's actions were what gave away that she was deeply distressed.

"Keep your hands off me, or I will make you regret it."

"You usually let me do this because you know I will find very little, so why are you running away?" Valerie paused, causing Carwyn to halt as well, as she eyed her sister's beseeching frown. "This is the last time I will be able to do this with you, Valerie. Please, give me this."

Geryon leaned forward when Valerie hesitantly nodded, intrigued by the situation. *What will be revealed?*

He could hardly wait to know.

Carwyn stepped forward and gently cupped Valerie's cheeks. There was a long pause, a long, silence-filled moment where nothing happened, nothing was said.

Then, as clear as day, heavy tears began to fall from Carwyn's eyes. Her bottom lip began to tremble while her eyebrows drew together so tightly, it bowed her eyes. There was a shuddering sob that followed, the sound of a squeaking breath caught in lungs.

Carwyn looked as though she was in terrible agony, while heavy tears fell like they would never stop.

Valerie grabbed her wrists and pulled her sister's hands away from her face, her expression empty and deadened. Yet, she pulled Carwyn forward with one arm while placing her hand on the back of her head, bringing her in for a tight, comforting embrace.

"You are in so much pain," her sister sobbed, heaving against her. "You have shattered your heart into pieces."

"Shhh, shhh, it's okay," Valerie said, patting the back of her head. "You need not speak of it."

"I'm so sorry for teasing you. I did not realise the piece you gave to him burns you." She shook her head on a heavy cry. "Or that your heart aches for Mother, Aldora, Kaeylyn, and me. You know how much you will miss us. You are worried about what will happen when you are not here to protect us." She dug her fingers into the back of Valerie's dress. "You are filled with so much shame, regret, and guilt. You are not even allowing yourself to feel happiness at bringing Kaeylyn home."

"I can barely feel it, Carwyn. I mostly feel numb."

"You always say that," she laughed. "Why is it every time

we do this, you end up comforting me when it's I who should be comforting you?"

"Because your powers of empathy mirror the hidden depths in which I have buried myself. A cut only bleeds when it first happens. After that, it merely stings, and the longer you wear it, the less it hurts."

"You have always been so alone."

"I'm not alone, Carwyn." Valerie leaned back so she could face her. "I have always had you. You know I have always loved you dearly, and I think I will miss you the most."

She stomped her foot as she whined. "You are only saying that to make me feel better."

"Mayhap." She gave a small smile, a forced one. "But it's still true."

Then, like she couldn't help herself, Carwyn reached up to touch Valerie's cheeks, just so she could share in the truth with her sister. She once more began to sob.

Valerie turned to look at the sky, as if to pull strength from it.

Geryon wanted to back away from what he learned. *Her sister is crying for her pain.* Pain that Geryon didn't know she was holding.

*She's filled with shame, regret, and guilt?* To know she must be riddled with these emotions wasn't a comforting thought. He hadn't thought on how much she would miss her family when he took her away from here.

But there was one thing that was more damning than the rest. *She gave a piece of herself to me?* Something that was hurting her?

*I don't understand what this means.*

Her sister had spoken as if it was burning her now, aching her this very moment. *Did she feel more for me than desire?* Had she felt something tender? Did she still?

He'd originally planned to kill her once they left her home.

He couldn't let her be free. She knew his human face, knew what he was, where his hunting grounds were. By Dragon law, she must be killed or imprisoned in his lair. *I have not been to my lair in decades.*

So, what should he do with her? He feared his own answer was not what it should be.

They pulled away from each other, and Carwyn gave her a bright smile, even though she was still crying.

"I want you to step through the ward, Valerie." She motioned her hand behind her.

"No, I would much rather not know the truth if it's unpleasant."

Carwyn walked around her and began to push her towards the house. Valerie fought her by digging her heels in.

"You are still a white Witch, and I plan to prove it!"

She shoved her hard, and eventually, they both went tumbling to the ground.

Carwyn sat up and pointed to her. "Ha! I told you. You are not turning yet."

Valerie looked at her position, where she was sitting in the clearing, and gave a singular laugh. "It appears as though you are right. I was able to pass through the ward."

Geryon eyed the sheen of the magic barrier he could see now that he knew about it. *She did not want to know if she was starting to become corrupt?* Did that mean it kept dark Witches out specifically?

Valerie stood, brushing off her pale green dress. It was light and simple, nothing like the intricate dresses she'd been wearing. She wore no shift, so the dress sat around her shoulders and revealed the bare skin of those rounded joints, as well as the top half of her chest.

"You are planning to leave now." Carwyn's saddened eyes fell away.

"Yes. I cannot remain here any longer. Mother is not out

here, so she does not intend to kill me like she is supposed to."

Geryon's claws dug into the bark of the tree. *They are so complicated!* Her own mother was supposed to kill her? He couldn't believe his ears!

"She has chosen banishment."

"You don't have to go, Valerie." Carwyn reached for her. "If the Witch's curse works, then you may not grow dark at all."

"I will not risk you all. I chose to go after Kaeylyn alone because I did not wish to possibly infect you all. This is the sacrifice I made." She paused, looking to the ground in thought before she said, "Just make sure Kaeylyn does not blame herself. It's not her fault people took her. She was a child who was playing. She's not at fault for that. Make sure she understands this, make sure she understands I did this because I felt like I had to, that I would have done it if any of you had been stolen."

Carwyn shook her head. "You could have taken us with you, Valerie."

"I did not want to risk anyone being killed or turned. Someone had to do it, and it had to be me." She brought her sister in for one last hug. "Tell Aldora I'm sorry I became the one thing she resents the most."

Valerie turned away from her sister, from the cottage that had been her home since she was a girl, from the clearing in which she'd played and used magic all her life. She walked away from the place that had brought her joy, a place where she'd been surrounded by love, despite her coldness.

Valerie walked away, knowing her heart was bleeding as

she did.

Yet, she did so with an expressionless face, like she didn't care. It wanted to fall; she could feel it trying to slip away so she could cry. Had she been alone, she may have, but she wasn't. She knew Geryon was watching, so she refused, keeping her composure as she left her home.

Once she was outside of the forest wards, Valerie moved until she stood in a space large enough for a Dragon to stand in it at any size.

She wondered if she'd lost him when he didn't approach straight away. *Did he get confused in the warding spells?*

He came out a few long moments later. He appeared in front of her, towering at his full height. The sun was setting, but she could still see him clearly in the light. It was the first time she'd seen him in so much brightness.

*His scales glitter like his eyes.*

He was staring at her in an assessment, an intense gaze of observation and thought. She knew why.

"What you heard–"

"Is it true?"

She didn't know why she looked away. Perhaps it was because she was ashamed. Perhaps it was because she didn't want to be honest with him. Usually, she averted her gaze because she didn't care about the conversation much.

This time, she knew it was because she couldn't look him in the eyes.

"It does not matter."

He curled his tail around her body and pulled, forcing her to face him. "Is. It. True?" He sounded each word out, his eyes narrowing.

"Yes, everything Carwyn said is real." She tried to slap his tail away to break eye contact, and she gave him her side. "She has the power of empathy. It allows her to feel for others, and she has become perceptive enough that she has taught herself how to read me when she's not touching me. When she is, she feels exactly what I feel."

This power was strong, rare. It meant she didn't require any spells, items, or chants to use it. Power like this always came with a sacrifice. Powers of telepathy, foresight, the ability to speak to animals – all of these were rare and amazing gifts only a handful could ever master.

Carwyn liked to tell her what she was feeling because she thought it would help her process it, like she needed assistance. In some small way, Valerie thought she may be right.

Valerie wasn't as cold and unfeeling as people thought.

"But like I said, it does not matter, and I know that." She turned to Geryon, knowing he would never reciprocate the tenderness she felt for him. "I'm ready to die now." She turned her chin up and folded her arms. "I believe I have already revealed how I wish to go."

Valerie wanted her body cleansed by dragonfire, hoping it would help her to go where she wanted in the afterlife. She still wanted to be with Faerydae, wanted to be in that plane with him. That's what they believed, that all Witches returned to their Dragon ancestor if they were pure or purified in death.

She watched his puffy Dragon lips thin, just as his eyes narrowed.

"No," he growled.

# 30

With the bottom of her fist, Valerie bashed on the boulder that had been rolled in front of her prison cell. "This is not what was promised to me, Dragon!"

She could hardly call it a prison cell, though.

Valerie had no idea where Geryon had taken her, but it wasn't to her death. *I must be in his lair.* What else could these cave walls mean?

After telling her he wouldn't kill her, he'd wrapped his tail around her torso and lifted her off into the sky. She could remember the high-pitch scream she gave, one that turned into shouting at him to put her down as she was flown across the heavens. Powerless, with no weapon to defend herself, she'd been nothing but a rag doll.

Once he'd landed at the top of a mountain, one any human would struggle to climb, he changed his size. He'd made it so that he was only just slightly larger than her and squeezed them both through a small hole. Then the bastard grew big again and dragged her along the ground.

Talk about a difficult way to enter one's own lair. Then

again, it meant it was well hidden.

The moment he'd entered, he grew large again and uttered a spell. A few of the torches along the walls lit up feebly, as though it had been far too long.

Inside was like a labyrinth. He'd seemed lost as he carried her around with his tail, like he could barely remember the way. When she'd asked why it was carved like a maze, he told her it was because he wanted it to be confusing. *Confusing enough even for himself.* From the large grin he'd been wearing, she had a feeling he enjoyed it.

Once he'd found the boulder he wanted, he rolled it around his lair, still carrying her. Then, he tossed her into a room full of blankets, pillows, and furs – like a collection of soft treasures – and rolled that boulder in front of it!

Valerie knew what this meant: he was intending on imprisoning her rather than killing her.

So, here she was, bashing her fist on this rock like a weak, feeble human, when she would have been able to move it with her witchcraft easily. *Bastard!* She didn't want to be a prisoner; she would much rather be dead.

Valerie wanted to escape what she'd done, and she wanted to do it before there was a possibility the Witch's curse didn't work, meaning she'd failed and would turn corrupt.

*The only thing that can purify me is fire.* It would be painful, morbid, but it was the only way she could be cleansed of her sins. *To burn away the darkness with unimaginable light.*

Knowing it was useless, she walked over to the cushions and pillows. She fell against them with a huff, folding her arms across her chest.

Geryon already made sure the dust in the room was taken care of, since there had been a large poof of it when he tossed her. When he realised, he'd flapped his wings inside the alcove until it was gone, pushing it out of this space and sending her into a coughing fit.

She eyed the curved ceiling with a glare, noting it must have been carved by sharp claws, since she could see gouge marks. Valerie knew Dragons found a cave and then shaped it to their liking. *Why did he bring me here?*

After some time passed, the boulder was rolled out of the way. Her eyelids flickered, not expecting the sight in front of her.

*He... He is human?* Geryon opened her prison in his human form.

He wore brown leather trousers that hugged his legs so tightly they left little to the imagination. A loose, crisp white tunic with a vee-shaped neckline cut down his chest, revealing strong muscles. He even wore an embroidered black coat that wasn't buttoned up. He wasn't wearing shoes, and his entire ensemble said he'd thrown everything on quickly.

A plate of food wafted with spices and herbs in his hand, and she hated that her mouth watered.

"Thought you may be hungry," he said, as he slowly, cautiously, approached.

Considering Dragons thought themselves weak in their human forms, her eyes drew over him in confusion. She knew he was more comfortable this way than most, since he lived with King Bradwick as a human, but she was a Witch, one he'd recently been deceived by.

*He could have given me food in his beast form.* Valerie never expected to see this side of him ever again.

Too busy gaping at his face in shock, her hands were slow in taking the plate and simple cutlery. When her fingers finally did touch it, he released it and she looked down.

It was a meal of meat and a wide variety of vegetables. She blinked at it since it was hot.

"Where did you get this?"

"Took some time to go down to the town to get supplies,

since I didn't have any." Her gaze flicked back up to his face. "I have learned much while being human."

"You cooked this?"

She brought it closer to her face and eyed it with uncertainty. Eating a meal made by a Dragon? She half-expected to die of food poisoning.

Yet, it looked delicious, which only made her wonder why he would cook such a grand meal for a prisoner. Honestly, she was so hungry right then, she didn't care if it was poisoned.

Curious about how Geryon's cooking would taste, she turned to plop herself onto the many cushions and pillows.

"No. I merely prayed to the gods, and they gave it to me."

She didn't laugh at his joke.

She examined his attire while she ate. She thought she was being sneaky, but he came closer to crouch a few feet from her. Collecting a stone from the ground, Geryon played with it while they spoke.

"I thought you intended to kill me," she said, bringing her first mouthful of food to her lips. Her tastebuds wonderfully sparked to life.

*Dear heavens, he knows how to cook something tasty.* It wasn't as good as hers or her mother's cooking, but it had the right kind of herbs and spices for what was available.

"Yes, that was originally my plan." He rested his elbows on his knees, keeping himself balanced on his toes. "But I have changed my mind. I can see you are not filled with evil."

"What do you plan to do with me, then? This was not a part of our bargain." Her tone was dull, letting him know she wasn't impressed.

"I have not made up my mind yet." Then a large, mischievous grin formed across his features, one she didn't trust.

"And why is that?"

"Because I wish to return to Bradwick's palace, to keep it

as my hunting grounds." His eyes followed her fork every time she speared it into her food. *He wants me to tell him what I think of his cooking.* She refused. "I have many years left there, and I don't know how to incorporate you into that."

"Then just kill me. I'm giving you permission."

He shook his head, his blue-black hair swaying. "I no longer wish to kill you."

"Then give me to the Elders."

When she stopped eating, her stomach too queasy with emotions to finish it, she placed it on the ground near her feet.

"It truly amazes me how much you know of my kind." He gave a laugh. "You may be one of the most informed Witches I have ever met, and for that reason alone you are quite the threat."

She looked at the pillows around her nervously. *Could I be endangering my family by revealing how much we know?* Damnit. Valerie hadn't thought about that possibility.

"No, I don't plan to hand you over to them." With his metallic blue eyes firmly on hers, he stepped closer in his crouched position.

"Then, what do–"

"I have learned much about you these past few days."

He tilted his head when she turned hers to the side to dismiss him. She wasn't bothered by what he learned. *Except for my feelings. I had wanted to keep them hidden.*

"Your family is odd. *You* are odd. I may not speak to Witches often, but even I know your family is different."

"So, you wish to keep me as a prisoner out of curiosity?" *Like dance monkey, dance?* She folded her arms, her fists bunching; she didn't appreciate such a thing.

"Oh, curiosity is definitely part of it," he grinned. "But your family's strange ways are not the main reason. I'm curious about *you* in particular."

Her brow twitched with the urge to frown. Despite her head

being turned, her eyes fell back on him. Valerie almost felt like a cornered mouse. If she wasn't careful, if she didn't keep her gaze on this predator, it might eat her – and not in the way she'd asked for.

"You have made your beliefs obvious, and I can see why you want to walk the path you wish to. You want to erase what you have done, even if it means your death. I find that noble. I wonder, though, did you kill the creatures you stole from?"

"No," she answered quietly. "I could not go that far."

"We don't know what it's that creates the poison in your kind, whether it's the use of dark magic or the death that comes directly before it. There are theories that the death of a magical creature lingers for a short while after its demise, that they try to curse those who have harmed them before they disappear from the world."

"Regardless, I still harmed when I should not have."

"You feel guilt over it, but you don't regret it, because the price was the safety of your sister." He crawled a little closer, and Valerie didn't know if his slowness was out of wariness, or to not spook her. It was like he was approaching an injured animal that might lash out. "So, what is it you truly regret? Why is it you feel shame?"

*Damn you, Carwyn.* She just had to speak out loud and reveal her true feelings for all to witness.

"I feel shame because I allowed my sister to be taken in the first place. If I had just protected her from the beginning, I would never have had to walk this path."

He opened his mouth to say something, but then immediately closed it. He cocked his head. "Then what of your regret?"

"I have hurt people who did not deserve it. It's hard not to feel regret over that. I deceived people, used evil magic. The soldiers who came to the castle with me must have been terribly confused when I released them from my spell. I worry they will be punished for not protecting the real Cecily. I don't even know if she's alive. She may be dead because of me."

"Do you feel regret in tricking me?" He twisted his head once more, and Valerie found it hard to look away from those metallic blue eyes, particularly when he was watching her so intently.

As before, she found them spellbinding. Her heart quickened a little.

"No," she lied, causing him to pout cutely. "Since you were also deceiving me."

A wide grin spread across his lips. "I think you do."

"Believe whatever it's you wish to. It still does not change what I have done – to you, to my family, to those in the palace." She unfurled her arms to point at him. "Don't forget I threatened King Bradwick. I threatened his balls, his eyes, his face, and then I tied him up."

"But you did not kill him when many others would have."

She made a face. "Of course not. I only wanted my sister. I did not care who took her or why she was taken, only that I found her, and we returned home."

"Now that you know what I am, what would you have done if you discovered I mistreated her?"

*He gave her toys.* She'd even looked healthy, had a bed, and must have been fed regularly. Kaeylyn had been healthy, despite where she was. She'd been unharmed; there hadn't been a single bruise, cut, or welt on her.

"Hated you without a doubt."

"But you don't, do you?"

Her voice pitched, almost spitting the words. "What is it you want from me, Geryon?" She turned her head to the side, needing to look away when confusing emotions arose. "You have approached me in your human form, and don't think I have not noticed you crawling closer. What is it you seek from me? Why have you imprisoned me instead of killing me like you promised?"

Why was her pulse wildly picking up speed the closer he got? Why did Valerie feel the unbearable need to retreat?

It didn't help that he had a certain look in his eyes. She thought she saw heat, but she didn't dare believe it.

"I don't care why you hide your emotions; all I know is you do." He was near her feet now, so close, and she tucked them away. "You show you are unfeeling, but you are not unsusceptible to whatever it's you have buried inside you. Perhaps you *are* uncaring most of the time. I can see it, times where you don't truly feel."

"And you wish to change me?" She gave a singular, mocking laugh. "Do you know how many people have tried? To coax me to become a friendlier or more compassionate person and have failed?"

Valerie finally retreated. She scooted backwards when he placed a knee next to hers to kneel.

"Changing implies a permanent shift to your personality, and I have no desire to change what I like for the benefit of others." He grabbed her knee to stop her, then reached forward to grab her around the base of her neck. "I plan to *break* you, for me and me alone."

Valerie tensed when he closed the space between them; he was so close, in fact, she was able to take in his sweet scent. Then he tilted his head and ran his tongue across her closed lips. She flinched at his touch.

"Break me?" she whispered, pressing the bottom of her fists against his chest.

Geryon wrapped his arm around her and cupped the back of her head, tilting it to the side with his hand. She pushed at him with shaking arms, a raspy gasp breaking through when he ran his tongue against her wildly beating pulse.

She didn't understand; it was not just his words, but his actions as well. *I'm so confused.* That confusion alone was

enough to derail her from that wet tongue's trance, despite
how her nipples pearled.

"Yes. You have not given me what I want, but you started
to, back in the palace. Every time you look at me with that
cold stare, something inside me demands I rip that mask from
your face."

He started to trail light kisses down the side of her neck,
and her body went warm – not just inside, where desire flipped
in her stomach, but also from the heat radiating from him.

"It angers me that someone else has seen under that mask."
*He's speaking of Carwyn.* She tried to get away, to stretch her
body from his touch. "I want to see under it, too. I want it to
slip away, to show me the passion you have hidden."

Her lips fell apart when she realised what he wanted. *He
wants to be intimate with me?*

"I'm a Witch, Geryon. Why do you even want this from
me?"

"You are hardly a Witch with this hex on you." He placed
his fingertips against the cold, burning symbol on her back –
the one locking her magic away. "Regardless, you are not
filled with darkness, which is what I truly hate."

"No spell can change what I was born as or what I have
done." *If only it was that simple.* "You are a Dragon; you hate
my kind. I tricked you; you should not want this from me."

"Don't tell me what I should or should not do or want. Like
I said, I learned much about you over the last few days, and
what I now know makes me crave you just as much as I did
before."

Then, to her surprise, he bit the side of her neck.

Valerie flinched from the strength of his bite, from the
words he uttered. *I must get away.* She pushed harder against
him, trying to force them apart.

*He's not thinking clearly.* He couldn't be. What he was
saying went against his nature, against the hatred his kind

held. Bedding a Witch? Knowingly and willingly?

"You are toying with me." Clearly, he was doing this because he learned she'd grown to care for him.

The fact he'd pulled her desire from her, made her feel warm and fuzzy, had been a strange sensation. No one else could make her heart race in the way it did when he touched her... like it was starting to now.

Valerie refused to be made a fool of.

"Am I?" He grabbed both her hands and pushed her down by her wrists, forcing her to lie back against the pillows around her. "I don't think I would be this hard if I merely wished to toy with you."

To punctate his statement, he lowered his hips to press his hardened cock against her. With one of her legs between his, she felt him slip over her thigh, and her chest flushed, both in shock and, surprisingly, arousal.

"The only game I wish to play is the one where you pretend you don't want me, which only makes me more desperate." He brought his mouth up higher to dart his tongue against the shell of her ear. He lowered his voice to a whisper when he said, "And yet I smell it on you."

A strangled noised squeezed its way past her throat.

Before she could say or do anything, he moved his mouth to bring it over hers. Geryon kissed her deeply, and her lips moved under the force of his own.

*He still tastes so sweet.* Like the sweetest candy. A rush of goosebumps trailed over her skin, and she couldn't deny herself just a sip of his mouth.

*What am I doing?* She asked herself this, yet her lips were moving of their own accord, kissing him back. *I need to stop this.* His tongue gently came to sweep against hers, and her stomach clenched. She lapped it with her own in greeting.

Why was it every time he kissed her, made her take in the taste of his mouth, Valerie lost her sense of reasoning? Did he even know he held this kind of power over her?

He came closer, sliding his legs down so that he rested more firmly against her.

He tilted his head the other way and deepened the kiss further, just as he thrust his hips against her. The upward movement caused his thigh to rub directly against her folds, and a spark shot through her.

Valerie was getting wetter with each touch, but she fought against it, her need for logic overpowering her arousal.

*He's using my feelings against me, manipulating me.* She clenched her eyes tight. This was why she didn't like revealing what she hid in the depths of her soul.

She broke away from the kiss by forcing her head to the side.

"Stop." She fisted her hands. "Remove yourself from me."

He chuckled and merely pressed his lips between her cheek and ear.

"You know what I am now. That means I can be open about what I can sense from you." The tip of his nose tickled the tightened ridge of her neck from her stretched position as he trailed it down her skin, his tongue following behind. "Delicious. I much prefer your scent to the human's you hid behind. It's stronger when you are aroused; it smells warm."

She wished she'd managed to contain the deep breath that fell from her. She knew she hadn't revealed any of her body's inner turmoil, but the fact he could scent it on her was disconcerting.

She feared she was beginning to reveal it in her voice, too.

"Your life is much longer than a human's."

Around his eyes, she could see a crinkle of enjoyment. Or was it humour? She wasn't sure, but it was there.

"So?"

"I wanted to keep you when you were human. Now, I can do so for much longer." He licked at the seam of her lips.

"Their lives are so fleeting. I'm sure you have at least a hundred years before your beauty even begins to fade." A grin spread on his face as his eyes darted over hers. "I'm sure I will not care when it does."

Then Geryon's lips were upon hers again. This kiss held more passion, more need as he panted into her mouth.

There was a level of shock she couldn't keep from her features. Sometimes, even Valerie couldn't hide what she felt, not such a sharp spike of emotion. Her eyes widened at the clench in her heart.

*He plans to keep me... for a hundred years?* To play this game? The one where she was his prisoner, a plaything? To touch her with his hands and mouth like this? *To be intimate with me?*

Valerie didn't know what he felt for her. Yes, she desired him, and that was from where her tiny piece of affection had grown. *But all he wants from me is my body.*

Her heartbeat sped up in a terrifying mix of emotions.

*He plans to keep me, like... like... some sort of perverted sex slave?* That was not something she wanted.

He released one of her hands so he could begin lifting the skirt of her dress. It took her longer than it should have to respond, but his lips against the sensitive skin of her throat while he sucked were just so damn distracting.

"Wait." He didn't.

He brought her skirts up higher, his lips trailing lower to flutter against her chest. It was only when his palm touched the skin of her outer thigh did she finally remember that damn word she always managed to forget.

"No."

He stopped completely, immediately, his eyes moving from the flushed skin of her chest to meet hers.

"No?" His tongue darted out, like he couldn't help himself from taking one last taste before he pulled away. He removed his hand from under her dress so that he could be on his hands and knees above her, caging her in, his nose only inches from hers. "Why not?"

He was huffing, his cheeks pink, like he was flushed with arousal. Geryon was turned on, and he had no shame about revealing so. Her eyes darted down for just a second before they came back up; she managed to catch that thick erection bulging tightly against his trousers.

"I don't have to give you a reason."

His lips thinned.

"This is true."

He brought one hand forward and brushed it over the side of her face softly. It was a caress, a touch of affection one would usually do to a lover. *Why did he touch me so gently?*

"But I can scent that you are turned on." His eyes trailed down her body, to what she guessed was the redness across her chest, her hardened nipples tight against her thin dress. "I can see it."

"My body may want something, but my mind might be averse to the idea."

He rolled his eyes at her words. "Humans and Witches are so strange. Dragonkind do what we want and think later."

That was because, deep down inside, they were truly a creature. They thought with instinct. Even though her family hadn't seen one in centuries, their temperament wasn't unknown.

Sex came easy to Dragons. When they desired another, they were generally demanding with it.

She lifted her head higher to bring herself closer, refusing to show any of her hesitancy or fear – even if she felt a little of both. "You must not have wanted me when you first discovered what I am."

His lips thinned once more.

"Well, yes." His grin was quick to brighten his handsome

features again. "But I desire you now that I know you are not despicable like dark Witches. You also cannot harm me with your magic, which was what made me apprehensive."

She let her head fall back, exasperated. "Your mind was still averse to it, though."

"You were not this against me in the palace. Is it because you know what I am?" He pulled back to sit on his heels, finally releasing her other hand. Then he had the audacity to pout like a child and turn his head away, grumbling. "I had hoped since you knew I was a Dragon you might take me in that form. I have never done so with something human shaped."

"No, it's not because you are... a..." Valerie trailed off, fully registering what he said.

*He wanted to have sex with me as a Dragon?* She started to crawl out from beneath him. *Someone help me, for I'm in danger with this male!*

The fact that he was even considering it meant he was clearly unhinged.

She wasn't against the idea of being intimate with him in his Dragon form, although it was something she'd never considered, even in her wildest dreams. The idea didn't send dread through her. With the way her family worshipped Dragons, held them sacred, it would be considered an honour.

She knew it was possible, that he could shift his size to something she could accommodate.

No, the reason she thought he was unhinged was because he wanted to be that open, in that form, with a Witch. Her, no less! Someone who had cast dark magic and deceived him.

"Wait." He grabbed her hips and pulled her back to him, and her arse accidentally ground against his erection, making him groan. "You did not answer my question."

"No, I don't wish to."

She didn't want to give him more ammunition to

manipulate her.

He released her again. Since she'd still been trying to climb away, she lunged forward and quickly turned to her side. She was surprised he'd let her go.

*'No' works for other things as well?*

She blinked, realising Geryon held the word dearly, not just sexually, but within other boundaries as well.

His gaze was averted while he looked around the room. He appeared frustrated but not angered from her rejection, and maybe... even a little hurt. Why did the aftermath of this, his firm reactions to that single word, the way he was looking now, betray her by making warmth spread through her chest?

# 31

The problem Valerie faced was although he released her when she uttered the word 'no', Geryon would eventually return to try again. That in itself wasn't the problem; she knew he would. He'd done so in the palace to coax her desire out, and she knew she could stop him whenever she pleased.

No, the problem was the more he tried, the further Valerie let him go. And just like in the palace, her resolve was faltering.

She couldn't hide it from him either, especially when it was made obvious when she let him get close enough, let him kiss her, touch her.

*I want him. I want Geryon inside me.* She wanted him to take her how he once did, when they'd been alone in that private room.

She didn't care what he was. He was the same man as before, the one who would touch her gently with his hands, causing her to arch into his touch rather than away, but his mouth would be like fire, leaving tingling traces in its wake.

His mouth was like poison, and whenever he kissed her,

she would lose herself to it. She knew it spurred him on if she stopped pushing him away and started to hold onto him, like her hands were desperate to reach for him. Even her nails dug in like she didn't want him to escape, as though he were prey she wanted to keep her claws in.

A desperate ache rose inside Valerie as time slowly dragged on.

It didn't help that he would be kind to her between his attempts.

He cooked for her, always carefully noting her preferences. If she didn't eat a certain item on the plate, she would never see it on one again. He was making sure he fed her things she liked; he was being attentive.

*He takes me outside.* She was a prisoner, and yet he offered to occasionally take walks so she could sit in the sun. It was like he understood that because she was a Witch, she needed to feel the outside world, even if she could no longer draw energy from it.

She'd seen more of his lair, but she noticed he never had a ward at the front to keep her in, or other Witches out.

When she asked him about it, he refused to answer her. It made her wonder if he could.

Not all Dragons were adept at magic, in the same way not all Witches were. He never warded the room holding her sister caged, either.

Because he'd seen her read at the palace, he brought her books. There was a pile steadily growing, offerings to try and keep her happy. He even tried to gift her jewels and gold, like she was a hoarding Dragoness sitting on pretty, sparkling treasures.

It would be easier to deny him if he didn't show her such consideration or kindness. *He's acting as though he cares for me.*

She didn't hope to believe it.

"You do these things in the hopes of softening me so I will cave to you," is what she told him the third time he allowed her to go outside.

His answer surprised her.

"You will cave regardless," he laughed, his eyes full of mirth. "I do them because I want to. Do they not bring you comfort or joy?"

They did. They also furthered her uncertainty. It was easy to deny a man who only came to her in an attempt to bed her. Geryon didn't.

She rarely spent any time alone; he would come to converse with her often. When questioned on why he didn't in the palace, he told her it was because he hadn't wanted to raise suspicion.

Then, he reminded her they'd spoken a great deal the day he showed her the dungeons, as well as the night they were intertwined. She barely remembered that. She'd been too fixated on the powerful emotions stirring because he was buried between her legs.

Now, he would speak with her often. It wasn't always just before he tried to bed her; no, it was as if he just wanted her company. He even stayed with her when she rejected him. He would grow flustered, but he wouldn't lash out at her for it like she expected. Instead, he'd make himself comfortable by laying back on the cushions and pillows, asking her assorted questions about her life, her family, her likes and dislikes.

Hell, he even asked her what her favourite colour was, displeased to hear it was green. The short, unhidden chuckle that had fallen from her was only because he demanded it be blue because of his scales.

The only reason she answered his questions was because he'd been unafraid to share those she asked of him. It was as though he wanted them both to reveal themselves with private little details only lovers would share.

*What is it about him that makes me crave him so dearly?*

Because, human or Dragon, Valerie still wanted him. When he held her down by her forearms, she didn't resist him. When he licked across her lips, she willingly parted them, and the sweetness she tasted in his human form was even stronger now, in his Dragon form.

The warmth she could feel from his scaly body was so smouldering, she found herself relaxed and docile beneath him.

*His touch is so light.* Even with his fangs and claws, she only felt them as soft points rather than razors. They became even gentler when he settled his body between her thighs and slipped his scaled hand under her dress to lift it.

His claws tickled her thigh as he lifted higher, until instead of fabric, it was his body, the scales here rougher than underneath him, that tickled her instead. The belly of him was smoother, more vulnerable, and slipped over her like silk. It was so soft, she barely registered anything other than how nice it felt.

*Yet he's so dominating.* Dominating by how, once he finished pulling her skirt up, he lifted himself higher to allow his tongue to go deeper within her mouth. Then, the next thing she knew, something hard entered her, but with his cock resting against her uncovered belly, hot and thick, she knew he hadn't entered her.

"W-what is that?" she rasped, trying her hardest not to moan.

It was textured, a little rough, but not painful. It was hard, impossibly long, thick, and it even wriggled a little. The last sensation was the one that had her legs parting for more, had her skin flushing terribly until she thought she'd combust.

"You are still fighting me," he rumbled teasingly against her ear, since she'd broken away from their strange kiss. "I did not want to enter you until you were ready." He swirled his tongue against her ear, making it tingle and causing a shiver to assault her spine. "I thought perhaps I should put the ruined tip of my tail to good use."

Her lips parted in surprise, understanding that the wriggly, slightly bendy thing inside her pussy was the stump of his tail. She'd seen the weaponised spike or spade had been removed from some sort of battle, and she could barely believe it was now inside her.

"I always hated my brother a little for biting off the end of it," he chuckled when she reached up to dig her nails into his sides. "But now I think I should thank him for allowing me to fuck you with it."

*Oh heavens,* she thought, clinging to him as she started bucking her hips against it, only for Geryon to throw her higher into pleasure by resting his cock between her folds and working the length of it over her clit.

"You seem more receptive to me as a Dragon." The humour in his tone was unmistakable, and the masculine vibration of pride in it twisted her stomach. "Would you prefer my Dragon cock over my human one, Valerie?"

Her name, spoken in his rough voice, had her inner walls clenching his tail. It also rendered her silent, unable to deny him. Did she prefer him as a Dragon? She wasn't sure, but knowing he was one... his heat, scent, even his scales had her melting quicker than usual.

When alone, Valerie had begun to ache for the moments he would come to try and take her. She wanted him, wanted to feel him. His cock was still rubbing over her clit, lashing it with pleasure as he attacked her most sensitive places any way he could. Even his bowed chest was scraping against her nipples, making them pound with need.

Everything felt so strange, it had her mind going blank.

His tail and cock worked faster, and she shivered against him. *I'm about to come.* She could feel it in the way her body ached, how it tightened, how her knees buckled and her hands trembled.

Like in the palace, she was allowing Geryon to sweep her away. The only difference now was, instead of gripping his back or his shirt, one of her hands gripped the base of a wing while the other clung to a head spike.

It was like he knew exactly how to touch her, knew how to make her legs tremble. Even now, his tongue moved away from her ear so he could slip it against her wildly beating pulse, the skin there so sensitive, it forced her breath to stutter.

With the dexterity he had in his tail, the moment he changed the angle upwards, Valerie fell apart. Her moan was silent – she made it so – but she buried her face against the side of his thick neck as she clenched around him. Hiding it was pointless; his answering pleased growl as liquid squelched from her pussy informed her he knew just how hard she was orgasming.

*It's too much.* She craved what she knew he would give her, that tingling rush of pleasure that threatened to make her cry out. She wanted him to replace his thrusting tail with his cock, because... despite how good this felt, she desperately wished for him to come apart as well.

She wanted to hear him unabashedly groan, to shudder, to stop being so sly, instead so heated that he could barely speak from that wicked mouth. What had started to undo Valerie's cold exterior was how open Geryon was with his desires, his fierce reactions. They fuelled her.

When she came down from bliss, her body went languid while her heart raced frantically. It picked up even more so when he pulled back and looked down at her, the scales around his metallic blue eyes crinkling as his grin turned lopsided. With his fangs glinting, he appeared devilish.

*I cannot do this anymore.* For days, he had been giving her such sweet attention, and she knew... she knew at some point, she would give in to him.

The only thing stopping Valerie was that she was averse to the future he presented for her.

*I wanted to be cleansed.* Why should she have this Dragon when she felt impure? *I wanted to be cleansed and die for my sins.* Not be on the receiving end of this beautiful creature's touches, devious tongue, and *tail*.

*What he wants is wrong.* To be doing this with her, wanting her for whatever reason it was; she knew it wasn't supposed to be this way.

Even now, he was still rubbing her clit, and her selfish desire made her spread her thighs just a little more so he could press harder. Her heart was beating so fast, she could barely think anymore, and it was so loud in her ears.

If he was to pull his tail away now and draw back, she knew she would beg for his cock. *I crave it when I should not.*

Which was why Valerie reached behind her and pulled the needle of her clip from her hair.

*I will not be able to deny him next time.* She knew, even if she uttered 'no' now, she would be forced to deal with the ache that would follow afterwards. In between his attentions, she would remain wet and wanting for this man.

Valerie selfishly wanted satisfaction.

*I'm so sorry.*

Geryon's body tensed when something sharp lanced the side of his throat. Silently, slowly, he pulled his tail from the woman whose delicious smelling orgasm lingered on it. He pulled further away so he could step back and plug the profusely bleeding hole she'd punctured in his jugular with a clawed finger.

He stumbled back when he saw something glinting from the bottom of her fist: the sharp point of her raven hair clip.

*She stabbed me?* Confusion sailed through Geryon, since he didn't understand at first why she did, before rage took hold as she bolted from the alcove.

Most importantly, Geryon felt undeniable lust that she'd done so. He was visibly shaking with it.

*She was giving in to me.* Instead of allowing him to win, she took it into her own hands to find a way out of it. *She knew she was not going to be able to deny me any longer.*

Geryon had won.

He wouldn't let her escape now, not when this woman was almost in his grasp. Geryon blew a ring of fire outwards and chanted the word, "Shift."

Within seconds, that fire came back to encase him in flames so he could revert to his human form. He would be unable to heal his wound in his Dragon form.

Focusing magic into his free hand, he blew fire at it until it stuck before he pressed one of his fingers into the hole to burn it. Quickly, before he passed out from the main artery being punctured, he healed himself using the same spell he'd used to heal her sister.

She had a head start on him, since he needed to shift and heal first, but eventually, he joined in the chase.

When he caught her, he knew she would take him.

It wasn't hard to track her with her rich, mouth-watering scent leading the way.

*She already memorised my maze.* She'd been memorising the paths she needed to take from when he would take her on walks. *So smart, so clever, so wonderful.* He panted as he followed, his shaft throbbing at the chase, at what she'd done to him. *Want to fuck her so hard.*

For the past few days since he'd brought her into his lair,

his home, Geryon had been vibrating with want for her. Maybe he was unhinged, but something about that woman had him outrageously aroused.

The more he touched her, tasted her, felt her, gained even the slightest reaction, he increasingly understood what he really wanted.

*I like her. I wish to keep her.* Her doing this just proved it to him more.

He would tell Bradwick whatever he needed to in order to keep her there, but he would be damned if he didn't have both of the things he wanted.

Gaining on her, he came upon her in the last main room, right before the exit tunnel.

She must have heard him coming because she ducked to the side and lunged for the pile of old armour and weapons he carelessly placed there years ago. There were also human remains from when he would regurgitate what his stomach acid couldn't eat away because of the armour. He'd never cared about keeping his lair neat, since he rarely spent time in it.

Once she was at his discard pile, she withdrew a sword from it and then pointed it at him!

He gave her a large grin when they began to circle each other.

"I thought you did not harm Dragons," he chuckled, watching her carefully.

Her features were firmly composed, showing no fear, no worry, no hesitation. He licked at his lips slightly, the scent of desire still rolling off her, cloying and thick from her. She could lie with her face all she wanted; her body was screaming the truth.

"Kill," she panted, her chest heaving from sprinting. "I don't kill Dragons."

They circled each other enough that he also made it to the

pile, and he picked up his own sword to point back at her. Her head tilted, and he figured that was her way of acting surprised.

"You don't truly wish to harm me, do you?" He stepped closer to draw her attack. "I have two swords on me, and I only plan to slam one of them inside you this day."

And it was not the one in his hand.

Her scent deepened at his words, and he couldn't stop himself from groaning. Still unclothed, he grabbed his cock and gave it a needy stroke, wishing to feel her heat around it rather than the cool air of his cave.

*Her face does not match her body.* Both were extremes of each other. *She makes me feel crazed.*

He stepped even closer, until the points of their weapons were almost touching. He tapped hers lightly to play with her.

His eyes crinkled with deep-seated humour. "Come now, we are being ridiculous. We both want me inside you."

"I'm not going to be some whore for you to play with."

She finally swung at him, knocking his sword sideways. He tightened his grip, following the swing so it didn't fly from his hand.

"Well, that's a rather grotesque way of putting it." He gave his own swing, and she narrowly missed it on purpose so she could swipe her blade downwards. It forced him to step back. "By your logic, would I also not be your whore?"

Her motions stuttered in surprise.

However, she swung up, and once again, he had to step back to miss it. "This was not what we agreed."

*She's a lot better with a sword than I thought she would be.* Already, he could tell she was better than most human men he'd fought.

"Did you not say you did not care what happened to you after you returned your sister home?"

He slashed his sword forward, and hers came up to deflect

it. A loud ringing filled the space, bouncing off the cave walls.

"I meant in the terms of my death."

She swung, and he deflected it this time.

She was swift and much more agile than he was. He was also not using much force, since he had no intention of harming her. He could tell she wasn't putting in all her effort, either.

"I would much rather burn you with my passion than with my flames." He swung up, knowing she would block him. Since they were so close now, she stepped back when he tried to grab her wrist with his free hand. "I'm rather fond of the idea of keeping you."

"I will not be a prisoner."

"Perhaps I don't want to keep you as a prisoner." There was a pause shared between them while she tried to understand what he meant.

The next time she swung at him, he was prepared.

It was a downwards swing, and he dodged it by stepping sideways while dropping his own sword. The blade sailed through the air next to him and hit the ground.

She hadn't expected him to come so close so suddenly, and Geryon managed to tackle her. He curled his arms around her head and midsection to protect her precious body from the ground.

Her sword was lost, clanking against the cave floor while he pinned her forearms down.

"Got you, my butterfly with fangs," he said down to her before he crushed her lips with his own.

Geryon groaned against her mouth and thrust his cock between her legs at the feel of her, the scent of her, the taste of her. *So unbelievably soft.* There was even a tiny moan in return, and his shaft twitched to the sound.

When her lips moved beneath his, he cupped the sides of her beautiful face with one hand to deepen the kiss. Her fingers dug into his back, and she bucked against him, the wonderful slide of her body slipping against his.

"I want inside you," he whispered against her lips before he slipped his tongue inside her mouth, just to feel her twirl it against her own.

His free hand began to lift the skirt of her dress up so he could grip her thigh and pull it to the side. He didn't know where one of her own hands went as it slipped away from holding him, but he was too focused on caressing her thigh to care.

*I want her naked beneath me.*

Geryon was conflicted. He wanted to rush so she wouldn't escape him, yet he wanted to be slow just so he could feel her.

The answer to where her hand went came flying at him – in the form of a stone against his temple.

Pulling away from her mouth with a huff of pleasure, he brought his tongue to her throat to sweep it in a long, flat stroke. He could feel a trickle of blood running down the side of his face.

"I told you a long time ago: whenever you say or do things like this, you will not get the reaction you want from me." He thrust against her again to punctuate his point, his entire body begging to have her glove him with her wet pussy. "With your scent the way it's, it only makes me want to bury my cock inside you more."

This is how a lot of Dragonesses liked to play. They liked to be dominated, wanted to be overpowered to make sure the male taking them was worth bedding.

If she fought him when he couldn't sense the arousal from her, he would back off. Geryon wouldn't persist or play this game with a woman who obviously didn't want it.

But the scent was thick from her, and just taking it in made him tingle all the way down his spine. It made him harder that she wasn't denying out of lack of desire.

It was something else, something he wanted to overcome. *But she will not show me, nor will she tell me.*

How was he meant to overcome something he didn't know? He was trying to face a problem blind. Geryon hoped if he finally crossed this barrier, he might come to understand why she was being infuriatingly hesitant.

"Stop," she said quietly, and yet he only chuckled.

*She did not say no.* Every time, it made him laugh.

They both knew what she needed to say to truly stop him.

"Let me be fond of you," he whispered softly.

He lifted himself to take her mouth, hoping it would calm her like it often did.

She hit him again, and a growl came from him. More blood welled against his temple, and he nipped her bottom lip with his front teeth.

He pulled his face back while he curled his arms around her head as if to pillow it. He was huffing wildly, vibrating with yearning. His eyes were half lidded as he simply held her.

Geryon gazed down at her, wishing, hoping to see something that would give him the answer, willing her to tell him.

"Why do you fight it?"

He wasn't. He knew he should be, so he didn't see why she should. They wanted each other, that was obvious, so he didn't understand why she wanted to reject it.

Staring down, he watched her bottom lip give the slightest tremble as her eyes flickered. *She wants to give in.*

Instead of answering him, she smacked him harder, successfully this time.

He'd really hoped she wouldn't have the strength behind her to actually send him into unconsciousness. Her tall but petite body was deceiving of her strength.

Geryon didn't know how long he'd been out, waiting for his magic to heal him. He likely wouldn't scar, since it wasn't a deep wound, but it had been enough to knock him out.

Something did wake him, however. Rather, someone. With much force, he was slapped back to consciousness – repeatedly.

"Okay, okay, I got it." He slapped the person's meaty hands to stop them. "I'm awake."

Geryon glared up at Rurik, who was human, naked, and straddling his torso. He really tried not to think too hard on the fact his cock and balls were pressing against him.

"What do you want, dear brother?"

He let his lifted head fall back against the ground, knowing he'd never be able to push him off; it would only anger him if he tried. Rurik was easy to predict in that way.

Rurik slapped him again. "Why do you smell of a Witch?"

"Because I had one." Rurik slapped him again, harder, which only caused Geryon to sigh in disappointment. "Why must you take your rage out on your own family?"

Rurik was Geryon's older brother by decades, making him the youngest sibling of them all. He had two other brothers and a sister as well. He once had many other siblings, but most had been killed by dark Witches.

"And you lost it?" He shouted it with his nose crinkling, making the long, deep scar across his nose and cheeks more prominent.

With a coy expression and a single finger lifted, he stated, "Momentarily."

Geryon would find Valerie. He would track her down and bring her back.

He was slapped again, and this time, he slapped back.

Rurik leaned closer with an intense, hateful glare full of menace and barely controlled rage. "Why do you smell of its arousal?"

Geryon's lips curled into a large, cheeky grin. "Why else would I smell of it?"

Rurik smacked his face into his palm in disbelief while he stayed on top of him. He rubbed his clenched eyes.

"How...? Why...? What were you thinking, brother? I came here because we organised that I would collect a witchling, and instead, I find you don't have it, smell of a different Witch, and smell like you have been trying to bed it."

"We both failed to detect her when she was at the palace, and she's quite the woman. Pure-hearted Witch, obviously."

Geryon genuinely thought this.

No matter what Valerie had done, he didn't think she was corrupted. He didn't know if that was truly because they had locked her magic away, but for now, that was what she was.

"The witchling was her sister, and she wanted to take her home."

"And you let her?"

Geryon caught Rurik's fist before he could punch him, similarly catching the other when it came flying. *See? His anger makes him predictable.*

"Why not? You told me you have been releasing Witches, so why cannot I?" Rurik narrowed his silver eyes, but he couldn't come up with a good enough rebuttal. "They are Faerydaes, Rurik. I have much to tell you."

"I don't care who their ancestor is! You let a Witch go free when she knows of your face, your lair? It's like you wish to be punished by the Elders. Why are you even trying to bed her?"

"You have a Witch. Why cannot I bed one for my own enjoyment?"

Rurik's head reared back while his eyes widened in shock.

"You cannot be considering that! Amalia is special. She's different, and she has proved that she will never turn." Then he leaned forward to snarl at Geryon. "Yours has knocked you unconscious with this rock and run away."

He grabbed the rock Valerie must have hit him with – it smelt of his blood. Rurik let it roll from his palm carelessly onto Geryon's face, and it smacked him straight in the nose. *Ow! Barbarian.*

"It's like she's begging me to fuck with her." Geryon sighed, falling back to let his eyes droop heavily.

*I can barely wait to catch her, to punish her with my cock.*

"You are an idiot!" Rurik shouted, and Geryon raised his brow in response, considering he wasn't the brightest himself. He may be a better warrior, but Rurik's short temper made him careless and impulsive. "Why must you always choose the most difficult path?"

That was the problem, wasn't it?

Geryon liked things that were difficult. His food, his clothing, his lair. Even his hunting grounds were a pain, because it meant he needed to be patient, or set up traps and lures.

Valerie was wild, extremely difficult, and it made him

undeniably and irrevocably smitten, in a crazed sort of way.

Unlike Rurik, Valerie wasn't predictable, which made her exciting. *I don't think I will ever tire of her.*

Chasing after her was more problematic than Geryon anticipated.

He thought, with her witchcraft locked away, she would be easy to find. *How hard is it to chase a human-like woman on foot?* One who would have needed to climb down the side of his mountain cliff, which was not an easy feat.

*Very.* He was finding it *extremely* hard.

The moment she hit the forest, her scent faded, as though she'd rubbed it away, right before it disappeared completely at a passing road. He'd been able to smell horses and the polished wood of a carriage, but not her.

Valerie had managed to hitch a ride.

When he followed it to the end of its path, her scent wasn't there, and he realised she'd hopped out of it earlier than its end destination.

Since then, he would pick up trails of her scent and then lose it.

She'd taken the sword she threatened him with. It at least brought him comfort, knowing she had something she could use to protect herself. He'd seen it the one time he managed to catch up to her and then, somehow, lost her again. They'd managed to have a conversation, though.

Her scent had been masked, dulled by a sickly sweet perfume that tickled his nose. Human-made and pungent, it was near impossible to smell through. Unfortunately for her, he'd taken in her scent directly; not just through his nostrils, but also with his tongue, his mouth.

Geryon would never forget it again.

Tracking her to just outside a town she must have stayed in for the night, he found her walking through the forest, rather than along the road.

She didn't hear him approaching as he came near on foot, knowing she'd run if she heard his wings. They created heavy, loaded whooshes that could be heard from a distance if one understood them.

Instead, he'd flown in his smaller size until he was close enough, then shifted.

Like any smart Dragon, he'd been carrying a flying pouch, something that could carry clothing, human weapons, and anything he desired. He slung it over his torso when he was medium, and carried it in his paws when he was small or overly large.

Knowing that approaching her naked may spook her – plus, the idea of chasing her unclothed while she had a sword wasn't wise – he donned his trousers.

He only got a few metres away from her before she swiftly turned to him, her short sword poised. She paused upon realising who had found her.

A loud trickle of water could be heard in the distance, and she'd been heading towards it. *She was intending to wash in the stream to clear her scent.*

"Have you come to finally do what you promised?" she asked, refusing to lower her weapon.

"What are you doing out here?" He watched her warily, his brows furrowing with deep confusion.

Why was Valerie choosing to run through the wilderness? She only occasionally stayed in human towns. *Would she really prefer this to me?*

"I can do whatever I want. You don't own me. You also did not answer my question."

For some reason, Geryon thought she would try to return home, but she never had. Her scent never went near those woods, and he'd been unable to find her family home by himself. He knew he must have gotten close a few times, considering he constantly got lost in the powerful magic surrounding it.

He stepped closer, shuffling his feet forwards, and she raised her weapon higher.

With his hands raised in submission, despite it being a façade, he twinkled his fingers at her. "I can grab you, you know," he chuckled, humour crinkling his eyes.

"Try it, and my sword will cut you. You can heal, so as long as I don't slit your throat or cut your heart or lungs, you will survive." Her eyes darted to his feet when he came just the tiniest bit closer. Her grip tightened on the hilt of her sword. "I know I'm your prey, but I will not willingly be your prisoner."

"I told you: what if I don't want you to be my prisoner?"

Her eyes squinted for a split second before she schooled her features. "I have no idea what that means."

Geryon stepped forward, and she swung that sword dangerously fast, like she truly would cut him with it.

Like a foolish, idiotic man, he crept even closer. "I'm saying... stay with me."

"Have you ever been hexed to not return to your Dragon form?"

"Of course I have." He gave a laugh, shaking his head. "It's a popular hex dark Witches use against my kind."

"How does it feel?"

He had to hide the urge to shudder at the memory.

"Appalling. I'm a Dragon before I'm a man, and not being able to shift to what I really am is abhorrent."

Being comfortable in his human body was one thing, but not being able to access the beast side of him was another. He'd been hatched from an egg. The first time he felt the world was with his soft, baby scales.

"Imagine it being permanent."

Geryon's expression hardened. "No. I would never allow it, and I would much prefer not to imagine it."

Her own face softened with mocking humour. "That's the future offered to me, and I don't want it."

He tilted his head sharply with a frown, not understanding how she would be affected by such a hex. "I don't–"

"I'm without my magic." She looked down to her free hand, clenching and unclenching it. "It's the same. As you need that side of you, I need to feel my magic coursing through my veins."

"But you were the one who wanted this."

She swiped her blade, even though he hadn't come closer.

"Until my death! Which I did not think was going to be long after." She gave a shake of her head, and her beautiful long brown hair swayed around her small shoulders. "My body aches for it, like an itch that's never scratched, like a thorn that cannot be pulled, like a cut that never heals. It nags constantly, and I don't wish to tolerate it for the next hundred years just to satisfy your desires." She turned her gaze to the side. "Or my own."

His mouth went dry at what he'd just heard.

*She wants her magic returned to her?* He thought she was afraid she would turn if she could feel her witchcraft. *How do I feel about this?*

Did he really want Valerie to the extent that he would allow such a glaring risk? *I don't think she will become corrupted.* Rurik's mate hadn't, and she'd cast blood magic. Everyone could tell she was still pure hearted, although she had only ever used her own blood to cast – except for one time, recently.

Amalia had been offered a heart to eat by a Dragoness who had become fond of her. That was a few years ago, and even now, she was still pure.

However, Geryon also needed to think on if he could trust her enough to bed her if she were filled with magic. The idea didn't repulse him like it should, though he would be far more careless and vulnerable. Could he trust Valerie that deeply?

"What... What if I were to release it?" How bad could it be to at least contemplate such a thought?

"No." She took a step back, but her brows knotted deeply –she was confused he even offered. "I don't want that either."

*Then what does she want?*

His eyes widened before he slowly pointed to himself. "*I* am the problem?"

Something sunk inside his chest; a creeping sadness, a feeling of rejection.

"No, you are definitely not the problem." She snorted a single laugh. "But that was self-absorbed of you. There is another reason, one I will not share with you because you will use it against me. I have two paths available, and I have decided which one I will walk."

Geryon gave a snarl, stepping closer regardless of her blade.

"For three weeks I have been chasing you, and I will have you!"

He'd decided on what he wanted, and he very much desired it. He would pluck her from this forest, take her back to his lair, and figure out why she was so hesitant so he could mitigate her fears, her uncertainty. Until she told him what the big fucking issue was, whether it be him or something else, Geryon knew he wouldn't stop.

At his shout, Valerie turned and ran. He quickly gave chase, but before he could get his arms around her, hoping he could figure out a way to convince her to stay with him, she jumped.

Valerie leapt off a small cliff and into a rushing river of rapids.

*Crazy woman!* On foot, he followed along the river to see her head pop up. When she didn't emerge, he shifted to see her from above.

He followed the river, came back around, and yet, he couldn't find her. The water was shallow enough he could see through it, but he couldn't spot her.

She had managed to climb out of the water while he was looking elsewhere and fled into the forest. With her scent washed away for the moment, it took him too long to pick it up again. By then, it was light and faded.

Her scent had become old, and he was once again hunting a trail that was difficult to track.

**2 weeks later**

Geryon followed Valerie's scent to a tavern. Like most of his kind preferred, he wore a cloak to hide his strange-coloured hair and identity. Dragons who travelled often liked to keep themselves hidden to protect themselves. It wasn't the humans who worried them, but the odd Witch they could come across.

Usually, Geryon would make quick work killing a Witch if he sniffed one close by, but this time, he didn't. He was too preoccupied with the one he was already hunting.

When he entered the tavern, he discovered she wasn't there, but her scent was fresh. She'd spent an extended period inside the establishment.

Obtaining answers about her was more of a hassle than he thought it would be. It was only when he noticed the wanted papers on the wall and the other heavily armed occupants, that he realised it was a place mercenaries often frequented.

Their secrecy had been infuriating.

The only reason he'd gotten any information at all was because it was used to mock him.

A young woman approached to tap him on one of his cheeks, like she had the damn right to! The sultry, devious smirk she gave him showed she wasn't interested in bedding him, but was up to mischief.

"I would not follow her, if I were you. She made quite the impression when she arrived."

With his nose crinkled, he leaned down to bring himself to her level. Her eyelids flickered with unease, realising he wasn't some simpleton.

She shied away from him, as most humans did, at the fierce, deadly gaze his eyes held. "You underestimate a stranger."

"The pretty woman with the dead eyes has been taken by the Caddel brothers," she told him. "They were impressed by her, and they are hard to please. If anyone tries to approach her, it will mean certain death."

His head reared back. *Impressed by her. Hard to please?* Such words could make him think things he would much rather not believe. *She has taken men as her protectors?*

*Blasted!* She really intended to make this as hard as possible.

He wasn't surprised she managed to find help. She was exceedingly clever, and he knew she could wrap anyone around her pale, nimble fingers. Like a spider with its web, she could weave strings of deceit.

Unfortunately for him, she'd added an element to this hunt – one he didn't like.

As much as he liked things difficult, he was growing aggravated. There was a limit to what one could take before things stopped becoming fun, and his heart was losing its enthusiasm when his arms ached with a loneliness, begging to hold her again.

*Why is she so against this? Where is she heading, and why?*

The Caddel brothers. Nice men, if you could call obvious marauders and murderers nice. They were tall, dark, and much older than Valerie. Both were covered in scars, which only added an evil hint to their constant scowls.

They were two strong humans in their late thirties. They didn't speak often, and what she liked about them the most is that they never asked why she hired them.

It was a beneficial contract. She needed to go east and people to travel with, and they were already heading that way and needed easy money.

It wasn't hard to convince them. Valerie had gotten into a fight with a man when she'd been sitting down for her evening meal in the tavern. *Apparently*, she'd stared at this young, roguish human wrong.

What he thought was an invitation to sit with her and attempt to get under her skirt turned into her bending his wrist so far back, she'd heard the bones crack. Then, she slammed his head against the table, all the while still attempting to eat her food, before she kicked him to the ground.

Her actions earned her these two brothers inviting themselves to sit with her. They hadn't said anything, and she'd gotten the impression they did it to ward other patrons away.

There had been two questions shared between them.

"Where you headed, young lady?" Neil, the older one by a year, had asked. His hair was black, his eyes brown, and he bore a scar over his empty left eye.

"Furthest borders of the east kingdom," she answered.

"Got money for protection?" Holden had asked, his hair dark brown and his eyes a darker shade than his brother's. He had a short beard, which made it difficult to tell if he also bore scarring on his face. "Area is dried up, and we were thinking of heading to another place."

Without a word, Valerie threw the last of her coin on the table. Neil had swiped it, checked what she had, and they nodded to each other.

She would have preferred to travel alone, but the moment they made the offer, she realised this was her perfect opportunity. She wished she'd thought of this kind of arrangement sooner.

After that, they'd become travelling companions.

She told them one thing and one thing only about what she was doing: she was being followed and if that person caught up to her, they weren't to get in their way. No matter what they heard or saw, she could handle him.

They'd raised their brows at her, but she explained she didn't need protection from that person, only others on the road.

*Geryon may kill them if they get in the way.* And she *did* like her travel companions.

They were rough around the edges, but they were respectable enough. They didn't hassle her, barely spoke to her, and she knew they appreciated she also wasn't chatty. Not once did they ever attempt to get under her skirt.

They looked like thugs, covered in scars and dirt. They spoke rudely, crudely, brashly. They often replied in grunts, but they were nice men. It was people like that who often gave her faith in humanity when she'd been dealt harm.

She once tried to teach Aldora that, to not think with bias, but she'd been too traumatised to see past her pain.

Since they knew she was being followed, they often split up. One would ride their horse along the road, and the other she rode with by the tree line.

She knew Geryon would follow her scent eventually to the tavern and someone would reveal she had left with these two. They were making it appear as though they were single riders, rather than a trio of people, from the skies, at least.

That's where the Caddel brothers really came in.

Valerie was using them to hide her scent alongside the perfumes she regularly changed. Geryon wouldn't know their scents, wouldn't know the smell of their horses.

With her riding behind one, they shielded her. It wouldn't last forever, but she just hoped it was enough to get her safely to her destination.

Valerie was facing backwards, like she usually did, and leaned against the back of the rider. Today, she was with Holden, and he paid no mind to what she did on the back of his horse.

She turned her head up towards the blue sky she could barely see through the canopy of leaves above.

*I hope I reach my destination before he finds me.* The piece of herself she'd given to Geryon burned worse than it did before.

It hadn't been able to grow in King Bradwick's palace, since she knew she had to leave after she found her sister. Afterwards, he had detested her.

It had been nothing but a sweet memory, a lovely thing she shared with another and cherished.

She may have regretted it for his sake, but that was no longer the case. Instead, the time she'd spent with him in his lair had forced it to grow, to spread into a bigger piece. It burned constantly. It took her a long time to realise she liked his attention.

*Do I miss him? No, no, that's not possible.* That was at least what she told herself.

Knowing he was out there, trying to find her, for whatever reason, made that piece ache worse. *Why does he keep chasing me?*

She didn't think it was only because she was his escaped prey. If that were the case, he would have done so with anger, with wrath. He wouldn't have approached her in the forest cautiously to have a conversation.

What he was offering sounded enticing. A life of pleasure? Some form of companionship other than what she planned at the end of this journey?

But she couldn't do that, and she knew it. What he wanted from her right now could be temporary. She wouldn't let him play her with emotions... with her heart – the one she was always desperate to never feel.

*I'm not unfeeling.* Valerie never had been. There was just something broken about her. For some deep reason, she'd never felt comfortable sharing herself with the world, had buried what she did feel deep inside.

Sometimes even to the point where she barely registered them.

Now, only strong emotions, sharp ones, could pierce through her façade. She mostly just felt numb.

*He's using what he knows about my feelings against me.* She wondered if he thought she was easier to control because of it. There was no way he would reciprocate those feelings and, therefore, Valerie didn't want to be intimate with someone who would only hurt her in the end.

*What is the point in allowing someone in?* Especially now, especially this person. The more her tenderness grew, the more desperate Valerie was to escape him. She was afraid.

At the end of this journey with the Caddel brothers, Valerie was going to take it out of his hands.

*I have made my decision and I will stick to it.* She wondered if Geryon would be upset when he discovered what she had done. *Most unlikely. He's a Dragon, after all.*

She would always be a temporary thing for him. She was seventy-three, and she had about a hundred years before she would truly start to wither with age.

Witches grew quickly in the beginning of their lives, matching humans, and then there was a quick decline. They would still age, but they would remain mostly youthful until they reached a hundred and seventy. Then their ageing would accelerate significantly.

She didn't know how old he was, but she was sure Geryon would live at least another five hundred years. There was no point to what they were doing, and Valerie knew it.

*That does not mean it does not make me sad.* Her face didn't convey such an emotion as specks of sunlight glittered through the leaves above her. Her lids flickered when one sparkled right in her eye, piercing it with light.

Holden whistled, calling Neil back to them to hide in the tree line. "Night will fall soon. We should set up camp."

Valerie put her thoughts on hold.

They would make a small fire so they could see and cook their food, then they would sleep out in the open.

The Caddel brothers would lie on either side of her – not too close, but enough that it would be hard to approach her without one of them noticing. What they didn't know is she would notice first. She appreciated the gesture, though.

*Such sweet men.*

**1 month later**

The eastern territory. The kingdom was large, flat, and forest covered everything except around its borders, where five main mountain ranges circled it.

Valerie had finally made it to the easternmost one. The land on the other side eventually turned to sea and islands, but the beaches wouldn't be seen for many weeks of riding.

There was one last town before it became a no-man's-land, and people feared going further east, feared going anywhere near the mountain. She knew she'd come to the right place when she heard rumours of demons and monsters that crawled the dense forestry.

Cattle mysteriously went missing from farms nearby, occasionally people as well. What kept people coming here was that the mountain range was rich in minerals, and they mined at the very base of it.

*I will never make it through the forest before nightfall.* Valerie needed to be able to see in the light of day for what she searched for.

Unfortunately, it meant she had to stop in town and pay for a stay at the inn. It was a hefty price, but the Caddel brothers had voiced no issue in helping her obtain more coin along their journey. They stole it from other travellers.

Getting here took longer than expected. From the northern kingdom, they had to go directly south and then travel east. The east was too hard to get to with the mountain ranges surrounding it.

It would be hard to instigate a war against it, which is why she thought the country had a long standing of peace.

Neil and Holden planned to stay a few nights in the town before they left. Valerie was intending to separate from them today. They were aware of this, and they'd already been paid.

To her surprise, Neil blubbered like a child at having to leave her, sentimental about their month together. She didn't know why; they'd rarely spoken.

They never discovered she was a Witch, but she had a funny feeling they wouldn't have cared. They saw a young woman who might have needed help and were already on the move.

Leaving the brothers to drink wine and eat by themselves, she paid the innkeeper to supply her with a warm bucket of water so that she could bathe before she slept. She planned to be up and out before the sun rose.

*It's getting colder.* Winter had finally come. *My favourite season,* she thought while she wiped her face and body clean. *I hope I see snow while I travel.*

Since she was alone, she allowed herself a small, sad smile.

With her remaining water, Valerie attempted to wash her spare clothes. She didn't have a nightgown. There wasn't a need for something so silly while she was travelling. She had needed to travel light.

She pulled out her last clean, dry dress from her pack. They'd often had to wash their clothes in streams, but it was better than not doing it at all.

She sniffed her dress. *I can never get the smoke of campfire out of my dresses.* Oddly enough, she liked the sweet aroma of it.

Now that she was clean, refreshed, and calm, Valerie pulled out a map she managed to acquire of the eastern kingdom. She fingered where she thought she would have to walk to find what she was searching for.

*If I go southeast of the town and circle north through this ridge of hillside, it will take me to the highest point of forest before it becomes rocky mountain.* She wondered if this was the best route to take. *I don't really know where I'm going, but I should find what I want if I follow the mountain around.*

If not, hopefully it found her.

Something *tinged* against the ground, like a metal coin dropped from a high place. It snapped her attention, and she turned around to find the key that had been in the door was now vibrating against the ground as it waited to settle. *Ching. Ching. Ching.* Before she could walk forward and reach for it, the door flung open.

Someone had used magic to unlock it.

A grumpy-looking man entered the room.

His eyes narrowed on her when he stepped inside before he slammed the door shut once more. It bashed against the door frame with a deafening boom.

"Found you, little mouse."

He pushed the hood of a cloak off his head to reveal a sour expression. His nose was crinkled, one side of his upper lip raised over his teeth.

Her face paled at seeing Geryon; not even she could control her shock. Damnit. Valerie was almost where she needed to be, was so close to completing her task.

She didn't know what emotion it was that quickened the steady beat of her heart, but it began to pound when he stepped closer.

"How did you–" She quickly scrunched up the map behind her back before he could see it.

She should have lunged for her sword instead.

He didn't stop growling, even when he closed the small space and threaded his fingers through her hair. He forced her head back with a yank, and... sniffed her temple?

She blinked at the unexpected action.

He began to sniff down the side of her face. It tickled when he did it to her neck, right behind her ear.

"What are you doing?" She tried to press her shoulder to her ear, closing the space to stop him from tickling her further.

"You are covered in a mixture of smells. I'm trying to figure out what is what."

He was being aggressive. She'd only ever heard his voice this deep when he was angry.

"Why?" Why were they having this strange start to a conversation?

"You have surrounded yourself with men. I'm trying to determine if your scent is *clean*."

"You... you!" She rose her hand to slap him.

He quickly caught her wrist before she made impact.

"I learned a long time ago not to make assumptions with you. Trying to figure out the truth first."

She pushed against his chest with her free hand when he drew his tongue against the centre of her throat. Then, she felt his lips moving, as though he was speaking against it, and warmth radiated all the way around it. *He used a spell?*

"Has another man touched you?"

"N-No," she whispered, unsure of why she was answering his rude question.

His growling finally settled, and he released her wrist, wrapping one of his arms around her midsection while the other slipped across her shoulders. The position forced her face into the crook of his neck.

"Good. I was not sure if I would be happy with what I discovered at the end of your trail."

*He has always been jealous and possessive.* She'd always known it would bother Geryon that she hired the Caddel brothers, but she'd needed their assistance.

"You used a truth speaking spell."

She bashed on his back. *How dare he.*

She could have fought against his weaker magic if she still had access to her own to chant a counter-spell. This was one of the reasons Valerie hated having her magic locked away – she couldn't defend herself properly. She couldn't stop herself from being a victim of another magic wielder's spells.

He pressed his lips against her throat again, and that warmth radiated down her side. "Were you harmed?"

"Y-Yes." The answer was stolen from her, no matter how hard she fought against it.

She and the Caddel brothers were attacked by other bandits, who were running low on supplies. Although it was a minor wound she could heal even without witchcraft, she was slashed against her lower back.

She'd been snuck up on and managed to lunge forward quick enough to only receive the tip of the sword.

Geryon held her tighter, his growl returning. "What was the point in hiring men if you were injured anyway?"

Whenever he moved his lips away from her throat, the warmth faded, and the spell wouldn't push for her to answer.

Valerie couldn't handle the affectionate embrace, the way it made her stomach flutter. She fought to free herself. When she struggled hard enough, he finally pulled back.

"You are too clever for your own good! For an entire month, I have been searching for you." His lips thinned while his eyes narrowed again. "I'm not pleased."

"I did not ask for you to come after me." She shoved at his

chest, and his eyes squinted further when he stumbled back. "Why will you not leave me alone?"

Ever logical, Valerie was refusing to listen to the deep pound of her pulse, the way it quickened at his touches, at merely the sight of him. She always listened to her head over her heart.

She was at the end of her patience with this, with him, with everything.

"Why are you here embracing me rather than killing me? Is it because you think it's entertaining, because you discovered I foolishly garnered tenderness for you?" She turned her head away, her fists clenched. "I don't want the empty future you have offered me, and I will not let you take me by force. Just leave me alone."

Rather than be angry, Geryon laughed. "You seriously have not figured it out yet, have you?"

"What is there to figure out? You are obviously deranged."

He had to be. He was a crazed beast who couldn't think rationally.

"That very well could be true," he pouted. From the corner of her eye, she saw him run his hand through his hair, rubbing the back of his head. It appeared awkward, as though he was shy and embarrassed. Even his cheeks pinkened slightly. "Do I have to be direct with you then? Is that what I must do?"

There was a small pause.

"Valerie..." Her head quickly shot to him at the beseeching way he said her name, only ever hearing him say it one other time. "You silly Witch! I care for you."

Her brows slowly drew together tightly. *He cares for me?*

"Why do you think it's I have been chasing you? Why do you think it's I want to touch you, regardless of what you are?" He stepped closer, and she was too shocked to stop him. "I have been fond of you since the palace."

He pressed his fingertips against the skin of her chest, right over the left side of it. "You are not alone in this burning sensation you feel, and I would prefer not to be wounded by what I hold any longer."

"But I'm a Witch, and you are a Dragon."

"And before I thought you were a human, and I was a Dragon. It still did not matter to me. I had planned to court you and spend whatever little human years you had with you."

*This is wrong.* Valerie stepped back, feeling like someone was trying to tug on the tendons holding her heart firmly in place. It wasn't the muscles she felt it against, but the hard layer of stone she had placed around it. *It's still not possible.*

"This mark does not erase what I am. I still cannot—"

He followed her, and before she could finish speaking, he cupped her hands and pushed them against his chest, holding them both with one of his own.

"When will you accept that I don't care what you are, or what you have done?"

He leaned down to press his lips against hers while he slid his free hand around her body once more. The kiss was gentle when she thought he would be rough. When he squeezed her fingers lightly, her lungs tightened in her chest.

*He... cares for me.* Just knowing that made the burning piece of tenderness within her spread with welcoming warmth instead.

The moment she parted her lips to return his kiss, his tongue swept inside her mouth. Geryon wasn't patient enough to go at her pace, his kisses hungry and messy.

She took in the sweet taste of him, and desire flipped in her belly, blossoming to life. *I want him.*

She had feared him catching up to her, because she knew if he did, Valerie wouldn't want to fight it. After his words, she wanted to fight him even less.

Her head could deal with this later.

Right then, right now, all she wanted was to believe his

words, even if it was just for a moment. She wanted to believe he shared in her feelings. She wanted to believe what she had done didn't matter, that darkness was not lurking around the corner to grab her in its ugly clutches.

For once in her life, Valerie wanted to let her heart take over. She was confused, uncertain, but just for one night, she didn't want to experience this terrible pang in her chest.

She wanted to ache in other ways.

Valerie slipped her arms around his shoulders and pressed her body against his, arching into him.

*I don't have to promise tomorrow.* But she could let him have now.

He gripped her tighter as a groan fell from him. "Nhn. Your scent..." He pulled back to shudder. "Changed so rapidly."

Taking his hand away from her, he pulled on the tie of his cloak while he pushed her back against the desk she'd been using earlier. It slipped from his shoulders when he crashed his lips against hers again.

This time, his gentleness faded, leaving scorching kisses in its wake. He spoke between them with such a haunting croak, it made her ears tingle.

"Are you going to try to run from me, force me to shove this" – he thrust his cock against her, showing her how hard and long it was already – "inside you before you do?" His hand lowered to grab her backside and grip it tightly, almost lifting her. "Or can I unclothe you first?"

Instead of answering, Valerie pulled Geryon so she could crash their lips back together, her tongue slipping inside his mouth. She lowered her hand and rubbed her palm over the bulge of his shaft. It was her own way of silently telling him she had no intention of stopping.

He gave a pant and broke away from her mouth to bring his lips against her neck. He started to undo the ties at the front of her simple dress at the same time.

"No more running away," he demanded.

She thought he was going to be soft with his mouth, would give her the little kisses that sometimes stole her breath. Instead, he bit her hard, like he once had on the back of her neck.

Skin tore. Blood welled. A gasp left her, and she tensed against him – accidentally squeezing his shaft she'd been stroking.

She stemmed her grimace when his teeth dug deeper. *It hurts.*

She was so distracted by the pain that it was only when he released his bite that she realised he'd pulled her dress to her waist. It caught on the slight flare of her hips.

When he licked at the wound, a ripple of goosebumps cascaded wildly down her body at the titillating sting. He brought his free hand forward to rub the pad of his thumb against one of her nipples, and it tightened under his touch.

His other hand rose to caress the bare skin of her back, his fingertips a feather-light touch against her.

One of the things that always drove her to Geryon was he was contradicting with his touches. One part of him would be rough, like his mouth and teeth, while others would be such a gentle touch that it tingled her skin. Her muscles leapt at each sensation in different ways.

It satisfied all parts of her. Soft, and yet mean. Rough, yet gentle. Forceful, yet coaxing.

Another shiver ran down her spine when he skimmed his hand over her hips and under her dress with such a silky touch it had her softening. He pushed her dress further down, and it eventually fell from the curve of her backside so he could grasp her freely.

Her thighs twitched at each flick of his thumb over her nipple, her abdomen tightening. Every time she felt desire roll, that growing pool of wetness at her core became damper.

She pulled her hand from around his shoulders to lower it to the other, fiddling with the buttons of his breeches. When she opened them, she was about to pull his cock from it when he lifted her off the ground.

Holding her tightly against him, Valerie was forced to wrap her legs around his waist as he walked them to the bed.

They fell against it, but he didn't stay with her. He lowered himself while trailing kisses down her chest. Pausing at her breasts, he brought almost the entirety of one into his mouth.

His breath was warm, and her chest flushed when he swirled his tongue around a hardened bud. He gave it a firm suck, squeezing the other with one of his rough, calloused palms before his head travelled lower.

The tips of his hair brushed across her skin and made her arch against him.

She heard the thud of a boot fall against the ground like it had been kicked off. A second thud followed.

"I have wanted to fuck you with the taste of your pussy on my tongue since I tasted it." He slipped his tongue over prominent the edge of her hip bone, and a strangled noise squeezed its way from her lungs.

*Such a carnal male.* It was one of the reasons Valerie found it so hard to resist him.

She opened her legs for him before he could get the chance to even try separating them himself. He grinned up at her, only occasionally darting his eyes away from her face to see where he was going as he made his way down.

Her pussy clenched in anticipation. *Don't fight, Valerie.* She wanted this, wanted this night, wanted this man.

A deep breath fell from her parted lips when he ran his tongue through her folds, a thorough and deep delve. Then, he was at her core, tonguing and slurping at her entrance.

Her nose felt fuzzy, like her sinuses went on the fritz at the sudden onslaught. Her body grew hotter in a rush, her back arched as a stifled moan escaped.

Valerie had wanted to be like this with him again, to let him freely touch her like that night in the palace. His tongue swirled at her entrance before he then did it to her clit.

Just like before, she gripped his hair to pull him harder against her as she lightly bucked. She throbbed, she ached, and Valerie was now at a point of no return.

*I'm... going to come soon.* Already she was toeing that line into sweet bliss.

She curled her body forward and brought her knees up so she could cup the sides of his head with her thighs and calves. Gripping his hair firmly with both hands, she watched him pleasure her with his tongue, unable to look away.

Yet, her head threatened to fall back whenever he sucked that hard nub of her clit or pushed the tip of his tongue inside her empty core.

When she detonated, he had to fight against her uncontrolled tugging of his hair to keep his mouth on her so he could steal it. He snarled against her folds, licking and sucking.

Her channel spasmed around nothing, disappointingly empty, and she was now hungrier to be filled. She had to close her eyes when they rolled back, her body twitching. Her orgasm was making her more aroused rather than satisfied.

*I need him inside me.* She needed something big, hard, and pounding inside her empty core, and it had to come from him and him alone. No one else could make her feel this way.

He rose above her, licking at his lips as he removed his tunic. Slowly, he revealed the muscled planes of his stomach, his torso, his broad chest. His hard body flexed beautifully when he pulled the fabric over his head.

She wanted to trail her tongue over the deep vee-line of his hips, the one that maddened most women because it always led to somewhere wonderful.

She didn't know when he managed to remove his breeches, but her eyes were riveted to his jutting erection. It looked as hard as steel, thick and visibly throbbing. The veins on the sides were twitching, showing her just how deeply his blood was excitedly pumping.

Her body wept for it, and her eyes darted up to his face.

Something had risen inside her chest, making her feel desperate; a deep-seated yearning, and she couldn't focus on anything but Geryon.

Her core throbbed to feel connected to him, her fingers itched to touch his body. Her skin wanted to be warmed by him. Her ears twitched to hear him groan. Her eyes were greedy to drink him in.

He ran his rough palm from her knee down her inner thigh, like he wanted to be gentle with her, slow.

She couldn't handle that right now.

She lifted and wrapped her hand around the side of his neck. Kicking her leg over while pushing him, she forced him to his back.

"Valerie?" Why did hearing him say *her* name make her chest feel tight?

She kissed at his chest when she finished straddling his waist.

Looking up at him, she watched his frown of concern turn into a grin of satisfaction. His mouth, and even cheeks, were wet from her orgasm, and she turned her gaze down to his chest.

*Magnificent.* Muscled, strong, lightly dusted with hair. She nipped her teeth into the squishiness of his pectoral muscle. He gave a grunt the first time, but the second time she did it, he ground his shaft against her just as she slipped her folds against him.

She had been trying to grind the sensitive nub of her apex against his cock.

Valerie didn't want to wait any longer. She swept her hands down the wonderful sides of his body and lifted her hips.

When she gripped his shaft, she didn't slowly lower her hips, didn't draw this out. She sat back from leaning over him so that she could mount his cock in one go.

A loud gasp fell from her, and her knees tucked in against him. *Dear heavens!* She dug her fingertips into his stomach. That aching emptiness was suddenly filled with all of Geryon, and all she wanted to do was melt around it.

*How can he feel this good?* She wasn't even moving yet, but her core was already quivering around him, the length, the girth, that unyielding hardness. He felt bigger than she remembered, like she'd forgotten the remarkable feeling.

Valerie was trying to hold on, to not completely lose herself to this. She knew it was over, though, when he gripped her hips and pushed her up the length of him, only to pull her back down as he thrust up.

Pleasure radiated all the way up her body to even the tip of her head. She threw it back. *Yes!*

Geryon only needed to spur her on once to get her to move her hips before she did, and by his great ancestors, did she.

She'd surprised him when she forcibly demanded to be on top. He'd almost denied her, almost rolled her over so he could take her the way he wanted. He'd wanted this for months, chasing her all over the world for another taste of her, to feel her like this.

*I promised myself I would punish her with my cock.*

Still, he'd noticed she was jittery. Her hands had been trembling, her breaths shallow, quick and shaky. For the first time, the flush of her arousal had pinkened her cheeks.

Seeing her like this had made him wonder what she would do if she were to control his cock, to ride him.

That first movement caused her to throw her head back, and she hadn't brought it forward since. He tried to match her pace. He tried to thrust up, to thrust deeper.

Geryon couldn't keep himself still even if he wanted to.

*Wanted her so badly.* His hands gripped her tighter.

She was grinding against him, moving back and forth,

moving his cock in and out of her gripping channel. It was gripping, tightening around him at intervals like it didn't want to let him go.

A shudder radiated all the way from his fingertips to his toes as he watched her ride him. Her small, perky breasts bounced, begging for his attention, but he couldn't get his hands away from her hips. His mind was too focused on her pussy wrapped around him to move away from where they were connected. It felt too intense, distracting from everything else.

*Her body is warm.* She was wet, and the sound of her arousal squelching made his mind feel hazed. Feeling it was even better.

He helped her move at a pace that was better suited while she kept her hands rested against his torso to keep her balance. Her fingers dug in when she arched her back occasionally.

There was one thing that caused him to groan loudly, his nose crinkling so tightly on one side it curled his lip back. He pulsated heavily, releasing a bubble of pre-cum.

It gave him a clear indication of how hard he knew he was going to spend when he did.

*She is moaning.*

It was soft, light, but he could hear it every time she rocked back onto him. She did it every time the head of his cockhead prodded against the swelling ridge of her G-spot. He wondered if she was even aware she was making such erotic noises.

Her lips were parted, but he couldn't see her face. All he knew was she was letting out little cries she never had before.

He wanted to roll her over so he could slam into her body and force her to be louder. Geryon craved to make her cry out in abandon.

*She's loving my cock inside her, riding it.* She was so wet the only resistance between their bodies was that she was so snug. *Been so long since I felt her.*

He expected they would need to take their time at first. Instead, she was riding him like she was unable to get enough of him moving inside her.

The more she moved, the warmer he felt. It was like paradise.

Geryon began to pull her down harder. Her back bowed as she tried to move faster. He was deep, had been deep the entire time. She barely moved a quarter of the way up his cock, like she didn't want to be without the feel of him for one moment.

Her breath caught as he watched her shiver.

Her core squeezed him for a moment. *She's about to come.* He made her come down quicker. *Want it all over me.* He tried to send his cock up faster. *Want her to–*

He never finished his thought. Her breath caught again, and she clenched around him unbelievably hard.

*Heavens!* His body tensed in reaction, his chin falling to his chest so he could watch where she orgasmed around him. *She feels so good.*

The feeling was slowly absorbed, since he wasn't pounding her through her orgasm. It meant he was able to perceive the way her walls spasmed around him.

Her legs trembled, and he had to keep her moving while she came, since she was too busy squirming. Her moan was silent, but he didn't think it was because she was trying to hide it; she was just too busy tensing.

Geryon let out a groan, feeling his balls draw up. *I have not come in months.* And here he thought he would be able to last.

His cock was laden with seed, and she was drawing him ever close to release.

He wanted to keep watching her ride him. He wanted to watch her use him to bring herself release over and *over* again. The usually cold woman, moving on him like she was hungry to come.

It was only when she stopped clamping down on him did he notice that her toes uncurled. He slipped his hands further back to grip her backside, kneading both cheeks.

"Don't stop," he groaned with a heavy shudder. *I'm close.*

He didn't care if she wanted to go limp or needed a moment to collect herself. If she paused now, she would leave him in agony.

His back arched, the muscles of his biceps and thighs twitching. He tried to get her to hit harder while she rolled her hips, and that press of his cockhead slamming deep radiated across his abdomen. *I want to come inside her.*

"So deep," she softly moaned.

She was trying to mirror him, to give him what he wanted, what he *needed*. Sweet, long-awaited release.

Geryon threw his head back against the bed. His back arched so tightly, it even came off the mattress when the first burst of his seed finally broke free. He let out a strangled groan as his engorged cock released, *finally*.

Even though he was frozen, unable to do anything but grip her backside tightly and push her down as he came, she kept rolling her hips. She was stirring him around, sending his pulsating, throbbing cock through her dripping core while he released.

It felt remarkable, made the experience even better.

*She rode me.* Geryon hadn't expected her to, thought he would have to fight her for something like this. *She rode me until I came.* It was a spine-tingling orgasm, barrelling through him while she continued to buck her hips like she wanted to completely empty him. *Rode me* as *I came.*

She stopped when she must have felt him softening. She leaned over, kissing his chest with her pale pink lips, and the softness of them moulded against his muscles.

Then the heat of her body began to slide up his shaft. *No, I need more.*

He still wasn't done with this exquisite woman, and he worried if he let her go now, she would try to flee. Fear struck. Geryon grabbed her wrist tightly as his shaft fell from her.

She didn't stop what she planned, though. She didn't even look up at him. This enchanting Witch crawled down his body while he had her wrist trapped and slammed her mouth around his semi-hard cock.

*Fuck!* Geryon released her to fist the back of her hair with both hands, unable to stop himself from rolling his hips into her welcoming mouth. Valerie was licking his cock clean of his seed, of her own orgasms. It was sensitive since he'd only just stopped coming a few seconds before.

He could feel her tongue swirling around the tip when she drew back, and it shot pleasure all the way back down his cock to spread across his groin. He let out a fluttering breath, his body vibrating with desire. His mouth fell open wide in a twisted 'o' shape, the entire bridge of his nose crinkling.

*She's not done with me.* For once, Geryon was at the mercy of her, rather than the other way around.

He was growing hard again, her teasing mouth making it difficult not to. It was impossible for him to deny.

She wasn't able to take all of him between her lips, so she brought her hand around the base and stroked in time with her tight suction. She cupped it with her tongue, her teeth grazing over the sides as she deliciously bobbed her head.

It was over for him when she finally took her eyes away from his pelvis to look up at him. There was a brightness in her pale eyes, one he'd never truly seen before. She even panted around his cock, and he felt it like a wave.

Having this woman, who had denied him so relentlessly, suck him with quick strokes like she wanted to taste him, had already been enough to spur him into a state of desperation.

Watching her do it, though, someone who usually looked cold, wearing a look that said she just wanted him back inside her, drove him to a place he'd never been.

Geryon ripped her mouth away, tugging her hair. There was a deep throb in his shaft, one that was growing by the second.

*I need to fuck her.* And he needed to do it *his* way.

He needed to release this pent-up frustration that had been building inside him, an aggressive lash of need.

She made a noise of disappointment that tightened his skin. Before she could say anything, do anything, think about anything, he flipped her onto her back and slammed his cock home.

She gasped loudly while his breath caught in his chest.

He gave neither one of them a chance to adjust. With his hands circling her slender waist, forcing her to be still, he began thrusting.

She was still dripping from her last orgasm and his seed. There was a sucking sound every time he withdrew, and a deep slapping sound whenever he thrust in. The sound of it, the feel of it, the scent of it, drove him into an uncontrollable need. He felt mindless with it.

He threw his head back as he pounded, his mouth falling open against the feel of Valerie's plush heat. The harder he shoved, the better it felt.

*She smells wonderful.* She felt tremendous.

A bubbling groan ripped its way from him when he felt her coming around his deep pounding, and he could barely keep a hold of himself.

Then his eyes widened in shock...? Surprise...? Disbelief...? His head fell forward when he heard a loud, pleasure-filled cry.

What he saw was damning.

Her back was arched so harshly, it showed the bottom of her ribs, the ridges of her hips. Her hands were beside her, so she could grip the sheets below her and tug on them heavily.

Her wetted lips were parted, her brows drawn into a deep furrow. There was a crinkle to the corner of her eyelids, a pinkness across her nose that made her unfocused eyes seem more dazed.

She was trembling, her legs jerking around his hips, and her arms shaking as she clawed at the sheets tighter.

Valerie had finally let go.

There was nothing hidden. Her crying scream was sweet, high pitched, and growing with each thrust of his cock. Her mask was gone, revealing a woman who had lost sense of herself.

*Dear lords of fire.* Geryon finally got what he wanted.

Her brown hair was haloed around her head, and it dragged with each arch of her back and slender neck. He could feel her ankles trying to lock around him, like she feared he would stop thrusting through her orgasm. He went faster – he had no intention of breaking away from her.

To see this made his chest tighten with emotions, his breaths coming out more laboured than before.

When she settled, he shot forward and rested one hand against the mattress, slamming the other against the headboard. Gripping it tightly, he used it to help him go harder, faster, deeper, anything to get her to fall deeper.

*Mine. I want to see this forever.* Valerie had finally showed him this hidden side, and he now knew he wanted to fight her for this again, to experience her at this peak of a wild, frantic state.

Her eyes rolled before she shut them as she began to come again. She was helpless not to, with how he gave her his cock. Moaning and panting in abandon, her head thrashed to the side even as she tried to throw it back.

He snarled loudly, deeply, that spasming clutching pressure making his cock drum with each aching throb of his dangerously beating heart.

*Waited so long. I knew she would be like this.*

His bottom jaw shook as he let out juddering groans, watching her like a fever had come over him. Geryon had known Valerie was full of passion and fiery heat, knew she would drive him crazy if he managed to get her there.

Like she couldn't help herself, she dug her nails and fingertips into his abdomen, close to where they were connected. They deliciously cut into him.

She even threw her head forward to watch. When her eyes flicked up to his, she gave him a shaking moan while her lids fluttered.

"Oh, Geryon!" She moaned his name, fucking yelled it!

The headboard cracked under the pressure of his hand when it tightened in reaction. At this rate, he was going to break this flimsy bed. He was sure it dully bashing against the wall would either cave it in or disturb their neighbours.

Though he didn't want to stop, it didn't matter. He didn't know when his balls had started to draw up. One minute, he was pounding into her wonderful core, crazed and lost in her, and the next, he was filling it with his seed as she clenched and swelled around him.

He let loose a bellowing roar, his body wracked with violent tremors. He struggled to hold onto the headboard and had to quickly sit back and grab her hips to drag her with him. It was like he had to have her pinned to him as he released one of the most mind-shattering cumulations of his life.

It felt like his soul was being ripped in two.

Breathing at this point became optional. His sight darkened, and his vision wavered from the strength of it.

All he could feel was her. Every squeeze of her body, every tremble, every tightening of muscle, like it was designed to heighten his pleasure. All he could scent was her and him mingled into one. All he could hear was her soft cry while she wriggled from him flooding her once more with his seed, coming with him.

He was coming so hard, it bordered on pain.

By the time they were done, they were both panting loudly.

Nothing could stop him from taking her lips with his own. *Appreciate her so damn much.* He appreciated this, that she had finally let go with him, and he knew he would get to experience more of it this night.

*She's so lovely.* He kissed her deeply as he swirled his tongue against hers. She was desperate to taste him, refusing to let him back away so he could kiss at her throat. She sucked on his tongue, making him groan.

Geryon was frenzied for this woman. Body and soul, he wanted it. *I will have all of her.*

*Stay with me.* They were the words Geryon had spoken to her before he fell asleep.

Like he feared she'd run if he didn't hold onto her, he'd slid one arm underneath her to grasp her shoulder – it was a firm hold, but not uncomfortable. His other hand wrapped around her from above until he had slipped it under her waist. Even his legs were threaded through hers.

He buried his face against her hair like he wanted to be surrounded by her scent.

There was a huff of contentment from him.

In this embrace, Valerie wouldn't be able to get away without waking him – except for the fact that she may have lulled him into a deeper sleep with a spell.

At first, she didn't know why or how she obtained strange magic, one that didn't belong to her. It didn't feel like witchcraft, didn't feel natural to her senses.

It started as a warm pool in her stomach, swirling magic that sizzled like electricity but was made of flames flickering to life. She felt something building inside of her.

The more Geryon took her throughout the night, the more she grew in strength.

Trying to understand what was happening to her through mind-scrambling, uncontrolled orgasms was near impossible. She did scream, repeatedly, while he tried to get her to be louder, to do it more frequently. He had been unstoppable.

She eventually figured it out.

When he'd been dozing off, giving her satisfied little huffs as he nuzzled the back of her neck, she finally realised what it was and where it came from.

*It's dragoncraft.* It was purer than any magic she'd ever wielded, and she knew she must have obtained it from Geryon somehow.

*My kind hunts his because every part of them is filled with magical essence.* Every. Single. Piece. Geryon had been feeding it to her periodically throughout the night by coming inside her, sharing his inner essence with her.

It was strong, a fluttering power that gave her energy, made her feel alive with strength. Without needing to do anything, she could even wield it.

*The hex only contains my witchcraft; it does not stop me from using this.*

The first thing Valerie did was bask in the warm, lovely embrace that was him after she softly sang, imbuing her voice with magic. He'd already been falling away, but this spell entranced him completely, no matter how much she moved.

*He's always blissfully warm.* It was hard to resist something this wonderful. She even turned her head back and nuzzled her cheek against the side of his face in affection, since he wouldn't know that she had. *I want to stay here more than anything.*

Valerie turned in his embrace, his spell-bound body relaxed against her movements. She stroked his lips, his cheek, his jaw while she gazed at him.

*He has a wonderful face. S*he really could stare at it forever.

"I'm sorry." She leaned forward and pressed her lips to his, deeply kissing his unresponsive mouth. "But one day, you will thank me for this." She wrapped her arms around his neck and kissed him harder, a lasting taste. "Thank you for tonight. I treasured it more than you will ever know."

She had wanted to share a piece of herself she'd never been able to with another. Geryon was the first man who brought her to a place of such heightened desire, and she hadn't wanted to keep it hidden from him.

Valerie wanted to gift this to the one person who deserved it. He'd told her he wanted to break her, and she let him.

Valerie let go of him. Rolling over to the edge of the bed, she placed her feet against the cold timber and stood.

The sun would rise soon, and although she didn't sleep a wink, she was determined to make sure she was ready to go before it did. Collecting one of her clean dresses, her sword, and the map, Valerie turned her head to look at him one last time.

Then she closed the door behind her to leave. Since he was enchanted into a sleep where nothing but time could wake him, she used more of the strange magic she obtained to cast a ward.

It would protect him from anyone who tried to enter the room.

Where was she going? Deep into the forest in hopes she would make it to the mountainside. Valerie was searching for someone in particular, and she was thankful she still had a small amount of dragoncraft left to help her find the way.

If it wasn't for the fact she had studied all kinds of magic, she wouldn't have known how to use it – most Witches didn't know Dragon spells. Her family had kept that knowledge sacred, teaching them to each child through the generations.

She used that knowledge now.

The magic was gone when she finally came across someone she would have much rather not come across first.

It was late in the day, and Valerie grimaced when she startled a woman holding a small infant in her arms.

The woman was speaking to it, rather than listening to her surroundings. She'd been walking through the forest, showing the baby cradled in her arms the trees and plants while it cooed and giggled.

The small squeal of surprise she made when she saw Valerie was ear piercing and loud. She quickly covered herself in a magical barrier, the shield glittering in the sunlight.

"I mean you no harm," she told her with both hands lifted to show they were empty, to appear non-threatening. "I did not mean to frighten you."

"Who are you? Why are you in these mountains?" She shielded the child further with her hands, like she feared Valerie was here for it.

"My name is Valerie Faerydae and I seek–" The sound of large footsteps stomping against the ground cut her words short.

It was heading towards them, and she cringed, her nose crinkling when she noticed a growl accompanying it.

"Get back inside! I smell a Witch," a deep, booming masculine voice shouted before he emerged into the clearing.

He and the woman were just within the trees, with a clearing and mountainside backing them. The woman's face paled as she stepped back, fearful now that she knew what Valerie was.

Valerie immediately got down on her knees and bowed to the male in front of her. She laid her forearms and head against the ground to appear submissive and, once more, non-threatening.

With her face pressed against the dirt, she said, "Rurik the

WitchSlayer. I have been seeking you."

The full-sized Dragon snarled.

She peeked her head up to stare at the large creature standing over her.

His scales were a dark purple, his head and body covered in large spikes. His tail was heart-shaped, unlike Geryon, who had a stump from it being severed. The scars marking his body made him appear more frightening, badges of his strengths and feats. The cold silver in his eyes was filled with obvious hatred, so much so, they could freeze over flames. That hatred was cast towards her.

He looked more frightening than Geryon ever had.

Valerie let her eyes fall upon the Witch next to him. He lifted his paw in front of them to cover her and his child, to protect them further.

"And what does a *Witch* want with me?"

She thought she should get the most important thing out of the way first.

"I intend you no harm." Without lifting her body, Valerie untied the front of her dress and shimmied it down enough to reveal the mark on her back. "I have allowed pixies to hex me, so my magic is bound. I cannot harm either of you with witchcraft."

He cautiously leaned forward to see it better. His eyelids flickered quickly, and she knew he must have been using a spell to see.

"It's true. I can see your magic is not flowing freely." His spikey brows drew together into a deep frown. He came a little closer, his puffy snout making quick sniffs before he gave a subtle sneeze. "I know that scent. So, Geryon caught back up to you, did he?"

Surmising it was safe to do so, Valerie lifted to her knees while shifting her dress to hide her exposed chest. "You know him?"

"Of course, I do!" He stomped a paw forward. "I was the Dragon he was going to hand your sister over to. I know all about you, your family, and what you have done." He gave another growl, curling his lips back over his fangs. "It seems he is still being idiotic with you. You reek of his scent, of seed and sex. Why have you come here?"

She sat back on her feet, laid her hands in her lap, and lifted her chin defiantly. "Because I want you to cleanse me in dragonfire."

His head reared back at her request. "Excuse me? You wish for me to burn you?"

His surprise was not unexpected.

Valerie sighed before averting her gaze to the side. "You are the only Dragon I knew the whereabouts of."

Horrified to discover she knew the location of his lair, his eyes widened before they quickly narrowed.

"How could you know such a thing? My home is guarded with wards and spells. My magic is strong; no one should be able to see through them!"

She brought her eyes forward to meet the sweet, innocent-looking blonde Witch next to him.

"I'm not sure if you remember me, but I have met you before, Amalia." She shook her head to say she didn't know who she was. Valerie was sure, at the time, Amalia found her insignificant, but it had not been so for Valerie. "When I had heard of the prophecy involving you and this Dragon, I originally came to kill you."

Valerie let her eyes fall to the child in her arms.

"I feared that a DragonWitch being born would mean the end for all Dragons and wanted to protect them." She gave a reassuring smile, since they both looked concerned. "Yet, when I saw you helping the humans in the village near your cottage, the animals you took into your care, I doubted you would ever turn. I could not see you casting dark magic when you seemed purer at heart than most I have met. Still, my family and I have been watching you for a long time."

They'd been scrying for Amalia ever since Valerie had obtained a small amount of her hair. It wasn't dark magic, but it required the power of her entire coven to conjure such an advanced spell.

"We were watching you both the night of the black moon. How could we not with what had been predestined? I saw what you did, and I was able to watch him bring you here to save you."

It had been prophesied that Amalia would take the heart of Rurik the WitchSlayer and birth his child. Many believed she would take his heart with a knife, not win it by gaining his love and then raise that child with him.

Valerie knew people often misinterpreted fortune-tellings. The Witch would speak out loud but would forget what they saw instantly. Often, foretellings were unknown, since the Witch would speak it when they were by themselves.

On the night of the black moon, just over twenty-five years ago, Rurik and Amalia had both been captured by Strolguil the Vast, the evillest Witch ever born. He forced her to ride Rurik for his seed so she would fall pregnant, and he gave her a blade to take his heart.

After she rode him and was given the blade, she instead stabbed herself and freed him. She almost died because of it, had sacrificed her life for his. In the end, that was the reason he'd come to trust her, since he was known for his hatred of their kind.

Her entire family had watched the events play out.

She turned her gaze back to Rurik.

"This is how I knew where you were. I cannot see past your wards, though. We have stopped watching since she's rarely outside of them, and we had no reason to."

He raised a brow. "You say you were intending to kill her.

Was that to protect us from the potential of an evil child who could hunt Dragons? You would have hunted her if she turned on me and our child?"

"Yes. My family usually stays out of external matters that don't involve us, but even we feared such power. After the night of the black moon, when Amalia sacrificed herself to save you, we knew we had nothing to fear."

"Hmm." He trailed an assessing eye over her before he twisted his head in thought. "Geryon did tell me your family is odd. He told me you have performed dark magic. Is this why you seek to be cleansed in dragonfire?"

She saw no point in lying to him. "Yes."

"Why not ask him to do it?" He gave a huff of irritation. "Why bother me with your request when you already have a Dragon on your tail?"

Valerie looked down at her hands in her lap, wishing her heart didn't radiate with an ache. "Because he will not do it. I thought that would have been obvious by my scent."

Rurik tapped one of his claws against the ground.

"He will not do it because he is interested in you." He licked inside his mouth, his eyes squinting. She could tell he was annoyed. "He believes you are a white Witch still. Amalia has used blood magic but has not turned."

"Has she ever harmed another to do so?"

"Well, no."

Valerie shook her head. "I have. I have stolen blood and magic from pixies and fairies. I have harmed others. We are not the same."

"Usually, I would not hesitate to take your life, but you are not my prey, and I can scent you have not become corrupted. I no longer kill white Witches." Rurik flicked his scaled hand forward. "Go back to Geryon; let him deal with you."

"Please." Her heart leapt into her throat, and she bowed down once more. "He will not do it." She tore at the grass in front of her with her nails. "He has told me he wishes to keep me."

"And you don't want this?" He snarled as he lowered his head to appear more menacing. "You should consider yourself lucky rather than disgusted!"

"We are not you and Amalia. Geryon is not the great WitchSlayer who killed Strolguil the Vast. I'm not Amalia, the Witch who sacrificed herself for a Dragon." Her eyes slipped along the grass. "No, I have used dark magic with callous actions. The Elders will never approve, no matter how I feel about him."

"And how do you feel?"

Valerie didn't answer, refusing to admit anything out loud. Instead, her hands clenched tighter, dirt beginning to mould around her fingers. "It does not—"

"You care for him..." This time, Amalia was the one to speak. Valerie's head shot up to face her. *Is it that obvious?* "You fear you will turn, and you wish to protect him."

"He will not stop chasing me, no matter how much I deny him." She turned her gaze to Rurik again. "He cannot chase a dead person."

"No, but he can mourn you," Amalia said, appearing more relaxed now as she began bouncing the child in her cradled arms.

Valerie drifted her eyes over the black Dragon mark on the front of her throat, making it obvious that Amalia was claimed.

"I'm not his mate. He will forget me, and when he has chosen his female, he will be thankful I'm not in the way." She lifted back up once more to sit on her heels. "I'm without my magic. I'm sure you would not enjoy that. I wish to protect him, I wish to make up for my indiscretions so I can be with my Dragon parent, but I also don't wish to suffer without it in this life. My decision is partly noble, but selfishness also compels me."

"I don't care. I will not take your life," Rurik said, turning his sights to the sky in thought.

She thought he was dismissing her. Valerie quickly stood and pointed her finger at him.

"You are not my last option. I would prefer dragonfire, but any fire will do."

She turned to walk away, fearing at any moment Geryon would turn up and ruin her plans. *That sleeping spell will not last forever.*

She wasn't afraid of death, and she wasn't afraid of the searing pain that would welcome her. She feared him coming along and stopping her.

"What if I were to take you to the Elders?"

She spun around, her lips parting. "You would take me to the Pinnacle of Dragons?"

She watched him shudder.

"It concerns me how much you know of my kind. It's rather off-putting." He nodded his head. "Yes, I will take you to the Elders and let them decide your fate."

The disappointment Geryon felt upon waking up to an empty bed only warmed by him was enough to make him want to claw his own face off. Frustration boiled; his stomach was knotted.

He'd fallen asleep satisfied, pleased, and thoroughly content with Valerie in his arms. He knew he'd wrapped himself around her so she couldn't escape.

*How did that sneaky bunny escape me?*

With a dejected sigh, he let his head fall against the bed,

thinking back on the night. He let out a groan, his nose crinkling on one side.

His shaft jerked in memory, despite his terrible mood.

He would have preferred to wake up and bury himself in her, rather than having to go chase after her. Still, he rose his naked human body from the bed in search of his clothing.

Once he was dressed, his shoulders slumped.

*Why did she not stay?*

He didn't understand why she'd run away again, not after how she had been with him. She'd enjoyed being underneath him all night.

Scratching the back of his neck, he thought once more on the night, but this time, in search of what he may have done wrong.

He didn't know.

He'd complimented her, told her how he felt about her, despite how embarrassing he found it to do so. Geryon had tried to be affectionate as he made *love* to her.

Regardless, he would still go after her. Call it an obsession, but he wasn't ready to let her go, not when he hoped he could eventually convince her to stay with him.

*I could imprison her again.* He rolled his eyes at himself; he'd seen how well that had worked out the first time.

Unsure as to why he'd slept for most of the day, the sun already trying to set, he shielded his eyes from the glowing red ball as he stepped outside.

Her male travel companions were gone, and they weren't with her, since he could smell she had gone into the forest on her own.

*Does she not realise who lives in these mountains?* He shook his head as he followed her scent through the forest. She had come through here hours before him.

Suddenly Geryon paused.

*What if she does know...* His eyes widened when he looked

in the direction she'd been travelling, realising it was directly taking him to a certain ill-tempered brother of his. *What if she's seeking him?*

That's when he understood why she had come here.

*She plans to ask Rurik to do what I will not!*

While he sprinted, he chanted the one word he needed to morph. "Shift!" he flung out impatiently as he finished blowing his ring of fire.

He didn't care his clothing was burned away when those flames came back to encase him, not when Valerie was in severe danger. *I must be quick. Rurik will do as she asks.*

He wouldn't care for Geryon's feelings, not when it involved a Witch who had used dark magic.

Within a matter of moments, he morphed into a Dragon and took to the skies. He was faster in the air, using his wings, rather than on foot as a man.

Flying straight for Rurik's lair, anxiety filled his chest. *Don't tell me I'm too late.*

What would have taken an hour or two on foot took him only a few minutes in the air with the way he flew.

Geryon landed out the front of Rurik's lair and instantly picked up that Valerie's scent was here. There were no charred marks, but that didn't mean she hadn't already been burned. He needed to know, needed to be told if he was too late.

"Rurik!" he shouted, running straight for the lair entrance and bashing headfirst into a ward designed to keep all but the caster out. *Ow! Fuck!* "Rurik!"

The one who greeted him was Amalia. She was alone, and she eyed him cautiously as she approached him from the cave tunnel. She never ventured past the ward.

"Geryon?" she asked quietly, her personality radiating soft and kind – as it had the small number of times he'd met her.

"Amalia, where is Rurik? What did he do with the Witch who came here?"

He tried to see past her in the hopes he would come up the tunnel behind her... Yet he couldn't hear any shouting or snarling like usual when Rurik had an uninvited guest bothering him.

"You are speaking of Valerie?"

His chest tightened at hearing her name. He became unsettled on his paws, shifting his weight back and forth.

*Why was I asleep for so long?* She'd managed to come here and introduce herself, had time to have a conversation with them.

Her scent here wasn't old, and he knew she had only recently been here. *Maybe an hour.*

"Yes, where is she?"

Amalia looked away.

His chest tightened further, the pain he felt crawling across his torso near suffocating.

She slowly brought her eyes back to him. "I'm sorry. He refused to do what she wanted, but he offered to take her to the Elders."

Geryon's wings drooped as his jaw fell open.

"The Elders? Why would he do that?"

The Elders could give her any kind of punishment, and there would be nothing Geryon could do about it. He'd been intending to keep her a secret from them, most likely forever.

"Blasted WitchSlayer," Geryon snapped, turning away from Amalia so he could take flight.

He didn't know how much time he had, but he needed to get to the Pinnacle of Dragons before her fate was decided. *They will not hesitate to act on their decision.* Once the Elders decided upon something, it was usually enacted the same day.

*Why would Rurik take her to the Elders? He hates them.* Just like how he hated everything. He usually liked to keep family issues within the family.

*I'm his fucking brother! Could he not have just waited for me?*

No. Instead, he'd taken Valerie to the one place Geryon would much rather have avoided.

After they landed at the top of the magnificent mountain island, Valerie was allowed to walk beside Rurik. The entrance to the Pinnacle of Dragons was near the edge of a cliff overlooking the sea. She knew if she had fallen off the edge, it would have been to her death. However, she wasn't looking for death in particular; she just wanted to be cleansed. She knew no other way than fire.

Rurik only gave her a moment to look over the expanse of ocean before he ushered her through the entrance archway, one that had strange Dragonian symbols around the outside. It was large enough to fit two full-sized Dragons walking side by side.

The path was twisty, and it began to spiral downwards inside the mountain. They didn't pass many Dragons, but there were some who peeked out from humongous alcove rooms to look at them.

Valerie mostly kept her eyes on Rurik, unless something wonderful came into sight. Something like the large rooms filled with tapestries she would have loved to read until the world around her crumbled away. There was also a room filled with statues and art that had obviously been created by large, inhuman hands.

She never thought they had culture and enjoyed things like this. *There was still so much to learn.* But she wasn't sad about knowing that.

She was seeing more than any of her family had for eons, *would* see for eons. *I'm blessed just to be here, even if it's the last place I will see.*

The ceilings were painted with an array of patterns and colours. Tapestry rugs of Dragons flying in the skies, or just nature in general, hung along the path they were walking. Even the ground they were walking on had a neat stone path. Large, round firepits floating with magic lit the way for them.

Everything inside this place was cared for and cleaned. Magic radiated from every room.

Then, for a long while, there was nothing important to look at as they descended deeper into the belly of the Pinnacle of Dragons.

"What are you staring at?" Rurik barked when she'd been ogling him for too long.

There hadn't been anything else to look at as they ventured further inside. He raised his brow when he got no reaction from her.

"I thought Geryon was magnificent, but I did not realise you all were." She didn't smile, but she also didn't look away. "I did not realise you would be as frightening to look at in particular."

His eyes squinted. "Are you saying I'm unsightly?"

"Not at all. Quite the opposite, in fact. Seeing your scars makes me realise just how strong and powerful you are. No wonder many Witches have fallen to your claw."

"Are... Are you complimenting me, Witch?" He growled as though he didn't appreciate it, but even she could tell it held no real hostility.

"Think nothing of it." She finally turned her gaze away to look forward. "I just never imagined I would meet a Dragon and not receive immediate death. I also never thought I would get to visit this place."

"You speak as though you are joyful, even when you are about to ask for your death, and yet your face holds no emotion. Are you cursed to appear unfeeling?"

"No. It's just who I am."

"Interesting," he answered, and for the first time, she heard humour in his voice. His silver eyes and puffy mouth crinkled at the edges with it. "I'm beginning to understand."

She would never know what he meant, since he never elaborated, and before long, he halted in front of two large doors at the bottom of the path. They were made of steel and stone, taller than Rurik himself.

*I would never be able to open such doors.* She doubted even her magic could open them, yet he opened them with ease by pushing on them with nothing more than his two front paws.

The room she was taken to was carved like a cave alcove. There were no brick stones on the ground, but one side was covered in fur rugs and pillows that were crafted for something of their size.

More fire pits lined the walls, and between them were more tapestries. They were generalised histories of their kind, of Dragons. The story of her origins, of Faerydae and his human female – who eventually birthed the first Witch – caught her eye. She stared at it for a long while.

"Rurik, my dear boy," a blue female Dragon greeted from her position on the pillows.

She looked old, her scales withered and wrinkled on her body rather than tight. She must have been resting her tired bones and muscles.

"Nayana," he sneered before his eyes moved over the three other aged Dragons lazing about with her.

Valerie watched as the bright blue one got to her feet before the others followed.

Rurik leaned his head down to her.

"The blue one is Nayana the Loathsome. The golden one is Aneirin the Great." Valerie watched them approach as he introduced them to her. "The pink one is Kelherian the ClawStriker and the grey one is Eridile. He has no title. You are lucky Fionnlagh has been dead for quite some time; he was stubborn as an Elder."

"Why have you brought us a Witch, Rurik?" Nayana asked him, raising her brow.

Her silver eyes roamed over Valerie with curiosity.

"One who smells of indecent actions with a Dragon," Eridile added, giving a huffing sneeze through his nose.

"I thought you would be faithful to your Witch mate." Nayana shook her head. "Do you wish for a harem of them now that you have gotten a taste? Should we start calling you the Witch*Layer* instead of Witch*Slayer*?"

"What the fuck? I would never betray Amalia!" he roared, stamping one of his paws forward. His claws dug into the ground to show just how offended he was at such a statement. "If you four are too old to realise she has the scent of another, then you are all hopeless and useless as our Elders."

"Why is it you have brought her here?" Aneirin asked. She got the feeling he wished to interject before it got out of hand.

Rurik huffed loudly and turned his head up and away dismissively. "She wished for a trial with the Elders, and I graciously thought to comply."

*I did not ask for a trial with them.* She didn't dare correct him, though.

"And why would you do anything for another, a Witch no less?"

He rolled his eyes as he brought them back to the Elders.

"My reasons are my own." He waved his paw towards her while stepping back. "You will be interested in speaking with her."

Now that she was to be spoken with directly, Valerie dropped to her knees and arched her body over the ground.

"She got to the ground like a frog," Eridile commented, and she could hear the confusion in it.

"She's bowing to us like the humans used to," Aneirin frowned. "I have never known a Witch to do this."

"Why are you bowing like a frog?" Nayana asked with quick blinks.

Valerie suddenly sat upright on her knees, surprised to feel the heat of embarrassment in her cheeks. She never realised bowing like that was so strange. It was only then she realised both Geryon and Rurik had seemed puzzled when she bowed to them as well.

"It's the easiest way to show my respect to those greater than me," she answered calmly, despite her hands jittering with nervousness. "I apologise. I did not realise it was odd."

They whispered among themselves for a moment.

"Who are you?" Aneirin asked while tilting his head at her. She thought the golden one was the most thoughtful, since he usually spoke deliberately and with much intonation.

"I wish to inform you now that I intend you no harm, I have gotten pixies to seal my magic away. As for my name, it's Valerie Faerydae."

"Faerydae, as in *the* Great Faerydae offspring?" asked Kelherian, the pink one. He seemed quieter than the others.

"I know it may be hard to believe, but yes. I'm a descendant of the white Dragon, Faerydae the Destroyer, the one who mated with Farrah the human after he became infatuated with her beauty."

Rather than eating the offering sacrifice he'd been given,

he'd chosen to bed her. Eventually, Faerydae the Destroyer fell in love with the pretty human and spent all her human years with her until she finally died of old age.

He never mated with another, and it was rumoured he also never bedded another after her. Instead, he raised their daughter and spent his time teaching the first Witch how to wield her magic. They had learned together.

The tale was one of Valerie's favourites.

"She knows of Farrah," Eridile whispered to the others. "Not even many Dragons know her name."

The other three began to nod.

"It's decided. We believe you are who you say you are," Aneirin told her.

*Why must I always be met with scepticism?* It was irritating and rather offensive.

Before she could even open her mouth to ask her request, the blue female stepped forward to sniff at the air.

"Whose scent is that on you?" She came a little closer. "It seems familiar."

To everyone's surprise, Rurik slapped his tail forward through the air to land in front of her.

"Your sense of smell is fading." He shook his head, like he couldn't believe what he was witnessing. "The fact you cannot sense who it belongs to is beyond disappointing."

"Well, who does it belong to, Witch?" Eridile came forward as well. "I'm also curious."

"It does not matter," she told them, squaring her shoulders back with her chin lifted. "I would much rather speak of why I'm here."

"But it matters to us," Aneirin answered, raising his brow. "This is considered an offense."

Valerie's eyes hardened in their direction. "No."

"No?" Rurik said as he turned his head to her. "They will punish you for defying them."

She turned her cold stare towards him instead. "I don't care what they do to me, as long as they fulfil my request."

Valerie didn't want to get Geryon in trouble. She didn't wish for him to be punished because of her, and she very much hoped Rurik would keep to himself what he knew. She softened her gaze, beseeching him silently.

He gave her a mischievous grin. "Well, it seems you are all able to take care of yourselves. I can see I'm no longer needed."

"Rurik," Nayana snapped sharply. "You will tell us who has been bedding this Witch."

Rurik chuckled. "Why, Mother, I have absolutely no idea." His grin grew as his eyes drifted over each of them. "I thought you lot would be able to tell me whose scent it belongs to, since you have, *apparently,* met all."

Nayana's eyes narrowed in disbelief. Regardless, she nodded. They all did, and Valerie figured it was because they couldn't force him to tell them.

*Nayana is Rurik's mother?* She quickly compared the two before he left the room to stand outside the doors, closing them behind him.

She was dark like him, but his scales were purple, whereas hers were blue. They didn't have similar spikes jutting out from their heads, but she did notice they had similar facial structures. Her eyes were silver like his; it was their most comparable feature.

Actually, Nayana closely resembled Geryon in colouring and spikes. She'd nearly had a heart attack when she first entered the room, thinking it was him.

"Why have you come here covered in the scent of a Dragon, but Rurik is the one who brought you here? Where is the one who has been bedding you?" There was a small growl from Kelherian. "What have you done with him?"

"With the dragoncraft given to me by him" – none of them

gasped or batted an eye at her words, so she figured they must already know about this – "I was able to put him to sleep for a short while so he could not come after me before I found Rurik. I have done nothing to harm him." She looked towards her folded hands. "I have come here because I used dark magic. I have never harmed a Dragon, but I took from pixies and fairies. I did it to save my sister, but I fear it means I'm no longer pure hearted." She turned her gaze up to them once more. "I come here with the request that I be purified by dragonfire. He will not do so, and Rurik has told me he will not either. I hope you will give me that blessing so I may be with my Dragon parent in the next life."

"You wish to escape what you have done. How selfish," Nayana sneered.

"Not at all," Valerie quickly answered. "If there was any other way to remove the corruption that will eventually take me, I would. Fire is the only way we know, and the pain I will receive will be enough of a punishment for my actions. I have never killed for the blood magic I used, but I still made the creatures I took from suffer."

"You never killed them?" Aneirin frowned, twisting his head at her. "And you did this to save your sibling?"

"Please, don't pity me or think lightly on this. I'm not asking for a trial; I'm asking for assistance."

"And yet it's a trial you are being given." He twisted his head the other way. "You did not kill. We don't know what truly makes your kind turn. You may not turn at all."

"Regardless, I have done unspeakable things."

"If she wishes to be cleansed, then so be it," Kelherian cut in. "Why should we care for the life of a Witch? We would never hesitate to take one of their lives in the wild."

"No, I still wish to know who this Dragon is," Eridile snapped. "Afterwards, we can put her to fire."

"So, it's agreed. Fire is her fate," Nayana said, while

Aneirin nodded as well.

An overwhelming sense of calm rushed over Valerie, and she closed her eyes in relief. *Finally.* Finally, she would get what she wanted.

She bowed just her head. "Thank you. I appreciate this decision."

"It's strange for a Witch to thank us for something like this," Aneirin said with a crinkle of his snout. "You truly want fire?"

"Enough of this! Tell us who the male is!" Kelherian shouted, stamping his paw. "I will not wait any longer to know who will be put on trial next."

"My apologies, but I will not reveal who it's. I don't wish for them to be punished when my death is imminent."

There was a growl from him and the blue one. "You will tell us."

"Or what? You will put me to fire?" Valerie gave a singular, mocking laugh. "You can torture me for information, but I will not allow you to harm someone I care for."

The words slipped out by accident, and she cringed. *Oops, I was intending to keep that secret from them.* She was feeling too relaxed now that she knew she was going to get what she wanted. *I just don't care anymore.*

"Ah, what I mean to say is–"

"If that's how she truly feels, then she will not tell us," Aneirin sighed. "Rurik knows; we can find out from him."

"Fine," Nayana growled. "We will ask Rurik once we are done here."

All four of them stepped forward, and she turned her face up towards them with her eyes closed. She awaited the fire that would take her to her ancestors.

Her hair billowed forward when there was a rush of air from behind her, like the door had been flung open.

Instead of flames wrapping around her, something cooler

and rougher enveloped her instead. The sounds of growling and quick huffs, like someone had exerted their body and was struggling to breathe, were loud.

She opened her eyes to find herself facing the back of a Dragon. Their tail was wrapped around her body protectively, the stumpy tip between her and the Elders.

The moment she saw dark blue scales shimmering in the firelight, she knew exactly who it was. Her mouth fell open with unhidden shock.

"Geryon, what are you doing?" Nayana shouted, before her eyes nearly bulged out of her skull in realisation. "It's you! You are the Dragon she has been with."

"I know what she has requested, and I will not allow it," Geryon snapped.

He lowered himself as he curled his body around her further, walking in a circle, much like how a snake would coil itself around prey, in order to put himself between her and the Elders. Then he covered her with his wing, shoving her into darkness and completely protecting her.

*Why is he here?* She thought he wouldn't come. If she knew the rules, then so did he. *How could he do something so stupid?*

"That's not your choice to make. She has made her request, and we have accepted it. As for you, you will be punished for what you have been doing with her." Nayana sounded furious. "She has seen your human face. You *know* letting her free is not permitted. She's to either be imprisoned in your lair or killed, and yet you decided to bed her."

"Because she is mine!" he roared, his tail coiling around her tighter. She lifted her hands before he could clamp her arms to her sides with it, but she did grimace at how much he was squeezing her now. "I will claim her."

Valerie paused with her pulse quickening. *What does that mean?*

"You are not Rurik, Geryon. You cannot have a Witch just because you say so."

"Just try and stop me." He let out a ferocious warning growl, snapping his jaws forward. Valerie could tell he lowered his body even more, as if readying himself to fight. "I have made my decision."

His tail tensed, like he was prepared at any moment to pick her up with it. *Is he planning to fight them for me?*

That's when Valerie understood everything.

She covered her mouth to hide the strangled noise that squeezed its way through her lungs.

*He wants to claim me... as in make me his mate?* Was that why he'd been chasing her so relentlessly? Was that why he wanted to be intimate with her, hoping she would open up to him?

*Geryon has chosen me as his female? But why?* Why did he want this from her, of all people?

And why did it make her heart pound like a storm in her chest?

Then, she realised she'd been asking someone who wanted to bond with her to take her life. *No wonder he has been so against it.* No wonder he was here now, trying to stop it.

"She's a Witch who has used dark magic. We cannot accept this bond," Aneirin said, but he didn't seem angered. No, he sounded rather disappointed for him, like he knew the law and the ways of their kinds wouldn't allow it.

There was a ring of agreeance, every Elder confirming they also didn't approve of them.

*I knew they would not approve of Geryon keeping me as a plaything, let alone as his chosen female!*

Heat surrounded them both, and even though she was tucked away and unable to see, she knew all four Elders had unleashed fire against them. Geryon's wing protected her, but he flinched under the sudden heavy assault.

She covered her head. Valerie was torn with what she wanted. She wanted to sit here in Geryon's protective embrace. Yet she wanted to lift his wing and force the dragonfire to take her so she could be cleansed.

If she hadn't known the truth about his feelings, she would have escaped him into the fire. Instead, she sat there immobile and utterly speechless for the first time in her life.

*"What is it you want?"* a male voice, unknown to her, whispered in her small, shielded space of darkness.

It swirled around her, so loud and yet so unimaginably quiet at the same time – like a voice that spoke and the echo that followed.

She tried to figure out where it was coming from as she frantically looked around.

*"Do you wish to be with this Dragon?"*

"I-I don't know," she answered truthfully. She didn't care to ask who it was. Would the invisible force even tell her if she asked? "I care for him, but I don't wish to be without my magic. I fear I will turn if it's released."

*"Is that all that's holding you back, my child?"* The voice was coming closer. Still, it was a gentle, gruff voice, and she wondered if anyone else was able to hear it over the crackle of the fire around them.

Now that she knew the truth? "Yes," she whispered back to the voice.

*"Then so be it."*

There was a swirl of energy that began to spiral around her, like it came from within her. She knew it made all within the room pause when the heat and fire dissipated. Then, the energy burst like wind as a great form began to take shape, taller than all the massive creatures standing in the room.

The wind forced Geryon's wing to lift away from her, but it was hard to make out what she was sitting inside of... until all that strong power settled.

It was like she was sitting inside the belly of a Dragon made from ghostly, fiery essence. It didn't burn her nor Geryon as it loomed over them.

With long, twirling horns pointing towards the rock ceiling, he was magnificent. A round ball with spikes, like a mace, tipped his tail as it slowly slid back and forth over the ground. One of his wings was torn to the point she imagined it would be difficult to fly, although not impossible.

The great Dragon was protecting both her and Geryon, and she could feel its magic twinkling around them with floating specks of glitter dust.

"What in the heavens is that?" Eridile yelled, scuttling backwards to the point he almost fell on his backside.

The other Elders stepped back warily as well.

Valerie tapped Geryon's wing so he would lower it. She wanted to see what was going on and what had come from her properly.

When he did, she spoke to it. "Who are you?"

The ethereal Dragon turned his horned head down to her with a raised brow. His teeth appeared sharp, and a few of them sat over his bottom lip even when his mouth was shut, as though he had a slight overbite.

"Dear child, can you really not see who your Dragon parent is when he appears before you?"

She couldn't hide the surprise as it sailed through her with a sharp exhale. "Faerydae the Destroyer?"

"How is this possible?" It wasn't any of the Elders who asked this question; it was Rurik.

He was standing in the opened doorway. He must have come in when he sensed a surge of power and the excessive magic that continued to radiate from Faerydae.

Even with her magic locked away, she could feel it.

Faerydae lowered his head and pushed it inside his own ethereal body. He carefully ran the side of his snout under her jaw in a display of affection, and she couldn't believe it was tangible – she could feel him!

It was an action that mistakenly forced her head to lift back and accept the touch. Geryon's tail tightened around her in fear.

"She and her ancestors have been feeding my soul magic since I died. They have given me the power to come here in her time of need, as all my children have been watched over."

Valerie lifted her hands to cup the bottom of his jaw and nuzzled her cheek against his snout. *I cannot believe this. How remarkable.* She couldn't help the small smile that played across her pale lips.

"Why are you here?" Aneirin asked with his brows furrowing.

"Why else would I be here?" He lifted his head away and turned to the Elders. "You tried to kill one of my daughters and have rejected this bond. I disagree with both of those decisions and have decided to make my presence known to dispute them."

"We are the Elders. Our decisions are law. You have had your time here in this world, old man," Nayana sneered. She sat back on her haunches and looked at her claws like they were more interesting than him. Him! A literal freaking ghost Dragon. "Go back to the afterlife."

"I do believe I'm the true Elder in the room, and with the magic gifted to me over these centuries, I can smite all of you with little care if you don't heed my command." He lifted a paw to reveal his claws in a threatening manner. "I was called 'the Destroyer' before my death for good reason."

"Why would you approve of this bond? One of your own children has used dark magic. If you have been watching the world since your passing, you would know why this is a terrible crime. Would you not prefer your own corrupt offspring to die rather than let it mate with one of your own?"

Aneirin asked, but his tone seemed more curious than anything.

Faerydae gave them a large, fanged grin.

"She will not turn. Regardless of what she has done, her will to be pure is too strong. It's why she still has not." He turned his head to Geryon. "ShadowHunter, you have chosen your female wisely. Valerie is a formidable Witch, and she will help you kill those who are truly evil if you seek to. She does not care for other Witches, and she has already killed many."

That's when her eyes fell to Geryon, who had been silent.

She could see his eyes flickering over the ethereal Dragon resting over them, his bottom jaw lowered. He was in awe of what he was witnessing, as most were. She didn't think any of them had ever spoken to a Dragon from the past.

*His name is Geryon the ShadowHunter?* He'd never told her what his title was. She wondered if it was because he shadowed humans to hunt Witches.

"And Valerie the Heartless loves him. That in itself is enough to show their bond is worthy."

Since she was already staring at him, she watched Geryon's eyes widen before he shot his head to her. Her nose crinkled when he twisted his head at her, at finding out the depth of her feelings. Once more, her cheeks heated, and she thought this day was the most she'd ever blushed.

She'd been intending to keep that a secret. *Figures I cannot hide it from Faerydae.*

"But–" one of the Elders started.

"You will accept this bond, or I will rain my terror down on you!" His yell pierced her ears before his roar shook the walls.

His wings even spread out, and he released ethereal fire to the cave ceiling, the heat washing over her as though real flames. He was able to cast fire and use magic.

When he settled, he shook his body while his wings folded neatly against his sides once more.

"Do I have any naysayers?" He narrowed his eyes in a silent challenge.

"Who am I to disagree with something ancient?" Aneirin sighed before sitting, as though he couldn't care less.

"Although I don't necessarily approve, I will not disagree with you," Eridile answered before he sat as well.

"I still don't approve, and I will make that known." Kelherian turned his head to the side with an irritated huff and refused to sit.

The last person standing was Nayana the Loathsome. She just stood there on all fours and glared.

"You can stand all day, Mother, but the trial has ruled in my favour," Geryon bit, taking her stare head on like a challenge.

As soon as he called her his mother, Valerie realised they looked so similar she should have seen it earlier.

"I'm merely disappointed that two of my sons have chosen Witches as mates." Her eyes trailed over them to see past their shoulders. "Rurik was a special case, but he has achieved so much greatness to have what he wants. As always, *you* have chosen to be a thorn in my side."

*She's Rurik's mother as well as Geryon's... That means...* Horrified, Valerie covered her face to hide it. *I walked to his brother's lair covered in the evidence of the night we shared and asked him to kill me.*

No wonder he said no. What were the chances?

Geryon looked up towards Faerydae still standing over them. He gave him a grin, the same cocky one he usually wore.

"Yes, but it does appear the gods and spirits are on my side, as always. I have never cared what you think, and I will not start doing so now." He looked down to Nayana as Valerie felt herself lifted from the ground by his curling tail. He made her face Nayana, who bared her sharp fangs at her. "This is the female I have chosen, and if you don't sit, you will not see either of us again."

"Geryon..." Valerie whispered.

Her words were cut short by him snapping his jaws in her direction to quiet her. She immediately shut her lips at the sharp, disturbing sound.

With a huff, Nayana sat, unhappy with his ultimatum. *She does not want him to disappear from her life completely.*

"So, it's decided then," Faerydae said, his wings lifting in triumph when his chest puffed out proudly. "If Valerie agrees to the claiming, then Geryon the ShadowHunter may take her."

"*If* she agrees?" Geryon asked, tilting his head to the side.

The ethereal Dragon turned his head to him with a warm chuckle.

"Just because she cares for you right now does not mean she may want to be bonded to you for eternity. You still have much work to do."

"You are jesting, right?"

"Do I look like I'm one to joke, boy?" He snapped his head to her. "He's overconfident, is he not? Are you sure you would not prefer flames, to join me?"

"I'm sure," she answered, much preferring the new path laid out for her.

*I can live, and Faerydae does not believe I will turn.* To know that warmed her heart more than it ever had been. She peeked over at Geryon. *I can live with this big, idiotic Dragon if I wish to.*

Nothing was set in stone, but it meant Valerie was absolutely free. She no longer had a reason to fear for her future.

Faerydae nodded his head at her and turned to the Elders,

making sure they all agreed.

In the background, Geryon lifted her so she was closer to his face and they could speak quietly. "He was joking, right? I did risk my wings being ripped from me to save you this day."

Valerie folded her arms and turned her head away. "I did not ask you to save me."

"Incredible." He shuddered. Then, to her abject horror, he drew his tongue over the side of her arm and face. "You sure do like to be difficult."

Valerie made a *blergh* face as she wiped his saliva away. *Disgusting! He licked me!*

"Why do you seem so happy about that?"

"You will be staying with me, but this will be a new game we will get to play."

She watched him dart his tongue out to lick his maw as he shifted his weight between each paw in excitement. *Such a strange male.*

She waved her hand like she didn't care.

"And what of King Bradwick? You told me you wished to return to his palace."

She highly doubted that was a possibility now.

"I will convince him to let you stay within the palace with me, or else I move to a new kingdom." However, a large smirk, one of confidence, crept into his features. "But he will cave to me. I have made sure he does not trust anyone as strongly as he does me."

Once Faerydae was finished conversing with the Elders, who were curious about him, he stepped away to face her. They walked away to laze about on their cushions, pillows, and furs, but they didn't seem as relaxed as before.

No, they were being very watchful.

"You remind me of Farrah. She was beautiful like you, with your brown hair and wintergreen eyes." His eyes drooped in memory of the human female he'd fallen for, before they refocused. "She had much more life to her, though; that's what truly captivated me."

Geryon set her down so she could speak to him properly. He didn't release her from his tail, like he still felt the need to protect her.

"What do you mean?" Valerie asked.

"She held not an ounce of fear when she saw me. Rather, she tried to warm me with her words of strength and encouragement before I was to take her life. She was easy to make laugh and smile, and in the small amount of time she was offered as a sacrifice, she had won me."

He paused as he thought on the memory for a long while. He even gave a short chuckle before he came back to the present.

"I have seen such life in you, but only recently." His gaze flicked briefly to Geryon. "It's for this reason alone I have stepped in."

Then, he leaned forward to place a claw under her chin to lift her head higher. She held onto it.

"You are the way you are, and I don't foresee you changing. However, allow yourself those moments, because you look so much like my beloved in those times, and you honour her by doing so."

"I did not know I look like Farrah. Her identity has always been a mystery."

"All my daughters have a piece of her. It's why I cursed my bloodline to only give birth to girls, so that I could see her for eternity in all our offspring."

"You truly loved her." Valerie let a real smile fill her features for him as his eyes flickered between hers.

"Yes, and our line has honoured me with their magic and allowed me to pull her from the human gods to my afterlife plane, where all our children come eventually. I have much to be thankful for. I have watched you care for your sisters and teach them the old ways. You made a sacrifice to save your sister, another one of my children, at great cost to yourself. You have done this many times. You deserved my assistance more than anyone else."

"Thank you. It's an honour to have met you." Valerie tried to bow her head for him, but he wouldn't let her with his claw.

"Don't bow to anyone. You have my blood in you. Those around you should fear and respect you instead." Her small smile grew, and he returned it with a bright one of his own. "I must go, before I drain all of the magic given to me."

"When my magic is released, I will make sure to feed you more."

"Please do. I could need it again one day." He gave a chuckle before his ethereal form began to fade, although much slower than how he'd entered.

"I barely believed he was truly your Dragon parent," Geryon said, and she turned to face him. "Shows I was wrong."

"Be thankful that you were! Otherwise, I would be a burned pile of ash and you would be punished."

"True, and now no one can dispute your bloodline." He turned, pushing his tail behind her so she could walk as well. "Come, we should leave. The Elders have not stopped glaring at us."

She peeked over her shoulder to see he was right. "Your mother is an Elder."

"My mother is a pain, and I have been avoiding her for years." He shook his head when they went through the doorway.

He closed the door behind them with his tail.

"I second that. She's rather off-putting," Rurik commented, now that they were standing in front of him.

The growl that came from Geryon alerted Valerie that

something terrible was about to happen.

"You bastard!"

Geryon reared back onto his hind legs and shoved Rurik in the chest. Taken by surprise, it knocked Rurik to his side, and he landed against the ground with a loud *thwack*.

Valerie practically had to dive out of the way when Rurik got to his paws and tackled Geryon around his scaly shoulders. He sat on top of him when he hit the ground and slapped him with his claws.

"Don't attack me, brother. I did you a favour." He snapped his jaws towards him in rage.

*Rurik has a really short temper.*

"She could have been killed before I arrived. Why would you bring her here? You hate the Elders."

Geryon managed to roll them over so he could get to his paws, his face bleeding from Rurik's claws. He didn't care as he bared his fangs, his growl so vicious it almost sounded like a hiss.

"Because you needed to face the Elders if you wanted her." He stamped his paw down before he lashed his tail forward. Geryon caught it with his own, but the lack of tip caused their tails to slip apart. "If I had to face them, then so did you. You cannot escape them and hide behind human armies. If they discovered what you had done, what you planned, they would have wiped out that puny human king and her along with him."

"You could have spoken to me first!"

With Valerie's back pressed firmly up against the wall to stay out of this foolish sibling fight, she watched intently as they circled each other. Moving so fast that even Valerie hadn't registered the action until it was completed, Geryon punched Rurik in the face with his ruined tail tip.

"As if you would listen to me! I flew here slowly for a reason." Rurik stepped back and wiped his scaled snout with the back of his forearm to check his mouth wasn't bleeding. "I knew you would catch up to us in time, but this needed to happen."

"You planned this?" Valerie piped up, causing both to turn their heads to her.

"Yes. The moment I smelled his scent all over you and learned he was not alone in his stupidity, I knew you two must face the Elders if you wished for a future." Then he sighed, running his paw down his face. "I did not foresee it going so poorly, but you were saved by Faerydae, which..." He paused to bring his gaze down and then back up her body. "I'm rather amazed by."

"That still did not give you the right to interfere," Geryon snapped, pulling his wing up to cover her from his view.

"No? She gained my approval when she asked for me to burn her with my flames. Would you much rather I had than this alternative?" Rurik raised his brow while tapping a claw against the ground impatiently. "Now you can do what you want with her, and the Elders will not care. Claim her, kill her; to them, it no longer matters."

Geryon brought his wing down with a sigh. "I have never needed your help."

"And I have never given it to you. Perhaps, occasionally, I should help my idiot younger siblings." Rurik harshly slapped him across the face with the flat part of his sharp, spaded tail tip. "Now, I'm leaving. I loathe this place, and I wish to return to Amalia and my spawn."

He turned to walk up the mountain pathway, leaving Valerie and Geryon alone together.

"I did not know you are brother to the famous WitchSlayer. Even Witches know of him and his exploits."

He scowled, licking the inside of his mouth in agitation.

"Please, do fawn over my brother. It does not bother me whatsoever." The sarcasm dripping from his tone was lethal.

*He does not like being compared to him.*

She turned her head up and gave him a bored look. "Then perhaps you should do something noteworthy."

"I think I got a much better reaction from you last night," he chuckled darkly, but she could tell he was still annoyed.

Valerie pursed her lips and began to walk up the mountain pathway. Even though she wanted nothing more than to remain and explore this wondrous place of ancient history and culture few of her kind would ever get the chance to see... She no longer wanted to remain in such a sacred place where a Witch like her didn't belong.

Geryon came up beside her with his large paws crunching against the stone. She could tell adjusting to her much slower strides was difficult, but he paced himself for her.

In her peripheral, she noted he kept his eyes on her, rather than their path.

"Is it true you love me?" He sounded jolly, his tone teasing.

She didn't answer, nor did she give away the truth in her expression or body language.

His toothy grin shifted into a self-assured smirk as his eyes brightened with mirth. "I will get you to say it one day, my fanged butterfly. We will have many years together, Valerie, and I will spend every day teasing you until it spills from your pretty lips."

Her heart betrayed her by fluttering in her chest at his words. *Someone save me, for I'm in danger with this overconfident Dragon!*

There was something about being back in King Bradwick's palace that brought Geryon a deep sense of contentment.

It had been a month since he returned and spoke with him. He explained his absence, as well as his intentions with Valerie – the Witch who had tricked them all.

He'd also informed him he would not be moved from his decision.

Of course, there had been an argument, but the threat that he was more than prepared to find some other palace to occupy had been enough to quieten the cocky king. Bradwick was learning that Geryon was higher in the chain of command than he originally realised.

He may be above other humans, but alone, he was nothing more than a man who was facing a creature who could vanquish him with nothing more than a fiery breath. He was also learning that what Geryon wanted, he would get.

*Now I have my home back,* as temporary as it may be, *and I have the female I want,* something he would make sure was not temporary.

He'd been earnest in his want to claim Valerie as his female and create a bond with her. Her much shorter length of life, however, was more concerning than he wanted it to be. When she was nothing more than a human, there was nothing he could have done about it.

He hadn't been intending to claim her as his mate because it would have been pointless.

*As a Witch, though...* They could indeed increase the length of her life.

Unfortunately, it required her to eat the heart of a Dragon every hundred years.

Rurik had found a way around the gruesome act by having an old Dragon gift their heart to Amalia upon their death. It increased the length of her life and she had caused harm to none.

*Must I do the same? I'm not Rurik...* He wasn't the great WitchSlayer. Who would give him their heart upon their peaceful death?

Still, he was investigating who was coming into their death to ask them if he could take their heart once they were no longer of this world.

He'd removed the binding spell that locked her magic away not even a day after meeting with the Elders. After Faerydae's affirmation that she wouldn't turn, her will too strong, he had confidence in her.

It meant she was free to use her magic. It was also necessary for her to do the spell that would lengthen her life.

*I still have to claim her.* His eyes fell upon the beautiful woman, who was currently being cold and callous to the nobles who plucked up the courage to speak with her.

They all knew what she was. Bradwick had already shared that she was a Witch who had infiltrated the palace before they'd returned. Some were frightened of her, others were curious. They all remembered how she had been.

They weren't sure how to handle her, especially since she had managed to spin them to somehow like her, much like she had during the gala.

As it had before, watching her interact with the court with her poised, lady-like features, but cruel and unfeeling words, made him shudder with want.

Even now, he was watching her speak with soft words to a baroness like she was being polite, yet she was insinuating that the woman was a snob.

*She gets my tail in a twist when she does that.*

It also didn't help that she was dressed like a snow maiden once more. She wore the silver dress she'd worn at the last ball, the one that caught the candles from the crystal chandeliers above and made it appear as though she wore a sheet of ice and glitter.

Her long hair was tied back into a half bun that revealed the sides of her long, slender neck, unveiling to all that Geryon had permanently marked it with his teeth multiple times.

She didn't seem to care that he had scarred her neck, shoulders, and chest with his bite marks.

Unless he was feeling possessive, possibly because she'd been speaking to a man who was getting too close to her, he usually didn't intend to harm her. Unfortunately, he also did it as a sign of affection, and he couldn't control his depth when he was feeling affectionate or fond of her.

Valerie wore his bites proudly, just as she was choosing to wear a thin red ribbon this night as well.

*She still reminds me of an elegant swan swimming across a lake.* He peacefully watched her flit around the ballroom on her own, his eyes drooping as he lovingly followed her with his gaze.

King Bradwick was throwing a ball in celebration of his marriage to Lady Wyetta, who was now the queen consort.

He'd waited for Geryon's return, uncertain about opening

his gates to the public without him. Since these were his hunting grounds, he'd made Bradwick a potential target of all his past traps in this kingdom.

It was a wise move on his part.

Geryon had already quietly disposed of a female Witch who attempted to gain entrance earlier in the day. She'd reeked of the foul scent that came from those who were corrupted, so she had been easy to find and remove.

Wyetta had easily forgiven Valerie for her callous actions on her departing day, and she quickly became her private confidante. Geryon knew that if Valerie hadn't punched the woman in the face, giving her a black eye, Bradwick would never have trusted Wyetta enough to marry her.

*She helped her win Bradwick's heart.*

"Are you sure about this one?" Bradwick asked when they could see Valerie blatantly ignoring a nobleman by turning her shoulder to him. It was rude, but she managed to make it not appear obvious. "I still cannot believe you not only attempted to steal one of the ladies from me, but when you discovered what she was, you still intended to keep her. You are lucky I'm forgiving."

"Attempted to steal?" Geryon chuckled, lowering his head to be level with him as he placed his arm around the top of the throne's backrest. "While you were distracted with the other ladies, I was under her skirt multiple times."

"It still does not please me to know that." Bradwick scowled, eyeing him suspiciously. "I thought you were loyal to me."

"I am." Geryon let his eyes fall to the pretty female sitting on her throne on the other side of them. "You have chosen the woman who is best suited for you, and I saw no harm in chasing after Valerie when I knew this would be the case."

Like she could sense they were speaking of her, Wyetta turned her head to smile at them both. Even Geryon could see the happiness she radiated.

"And I must add, it does appear that this one actually seems to care for you, rather than just the crown on her head."

Bradwick nodded, covering his mouth to whisper quieter.

"I do believe you are correct." Then he waved his hand to dismiss him. "Leave me. I wish to speak to my new wife."

Geryon did as he was asked, but only because he was already intending to leave the king's podium anyway.

Since he was using a spell to dull his hearing to stop from being overwhelmed by the constant chattering, he needed to keep his sense of smell sharp as he made his way through the people. There were many here he didn't know.

Grabbing the unsuspecting hand of his woman, Geryon lifted it to his mouth when it stole her attention from the person she was speaking to. Rather than kissing it, he nipped the back of her wrist with a coy smile.

"I do believe I once told you I wished I could dance with you," he reminded her, his eyes bright with humour when her face dulled to hide her true reaction.

She often did this, became more doll-like when he was near her in front of others.

It wasn't that she was hiding their relationship, since there was absolutely no way for them to hide it – not with how he chased her around the palace. No, she merely did it because that was just the way she was, not wanting others to know she was vulnerable to him.

"I was curious to know when you would finally come offer your hand."

She turned from the nobles she was speaking with and allowed him to lead her to the dancing area. He walked backwards carelessly, barging people out of his way.

There was no awkwardness or hesitation from either of them, even though they'd never danced together before. She placed her arm around his shoulders while he wrapped one of his around her waist, interlocking their free hands.

It was not the intricate dance others were doing, but he wasn't interested in putting on a show when he would rather just speak and spend time with her. It was the only thing he could really do while keeping an eye out for potential threats.

"You look rather beautiful tonight," she said quietly, making sure her voice was hushed.

He noted that her eyes trailed from his detailed navy dress coat before they ran over the features of his face. They settled on his eyes, and his pulse quickened.

*She never shies away from me.*

He gave a raise of his brow. "I do believe that's supposed to be my line."

She shrugged. "It's not my fault that you were too slow."

She began to tickle her fingers through the short length of hair on the back of his head. She twirled it, making goosebumps prickle down the nape of his neck and over his shoulders.

He also noted that her body was pressed firmly against his own. Each movement caused her hips to rub against his, and he wasn't sure if she was doing it on purpose or not.

"You have been cold to the nobles tonight," he said after he spun her out and then back to him.

Then he dipped his head to run his tongue over her throat. *I wonder if she knows I enjoy watching her with them.*

He felt her roll her body into his subtly in reaction, and yet the words that came out of her mouth next incited anger from him.

"I do think Lord Parika likes me. The number of times I have had to deny his hand for a dance was becoming irksome. If you had not come along, I feared I would be unable to deny him much longer."

Geryon's nose crinkled as he growled, his eyes searching for this apparent Lord Parika.

"You only say such things because you know I cannot leave my post this eve." *Evil wench!*

"Perhaps I say them in order to convince you, regardless." There was an emotion dripping in her voice, one that made his hackles rise and his growl quieten immediately.

Geryon slowly pulled back to take in the features of her face.

Her expression was blank – except she was letting her true intention fill her eyes. The skin of her chest was turning pink, and he knew, before long, he'd be able to smell a change in her scent.

"You are toying with me openly when you usually don't." To his dismay, it was working.

Geryon held her tighter against him when his cock jerked and began to harden.

"It's not my fault you look ravishing in this coat, or that you have been looking around like you are hunting." She leaned a little closer to add with a whisper, "It just reminds me of what you are."

"You are a cruel woman," he groaned.

She was making it increasingly obvious she was excited by the fact she knew he was a Dragon. It made sense, considering her coven respected them, although he still found that odd.

*She's just as insatiable for me as I'm for her.*

"Well, if you leave your post and King Bradwick was to perish, you would become a laughingstock, since you were chasing after women instead of protecting him."

He wished he hadn't come to dance with her when she raked her nails from the bottom of his skull to the top of his head. A shudder rippled through him. She was taunting him, playing with him, because she thought he wouldn't cave.

*She's playing a dangerous game.* Geryon was growing fonder and fonder of the idea of tossing her over his shoulder and taking her somewhere out of sight.

If she kept playing with him like this, he may not even consider leaving this room.

"One woman," he corrected with a dart of his tongue at the seam of his lips. "The only woman I would be chasing after is you."

"Oh, are you saying it's my fault?" She deliberately ran her knee between his legs so that her thigh would rub against his pestering erection.

"Valerie..." He wasn't sure if the warning came out as a groan or a growl or a mixture of the two, but he could feel his control slipping.

The reason he should be staying in this room was becoming less and less important to him.

Then she leaned forward to bring her lips to his ear. "I could always place a ward around the room to keep threats out while we are gone."

*Blasted!*

"Do it," he growled, releasing her hand so he could place it around her waist as well. "Quickly."

She brought her hands between their bodies to hide them, and he could feel the swirl of energy. Her eyes were shut as she silently chanted.

It usually made Geryon uncomfortable to watch her magic, but right then, he didn't mind. *Want her.* He was too distracted by the potential of what this magic could lead to.

When he watched the glittering sphere in her palms expand to the size of the room, he didn't wait. Geryon grabbed her hand and dragged her out of the ballroom.

He took her to the large hallway that led to one of the arms of the palace on the ground level. For now, it was empty of people, except for one guard, who he ordered to leave.

Turning them, he pushed Valerie against the corner while he brought his lips down on hers. They kissed deeply as he loosened the back of her dress, impatiently pulling on the ties.

He wasn't going to remove it; he just wanted to give his hands space to roam.

There was no hesitation on her part.

She even gave him a moan as she swirled her tongue against his. He knew if he opened his eyes, he would see her mask fading, like it usually did when they were alone and being intimate.

He wrapped his arms around her waist, one hand holding her shoulder while the other kneaded her backside.

"I want to claim you, Valerie," he said in between kisses. "Don't deny me any longer."

She'd been denying him for the past month. It hurt him each night she told him no, since he asked every day. She would still allow him to touch her afterwards, would allow him to taste her and be with her, but she wouldn't let him put his claim on her.

He'd been attentive, spending as much time as he could with her. Sometimes, he would steal her away from court to take a stroll with her, where they would converse about intelligent topics the people here couldn't care less about.

He'd made her laugh, tried to make her feel cherished.

"Why?" she asked softly before bringing her lips back over his.

His hands tightened on her as he pulled away to stare at her, his gaze intense.

*What does she want from me?* She asked him the same question every time he told her he wanted to claim her. Each time, he would tell her a different reason. *I want you. I want to make you mine. I chose you.*

None of these responses seemed to be what she wanted to hear.

Her pale green eyes flickered over his before she leaned forward to nip her teeth against his throat, bringing her lips close to his ear while she did.

"Why do you want to claim me, Geryon?"

With a growl, he grabbed the back of her hair and pulled her head back. His nose was crinkled, his teeth gritted, and yet she never looked afraid of him.

*I tire of waiting.* Geryon was usually a patient male, but he didn't want to wait for this.

"Why?" He pulled her head all the way back, exposing her throat to him and forcing her to submit physically. He wished it could get her to submit to him in this. "Because I love you, you silly Witch! Why else would I want to claim you as my female?"

"*Finally*, you get the courage to say it." There was humour in her eyes and in her voice.

Geryon frowned at her for it, for her words.

"I have told you of my feelings." He gave a dark laugh, one that didn't share in her humour. "I would not want to claim you if I did not feel this way, if I did not care for you."

"You care for King Bradwick. Do you wish to put your cock in him too?"

Geryon grew aghast, horrified even! "Not at all! That's absurd. You–"

"There is a difference between caring for someone and loving them," she butted in before he could get carried away. Then she averted her gaze momentarily. "You were told of my feelings, even though I did not wish to share them. I wanted to know the depth of yours."

"You have been denying me for this reason?"

He wanted to be angry, but he couldn't be.

Valerie was showing a vulnerability, and she never showed her vulnerabilities, not even to him. It was a rare sight, and it was usually because he had to catch her out on it.

This time, she was being forward about it.

He shook his head as a chuckle fell from him. He pressed his lips to her throat, still exposed from the forceful hold he had her in.

"Now that I have said it, will you accept my mark? You are beautiful in this dress, and I would like to take you in it."

He would always prefer her naked, but he knew trying to get under her skirts out in the open was hard enough as it was.

*The fact she's not trying to stop me now is remarkable.* This hallway was not often a thoroughfare, but the occasional person liked to wander through. Plus, there were many people here this night who were curious about the palace.

There were also guests who would be staying in the apartments further down, who needed to venture through it.

"Yes, you may claim me," she answered, and the sweet, unhidden smile she gave him was enough to undo him.

*Pretty woman.*

Instead of being sweet, though, Geryon spun her around. He pressed the front of her torso against the wall while he bunched the skirts of her dress up so he could snake his hands underneath it.

He kissed the back of her neck. "Apparently, it hurts," he warned her.

Just that fact alone was almost enough to make him want to wait until they were in the privacy of their lavish suite. They had been moved to a spacious room on the third floor.

He wouldn't wait any longer.

The night was still early, and there would be many more hours he would have to spend in the ballroom to keep it safe.

"I have been waiting for this since I discovered you wanted to claim me, Geryon." She turned her head to peek back at him. "I don't care if it hurts, so long as the mark is yours."

He had to settle his hands and press his forehead against her shoulder blade so he could groan against it. *She has been waiting for it?*

Why did hearing that make his cock throb deeply within his breeches?

Pressing his lips to the back of her shoulder, he shot his hands up until they rested on the centre of her back. He spread his fingers while he lined his thumbs together.

He felt the magic he needed come to life when he mentally recited the lengthy yet ancient chant. His heart. His mind. His body and soul. They all knew exactly what he wanted.

Under his palms, Valerie visibly flinched before she grew taught. A sharp gasp came from her at the warmth even he could sense in his hands. It would feel as though he was burning her skin, although he wasn't.

She didn't scream or cry. She persevered through it by gritting her teeth and pressing her face against the corner of the walls. Her strength called to him, and he knew he'd made the right decision on his female.

*Now, you are mine.* They were called the Flames of Binding. Eventually, these burns would turn into a black tribal Dragon marking against her back.

When the magic faded and her body grew lax once more, Geryon turned her without moving his arms from under her skirt.

"I don't think I have wanted you more than I do this very moment." He licked his lips, his tongue darting out.

*But if the pain was too much...*

Valerie wrapped her arms around his shoulders and jumped, forcing him to catch underneath her thighs.

"I did not think I would have to wait for your cock afterwards."

*Ungh! Wicked Witch!* If he didn't have to go back to the ballroom, he would have ripped his breeches open to free his cock.

Instead, he had to carefully unbutton the ones he needed to be able to free himself, a lopsided grin marring his lips. Vibrating with desire and love for the woman in his arms, he chuckled. "You are going to regret saying that."

**39**

Valerie rested against the many pillows cushioning the headboard of their shared bed. With her knees curled up, her feet tucked under her backside, her side laying upon the pillows, and a chalice of bitter wine in her hand, she awaited Geryon.

Naked, presenting herself for him, a small smile curled her lips, and she quickly had to hide it behind a sip of her drink.

Since she'd left the wedding ball earlier than him, she had already wiped herself down and stripped to await him in their bedchamber.

It was neither of their old suites, but one on the very top floor of this palace. Bradwick only permitted a select few trusted people to live on the same floor as him, and of course, Geryon was one of them.

The strange king threw whatever he could at Geryon to make him happy, despite always giving Valerie a suspicious side eye.

Of course, Valerie was happy to live wherever made her new 'mate' content.

She also wore what she knew would excite him the most, sometimes hating being dressed in elaborate clothing just for his enjoyment of trying to playfully get her out of it. His excitement as he grew more frustrated with each link or button in his way only caused his mouth to be hungrier on her lips, her neck, her earlobe.

There was little else Valerie wanted to do but be Wyetta's council and Geryon's female. Since she was able to use her magic freely, King Bradwick was finding her to be a useful tool in his arsenal, and she did whatever he demanded of her just to keep the peace between him and Geryon.

Her eyes fell upon the green walls, embossed with gold leaf, then the white ceiling. The furniture in this room was lush, far too expensive for her taste, but the carpet felt like the most wonderful bed of moss upon her bare feet.

Geryon liked it, and that's all she cared about.

The fire-lit lanterns outside the bay window almost made it appear as though the stars were floating along the earth. Many were moving as more people found where they were going to rest for the night, the front gates permanently closed.

"You are not watching me, *mate*," Geryon bit, despite his last word being filled with heat. She even saw him visibly shudder.

"I'm watching, I promise," she said as she brought her gaze back to him.

When their eyes met, proving that her sight had wandered, she brought her chalice back to her lips and stroked her fingertips between the valley of her naked breasts for him. She wondered if her humour could be seen in her crinkling eyes.

His attention was diverted to her hand, while his own finally moved off his elaborate coat. He then worked on his pants, having a much easier time with those.

"Are you sure this is a good idea?" she asked as she braved glancing around the room that could easily be set on fire.

Once fully unclothed, Geryon climbed inside the empty clawfoot bathtub.

"You promised that once I claimed you as my mate, I could claim you as a Dragon as well. I don't wish to wait any longer."

Valerie's heart stuttered at the idea, reconsidering her promise. She wasn't usually the kind of person to back out of a deal, but she was nervous about what it would be like. She knew he could match her size, so it wouldn't be too painful if they were careful, but the idea of having a Dragon rutting her was profound!

She'd never thought, not once in her life, that she would be opening her thighs for a Dragon while they were in their beast form. Someone with claws, and fangs, and hard scales.

However, she also couldn't deny how it caused her inner walls to tighten and grow wet.

She trusted Geryon, which is the only reason she didn't bow out.

"Are you sure you will be the right size?" she asked, looking around once again. "If you break our bathtub, they may ask questions."

"Yes, I'm sure," he said as he rolled his eyes at her. "The last time I shifted, I made sure I would be a suitable size for our room."

Valerie's lips pursed. The devious male had been planning for this day.

With one hand on the rim of the porcelain bathtub, the only place that could withstand flames and not be set on fire, he blew a ring of fire above his head. Then, he lowered his face, and he eyed her through his brows with a grin forming across his handsome features.

"Shift," he whispered, not taking his sight off her as the flames came back to encase him.

She saw nothing through the swirling fire until he poked

his blue snout through, the rest of his spiky head following. As soon as his paw keeping him steady on the edge of the tub was revealed, he dived forward.

The inside of the porcelain tub was completely charcoaled, and she hoped she could wipe it off later.

Geryon scuttled to her on all fours. His size grew slightly, as though he'd originally made himself smaller on purpose, just in case.

By the time he was climbing the side of the bed, she knew he had made himself the perfect size for her.

Her trepidation grew tenfold, but she didn't scurry away.

With a shaky hand, she reached behind her to place her chalice on the nightstand. Just as she was bringing her arm back, Geryon's clawed hand wrapped around her forearm to halt her.

"It's not often I see you nervous."

Valerie let out a scoff and turned to him. "I'm not nervous. Just a little tired from the ball."

His gaze was warm, his metallic blue eyes hinting at both humour and concern. That was, until he brought her arm forward and licked at the back of her hand and wrist.

"I will not hurt you," he rasped against her, before his puffy lips curled. "I will be as gentle for as long as I can. How is your back?"

Her back still felt as though it was on fire, like she'd been permanently seared. "Sore, but worth it."

"Atta girl," he purred, before he grabbed one of her knees and yanked her so she was beneath him.

A small squeak of surprise escaped her, and she was thankful he'd dragged her somewhat to her side. Despite him appearing to be the same size as her, maybe even slightly larger, she felt undeniably small beneath his four scaled limbs.

She let out a soft mewl when he dragged his tongue underneath her jaw, and she lifted her chin to give him more room. He nibbled at her neck, then her chest, his breath warm and comforting.

"I want you to say it to me," he said, just as he drew his tongue over one of her hard, aching nipples.

Valerie stifled a shiver, but it was more noticeable when he went to the other. He teased both with his tongue, dabbing at the small valley between them, and she arched her back slightly.

It was only when she placed her hands against his hard forehead and pushed him down that she finally answered him. "Say what?" she whispered.

Geryon started painting a path lower with his tongue. "You know."

Valerie looked down as she spread her thighs, already knowing what that wicked tongue felt like against her sensitive clit. Her stomach pooled with desire, and she ached for him to taste at her entrance.

"I'm yours?" she panted when he positioned himself between her legs.

"Yes, *now* you are mine," he rumbled, before licking at his jowls. "But no, that's not what I want to hear. Fuck, Valerie, you are very wet." His eyes lifted from her pussy to greet hers. "Looks like you wanted this more than you care to admit."

Before she could answer, Valerie threw her head back while digging her fingers around the crown of his spiked head, just as he swept his long, flat tongue all the way through her folds. Her moan was soft, instant, unhidden.

The moment he tasted her, Geryon groaned against her. He curled his arms around her thighs from underneath, laid down upon the bed, and darted his head down. She gasped when he shoved his entire tongue inside her core, and it bottomed out as his jaws parted around her.

The sharpness of his fangs tickled her arse, and she bounced.

He let out a shuddering groan, as though he was starved and finally ate something heavenly. His tongue was quick to slip back and forth, the flexible muscle swirling as it moved.

"W-wait, too fast." She palmed his snout and tried to push back.

He didn't relent, instead moving his tongue faster, faster, with a growly rumbling sound from his chest. Valerie's back arched as she let out a loud moan, digging her nails into whatever part of his scaled face she was touching.

Her moans turned higher pitched when her breath caught every time he slipped out to lash at her swollen clit. Valerie's thighs trembled around his head, one minute squeezing his skull, while the next she was trying to get them further apart so he could get deeper, go even faster.

It wasn't long before she was teetering on the edge of bliss, little sparks in her vision. She reached up to play with a breast, turning her shoulders to the side while trying to keep her hips flat for the safety of his fangs. She wanted to buck, and she was sure her grinding movements felt that way to him.

But even as her back arched, and she clenched, Valerie couldn't come. Instead, she was getting more wound up, aching to orgasm but unable to.

"Geryon," she whined, all her usual self-control and poised image completely shoved to the side. She tried to be free with him while they were being intimate or close, her own way of showing how much she cared.

Even as his tongue moved faster, his thrusts more persistent to get her over the edge, it didn't matter. When he realised it, he withdrew his tongue from her spasming channel.

"You cannot come?" he asked as he climbed above her. "Is your back hurting laying against the bed?"

Needy and desperate, Valerie shoved his shoulders. She knew her strength compared to him like this was nothing, but her kissing his neck at the same time had him caving. Geryon rolled to the side while taking her with him, being careful not to crush his wings.

The large wings tucked against him until he was on his back, and then he spread them a little.

The moment Valerie sat against his pink cock, already fully engorged and waiting for her attention, she began to grind herself along the entire length of it.

Now that her aching back was freed from the pressure, the throbbing in her pussy became a nagging need. With both hands on his armoured torso, thighs resting on either side of his hips, Valerie threw her head back and thrust against his cock.

It felt a little too hard, not as spongey as when he was human formed, but it was perfect. Her arousal pooled onto it, so much so that every time she moved, the glide became slicker, better.

"Say it, Valerie."

Geryon thrust upwards, mimicking her movements to help her as she slid back and forth. His forepaws gripped the sides of her ribcage, his claws slipping over her to tickle her flesh, causing goosebumps to prickle.

She couldn't say anything, not when her body tensed and all she could do was let out a sharp cry as she finally came. She bucked erratically, her hips twitching as liquid heat pooled over his cock as she worked herself on it.

When she finished, Geryon didn't cease grinding upwards, even when she stopped moving and just twitched above him. With her lips apart, a little moan slipping from them, she tilted her head forward to look down at him.

His snout was bunched, his fangs clamped tightly shut, as he watched his cock slipping between the lips of her pussy. She followed his gaze and noted the pink, pointed head was dripping a line of pre-cum.

He was panting wildly, his brows furrowed deeply, and

Valerie knew he'd enjoyed watching her masturbate with his cock.

Still riding the high from her orgasm, she fell forward with her hands resting on either side of his spiky, scaly head and she kissed his snout right between his slitted nose holes.

"I love you," she whispered softly, wishing her cheeks wouldn't burn at saying it out loud.

She hadn't said it to him personally, only through Faerydae, and it was only now that she realised this was what he'd been asking her to say.

Geryon paused to huff at her, his blue eyes dragging her under some kind of spell. His cock twitched against her sensitive flesh, producing another drop of pre-cum.

"Say it again," he said with a pathetically needy groan. His forepaws lowered to grab her arse, his claws precariously slipping between her cheeks as he pulled them apart. "*Fuck,* Valerie. Say it again while I'm inside you like this."

Geryon lifted her hips, his cock raising with it, and he lined her up before slamming her pussy down on him.

The gasp that rendered out of her was acute.

He was thicker than she thought he'd be, hotter than she could have imagined, and he was so hard that her core had no other option but to make way for him. Valerie tightened around him, spasming at the sudden stretch and intrusion as she took him all the way to his protective slit.

Geryon's back arched sharply. His tail twisted, and his wings kinked against the mattress. She heard something rip, like one of his spikes or toe claws, or even his wing talon, had shredded the blanket.

"You are so soft like this," he exclaimed with a feverish shudder. "But you are also so tight, so hot, so wet." It was like he was trying to push her away with his palms while his fingers kept her down, and yet his hips kept subtly moving his shaft up and down. "I almost came just from entering you."

*He has never done this before with someone human formed.* Valerie had forgotten that.

Watching his first experience of this, how much his eyes were trying to roll back in ecstasy, even with only minute movements, had her heart fluttering. She purposely clenched around him, and his face bunched as he let out a shaken huff in response.

Valerie started layering whisper-soft kisses against his face as she moved her hips back and forth. She ground her hips so his odd-shaped cock would hit all the right places, and each time it did, she made sure she moaned a little louder than normal for him.

She swept her palm over the left side of his face as she brought her lips down the right.

He was being gentle because he was trying to get accustomed to her like this. She knew giving him exactly what he wanted would send him spiralling.

Did she just learn a new way to tease him? One that she would withhold simply until she knew it would heighten his own pleasure? She hoped so.

She tried to move her hips a little faster, her body bouncing over him. "I love your cock inside me," she whispered right next to where his ear must be. "You feel so good like this."

His hips quickened for a few pumps, and she noticed the scales over his body became a brighter blue than they already were. Even just her bare nipples scraping over his armoured torso warned her how heated he was becoming.

"Valerie," he warned.

Preparing herself for whatever was about to happen, her lips quirked. She licked at his neck with a deep and longer stroke, hoping to send this male into a frenzy. It was nice that she wasn't the one about to go mindless.

"I love you, Geryon," she purred, her lips brushing against him.

Within an instant, his claws stabbed into her as he gripped the crease where her thighs met her arse cheeks. This, and his savage growl, was the only warning she got before he turned them onto their sides.

Geryon wrapped both his rough, scaled arms around her, one hand gripping her arse, the other clasping her opposing shoulder. Then he enclosed Valerie in both his soft wings, cuddling her snugly with them, as he began to wildly drive his cock into her.

She choked, her lips parting wide as she struggled to breathe. Her arms were clamped between them, and she was unable to dig her nails into him properly to help fight her tension.

The speed at which he fucked her was too fast. She didn't know when he was entering or withdrawing. All she knew was that it was hard, deep, and she could don'thing but take his swift rams.

Her head fell back against the cushion of his wings, and he used that to draw his tongue against the exposed column of her throat.

"There we go. Take my Dragon cock," he growled as he pressed his puffy snout against her. "Nice and hard and deep."

His maniacal thrusting was aiding him, whereas it was tearing her mind in two. Her ability to think was snuffed out as he took her, little else to focus on but his cock.

One minute, Valerie was relaxed and being swept away, and the next, she was screaming as she tensed around his cock in his arms. She bucked against him, unsure if she was trying to help him or get away as she used her heel against the back of his hips.

"That's right. Come for me, my vicious butterfly." He rubbed his snout against her, occasionally licking. "If you were a Dragoness, I would have bitten you by now, clawed you, pinned you beneath me so you would not be able get away as I took you. I want to. I want to sink my teeth into you with affection, but I cannot, so I will fuck your pretty pussy with my cock, my tongue, my tail, until you beg me to stop."

Geryon groaned deeply, his cock pulsating inside of her, as he whispered, "Unless you swallow my knot for me."

Valerie knew what swallowing his knot entailed. The tip of his cock would pierce her womb, allowing room for his extending cock to slip inside and swell. The whole idea sounded painful to her, but apparently, with a Dragon, it wasn't.

Anyway, right now, she was too busy clenching orgasm after orgasm around his pistoning cock that she didn't think she would mind if it happened. She was adoring this, and she couldn't believe she'd been so nervous when he felt absolutely amazing.

How was she supposed to go back to human Geryon when she knew the Dragon version of him could feel this good?

"Heavens," he whined. "Oh *fuuuck.*"

It only got better when his wings and arms tightened around her, when he held her closely, passionately, and bit back the roar she could feel in his quaking body – unable to release it in the palace like she knew he wanted to.

His pumping slowed, but he felt harder than ever before as he plunged deeply. She expected him to go deeper, but their bodies never lined up and instead, liquid heat began to burst inside her pussy as he kept thrusting.

She gasped in surprise at first before she melted, his hot come soothing her tender inner walls. Both their heads were tilted back in bliss as Geryon filled her and filled her, and she knew a small trail had leaked from her.

Eventually, he relaxed, panting against the pillows while Valerie had his biceps to lay her head upon.

His arms and wings were like a blanket of security that made her feel undoubtedly cherished, while his sounds made her ears tingle. She pressed her forehead against his sternum to nuzzle him, and she could feel how fast his heart was sprinting, how heavy his shuddering lungs were.

*Dear heavens... That was amazing.* She opened her mouth to tell him so, and then immediately shut it. She refused to give him an extra tool in his arsenal; he easily got under her skin by being a devious, roguish cad.

"I knew my mate would like that," he said with quick pants.

"It was okay," she answered, trying to sound bored just to nettle him, but instead, her voice cracked, tender from crying out.

Geryon gripped the back of her hair and yanked her head back. There was no glare, his stare lazy but ardent. He ground his cock into her, and a mew slipped from her lips.

He raised a spiked brow. "What was that again?"

"I said it was o–" Before Valerie could finish, he ground his shaft again and another moan slipped from her. "Please. Give me a moment."

"My cock will stay hard for a little while longer. I can tease you with it, or I can let you rest with you cuddling me. It will depend on you." When Valerie nodded in defeat, he licked underneath her jaw. "You did not take my knot. I would be disappointed, but that means I can take you again, and then again, if you still don't."

Valerie's aching core clamped down on him, and Geryon's following chuckle was warm and inviting. One side of her lips twitched, like she wanted to smile in contentment.

She was unused to being so emotionally free with someone, but she was thankful she had finally found that person, and that it was Geryon, of all people.

Someone who understood when she was trying to be teasing, rather than just a bitch. Someone who understood that instead of crying when they were hurting, she turned cold to hide it. Someone who, despite all her glaring flaws, still wanted her, desired her, somehow found a way to love her.

Even if she was terrible at showing it, Valerie utterly adored Geryon.

She reached up, palming the sides of his scaled face in a gentle caress before she wrapped her arms around his thick neck. She didn't mind the stabs of dull spikes; hugging him was worth it.

"I would like to do this again with you," she said, her face pressing against his shoulder. "Thank you for claiming me in more ways than one tonight," she muttered against him.

"How is your back?" he asked, releasing the fistful he had of her hair to tickle her side with his claws. "I thought being on our sides might be less painful for you."

Her heart melted in tenderness at his consideration of her.

A small laugh quivered out of her. "I'm fine, Geryon." Then she wiggled her backside, stirring his cock inside her while his wings pet her arse. "I really like having your wings around me."

"You do?" he asked with a huff of humour, rubbing the underside of his jaw against the top of her hair. "I was not sure if you would enjoy being confined by them, but if you like, you can sleep in them every night."

Valerie sighed contentedly. *I would like that very much.*

# Epilogue

Geryon usually woke each morning with a rush of worry that he would find his bed empty of his woman, and he wouldn't be able to track her inside the palace. Geryon still couldn't shake the fear that Valerie would try to run from him again, and he often fell asleep gripping the long length of her wavy brown hair.

He was always relieved when he found her still tangled with him in bed. This morning, however, he gave a huff of contentment when he woke and felt a soft and lax woman caught inside his arms and wings.

Last night, they'd both returned to the ballroom after he had claimed her and taken her against the wall. They hadn't gone completely unseen, a couple stumbling across them mid-act. They had both frozen at being caught – which was difficult for him, being moments from coming inside her warm channel.

Valerie had tightened in tension when they were spotted, squeezing him so wonderfully that he had to tell her to stop if she didn't want him to keep thrusting while people passed.

Since they hadn't been alone anymore, she'd given him that cold stare, hiding her pleasure-filled face behind her mask once more.

Helpless against the power she somehow had over him, he hadn't been able to stop from pumping himself into sweet oblivion. He completely forgot about the people in the hallway hurrying past as he drove into her, chasing bliss.

It wasn't the first time they had been caught being intimate out in the open. He was sure it wouldn't be the last.

What Valerie didn't know yet was that Geryon had come across many others doing the same thing in the years he'd been here. It even occurred in other kingdoms before his stay in Bradwick's. It wasn't an uncommon occurrence; one he wouldn't be shy about. If he wanted his woman, he would take her.

Back in the ballroom, he could tell she was uncomfortable with the pain in her back from his claiming flames. Still, she held her features as calm as ever, and he hadn't been able to stop his chest from puffing in pride at his chosen female.

It was deeply satisfying to watch her flit around the ballroom, knowing she had accepted his marking and was now claimed as his mate.

His memories of when he returned to their suite made his lips curl back from his fangs in a grin. It crinkled the scales around his cheeks and eyes, and he felt rather sated and satisfied.

The poor bed was now littered with claw marks; he didn't know how they were going to explain them – not that he truly cared.

He'd taken her twice more before they'd both begun falling asleep, the night long and late. She'd never taken his knot, but that just made him more excited for the next time they were intimate while he was a Dragon. There was something new for him to experience, and after how much she seemed to have enjoyed everything, he hoped she grew addicted to taking him like this.

He would just simply love taking her throughout the day as a human in every corridor of this palace, while at night they could be private and free enough for him to be his Dragon self. He was hoping Valerie would be the key to getting him back in touch with this side of who he was, an important part he'd been largely ignoring. It had been severely weighing on his thoughts.

He brought her closer and tightened his wings around her. Even his tail had curled around the leg she was laying upon, since it was straight. She was trapped, and yet her soft snores said she was as comfortable as she could be.

She was naked, facing away from him while deep in slumber. He revelled in being able to sleep with her on their bed while in this form.

His eyes lovingly swept over the parts of her exposed body he could see. She often kicked the blankets away because of the natural heat he emitted, and it meant he could always hold and see her freely.

He'd seen his burned palm prints on her back when he had taken her from behind.

Now, those marks had turned into a large, tribal Dragon, as though it was flying up the centre of her back. The tail started from the middle of her spine, its body where his palms had been touching. Its head was where his thumbs had been between her shoulder blades, with two great wings open over them.

It looked like she had her own Dragon wings.

*She does admire my kind. I do hope she likes how I have marked her.* It was exactly how he imagined it.

She rolled in his arms to escape the sunlight hitting her face from the window and nuzzled the scales between his neck and shoulder. Tranquil peace fluttered tenderness into his chest as he watched specks of dust float above her.

His life was finally where he wanted it to be.

The loneliness he'd begun to feel crawling into his lungs over the years, trying to choke him, was lifted away. He had his hunting grounds, a task he enjoyed, and now, a woman to keep him happy and sated.

He knew she would always interest him, and already, he could tell watching her from afar while he performed his duties gave him great enjoyment.

She also liked to play tricks and games with him in front of the court, who had no idea of her antics.

Some of them were like the game she'd played with him while dancing. Others were versions of how much she could blatantly ignore his existence until she irritated him into leaving his post. It would only make him fall deeper in love with her when she'd freely, although quietly, giggle for him when he caught her.

Finding her when she wasn't with court was also entertaining. Sometimes, it was just because he wanted to be in her presence. Other times, it would be to touch her, and she would deny him just to get him riled and pent-up for later.

Geryon adored her for it.

Holding her in his arms, he tickled his claws over the claim, knowing now that it had changed into a dark marking, it would no longer hurt her.

*It's a fitting mark for a Witch who has the heart of a Dragoness inside her, and the woman who has won mine.*

Also by Opal Reyne

## DUSKWALKER BRIDES
A Soul to Keep
A Soul to Heal
A Soul to Touch
A Soul to Guide *(Coming June 2023)*
A Soul to Revive *(TBA 2023)*
A Soul to Steal *(TBA 2024*
*(More titles coming soon)*

## WITCH BOUND
The WitchSlayer
The ShadowHunter
*(More titles coming soon)*

*Completed Series*

## A PIRATE ROMANCE DUOLOGY
Sea of Roses
Storms of Paine

## ~~THE ADEUS CHRONICLES~~
This series has been unpublished as of
20th of June 2022

Opal Reyne

If you would like to keep up to date with all the novels I will be publishing in the future, receive exclusive giveaways, and first grabs at ARCs, follow me on my social media platforms.

Facebook Page:
www.facebook.com/OfficialOpalReyne

Facebook Group:
www.facebook.com/groups/opals.nawty.book.realm

Instagram:
www.instagram.com/opalreyne

TikTok:
@OpalReyneAuthor

Made in United States
Orlando, FL
02 December 2024

54871153R00312